I0585063

Patrick O Shea

The sixth progressive reader, or Oratorical class-book

With a treatise on elocution

Patrick O Shea

The sixth progressive reader, or Oratorical class-book
With a treatise on elocution

ISBN/EAN: 9783741176050

Manufactured in Europe, USA, Canada, Australia, Japa

Cover: Foto ©Andreas Hilbeck / pixelio.de

Manufactured and distributed by brebook publishing software
(www.brebook.com)

Patrick O Shea

The sixth progressive reader, or Oratorical class-book

THE ILLUSTRATED PROGRESSIVE SERIES.

THE

SIXTH PROGRESSIVE READER;

OR,

ORATORICAL CLASS-BOOK.

WITH A TREATISE ON ELOCUTION, &c.

CAREFULLY

ARRANGED FOR THE USE OF SCHOOLS.

NEW YORK:
P. O'SHEA, PUBLISHER,
45 WARREN STREET.

PREFACE.

THE intention of the author in preparing this volume for the use of schools, is to confine himself strictly to what is really useful and interesting to the learner. The treatise on elocution is very easy and intelligible, and explains the inflections of the voice very clearly. The treatise on gesture is short; but it is believed to comprise all that is essential. The collection of pieces for reading and declamation are strictly adapted to that purpose. The best specimens of pulpit eloquence, from St. Chrysostom to Lacordaire; the most manly, moving, and impassioned efforts of the tribune, from Demosthenes to O'Connell; the most effective and persuasive triumphs of the forum, from Cicero to Curran, will be found embodied in the ORATORICAL CLASS-BOOK. The Dialogues, both grave and humorous, are such as Christian youth may speak, and polite and intelligent people may listen to without *ennui* or disgust.

The author hopes and trusts that the work, on the whole, will be found well suited for use in schools and seminaries

CONTENTS.

———

PART SECOND.

PRINCIPLES OF ELOCUTION.

ELOCUTION is an important branch of oratory; so important, that eloquence borrows its name from it. The theory consists of certain rules, which should be observed by all who read or speak in private companies or public assemblies. In practice elocution consists in the art of reading, or speaking, with propriety and elegance; or of delivering our words in a just and graceful manner; untainted with pedantry or affectation, and uncorrupted with any provincial sound or dialect.

It is absolutely necessary that every young gentleman should be acquainted with the science of elocution, especially those who are intended for the pulpit, the senate, the bar, or the stage; so that very few persons need be told, that a graceful elocution is of the highest importance. Everybody will allow, that what a man has occasion daily to do, should be done well; yet so little attention has sometimes been paid to this accomplishment, even from those, in whom (from their professions as public speakers) we have been led to expect a perfect model of the art, that it has tended to eclipse

all their other merits, however great; while others, of
inferior attainments, by the help of a tolerably good
style, and a just elocution, have risen to considerable
eminence.

A graceful elocution is, to a good style, what a good
style is to the subject matter of a discourse, an effectual
ornament: for, if the subject of a discourse be ever so
interesting, and the speaker's knowledge ever so profound, without a correct style the discourse must suffer
greatly in its reputation; and though the speaker's
abilities be of the first eminence, and the style good,
with a bad elocution, or delivery, it will fare little
better:—so great an effect have these exterior accom-
plishments over the public taste. Indeed, the great
design and end of a good pronunciation is, to make the
ideas seem to come from the heart; and then they will
not fail to excite the attention and affections of those
who hear us read or speak.

The principal design which we have in view is to show:

First. *What a bad pronunciation is, and how to
avoid it.*

Secondly. *What a good pronunciaiton is and how to
attain it.*

In the first place, it may be necessary to mention,
that a chief fault of pronunciation is, *when the voice is
too loud,* This is very disagreeable to the hearer, and
inconvenient to the speaker   It will be disagreeable to
the hearers, if they be persons of good taste; who will
look upon it to be the effect of ignorance or affectation.
Besides, an overstrained voice is very inconvenient to
the speaker, as well as disgustful to judicious hearers

.

It exhausts his spirits to no purpose, and takes from him the proper management and modulation of his voice according to the sense of his subject; and, what is worst of all, it leads him into what is called a *tone*. Every person's voice should fill the place where he speaks; but, if it exceed its natural key, it will be neither sweet, nor soft, nor agreeable, because he will not be able to give every word its proper sound.

Another fault in pronunciation is, when the voice is too low. This is not so inconvenient to the speaker, but it is as disagreeable to the hearer, as the other extreme. It is offensive to an audience, to observe anything in the reader or speaker that looks like indolence or inattention. The hearer can never be affected while he perceives the speaker indifferent. The art of governing the voice consists chiefly in avoiding these two extremes; and, for a general rule to direct us herein, the following is a very good one: "Be careful to preserve the key of your voice; and, at the same time, to adapt the elevation and strength of it to the condition and number of the persons you speak to, and the nature of the place you speak in." It would be altogether as ridiculous in a general, who is haranguing an army, to speak in a low and languid voice, as in a person, who reads a chapter in a family circle, or the narrative of any particular historical occurrence, to speak in a loud and eager one.

Another fault in pronunciation is, a thick, hasty, chattering voice. When a person mumbles, that is, leaves out some syllables in the long words, and never pronounces some of the short ones at all; but hurries on

without any regard whether he be heard distinctly or
not, or whether he give his words their full utterance,
or whether his hearers are impressed with the full sense
and meaning of them.   This, however, is frequently
owing to defect in the organs of speech, or a too great
tremulation or flutter of the animal spirits; but oftener
to a bad habit which he has not attempted to correct.
Demosthenes, the greatest orator Greece ever produced,
had, it is said, three natural impediments in pronunciation, all of which he conquered by invincible labor and
perseverance.   One was a weakness of voice; which he
cured by frequently declaiming on the sea-shore, amidst
the noise of the waves.   Another was a shortness of
breath; which he mended by repeating his orations as
he walked up a hill.   And the other was the fault we
are speaking of; a thick mumbling way of speaking:
which he broke himself of by declaiming with pebbles
in his mouth.

*Another fault in pronunciation is, when persons speak
too quickly.*   This method of reading is well enough
among lawyers, in examining leases, perusing inden-
tures, or reciting acts of Congress, where there is
always a superfluity of words; or in reading a news-
paper, where there is but little matter that deserves our
attention; but it is very improper in reading books of
devotion and instruction, and especially the sacred
Scriptures, where the solemnity of the subject, or the
weight of the sense, demands a particular regard.   The
great disadvantage which attends this manner of pronunciation is, that the hearer loses the benefit of half
the good things he hears, and would fain remember, but

cannot: and a speaker should always have a regard to
the memory as well as to the understanding of his
hearers.

As it is a fault to speak too quickly, so it is likewise
a blemish in elocution *to speak too slowly.* Some persons
are apt to read or speak in a heavy, droning, sleepy
way; and, through mere carelessness, make pauses at
improper places. This is very disagreeable: but to
hem, sneeze, yawn, or cough, between the periods, is
much more so. A too slow elocution is most faulty in
reading trifles, subjects that do not require much atten
tion. It then renders every sentence tedious. A too
slow elocution, however, is a fault rarely to be found,
unless in aged people, and those who naturally speak
so in common conversation: but in these, if the pronunciation be in other respects just, decent, and proper,
and especially if the subject be weighty or intricate, it
is more excusable, and is frequently overlooked.

*An irregular or uneven voice is a great fault in reading
or speaking.* This happens, when the voice rises and
falls by fits or starts, as it is generally termed; that is,
when it is elevated or depressed unnaturally or unsea-
sonably, without regard to the sense of the passage and
the meaning of the author, or to the points or stops in
a just method of punctuation; or in always beginning
a sentence with a high voice, and, on the contrary,
concluding it with a low one, or always beginning and
concluding it in the same key.

Another fault, which may be looked upon as the
direct opposite to this, is *a flat, dull, uniform tone of
voice; without emphasis or cadence, or even regard to the*

2

sense or subject of what is read or spoken. This is a habit which children, who have been used to read their lessons by way of task, are very apt to fall into, and retain as they grow up. Indeed, it is a great blemish when it becomes habitual; because it deprives the hearer of the greater part of the benefit he might otherwise receive by a close attention to the interesting parts of the sub ject, which should always be distinguished by the pro- nunciation: for a just pronunciation is a good com- mentary; and therefore no person ought to read a chapter of the Bible or a Psalm, in public, or a speech in a play, or a poetical extract, before he has carefully read it over himself once or twice in private.

The greatest and most common fault is that of reading or speaking with what is called a tone. There is not any habit more easy to be contracted than this, nor more difficult to be conquered. This unnatural tone in read- ing and speaking is very various; but, whatever it be, it is always disgustful to persons of delicacy and judg- ment. Some have a womanish squeaking tone; which persons whose voices are shrill and weak, and over- strained, are very liable to fall into. Some have a singing or canting note: others assume a high, swelling, theatrical tone; and, being ambitious of the fame of fine orators, lay too much stress or emphasis on every sentence, and thereby transgress the rules of true oratory. Some affect an awful and striking tone, attended with solemn grimace, as if they would move the hearer with every word they utter, whether the weight of the subject bear them out in that method or not. This is what persons of a gloomy or melancholy

east of mind are most like y to fall into. Some have a
set, uniform tone of voice, and others an odd, whimsical,
whining tone, peculiar to themselves, and which cannot
be well described; only, that it is an improper laying
cf the emphasis on words which do not require or deserve it.

Such are the common faults of a bad pronunciation.

We now proceed, in the second place, to point out
how a bad pronunciation is to be avoided. And to this
end, it will be exceedingly proper that a person should
not read in too loud nor in too low a voice. If a person
would not read in a voice which is too loud or strong,
nor in one that is too low, or faint, or weak, he should
consider whether his voice be naturally too low or too
loud, and endeavor to correct it accordingly in his daily
ordinary conversation; by which means he will be better
able to correct it in reading. If his voice be too low,
he should converse with those who are hard of hearing;
if too loud, with those whose voices are low. He
should begin his periods with an even moderate voice,
that he may have such a command of it, as to be able
to raise or depress it as the subject requires.

In order *to cure a thick, confused, cluttering voice,* a
person should accustom himself, in conversation, reading, and speaking, to pronounce every word distinctly
and clearly. He ought to observe with what deliberation some persons converse and read, and how full a
sound they give to every word; and closely imitate
them. He should never affect to contract his words, as
some have done, or run two into one. This may do
very well in conversation, or in reading familiar dia-

logues, but it is not so decent nor so decorous in **grave**
and solemn subjects; especially in reading the Scriptures, sermons, or extracts from religious books. It
appears, from the case of Demosthenes, that this fault
of pronunciation cannot be cured without much difficulty,
nor will the remedy which he adopted be found effectual
without a considerable share of perseverance.

To break a habit of reading or speaking too fast, a
person must attend diligently to the sense, weight, and
propriety of every sentence he has occasion to read, and
of every emphatical word contained therein. This will
not only operate as an advantage to himself, but be a
double one to those who hear him; for it will at once
give them time to do the same, and excite their attention when they perceive the speaker's is fixed. A
solemn pause after a weighty thought is not only beautiful but striking. A well-timed cessation or pause gives
us much grace to speech as it does to music. Let a
person imagine that he is reading to persons of slow and
unready conceptions; but he must not measure the
hearer's apprehension by his own. If he does, he may
possibly outrun it. And, as in reading he is not at
liberty to repeat his words and sentences, *that* should
engage him to be very deliberate in pronouncing them,
that their sense may not be misconceived or lost. The
ease and advantage that will arise both to the reader
and hearer, by a free, full, and deliberate pronunciation,
is hardly to be conceived. A too slow pronunciation is
a fault which very few are likely to fall into.

To cure an uneven, desultory voice, a person should
take care that he does not begin his periods either in too

high or in too low a key; for that will necessarily lead him to an unnatural and improper variation of it. He should have particular regard to the nature and quantity of his points, and the length of his periods; and keep his mind intent on the sense, subject, and spirit of his author.

It is very requisite that similar directions should be given to every young gentleman destined to read or speak in public, that he may constantly avoid a monotony in pronunciation; that is, a dull, set, uniform tone of voice: and, if the mind of the student be attentive to the sense of the subject before him, he will naturally manage and modulate his voice agreeably to the nature and importance of the subject.

In order *to avoid all kinds of unnatural and disagreeable tones, he must endeavor to speak with the same ease and freedom as he would do, on the same subject, in private conversation.* You do not hear any person converse in a tone, unless he has the accent of some other country, or has contracted a habit of altering the natural key of his voice when he is talking of some serious subject, of religion particularly. But I do not see any particular reason why, in common conversation, we speak in a natural voice, with proper accent and emphasis; yet, so soon as we begin to read or talk of religion, or speak in public, we should immediately assume a stiff, awkward, unnatural tone. If we are indeed deeply affected with the subject we read or talk of, the voice will naturally vary according to the passion excited; but if we vary it unnaturally, only to seem affected, or with a design to affect others, it then be-

comes a tone, and is offensive In reading, then, a
person should attend to his subject, and deliver it as he
would do if he were talking of it. This is the great,
general, and most important rule of all; which, if carefully observed, will correct not only these but almost all
other faults in a bad pronunciation; and give an easy,
decent, and graceful delivery, agreeably to all the rules
of a right elocution. For, however apt we are to transgress them in reading, we follow them naturally and
easily in conversation: even children will tell a story
with all the natural graces and beauties of pronunciation, however awkwardly they may read the same from
a book. Dr. Watts, in his "Art of Reading," says:
"Let the tone and sound of your voice in *reading*
be the same as it is in *speaking*, and do not affect
to change that natural and easy sound wherewith
you *speak*, for a strange, new, awkward tone, as some
do when they begin to *read;* which would almost persuade our ears, that the *speaker* and the *reader* were
two different persons, if our eyes did not tell us the
contrary."

It is necessary that we now pay attention to the
second principal head of our subject, and that is, *what
a good pronunciation is, and how to attain it.*

In this branch of elocution there are several things to
be adverted to; and, first, we must observe, that a good
pronunciation in *reading* or speaking, is the art of
managing and governing the voice so as to express the
full sense and spirit of the author, in that just, decent,
and graceful manner, which will not only instruct but
affect the minds of the hearers; and which will not only

raise in them the same ideas the speaker intended to
convey, but the same passions he really felt.   This is
the great end of speaking or reading before others, and
this end can only be attained by a proper and just
method of pronunciation.

And hence we may learn wherein a good pronunciation in *speaking* consists; which is not anything but
a natural, easy, and graceful variation of the voice,
suitable to the nature and importance of the sentiments
we deliver.

A good pronunciation, in both these respects, is more
easily attained by some persons than by others; because
some can more readily enter into the sense and sentiments of an author, and more easily discover their own,
than others can; and at the same time have a more
happy facility of expressing all the proper variations
and modulations of the voice.   Thus, persons of a quick
apprehension and brisk flow of animal spirits (setting
aside all impediments of the organs) have generally a
more lively, just, and natural elocution, than persons of
a slow perception and a phlegmatic cast.   However, it
may in a great degree be attained by every one that
will carefully attend to, and practice, those rules that
are conducive to the acquisition.

In a just elocution, a particular regard should be paid
to the PAUSES, the EMPHASIS, and the CADENCE.

With respect to the pauses necessary to be observed
in reading, a person will, in a good measure, be directed
by the points; but not perfectly, for there are but few
books that are correctly pointed, according to the true
principles of grammar and reason.

The points serve two purposes, viz., first, to distinguish the sense of the author; and, secondly, to direct the pronunciation of the reader.

A speaker or reader is not to draw or fetch breath, as it is termed, if it can be avoided, till he arrives at the period or full stop; but a discernible pause is to be made at every one, according to its proper quantity of duration. Where the periods are very long, the speaker may take breath at a colon or semicolon, and sometimes even at a comma, but never where there is no point at all. To break a habit of taking breath too often, in reading or speaking, a person should accustom himself to read long periods, such, for instance, as the first sixteen lines of Milton's " Paradise Lost."

> Of Man's first disobedience, and the fruit
> Of that forbidden tree, whose mortal taste
> Brought death into the world and all our woe,
> With loss of Eden, till one greater man
> Restore us and regain the blissful seat,
> Sing, heav'nly muse, that, on the secret top
> Of Oreb or of Sinai, didst inspire
> That shepherd who first taught the chosen seed
> In the beginning, how the heav'ns and earth
> Rose out of chaos : or, if Sion hill
> Delight thee more, and Siloa's brook that flow'd
> Fast by the oracle of God, I thence
> Invoke thy aid to my advent'rous song,
> 'That, with no middle flight, intends to soar
> Above th' Aonian mount, while it pursues
> Things unattempted yet in prose or rhyme.

It is frequently necessary to regulate the pauses, as well as the variations of the voice, by a careful attention to the sense and the importance of the subject rather than to the punctuation.

The emphasis is another peculiar branch of a just elocution, and is to be particularly regarded in reading or speaking. With respect to this portion of our subject, it is necessary that a person should be exceedingly careful that it be always laid on the proper emphatical word. When we distinguish any particular syllable in a word with a strong voice, it is called *accent;* when we thus distinguish any particular word in a sentence, it is denominated *emphasis,* and the word so distinguished is the *emphatical word.* And the emphatical words (for there are often more than one) in a sentence, are those which carry a weight or importance in themselves, or are those on which the sense of the rest depends; and these must always be distinguished by a fuller and stronger sound of voice, wherever they be found, whether in the beginning, the middle, or the end of a sentence, as in the following couplets :

> "Get *place* and *wealth,* if possible, with *grace ;*
> If not, by *any* means get *wealth* and *place.*" *Pope.*

> "Some have at first for *wits,* then *poets,* pass'd,
> Turn'd *critics* next, and prov'd plain *fools* at last." *Ibid.*

In these quotations, the emphatical words are put in italics; and which they are, the sense will generally discover.

It is necessary to be somewhat more particular on the subject of emphasis; and here I shall make a few brief remarks on matters of this nature.

1 That some sentences are so full and comprehensive, that almost every word is emphatical; and it is of the greatest consequence to mark the emphatical word by a different and strong modulation of the voice: as in the following instance of pathetic expostulation, in the prophecy of Ezekiel:

"Why will ye die?"

Here every word may be made emphatical, and on which ever word a person lays the emphasis, whether on the first, second, third, or fourth, it conveys a very different sense, and opens a new subject of moving expostulation.

2. Some sentences are equivocal, as well as some words; that is, they contain more senses than one; and which is the sense intended, can only be known by observing on what word the emphasis is laid. Thus: "Shall you ride to town to-day?" This question is capable of being taken in four different senses, according to the different words on which you lay the emphasis. If it be laid on the word [*you*], the answer may be, "No, but I intend to send my servant." If it be laid on the word [*ride*], the answer may be, "No, I intend to walk." If you place the accent on the word [*town*], it is a different question, and the answer may be, "No, for I design to ride into the country." And if it be laid on the compound word [*to-day*], the sense is still somewhat different from any of these, and the proper answer may be, "No, but I shall to-morrow.' Of such importance sometimes is a right disposition of the emphasis, in order to determine the proper sense of what

we read or speak. I shall illustrate this subject by introducing another example: thus, this short sentence, "Did Alexander conquer the Persians?" may have three different meanings, according to the manner in which the speaker places the accent; and the emphasis has, consequently, three different places: as, when the speaker knew that the Persians were conquered, but did not know by whom; then the emphasis is placed on the word *Alexander;* as, "Did *Alexander* conquer the Persians?" When it is known that Alexander attempted the conquest, but the issue is not known, the emphasis is then placed on the word *conquer;* as, "Did Alexander *conquer* the Persians?" When it is known that he conquered the adjacent countries, but it is not certainly known that he conquered the Persians, the emphasis is placed on the word *Persians;* as, "Did Alexander conquer the *Persians?*"

3. The voice must express, as exactly as possible, the very sense or idea designed to be conveyed by the emphatical word, by a strong, rough, and violent, or a soft, smooth, and tender sound. Thus the different passions of the mind are to be expressed by a different sound or tone of voice. *Love,* by a soft, smooth, languishing voice; *anger,* by a strong, vehement, and elevated voice; *joy,* by a quick, sweet, and clear voice; *sorrow,* by a low, flexible, interrupted voice; *fear,* by a dejected, tremulous, hesitating voice; *courage* hath a full, bold, and loud voice; and *perplexity,* a grave, steady, and earnest one. Briefly, in *exordiums* the voice should be low; in *narrations,* distinct; in *reasoning,* slow; in

persuasion, strong : it should thunder in *anger*, soften in *sorrow*, tremble in *fear*, and melt in *love*.

4. The variation of the emphasis must not only distinguish the various passions described, but the several forms and figures of speech in which they are expressed; namely, in a *prosopopœia*, we must change the voice as the person introduced would. In an *antithesis*, one contrary must be pronounced louder than the other. In a *climax*, the voice should always rise with it. In *dialogues*, it should alter with the parts. In *repetitions*, it should be loudest in the second place. Words of quality and distinction, or of praise or dispraise, must be pronounced with a strong emphasis.

5. The emphasis is often placed on a wrong word in a sentence. This is the most common fault, and most liable to be committed, and arises from the want of a thorough knowledge of the sense, and the writer's ideas : for, if the reader or speaker be not perfectly acquainted with the exact construction and full meaning of every sentence which he recites, it is impossible he should give those inflexions and variations of the voice which nature requires. Some persons, finding the difficulty of rightly placing the emphasis, have rejected all emphasis entirely, and read with a dull, stupid monotony, which is the worst fault of all.

Cadence is directly opposite to *emphasis*. *Emphasis* marks the raising of the voice, *cadence* the falling of it; and, when it is managed with propriety and judgment, it is exceedingly musical. But, besides a cadence of the voice, there is such a thing as cadence of *style ;* and that is, when the sense being almost expressed and perfectly

discerned by the reader, the remaining words (which are
only necessary to complete the period) gently fall of
themselves without any emphatical word among them;
and, if the author's language be pure and elegant, his
cadence of style will naturally direct the cadence of
voice. Cadence, then, generally takes place at the end
of a sentence, unless it close with an emphatical word
Every *parenthesis* is to be pronounced in cadence, that
is, in a low voice, and quicker than ordinary, that it
may not take off the attention too much from the sense
of the period it interrupts. But all *apostrophes* and
prosopopœias are to be pronounced in *emphasis*.

A careful regard to these things is the first rule for
attaining a right and proper method of pronunciation.

If a person would acquire a right and just pronunciation in reading or speaking, he must not only take in
or comprise the full sense, but enter into the spirit of
his author ; for he can never convey the force and full-
ness of his author's ideas to another, till he feel them
himself. No man can read an author he does not per
fectly understand; at least, not so as to be perfectly
comprehended.

"The great rule," says a distinguished writer and
orator, "which the masters of rhetoric so much press,
can never enough be remembered ; 'that to make a man
speak well, and pronounce with a right emphasis, he
ought thoroughly to understand all that he says, be fully
persuaded of it, and bring himself to have those affec
tions which he desires to infuse into others.' He that
is inwardly persuaded of the truth of what he says, and
that hath a concern about it in his mind, will pronounce

with a natural vehemence that is far more lovely than all the strains that art can lead him to. An orator must endeavor to feel what he says, and then he will speak so as to make others feel it."

The same rules are to be observed in reading poetry as prose: neither the rhyme nor the numbers should take off the attention from the sense and spirit of the author; for it is that only which must direct the pronunciation in poetry as well as in prose. When any one reads verse, he must not at all favor the measure or rhyme; that often obscures the sense, and spoils the pronunciation; for the great end of pronunciation is to elucidate and heighten the sense; that is, to repre sent it not only in a clear but a strong light. Whatever then obstructs this is carefully to be avoided, both in verse and prose. Nay, this ought to be more carefully shunned in reading verse than prose; because the author, by a constant attention to his measures or rhyme, and the exaltation of his language, is sometimes apt to obscure his sense; which therefore requires the more care in the reader to discover and distinguish it by the pronunciation. And if, when any one reads verse with proper pause, emphasis, and cadence, and a pronunciation varied and governed by the sense, it be not harmonious and beautiful, the fault is not in the reader, but the author. If the verse be good, to read it thus will improve its harmony; because it will take off that uniformity of sound and accent which tires the ear, and makes the numbers heavy and disagreeable.

In the *third* place; another important rule is, Study nature. By this is meant

1. *That a person should study his own natural dispo-sitions and affections;* and those subjects which are more congenial to his own feelings, he will easily pro-nounce with a beautiful propriety; but, to heighten the pronunciation, the natural warmth of the mind should be permitted to have its course under a proper rein and regulation.

2. *Study the natural dispositions and affections of others;* for some are more easily impressed and moved one way, and some another. An orator should be acquainted with all the avenues to the heart.

3. *A person should study the most easy and natural way of expressing himself, both as to the tone of voice and the mode of speech.* This is best learned by observations on common conversation; where all is free, natural, and easy; where we are only intent on making ourselves understood, and conveying our ideas in a strong, plain, and lively manner, by the most natural language, pro-nunciation, and action. The nearer, indeed, our pro-nunciation in public agrees with the freedom and ease of that we use in common discourse, (provided we keep up the dignity of the subject, and preserve a propriety of expression,) the more just, and natural, and agreeable it will generally be. Above all things, then, study nature, avoid affectation; never use art, if you have not the art to conceal it; for whatever does not appear natural can never be agreeable, still less persuasive.

In the *fourth* place, it is proper that a person should *endeavor to keep his mind collected and composed.* He should constantly guard against that flutter and timidity of spirit which is the common infelicity of young persons, and especially those who are naturally bashful, when they first begin to speak in public. This is a very great hindrance both to their pronunciation and invention; and at once gives both themselves and their hearers unnecessary pain. It will wear off, by constant opposition. The best way to give the mind a good degree of assurance and self-command at such a time, is, for a person,

1. To be entirely master of his subject; with a consciousness that he delivers to his audience nothing but what is worth their hearing: this will furnish him with a proper share of courage.

2. He should endeavor to be wholly engaged in his subject; and, when the mind is intent upon and warmed with it, it will forget that awful deference it before paid to the audience, which was so apt to disconcert it.

3. If the sight of his hearers, or any of them, discompose him, he should keep his eyes from beholding them.

Fifthly, it is proper to observe, that a person should keep up a life, spirit, and energy, in the expression; and let the voice naturally vary according to the variation of the style and subject. Whatever be the subject, it will never be pleasing, if the style be low and flat; nor, if the pronunciation be so, will the beauty of the style be discovered. Cicero observes, there must be a *glow* in our style, if we would warm our readers. The transition of the voice must always correspond with that of the subject, and the passions it was intended to excite.

Sixthly, in order to attain a just and graceful pro-enunciation, it is proper that a person should accustom himself frequently to hear those who excel in it, whether at the bar or in the pulpit; where he will perceive all .the forementioned rules exemplified, and be able to account for all those graces and beauties of pronuncia- tion which always gratified him, though he were unable to tell why. Indeed, the best mode of acquiring the art of pronunciation, like all others, is rather by imita- tion than by rule; but to be first acquainted with the rules of it, will render the imitation more easy. In fact, beyond all that has been said, or can be described, he will observe a certain agreeableness of manner in some speakers, that is natural to them, not to be reduced to any rule, and to be learned by imitation only; nor even by that, unless it be in some degree natural to himself as the hearer.

Seventhly, a person should frequently exercise him- self in reading aloud, according to the foregoing rules. It is practice only that can give him the faculty of an elegant pronunciation. This, like other habits, is only to be acquired by acts often repeated.

Orators, indeed, as well as poets, must be born so, or they will never excel in their respective arts: but that part of oratory which consists in a decent and graceful pronunciation (provided there be no defect in the organs of speech) may be attained by rule, by imitation, and by practice; and, when attained, will give a beauty to a person's speech, a force to his thoughts, and a plea- sure to his auditors, which cannot be expressed; and which all will admire, but none can imitate, unless they be first prepared for it by nature and by art   In short,

3

the great advantage of a just pronunciation is, that it will please all, whether they have no taste, a bad taste, or a good one.

THE INFLECTIONS OF THE VOICE.

Besides the pauses, which indicate a greater or less separation of the parts of a sentence and a conclusion of the whole, there are certain inflections of voice, accompanying these pauses, which are as necessary to the sense of the sentence as the pauses themselves; for, however exactly we may pause between those parts which are separable, if we do no. pause with such an inflection of the voice as is suited to the sense, the composition we read will not only want its true meaning, but will have a meaning very different from that intended by the writer.

Whether words are pronounced in a high or low, in a loud or soft tone; whether they are pronounced swiftly or slowly, forcibly or feebly, with the tone of passion or without it; they must necessarily be pronounced either sliding upward or downward, or else go into a monotone or song.

By the rising or falling inflection, is not meant the pitch of the voice in which the whole word is pronounced, or that loudness or softness which may accompany any pitch; but that upward or downward slide which the voice makes when the pronunciation of a word is finishing, and which may, therefore, not improperly, be called the rising and falling inflection.

We must carefully guard against mistaking the low tone at the beginning of the rising inflection for the falling inflection, and the high tone at the beginning of the falling inflection for the rising inflection, as they are not denominated rising or falling from the high or low tone in which they are pronounced, but from the upward or downward slide in which they terminate, whether pronounced in a high or low key.

RULE I.— *The falling inflection takes place at a period.*
EXAMPLES.
1. That man is little to be envied whose patriotism

would not gain force upon the plain of Marathon, or whose piety would not grow warmer among the ruins of Iona'.

2. The pleasures of the imagination, the pleasure arising from science, from the fine arts, and from the principle of curiosity, are peculiar to the human' species.

When a sentence concludes an antithesis, the first branch of which, being emphatic, requires the falling inflection; the second branch requires the weak emphasis, and rising inflection.

Note.—When there is a succession of periods or loose members in a sentence, though they may all have the falling inflection, yet every one of them ought to be pronounced in a somewhat different pitch of the voice from the other.

EXAMPLES.

1. If we have no regard for our own' character, we ought to have some regard for the character of others'.

2. If content cannot remove' the disquietudes of mankind, it will at least alleviate' them.

RULE II.—*Negative sentences, or members of sentences, must end with the rising inflection.*

EXAMPLES.

1. The region beyond the grave is not a solitary' land. There your fathers are, and thither every other friend shall follow you in due season.

2. True charity is not a meteor, which occasionally glares; but a luminary, which, in its orderly and regular course, dispenses a benignant influence.

RULE III.—*The penultimate member* of a sentence re quires the rising inflection.*

EXAMPLES.

1. We were now treading that illustrious island which was once the luminary of the Caledonian regions, whence savage clans and roving barbarians derived the benefits of knowledge', and the blessings of religion.

2. Mahomet was a native of Mecca, a city of that division of Arabia, which, for the luxury of its soil and happy temperature of its climate, has ever been esteemed the loveliest and sweetest' region in the world, and distinguished by the epithet of happy.

RULE IV.—*Every direct period, having its two principal constructive parts connected by corresponding conjunctions or adverbs, requires the long pause, with the rising inflection at the end of the first part.*

EXAMPLES.

1. If, when we behold a well-made and well-regulated watch, we infer the operations of a skillful artificer'; then none but a "fool" indeed can contemplate the universe, all whose parts are so admirably formed, and so harmoniously adjusted, and yet say, "There is no God."

2. Whenever you see a people making progress in vice; whenever you see them discovering a growing disregard to the divine law'; there you see proportional advances made to ruin and misery.

Note.—When the emphatical word in the conditional part of the sentence is in direct opposition to another word in the conclusion

---

* Penultimate signifies the last but one.

and a concession is implied in the former, in order to strengthen the argument in the latter, the first member has the falling, and the last the rising inflection.

1. If we have no regard for religion in youth`, we ought to have some regard for it in age´.

2. If we have no regard for our own` character, we ought to have some regard for the character of others´.

If these sentences had been formed so as to make the latter member a mere inference from, or consequence of, the former, the general rule would have taken place : thus—

1. If we have no regard for religion in youth´, we have seldom any regard for it in age`.

2. If we have no regard for our own´ character, it can scarcely be expected that we could have any regard for the character of others`

RULE V.—*Direct periods, commencing with participles of the present and past tense, consist of two parts ; between which must be inserted the long pause and rising inflection.*

EXAMPLES.

1. Having existed from all eternity´, God, through all eternity, must continue to exist.

2. Placed by Providence on the palæstra of life´, every human being is a wrestler, and happiness is that prize for which he is bound to contend.

Note.—When the last word of the first part of these sentences requires the strong emphasis, the falling inflection must be used instead of the rising.

EXAMPLE.

Hannibal being frequently destitute of money and provisions, with no recruits of strength in case of ill fortune, and no encouragement, even when successful´ ; it is not to be wondered at that his affairs began at length to decline

Rule VI.—*Those parts of a sentence which depend on adjectives require the rising inflection.*

EXAMPLES.

1. Destitute of the favor of God', you are in no better situation, with all your supposed abilities, than orphans left to wander in a trackless desert.

2. Full of spirit, and high in hope', we set out on the journey of life.

Rule VII.—*Every inverted period* * requires the rising inflection and long pause between its two principal constructive parts.*

EXAMPLES.

1. Persons of good taste expect to be pleased', at the same time they are informed.

2. I can desire to perceive those things that God has prepared for those that love' him, though they be such as eye hath not seen, ear heard, nor hath it entered into the heart of man to conceive.

Sentences constructed like the following also fall under this rule.

3 Poor were the expectations of the studious, the modest, and the good', if the reward of their labors were only to be expected from man.

4. Virtue were a kind of misery', if fame only were all the garland that crowned her.

---

* A period is said to be inverted, when the first part forms perfect sense by itself, but is modified or determined in its signification by the latter.

RULE VIII.—*The member that forms perfect sense must be separated from those that follow by a long pause and the falling inflection.*

EXAMPLES.

1. Through faith we understand that the worlds were framed by the word of God'; so that things which are seen were not made of things that do appear.

2. By faith Abraham, when he was called to go out into a place which he should after receive for an inheritance, obeyed'; and he went out, not knowing whither he went.

Note.—When a sentence consists of several loose members which neither modify nor are modified by one another, they may be considered as a compound series, and pronounced accordingly.

RULE IX.—*The first member of an antithesis must end with the long pause of the rising inflection.*

EXAMPLES.

1. The most frightful disorders arose from the state of feudal anarchy. Force decided all things. Europe was one great field of battle, where the weak struggled for freedom', and the strong for dominion. The king was without power', and the nobles without principle. They were tyrants at home', and robbers abroad. Nothing remained to be a check upon ferocity and violence.

2. Between fame and true honor a distinction is to be made. The former is a blind and noisy' applause; the latter a more silent and internal homage. Fame floats on the breath of the multitude': honor rests on the judgment of the thinking. Fame may give praise,

while it withholds esteem': true honor implies esteem mingled with respect. The one regards particular dis tinguished' talents; the other looks up to the whole character.

RULE X.—*At the end of a concession the rising inflection takes place.*

EXAMPLES.

1. Reason, eloquence, and every art which ever has been studied among mankind, may be abused, and may prove dangerous in the hands of bad' men; but it were perfectly childish to contend, that, upon this account, they ought to be abolished.

2. One may be a speaker, both of much reputation and much influence in the calm argumentative' manner. To attain the pathetic, and the sublime of oratory, requires those strong sensibilities of mind, and that high power of expression, which are given to few.

RULE XI.—*Questions asked by pronouns or adverbs end with the falling inflection.*

EXAMPLES.

1. Who continually supports and governs this stupen dous system'? Who preserves ten thousand times ten thousand worlds in perpetual harmony'? Who enables them always to observe such times, and obey such laws, as are most exquisitely adapted for the perfection of the wondrous whole'? They cannot preserve and direct themselves; for they were created. and must, therefore, be dependent. How, then, can they be so actuated

and directed but by the unceasing energy of the great Supreme'?

2 Ah! why will kings forget that they are men,
And men that they are brethren'? Why delight
In human' sacrifice? Why burst the ties
Of nature, that should knit their souls together
In one soft bond of amity and love'?

Note 1.—Interrogative sentences, consisting of members in a series necessarily depending on each other for sense, must be pronounced according to the rule which relates to the series of which they are composed.

EXAMPLES.

What can be more important and interesting than an inquiry into the existence', attributes', providence', and moral government' of God?

RULE XII.—*Questions asked by verbs require the rising inflection.**

EXAMPLES.

1. Can the soldier, when he girdeth on his armor, boast like him that putteth it off'? Can the merchant predict that the speculation, on which he has entered, will be infallibly crowned with success'? Can even the husbandman, who has the promise of God that seed-time and harvest shall not fail, look forward with assured confidence to the expected increase of his fields'? In those, and in all similar cases, our resolution to act can be founded on probability alone.

2. Avarus has long been ardently endeavoring to fill his chest: and lo! it is now full. Is he happy'? Does

---

* When the question is very long, however, or concludes a paragraph, the falling instead of the rising inflection takes place.

ne use′ it? Does he gratefully think of the Giver′ of all good things? Does he distribute to the poor′? Alas! these interests have no place in his breast.

Ruɪɪ XIII.— *When interrogative sentences connected by the disjunctive,* or, *expressed or understood, succeed each other, the first end with the rising and the rest with the falling inflection.**

EXAMPLES

1. Does God, after having made his creatures, take no further′ care of them? Has he left them to blind fate or undirected chance′? Has he forsaken the works of his own hands′? Or does he always graciously preserve, and keep, and guide‵ them?

2. Should these credulous infidels after all be in the right, and this pretended revelation be all a fable, from believing it what harm‵ could ensue? Would it render princes more tyrannical, or subjects more ungovernable′? the rich more insolent, or the poor more disorderly′? Would it make worse parents, or children′; husbands, ɔ· wives′; masters, or servants′; friends, or neighbors′? *or* would it not make men more virtuous, and, consequently, more happy‵ in every situation?

Note 2.—An interrogative sentence, consisting of a variety of members depending on each other for sense, may have the inflection common to other sentences, provided the last member has that inflection which distinguishes the species of interrogation to which it belongs.

EXAMPLE.

Can we believe a thinking being, that is in a perpetual progress of improvement‵, and travelling on from perfection to perfection, after

---

* When *or* is used conjunctively, the inflections are not regulated by it.

having just looked abroad into the works of its Creator', and made a few discoveries of his infinite goodness, wisdom, and power, must perish at her first setting out', and in the very beginning' of her inquiries?

Note 3.—Interrogative sent‿ces, consisting of members in a series which form perfect sense as they proceed, must have every member terminate with that inflection which distinguishes the species of interrogation of which they consist.

EXAMPLES.

1. Hath death torn from your embrace the friend whom you tenderly loved'—him to whom you were wont to unbosom the secrets of your soul'—him who was your counsellor in perplexity, the sweet ener of all your joys, and the assuager of all your sorrows'? You think you do well to mourn; and the tears with which you water his grave, seem to be a tribute due to his virtues. But waste not your affection in fruitless lamentation.

2. Who are the persons that are most apt to fall into peevishness and dejection'—that are continually complaining of the world, and see nothing but wretchedness' around them? Are they those whom want compels to toil for their daily bread'—who have no treasure but the labor of their hands'—who rise with the rising sun to expose themselves to all the rigors of the seasons, unsheltered from the winter's cold, and unshaded from the summer's heat'? No. The labors of such are the very blessings of their condition.

Note 4.—When questions, asked by verbs, are followed by answers, the rising inflection, in a high tone of voice, takes place at the end of the question, and, after a long pause, the answer must be pronounced in a lower tone.

EXAMPLES.

1. Are you desirous that your talents and abilities may procure you respect'? Display them not ostentatiously to public view. Would you escape the envy which your riches' might excite? Let them not minister to pride, but adorn them with humility.

2. There is not an evil incident to human nature for which the gospel doth not provide a remedy. Are you ignorant of many things which it highly concerns you to know'? The gospel offers you instruction. Have you deviated from the path of duty'? The gospel

offers you forgiveness. Do temptations surround you? The gospel offers you the aid of Heaven. Are you exposed to misery? It consoles you. Are you subject to death? It offers you immortality.

RULE XIV.—*The inflections at the note of exclamation are the same as at any other point, in sentences similarly constructed.*

EXAMPLES.

1. The Almighty sustains and conducts the universe! It was he who separated the jarring elements'! It was he who hung up the worlds in empty space'! It was he who preserves them in their circles, and impels them in their course'!

2. How pure, how dignified should they be, whose origin is celestial'! How pure, how dignified should they be, who are taught to look higher than earth; to expect to enjoy the divinest pleasures for evermore, and to "shine forth as the sun in the kingdom of their Father'!"

RULE XV.—*When the exclamation, in form of a question, is the echo of another question of the same kind, or when it proceeds from wonder or admiration, it always requires the rising inflection.*

EXAMPLES.

1. Will you for ever, Athenians, do nothing but walk up and down the city, asking one another, What news'? What news'! Is there anything more new than to see a man of Macedonia become master of the Athenians, and give laws to all Greece'?

2. What'. might Rome then have been taken, if those men who were at your gates had not wanted courage'

for the attempt?—Rome taken when I' was consul!—Of honors I had sufficient—of life enough—more than enough. '

RULE XVI.—*A parenthesis must be pronounced in a lower tone of voice than the rest of the sentence, and conclude with the same pause and inflection which terminate the member that immediately precedes it.* *

EXAMPLES.

1 Though fame, who is always the herald of the great, has seldom deigned to transmit the exploits of the lower ranks to posterity', (for it is commonly the fate of those whom fortune has placed in the vale of obscurity to have their noble actions buried in oblivion';) yet, in their verses, the minstrels have preserved many instances of domestic woe and felicity.

2. Uprightness is a habit, and, like all other habits, gains strength by time and exercise. If, then, we exercise' upright principles, (and we cannot have them unless we exercise' them,) they must be perpetually on the increase.

Note 1.—The end of a parenthesis must have the falling inflection when it terminates with an emphatical word.

EXAMPLE.

Had I, when speaking in the assembly, been absolute and independent master of affairs, then your other speakers might call me to account. But if ye were ever present, if ye were all in general invited to propose your sentiments, if ye were all agreed that the measures

---

* A parenthesis must also be pronounced a degree quicker than the rest of the sentence ; a pause, too, must be made both before and after it, proportioned in length to the more intimate or remote connection, which it has with the rest of the sentence.

then suggested were really the best; if you, Æschines, in particular, were thus persuaded, ('and it was no partial affection for me, that prompted you to give me up the hopes, the applause, the honors, which, attended that course I then advised, but the superior force of truth and your utter inability to point out any more eligible' course ;) if this was the case, I say, is it not highly cruel and unjust to arraign those measures now, when you could not then propose any better?

Note 2.—When the parenthesis is long, it may be pronounced with a degree of monotone or sameness of voice, in order to distinguish it from the rest of the sentence.

EXAMPLE.

Since, then, every sort of good which is immediately of importance to happiness, must be perceived by some immediate power or sense, antecedent to any opinions or reasoning', (for it is the business of reason to compare the several sorts of good perceived by the several senses, and to find out the proper means for obtaining' them,) we must therefore carefully inquire into the several sublimer perceptive powers or senses : since it is by them we best discover what state or course of life best answers the intention of God and nature, and wherein true happiness consists.

Note 3.—The small intervening members, *said I, says he, continued they,* &c., follow the inflection and tone of the member which precedes them, in a higher and feebler tone of voice.

EXAMPLE.

Thus, then, said he, since you are so urgent, it is thus that I conceive it. The sovereign good is that, the possession of which renders us happy. And now, said I, do we possess it? Is it sensual or intellectual? There, you are entering, said he, upon the detail.

HARMONIC INFLECTION.

Besides that variety which necessarily arises from annexing certain inflections to sentences of a particular import or structure, there is still another source of variety, in those parts of a sentence where the sense is not at all concerned, and where the variety is merely to please the ear. There are many members of sentences which may be differently pronounced without greatly affecting their variety and harmony

It is chiefly toward the end of a sentence that the harmonic inflection is necessary in order to form an agreeable cadence.

RULE I.—*When a series of similar sentences, or members of sentences, form a branch of a subject or paragraph, the last sentence or member must fall gradually into a lower tone, and adopt the harmonic inflection, on such words as form the most agreeable cadence.*

EXAMPLE.

Since I have mentioned this unaccountable zeal which appears in atheists and infidels, I' must farther observe, that they are likewise in a most particular manner possessed with the spirit of bigc ry. They are wedded' to opinions' full of contradiction' and impossibility', and at the same' time' look upon the smallest' difficulty' in an article' of faith' as a sufficient reason for rejecting it.

RULE II.—*When the last member of a sentence ends with four accented words, the falling inflection takes place on the first and last, and the rising on the second and third.*

EXAMPLES.

1. The immortality of the soul is the basis of morality, and the source of all the pleasing' hopes' and secret joys', that can arise' in the heart' of a reasonable' creature'.

2. A brave' man struggling in the storms' of fate',
   And greatly' falling' with a falling' state'.

RULE III.— *When there are three accented words at the end of the last member, the first has either the rising or falling, the second the rising, and the last the falling inflection.*

EXAMPLE.

Cicero concludes his celebrated books, *De Oratore,* with some precepts for pronunciation and action, without which part he affirms, that the best orator in the world can never succeed, and an indifferent one, who is master of this, shall gain much'greater' applause.

ECHO

Is here used to express that repetition of a word or thought, which immediately arises from a word or thought that preceded it.

RULE.— *The echoing word ought always to be pronounced with the rising inflection in a high tone of voice, and a long pause after it, when it implies any degree of passion.* *

EXAMPLE.

1. Augustin became a Christian! *Augustin!* who had mastered all the learning of his age, and whose subtle mind had anticipated the objections of future unbelievers.

Bossuet was a Christian! *Bossuet!* whose soaring genius and wonderful intellectual vision ar acknowledged and honored by all.

---

* The echoing word is printed in *italics,* and marked with the rising inflection.

THE MONOTONE,

In certain solemn and sublime passages has a wonderful force and dignity; and by the uncommonness of its use, it even adds greatly to that variety with which the ear is so much delighted.*

EXAMPLE.

1. High on a throne of royal state, which far
   Outshone the wealth of Ormus or of Inde,
   Or whēre the gōrgeous eäst, with rīchest hānd,
   Shōwers, on her kīngs barbāric, pearl' and gold',
   Satan exalted sat.

CIRCUMFLEXES.

The *rising* circumflex begins with the falling inflection and ends with the rising upon the same syllable, and seems as it were to twist the voice upward. This turn of the voice is marked in this manner, (᷎.)

EXAMPLE.

But it is foolish in us to compare Drusus Africanus and ourselves with Clŏdius; all our other calamities were tolerable; but no one can patiently bear the death of Clŏdius.

The *falling* circumflex begins with the rising inflection, and ends with the falling upon the same syllable, and seems to twist the voice downward. This turn of the voice may be marked by the common circumflex : thus, (᷅.)

EXAMPLE.

Queen. Hamlet, you have your father much offeɪded.
Hamlet. Madam, yoû have my father much offended.

---

* This monotone may be defined to be a continuation or sameness of sound upon certain syllables of a word, exactly like that produced by repeatedly striking a bell ;—such a stroke may be louder or softer but continues exactly in the same pitch. To express this tone upon paper, a horizontal line may be adopted ; such a one as is generally used to express a long syllable in verse : thus (–.)

4

Both these circumflex inflections may be exemplified in the word *so* in a speech of the Clown in Shakspeare's *As You Like It.*

I knew when seven justices could not take up a quarrel; but when the parties were met themselves, one of them thought but of an If; as if you said sŏ, then I said sô. O ho! did you sŏ? So they shook hands and were sworn brothers.

CLIMAX,

OR A GRADUAL INCREASE OF SIGNIFICATION,

Requires an increasing swell of the voice on every succeeding particular, and a degree of animation corresponding with the nature of the subject.

EXAMPLE.

1. After we have practised good actions awhile, they become easy, and when they are easy, we begin to take pleasure in them; and when they please us, we do them frequently; and, by frequency of acts, a thing grows into a habit; and a confirmed habit is a second kind of nature; and, so far as anything is natural, so far it is necessary, and we can hardly do otherwise; nay, we do it many times when we do not think of it.

ACCENT.

RULE.—*Emphasis requires a transposition of accent, when two words which have a sameness in part of their formation, are opposed to each other in sense.*

EXAMPLES.

1. What is *done'*, cannot be *un'*done.*

---

* The signs ('and ',) besides denoting the inflections, mark also the accented syllables.

Whatever inflection be adopted, the accented syllable is always

2. There is a material difference between *giv'ing* and *for'giving*

3. Thought and language *act'* and *re'act* upon each ether.

4. He who is good before *in'*visible witnesses, is eminently so before the *vis'*ible.

5 What fellowship hath *right'*eousness with *un*-righteousness? and what communion hath light with darkness?

6. The riches of the prince must *in*crease or *de'*-crease, in proportion to the number and riches of his subjects.

Note 1.—This transposition of the accent extends itself to all words which have a sameness of termination, though they may not be directly opposite in sense.

EXAMPLES.

1. In this species of composition, *plau'*sibility is much more essential than *prob'*ability.

2. Lucius Catiline was expert in all the arts of *sim'*ulation and *dis'*simulation; covetous of what belonged to others, lavish of his own.

Note 2.—When the accent is on the last syllable of a word which has no emphasis, it must be pronounced louder and a degree lower than the rest.

EXAMPLE.

Sconer or later virtue must meet with a *reward'*.

---

louder than the rest; but if the accent be pronounced with the rising inflection, the accented syllable is higher than the preceding, and lower than the succeeding syllable; and if the accent have the falling inflection, the accented syllable is pronounced higher than any other syllable, either preceding or succeeding

EMPHASIS

Is that stress we lay on words which are in contradistinction to other words expressed or understood. And hence will follow this general rule: *Wherever there is contradistinction in the sense of the words, there ought to be emphasis in the pronunciation of them.*

All words are pronounced either with emphatic force, accented force, or unaccented force; this last kind of force may be called by the name of feebleness. When the words are in contradistinction to other words, or to some sense implied, they may be called *emphatic,* where they do not denote contradistinction, and yet are more important than the particles, they may be called *accented,* and the particles and lesser words may be called *unaccented* or *feeble.*

EXAMPLES.

1. *Exercise* and *temperance strengthen* the *constitution*

2. *Exercise* and *temperance strengthen* even an INDIF-FERENT constitution.

The word printed in Roman capitals is pronounced with *emphatic* force; those in small Italics are pronounced with *accented* force; the rest with *unaccented* force.

SINGLE EMPHASIS.*

RULE.— *When a sentence is composed of a positive and negative part, the positive must have the falling, and the negative the rising inflection.*†

EXAMPLES.

1. We can do nothing *against'* the truth, but *for'* the truth.

2. None more impatiently *suffer'* injuries, than they who are most forward in *doing'* them.

---

* When two emphatic words in antithesis with each other are either expressed or implied, the emphasis is said to be single.

† To this rule, however, there are some exceptions, not only in poetry, but also in prose.

8. You were paid to *fight* against Alexander, and not to *rail'* at him.

DOUBLE EMPHASIS.*

RULE.—*The falling inflection takes place on the first emphatic word, the rising on the second and third, and the falling on the fourth.*†

EXAMPLES.

1. To *err`* is *human'*; to *forgive'* *divine`*.
2. Custom is the *plague`* of *wise'* men, and the *idol'* of *fools`*.

TREBLE EMPHASIS.‡

RULE.—*The rising inflection takes place on the first and third, and the falling on the second of the first three emphatical words; the first and third of the other three have the falling, and the second has the rising inflection.*

EXAMPLES.

1. A *friend'* cannot be *known`* in *prosperity'*; and an *enemy`* cannot be *hidden'* in *adversity`*.
2. Flowers of rhetoric in sermons or serious discourses are like the blue and red flowers in corn, *pleasing'* to *those`* who come only for *amusement'*, but *prejudicial`* to *him'* who would reap the *profit`*.

---

* When two words are opposed to each other, and contrasted with two other words, the emphasis on these four words may be called double.

† The pause after the second emphatic word must be considerably longer than that after the first or third.

‡ When three emphatic words are opposed to three other emphatic words in the same sentence, the emphasis is called treble.

THE ANTECEDENT.

RULE.—*Personal or adjective pronouns, when antecedents, must be pronounced with an accentual force, to intimate that the relative is in view, and in some measure to anticipate the pronunciation of it.*

EXAMPLES.

1. *He,* that pursues fame with just claims, trusts his happiness to the winds; but *he,* that endeavors after it by false merit, has to fear, not only the violence of the storm, but the leaks of his vessel.

2. The weakest reasoners are always the most positive in debate; and the cause is obvious; for *they* are unavoidably driven to maintain their pretensions by violence, who want arguments and reasons to prove that they are in the right.

RULE II.—*When the relative only is expressed, the antecedent being understood, the accentual force then falls upon the relative.*

EXAMPLES.

1. *What* nothing earthly gives or can destroy,
    The soul's calm sunshine, and the heartfelt joy,
    Is virtue's prize.
2. *Who* noble ends by noble means obtains,
    Or failing, smiles in exile or in chains,
    Like good Aurelius let him reign, or bleed
    Like Socrates, that man is great indeed.

GENERAL EMPHASIS

Is that emphatic force, which, when the composition is very animated and approaches to a close we often lay upon several words in succession. This emphasis is not so much regulated by the sense of the author, as by the taste and feelings of the reader, and therefore does not admit of any certain rule.

EXAMPLES.

1.
What men could do
Is done already: heaven and earth will witness,
If' Rome' must' fall', that we are innocent.

2. There was a time, then, my fellow-citizens, when the Lacedæmonians were sovereign masters both by sea and land; when their troops and forts surrounded the entire circuit of Attica; when they possessed Eubœa, Tanagra, the whole Bœotian district, Megara, Ægina, Cleone, and the other islands, while this state had not one ship, not' one' wall'.

THE INTERMEDIATE OR ELLIPTICAL MEMBER

Is that part of a sentence which is equally related to both parts of an antithesis, but which is properly only once expressed.

EXAMPLES.

1. Must we, in your person, crown' the author of the public calamities, or must we destroy' him?

2. A good man will love himself too well to lose' an estate by gaming, and his neighbor too well to win' one.

RHETORICAL PAUSES.

RULE I.—*Pause after the nominative when it consists of more than one word.**

EXAMPLE.

1. The fashion of this world *passeth* away.

---

* The place of the pause is immediately before each of the words printed in *italics*.

Note.—A pause may be made after a nominative, even when it consists of only one word, if it be a word of importance, or if we wish it to be particularly observed.

EXAMPLES.

1. Adversity *is* the school of piety.
2. The fool *hath* said in his heart there is no God.

RULE II.—*When any member comes between the nominative case and the verb, it must be separated from both of them by a short pause.*

EXAMPLES.

1. Trials *in* this state of being *are* the lot of man.
2. Such is the constitution of men, that virtue *however* it may be neglected, for a time *will* ultimately be acknowledged and respected.

RULE III.—*When any member comes between the verb and the objective or accusative case, it must be separated from both of them by a short pause.*

EXAMPLE.

I knew a person who possessed the faculty of distinguishing flavors in so great a perfection, that, after having tasted ten different kinds of tea, he would distinguish *without* seeing the color of it *the* particular sort which was offered him.

RULE IV.—*When two verbs come together, and the latter is in the infinitive mood, if any words come between, they must be separated from the latter verb by a pause.*

EXAMPLE.

Whether 'tis nobler in the mind *to* suffer
The stings and arrows of outrageous fortune;

Or to take arms against a sea of troubles,
And by opposing end them?

Note.—When the verb *to be* is followed by a verb in the infinitive mood, which may serve as a nominative case to it, and the phrase before and after the verb may be transposed, then the pause falls between the verbs.

EXAMPLE,

The greatest misery is *to* be condemned by our own hearts.

RULE V.—*When several substantives become the nominatives to the same verb, a pause must be made between the last substantive and the verb, as well as after each of the other substantives.*

EXAMPLE.

Riches, pleasure, and health *become* evils to those who do not know how to use them.

RULE VI.—*If there are several adjectives belonging to one substantive, or several substantives belonging to one adjective, every adjective coming after its substantive, and every adjective coming before the substantive except the last, must be separated by a short pause.*

EXAMPLE.

1 It was a calculation *accurate* to the last degree.

Note.—This rule applies also to sentences in which several adverbs belong to one verb, or several verbs to one adverb.

EXAMPLES.

1. To love *wisely, rationally, and* prudently, is, in the opinion of lovers, not to love at all.

2. Wisely, *rationally, and* prudently to love, is, in the opinion of lovers, not to love at all.

RULE VII.—*Whatever words are in the ablative absolute, must be separated from the rest by a short pause both before and after them.*

EXAMPLE.

If a man borrow aught of his neighbor, and it be hurt or die, *the* owner thereof not being with it, *he* shall surely make it good.

RULE VIII.—*Nouns in opposition, or words in the same case, where the latter are only explanatory of the former, have a short pause between them, either if both of these nouns consist of many terms, or the latter only.*

EXAMPLES.

1. Hope, *the* balm of life, soothes us under every misfortune.

2. Solomon, *the* son of David, *and* the builder of the temple of Jerusalem, was the richest monarch that reigned over the Jewish people.

RULE IX.—*When two substantives come together, and the latter, which is in the genitive case, consists of several words closely united with each other, a pause is admissible between the two principal substantives.*

EXAMPLE.

I do not know whether I am singular in my opinion, but, for my own part, I would rather look upon a tree in all its luxuriancy, and diffusion *of* boughs and branches, than when it is cut and trimmed into a mathematical figure.

RULE X.—*Who, which, when in the nominative case, and the pronoun* that, *when used for* who *or* which, *require a short pause before them.*

1. Death is the season *which* brings our affections to the tost.

2. Nothing is in vain *that* rouses the soul : nothing in vain *that* keeps the ethereal fire alive and glowing.

3. A man can never be obliged to submit to any power, unless he can be satisfied *who* is the person *who* has a right to exercise it.

RULE XI.—*Pause before* that, *when it is used for a conjunction.*

EXAMPLE.

It is in society only *that* we can relish those pure delicious joys which embellish and gladden the life of man

RULE XII.— *When a pause is necessary at prepositions and conjunctions, it must be* before, *and not* after *them.*

EXAMPLES.

1. We must not conform to the world *in* their amusements and diversions.

2. There is an inseparable connection *between* piety and virtue.

RULE XIII.—*In an elliptical sentence, pause where the ellipsis takes place.*

EXAMPLE.

To our faith we should add virtue; and to virtue knowledge ; and to knowledge *temperance ;* and to temperance *patience;* and to patience *godliness;* and to godliness *brotherly* kindness; and to brotherly kindness *charity.*

RULE XIV.— *Words placed either in opposition to, or in apposition with each other, must be distinguished by a pause.*

EXAMPLE.

The pleasures of the imagination, taken in their full extent, are not so gross *as* those of sense, nor so refined *as* those of the understanding.

RULE XV.— *When prepositions are placed in opposition to each other, and all of them are intimately connected with another word, the pause after the second preposition must be shorter than that after the first, and the pause after the third shorter than that after the second.*

EXAMPLE.

Rank, distinction, pre-eminence, no man despises, unless he is either raised very much *above,* or sunk very much *below,* the ordinary standard of human nature.

RULES FOR READING VERSE.

On the Slides or Inflections of Verse.

· 1. The first general rule for reading verse is, that we ought to give it that measured harmonious flow of sound which distinguishes it from prose, without falling into a bombastic, chanting pronunciation, which makes it ridiculous.

2. It will not be improper, before we read verse with

its poetical graces, to pronounce it exactly as if it were
prose: this will be depriving verse of its beauty, but
will tend to preserve it from deformity: the tones of
voice will be frequently different, but the inflections will
be nearly the same.

3. But though an elegant and harmonious pronuncia
tion of verse will sometimes oblige us to adopt different
inflections from those we use in prose, it may still be
laid down as a good general rule, that verse requires
the same inflections as prose, though less strongly
marked, and more approaching to monotones.

4. Wherever a sentence, or member of a sentence,
would necessarily require the falling inflection in prose,
it ought always to have the same inflection in poetry;
for though, if we were to read verse prosaically, we
should often place the falling inflection where the style
of verse would require the rising, yet in those parts
where a portion of perfect sense, or the conclusion of a
sentence, necessarily requires the falling inflection, the
same inflection must be adopted both in verse and prose.

5. In the same manner, though we frequently suspend
the voice by the rising inflection in verse, where, if the
composition were prose, we should adopt the falling, yet,
wherever in prose the member or sentence would necessarily require the rising inflection, this inflection must
necessarily be adopted in verse.

6. It may be observed, indeed, that it is in the fre·
quent use of the rising inflection, where prose would
adopt the falling, that the song of poetry consists;
familiar, strong, argumentative subjects naturally enforce the language with the falling inflection, as this is

naturally expressive of activity, force, and precision but grand, beautiful, and plaintive subjects slide natu rally into the rising inflection, as this is expressive of awe, admiration, and melancholy, where the mind may be said to be passive; and it is this general tendency of the plaintive tone to assume the rising inflection, which inclines injudicious readers to adopt it at those pauses where the falling inflection is absolutely neces- sary, and for want of which the pronunciation degene- rates into the whine, so much and so justly disliked; for it is very remarkable, that if, where the sense con- cludes, we are careful to preserve the falling inflection, and let the voice drop into the natural talking tone, the voice may be suspended in the rising inflection on any other part of the verse, with very little danger of falling into the chant of bad readers.

On the Accent and Emphasis of Verse.

In verse, every syllable must have the same accent, and every word the same emphasis, as in prose.

In words of *two* syllables, however, when the poet transposes the accent from the *second* syllable to the *first*, we may comply with him, without occasioning any harshness in the verse;—but when, in such words, he changes the accent from the *first* to the *second* syllable, every reader who has the least delicacy of feeling will certainly preserve the common accent of these words on the *first* syllable.

In misaccented words of *three* syllables, perhaps the least offensive method to the ear of preserving the ac- cent, and not entirely violating the quantity, would be to place an accent on the syllable immediately preceding that on which the poet has misplaced it, without dropping that which is so misplaced.

The same rule seems to hold good where the poet has placed the accent on the first and last syllable of a word, which ought to have it on the middle syllable.

Where a word admits of some diversity in placing the accent, it is scarcely necessary to observe, that the verse ought in this case to decide.

But when the poet has with great judgment contrived that his numbers shall be harsh and grating, in order to correspond with the ideas they suggest, the common accentuation must be preserved.

How the Vowels e and o are to be pronounced, when apostrophized.

The vowel e, which in poetry is often cut off by an apostrophe in the word the and in unaccented syllables before r, as dang'rous, gen'rous, &c., ought always to be preserved in pronunciation, because the syllable it forms is so short as to admit of being sounded with the succeeding syllable, so as not to increase the number of syllables to the ear, or at least to hurt the melody.

The same observations, in every respect, hold good in the pronunciation of the preposition to, which ought always to be sounded long, like the adjective two, however it may be printed.

On the Pause or Cæsura of Verse.

Almost every verse admits of a pause in or near the middle of the line, which is called the cæsura; this must be carefully observed in reading verse, or much of the distinctness, and almost all the harmony, will be lost.

Though the most harmonious place for the capital pause is after the fourth syllable, it may, for the sake of expressing the sense strongly and suitably, and even sometimes for the sake of variety, be placed at several other intervals.

The end of a line in verse naturally inclines us to pause; and the words that refuse a pause so seldom occur at the end of a verse, that we often pause between words in verse where we should not in prose, but where a pause would by no means interfere with the sense This, perhaps, may be the reason why a pause at the end of a line in poetry is supposed to be in compliment to the verse, when the very same pause in prose is allowable, and perhaps eligible, but neglected as unnecessary: however this be, certain it is, that if we pronounce many lines in Milton, so as to make the equality of impressions on the ear distinctly perceptible at the end of every line; if, by making this pause, we make the pauses that mark the sense less perceptible, we exchange a solid advantage for a childish rhythm, and by endeavoring to preserve the name of verse, lose all its meaning and energy.

On the Cadence of Verse.

In order to form a cadence at a period in rhyming verse, we must adopt the falling inflection with considerable force in the cæsura of the last line but one.

How to pronounce a Simile in Poetry.

A simile in poetry ought always to be read in a lower tone of voice than that part of the passage which precedes it.

This rule is one of the greatest embellishments of poetic pronunciation, and is to be observed no less in blank verse than in rhyme.

General Rules.

Where there is no pause in the sense at the end of a verse, the last word must have exactly the same inflection it would have in prose.

Sublime, grand, and magnificent description in poetry requires a lower tone of voice, and a sameness nearly approaching to a monotone.

When the first line of a couplet does not form perfect sense, it is necessary to suspend the voice at the end of the line with the rising slide.

This rule holds good even where the first line forms perfect sense by itself, and is followed by another forming perfect sense likewise, provided the first line does not end with an emphatic word which requires the falling slide.

But if the first line ends with an emphatical word requiring the falling slide, this slide must be given to it, but in a higher tone of voice than the same slide in the last line of the couplet.

When the first line of a couplet does not form sense, and the second line, either from its not forming sense, or from its being a question, requires the rising slide; in this case, the first line must end with such a pause as the sense requires, but without any alteration in the tone of the voice.

In the same manner, if a question requires the second line of the couplet to adopt the rising slide, the first ought to have a pause at the end; but the voice, without any alteration, ought to carry on the same tone to the second line, and to continue this tone almost to the end.

The same principles of harmony and variety induce us to read a *triplet* with a sameness of voice, or a monotone, on the end of the first line, the rising slide on the end of the second, and the falling on the last.

This rule, however, from the various sense of the triplet, is liable to many exceptions. But, with very few exceptions, it may be laid down as a rule, that a *quatrain* or *stanza* of four lines of alternate verse, may be read with the monotone ending the first line, the rising slide ending the second and third, and the falling the last.

The plaintive tone, so essential to the delivery of elegiac composition, greatly diminishes the slides, and reduces them almost to monotones; nay, a perfect monotone, without any inflection at all, is sometimes very judiciously introduced in reading verse.

On Scanning.

A certain number of syllables connected form a foot. They are called *feet*, because it is by their aid that the voice, as it were, steps along through the verse, in a measured pace.

All feet used in poetry consist either of two or of

three syllables, and are reducible to eight kinds; four of two syllables, and four of three, as follow:—

The hyphen – marks a long, and the breve ᵕ a short syllable.

Dissyllable.		*Trisyllable.*	
A Trochee	– ᵕ	A Dactyl	– ᵕ ᵕ
An Iambus	ᵕ –	An Amphibrach	ᵕ – ᵕ
A Spondee	– –	An Anapæst	ᵕ ᵕ –
A Pyrrhic	ᵕ ᵕ	A Tribrach	ᵕ ᵕ ᵕ

GESTURE.

THE ancients comprehended *action*, as well as *elocution*, under the term *pronunciation*. The action should be as easy and as natural as the elocution; and, like that, it must be varied and directed by the passions. An affected violence of motion is as disagreeable and disgustful as an affected vehemence of voice; and *no* action, as bad as no emphasis: which two faults commonly go together, as do the other two just before mentioned.

Those parts of the body which are to be principally employed in oratorical action, are the HEAD, the FACE, the EYES, the HANDS, and the upper part of the WHOLE BODY.

The HEAD. This should generally be in an erect position; turning sometimes on one side, and sometimes on the other, that the voice may be heard by the whole audience, and a regard paid to the several parts of it. It should always be on the same side with the action of the hands and body, except when we express an abhorrence or refusal of anything, which is done by rejecting it with the right hand, and turning away the head to the left. (Fig 1.)

(68)

The COUNTENANCE. In this is the seat of the soul, and the very life of action. Every passion, whilst uttered with the tongue, should be painted in the face. There is frequently more eloquence in a look, than it is possible for any person to express in words. By this we are awed, charmed, incensed, softened, grieved, rejoiced, raised, or dejected, according as we catch the fire of the speaker's passion from his face. In short, there is no end in recounting the force and effects of this dumb oratory; which Nature only teaches, and which persons of low passions lose all the advantages of. Let any person look well upon a good piece of painting where the passions are strongly delineated, and he will instantly conceive the power of it.

Fig. 1.

The EYES. These should be carried from one part of the audience to the other, with a modest and decent aspect; which will tend to recall and fix their attention, and animate the speaker's own spirit by his observing that attention closely fixed. But if their affections be strongly moved, and the observing it be a means of raising his own too high, it will be necessary then to keep the eye from off them; for, though an orator should always be animated, it is necessary that he guard against being overcome by his passions. The language of the eye is inexpressible. It is, in fact, the window of the soul, from which sometimes the whole heart looks out at once, and speaks more feelingly than all the warmest strains of oratorical eloquence; indeed, it comes effectually in aid of it, when the passion is too strong to be uttered.

The HANDS. The left hand should never be used alone, unless it be to attend the motion of the head and eyes in an address to the audience on the left side.

The right hand may be frequently used alone. When a person speaks of the body, he may point to it with the middle finger of the right hand. When he speaks

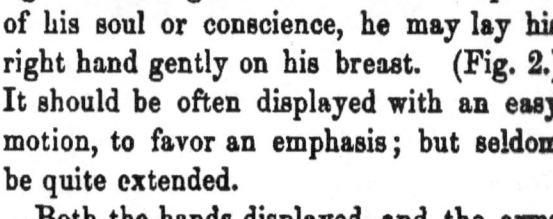

Fig. 2.

of his soul or conscience, he may lay his right hand gently on his breast. (Fig. 2.) It should be often displayed with an easy motion, to favor an emphasis; but seldom be quite extended.

Both the hands displayed, and the arms extended, is a violent action, and never just or decent unless the audience be noisy, and part of them at a considerable distance from the speaker, and he is laboring to be heard; and even then they should never be extended higher than the head, unless pointing at something above the audience. (Fig. 3.)

The motions of the hand should always correspond with those of the head and eyes, as they should with the passions expressed.

In deliberate proof or argumentation, no action is more proper or natural, than gently to lay the first finger of the right hand on the palm of the left. (Fig. 4.)

How considerably the proper motion of the hand assists pronunciation, and how many passions may be very strongly indicated thereby, when attended with that of the head and eyes, it is not easy to describe, but may be quickly observed even in common conversation.

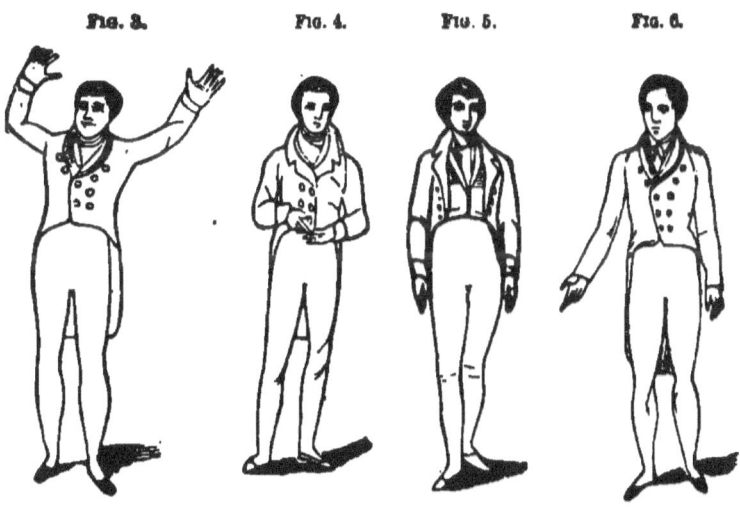

The posture of the BODY. (Fig. 5.) This should be usually erect; not continually changing, nor always motionless; declining in acts of humiliation, and raised in acts of praise and thanksgiving. It should always accompany the motion of the hands, head, and eyes, when they are directed to any particular part of the audience, but never so far as to let the back be turned to any part of it.

It is in the level parts of a discourse, such as narration, explanation, &c., that the speaker is most frequently at a loss for a graceful management of the hands. A slight elevation of the right hand, as in Fig. 6, is here appropriate. A slight elevation of both hands, as in Fig. 7, has a good effect, when the subject in creases in warmth and interest. This gesture is also adapted to demonstration, remonstrance, or an appeal to the candor of the audience.

In the unimpassioned parts of a discourse, it gives the orator an air of ease and self-possession to place the left hand on the hip, while he gesticulates in a moderate degree with the right, as in Figs. 8 and 9. In impas-

FIG. 7.   FIG. 8.   FIG. 9.

sioned parts of a discourse, this placing the hand on the hip is obviously wrong. An eloquent orator would find it impracticable to proceed, without having the left hand free, ready for use on the first strong impulse, in aid of the right hand.

The gesture indicated in Fig. 10 is in more frequent use than any other, since it is equally appropriate to any part of a discourse, which is not impassioned or earnestly argumentative.

Quintilian says, a moderate extension of the arm, with the shoulders thrown back, and the fingers opening as the hand advances, is a kind of gesture excellently adapted to continuous and smoothly flowing passages. In an attitude of apology or supplication, we naturally lower the hands. (Fig. 11.) In adoration we raise

Fig. 10.　　　　　　　Fig. 11.

them, sometimes even above the head, and this gesture is also applied to passages in which we describe what is elevated, vast, or sublime, in the moral, as well as the material world. In ordinary cases, the hands acting in concert express most feeling; stretched out but a short distance when we speak on inconsiderable, grave, or tranquil subjects, but extended to a greater distance when we treat of such as are important, exhilarating, or awful. In Figs. 12, 13, and 14, there is animated gesture with both hands; but it is only in Fig. 14 that they act strictly in concert.

As to the hands, says Quintilian, without the aid of which all delivery would be deficient and weak, it can scarcely be told of what a variety of motions they are

FIG. 12. FIG. 13. FIG. 14.

susceptible, since they almost equal in expression the powers of language itself; for other parts of the body assist the speaker, but these, I may almost say, speak themselves. With our hands we ask, promise, call persons to us and send them away, threaten, supplicate, intimate dislike or fear; with our hands we signify joy, grief, doubt, acknowledgment, penitence, and indicate measure, quantity, number, and time. Have not our hands the power of inciting, of restraining, of beseeching, of testifying approbation, admiration, and shame? Do they not, in pointing out places and persons, discharge the duty of adverbs and pronouns? So that amidst the great diversity of tongues pervading all nations and people, the language of the hands appears to be a language common to all men.

As to the motion of the hand, continues Quintilian, it commences, with very good effect, on the left, and stops on the right; but the hand ought to stop so that it may appear to be laid down, not to strike against anything; though, at the end of a phrase, the hand may sometimes sink, but so as soon to raise itself again; and it sometimes even rebounds, as it were, when we enforce a denial or express wonder. In regard to this point the old masters of delivery have very properly added a direction that *the movement of the hand should begin and end with the sense;* otherwise the gesture will either precede the sense, or will fall behind it; and propriety is violated in either case.

But when increasing warmth has given it animation, the gesture will become more spirited in proportion to

FIG. 15.   FIG. 16.   FIG. 17.

the ardor of the language. But though in some passages a rapid pronunciation will be proper, in others a

staid manner will be preferable. On some parts we
touch but slightly, throw together our remarks upon
them, and hasten forward; in others we insist, inculcate, impress. But slowness in delivery is better suited
to the pathetic; and hence it was that Roscius was
inclined to quickness of manner; Æsopus to gravity: the
one acting in comedy and the other in tragedy.

In Figs. 15, 16, and 17, are illustrated some of the
more animated gestures of the hands; fig. 15 being
suitable for narration, demonstration, or argument, fig.
16 for exhortation, and fig. 17 for grief, or an endeavor
to suppress emotion.

PART SECOND.

1. HAD I not just reason to set before Entropius the inconstancy of riches? He now has found, by his own experience, that, like fugitive slaves, they have abandoned him, and are become, in some measure, traitors and murderers, since they are the principal cause of his fall. I often repeated to him that he ought to have a greater regard to my admonitions, how grating soever they might appear, than to the insipid praises which flatterers were perpetually lavishing on him, because, "faithful are the wounds of a friend; but the kisses of an enemy are deceitful."

2. Had I not just reason to address him in this manner? What has become of the crowd of courtiers? They have turned their backs; they have renounced his friendship; and are solely intent upon their own interest and security, even at the expense of his. We submitted to his violence, in the meridian of his fortune, and, now he is fallen, we support him to the utmost of our power. The church, against which he has warred, opens its bosom to receive him; and the theatres, the eternal object of his favor, which had so often drawn down his indignation upon us, have abandoned and betrayed him.

3 I do not speak this to insult the misfortunes of

him who is fallen, nor to open and make wounds smart that are still bleeding; but in order to support those who are standing, and teach them to avoid the like evils. And the only way to avoid these, is to be fully persuaded of the frailty and vanity of worldly grandeurs. To call them a flower, a blade of grass, a smoke, a dream, is not saying enough, since they are even below nothing. Of this we have a very sensible proof before our eyes.

THE BEGINNING OF THE FIRST PHILIPPIC OF DEMOSTHENES.

HAD we been convened, Athenians! on some new subject of debate, I had waited till most of your usual counsellors had declared their opinions. If I had approved of what was proposed by them, I should have continued silent; if not, I should then have attempted to speak my sentiments. But since those very points, on which those speakers have oftentimes been heard already, are at this time to be considered, though I have arisen first, I presume I may expect your pardon; for, if they on former occasions had advised the proper measures, you would not have found it needful to consult at present.

2. First, then, Athenians! however wretched the situation of our affairs at present seems, it must not by any means be thought desperate. What I am now going to advance may possibly appear a paradox; yet it is a certain truth, that our past misfortunes afford a circumstance most favorable to our future hopes. And what is that? even that our present difficulties are owing entirely to our total indolence and utter disregard of our own interest. For were we thus situated, in spite of

every effort which our duty demanded, then indeed we might regard our fortunes as absolutely desperate. But now, Philip hath only conquered your supineness and inactivity; the state he hath not conquered. You cannot be said to be defeated, your force hath never been exerted.

3. If there is a man in this assembly, who thinks that we must find a formidable enemy in Philip, while he views on one hand the numerous armies which surround him, and on the other the weakness of our state, despoiled of so much of its dominions, I cannot deny that he thinks justly. Yet let him reflect on this: there was a time, Athenians! when we possessed Pydna, Potidæa, and Methone, and all that country round; when many of the states now subjected to him were free and independent, and more inclined to our alliance than to his. If Philip, at that time weak in himself and without allies, had desponded of success against you, he would never have engaged in those enterprises which are now crowned with success, nor could have raised himself to that pitch of grandeur at which you now behold him. But he knew well that the strongest places are only prizes laid between the combatants, and ready for the conqueror. He knew that the dominions of the absent devolve naturally to those who are in the field; the possessions of the supine to the active and intrepid. Animated by these sentiments, he overturns whole nations. He either rules universally as a conqueror, or governs as a protector; for mankind naturally seek confederacy with such as they see resolved, and preparing not to be wanting to themselves.

4. If you, my countrymen, will now at length be per
suaded to entertain the like sentiments; if each of you
be disposed to approve himself a useful citizen, to the
utmost that his station and abilities enable him; if the
rich will be ready to contribute, and the young to take
the field; in one word, if you will be yourselves, and
banish those hopes which every single person entertains,
that the active part of public business may lie upon
others, and he remain at his ease; you may then, by
the assistance of the gods, recall those opportunities
which your supineness hath neglected, regain your dominions, and chastise the insolence of this man.

5. But when, O my countrymen! will you begin to
exert your vigor? Do you wait till roused by some dire
event? till forced by some necessity? What, then, are
we to think of our present condition? To free men, the
disgrace attending on misconduct is, in my opinion, the
most urgent necessity. Or say, is it your sole ambition
to wander through the .public places, each inquiring of
the other, "What new advices?" Can anything be
more new, than that a man of Macedon should conquer
the Athenians, and give law to Greece? "Is Philip
dead?" "No—but he is sick." Pray, what is it to
you whether Philip is sick or not? Supposing he should
die, you would raise up another Philip, if you continue
thus regardless of your interest.

6. Many, I know, delight more in nothing than in
circulating all the rumors they hear as articles of intelligence. Some cry, Philip hath joined with the Lace-
demonians, and they are concerting the destruction of
Thebes. Others assure us, he hath sent an embassy to

the king of Persia; others, that he is fortifying places
in Illyria. Thus we all go about framing our several
tales. I do believe, indeed, Athenians! that he is in-
toxicated with his greatness, and does entertain his imagination with many such visionary projects, as he sees no
power rising to oppose him. But I cannot be persuaded
that he hath so taken his measures, that the weakest
among us (for the weakest they are who spread such
rumors) know what he is next to do. Let us disregard
their tales. Let us only be persuaded of this, that he
is our enemy; that we have long been subject to his insolence; that whatever we expected to have been done
for us by others, hath turned against us; that all the
resource left us is in ourselves; and that, if we are not
inclined to carry our arms abroad, we should be forced
to engage him at home. Let us be persuaded of these
things, and then we shall come to a proper determination, and be no longer guided by rumors. We need not
be solicitous to know what particular events are to happen. We may be well assured that nothing good can
happen, unless we give due attention to our affairs, and
act as becomes Athenians.

SPEECH OF CA'IUS MA'RIUS TO THE ROMANS; SHOWING
THE ABSURDITY OF THEIR HESITATING TO CONFER ON
HIM THE RANK OF GENERAL, MERELY ON ACCOUNT
OF HIS EXTRACTION.

IT is but too common, my countrymen, to observe a
material difference between the behavior of those who
stand candidates for places of power and trust, before

and after obtaining them.   They solicit them in one
manner, and execute them in another

2. They set out with a great appearance of activity,
humility, and moderation ; but they quickly fall into
slōth, pride, and avarice.   It is, undoubtedly, no easy
matter to discharge, to general satisfaction, the duty of
a supreme commander in troublesome times.

3. You have committed to my conduct the war against
Jugurtha.   The patricians are offended at this.   But
where would be the wisdom of giving such a command
to one of *their* honorable body ? a person of illustrious
birth, of ancient family, of innumerable statues, but——
of no experience !

4. What service would his long line of dead ancestors, or his multitude of motionless statues, do his country in the day of battle ?   What could such a general
do, but, in his trepidation and inexperience, have re-
course to some inferior commander for direction in difficulties to which he was not himself equal ?   Thus, your
patrician general would, in fact, have a general over
him ; so that the acting commander would still be a ple
be'ian.

5. So true is this, my countrymen, that I have, myself, known those who have been chosen consuls, begin
then to read the history of their own country, of which,
till that time, they were totally ignorant ; that is, they
first obtained the employment, and then bethought themselves of the qualifications necessary for the proper discharge of it.

6. I submit to your judgment, Romans, on which side
the advantage lies, when a comparison is made between

patrician haughtiness, and plebeian experience. The very actions which they have only read, I have partly seen, and partly myself achieved. What they know by reading, I know by action. They are pleased to slight my mean birth; I despise their mean characters.

7. Want of birth and fortune is the objection against *me*; want of personal worth, against *them*. But, are not all men of the same species? What can make a difference between one man and another but the endowments of the mind? For my part, I shall always look upon the bravest man as the noblest man.

8. If the patricians have reason to despise me, let them likewise despise their ancestors, whose nobility was the fruit of their virtue. Do they envy the *honors* bestowed upon me? let them envy, likewise, my labors, my abstinence, and the dangers I have undergone for my country, by which I have acquired them.

9. But those worthless men lead such a life of inactivity, as if they despised any honors you can bestow; while they aspire to honors as if they had deserved them by the most industrious virtue. They lay claims to the rewards of activity, for their having enjoyed the pleasures of luxury. Yet none can be more lavish than they are in praise of their ancestors.

10. And they imagine they honor themselves by celebrating their forefathers; whereas, they do the very contrary; for, as much as their ancestors were distinguished for their virtues, so much are *they* disgraced by their vices.

11. The glory of ancestors casts a light, indeed, upon their posterity; but it only serves to show what the de-

scendants are. It alike exhibits to public view their degeneracy and their worth. I own I cannot boast of the deeds of my forefathers; but I hope I may answer the cavils of the patricians, by standing up in defence of what I have *myself* done.

12. Observe now, my countrymen, the injustice of the patricians. They arrogate to themselves honors, on account of exploits' done by their forefathers, whilst they will not allow me due praise for performing the very same sort of actions in my own person.

13. He has no statues, they cry, of his family. He can trace no venerable line of ancestors. What then! is it matter of more praise to disgrace one's illustrious ancestors, than to become illustrious by one's own good behavior?

14. What if I can show no statues of my family? I can show the standards, the armor, and the trappings, which I have myself taken from the vanquished; I can show the scars of those wounds which I have received by facing the enemies of my country.

15. These are *my* statues. These are the honors *I* boast of; not left me by inheritance, as theirs, but earned by toil, by abstinence, by valor, amidst clouds of dust, and seas of blood; scenes of action, where those effeminate patricians, who endeavor, by indirect means, to depreciate me in your esteem, have never dared to show their faces.

PART OF THE SPEECH OF PUBLIUS SCIPIO TO THE ROMAN
ARMY, BEFORE THE BATTLE OF THE T. CIN.

That you may not be unapprized, soldiers, of what
sort of enemies you are about to encounter, or what is
to be feared from them, I tell you they are the very
same, whom, in a former war, you vanquished both by
land and sea; the same from whom you took Sicily
and Sardinia; and who have been these twenty years
your tributaries.

2. You will not, I presume, march against these men
with only that courage with which you are wont * to face
other enemies, but with a certain anger and indignation
such as you would feel if you saw your slaves on a sudden rise up in arms against you.

3. But you have heard, perhaps, that though they are
few in number, they are men of stout hearts and robust
bodies; heroes of such strength and vigor as nothing is
able to resist. Mere effigies! nay, shadows of men!
wretches, emaciated with hunger, and benumbed with
cold, bruised and battered to pieces among the rocks and
craggy cliffs; their weapons broken, and their horses
weak and foundered!

4. Such are the cavalry, and such the infantry, with
which you are going to contend; not enemies, but the
fragments of enemies. There is nothing which I more
apprehend than that it will be thought Hannibal was
vanquished by the Alps before we had any conflict with
him.

---

* Pronounced, wunt.

5. I need not be in any fear that you will suspect me of saying these things merely to encourage you, while inwardly, I have different sentiments. Have I ever shown any inclination to avoid a contest with this tremendous Hannibal ? and have I now met with him only by accident, and unawares ? or am I come on purpose to challenge him to the combat ?

6. I would gladly try whether the earth, within these twenty years, has brought forth a new kind of Carthaginians, or whether they be the same sort of men who fought at the Æ-ga'tes, and whom, at E'ryx, you suffered to redeem themselves at eighteen denarii per head ; whether this Hannibal, for labors and journeys, be, as he would be thought, the rival of Hercules ;* or whether he be what his father left him, a trib'utary, a vassal, a slave to the Roman people.

7. Did not the consciousness of his wicked deed at Saguntum torment him, and make him desperate, he would have some regard, if not to his conquered country, yet surely to his own family, to his father's memory, to the treaty written with Amilcar's own hand. We might have starved them in Eryx ; we might have passed into Africa with our victorious fleet, and, in a few days, have destroyed Carthage.

8. At their humble supplication, we pardoned them. We released them when they were closely shut up without a possibility of escaping. We made peace with them when they were conquered.† When they were distressed

---

* Pronounced, *Her-culeez.*　　　† *Konker'd.*

by the African war, we considered them, and treated them as a people under our protection.

9. And what is the return they make us for all these favors? Under the conduct of a hare-brained young man, they come hither to overturn our state, and lay waste our country.

10. I could wish, indeed, that it were not so; and that the war we are now engaged in concerned our glory only, and not our preservation. But the contest at present is not for the possession of Sicily and Sardinia, but of Italy itself. Nor is there behind us another army, which, if we should not prove the conquerors, may make head against our victorious enemies.

11. There are no more Alps for them to pass, which might give us leisure* to raise new forces. No, soldiers; here you must take your stand, as if you were just now before the walls of Rome. Let every one reflect, that he is now to defend, not his own person only, but his wife, his children, his helpless infants.

12. Yet let not private considerations alone possess our minds. Let us remember that the eyes of the senate and people of Rome are upon us; and that, as our force and courage shall now prove, such will be the fortune of that city, and of the Roman empire.

PART OF HANNIBAL'S SPEECH TO THE CARTHAGINIAN
ARMY ON THE SAME OCCASION.

On what side soever I turn my eyes, I behold all full of courage and strength. A veteran infantry; a most

---

* Pronounced, *lee'zure.*

gallant cavalry; you, my allies, most faithful and valiant;
you, Carthaginians, whom not only your country's cause,
but the justest anger, impels to battle.   The hope, the
courage of assailants, is always greater than that of those
who act upon the defensive.

2. With hostile* banners displayed, you are come down
upon Italy.   You bring the war.   Grief, injuries, indignities, fire your minds, and spur you forward to revenge.
First, they demanded me; that I, your general, should
be delivered up to them; next, all of you who had fought
at the siege of Saguntum; and we were to be put to
death by excruciating tortures.

3. Proud and cruel nation!   Everything must be
yours, and at your disposal!   You are to prescribe to us
with whom we are to make war, with whom to make
peace!   You are to set us bounds; to shut us up between
hills and rivers; but you are not to observe the limits
which yourselves have fixed!

4. "Pass not the Ibe'rus."   What next?   "Touch
not the Saguntines; Saguntum is upon the Ibe'rus; move
not a step towards that city."   Is it a smaller matter,
then, that you have deprived us of our ancient possessions, Sicily and Sárdinia?   You would have Spain,
too!

5. Well, we shall yield Spain, and then——you will
pass into Africa.   *Will* pass, did I say?   This very year,
they ordered one of their consuls into Africa, the other
into Spain.   No, soldiers, there is nothing left for us but
what we can vindicate with our swords.

6. Come on, then.   Be men.   The Romans may, with

---

* *hos'til.*

more safety, be cowards. They have their own country behind them ; have places of refuge to flee to ; and are secure from danger in the roads thither. But for *you*, there is no middle fortune between death and victory. Let this be but well fixed in your minds, and, once again, I say, you are *conquerors*.

SPEECH OF BONAPARTE, COMMANDER-IN-CHIEF OF THE FRENCH ARMY IN ITALY, BEFORE HIS ATTACK ON MILAN, APRIL 26, 1796.

SOLDIERS,—You have in a fortnight gained six victories; taken twenty-one stands of colors; seventy-one pieces of cannon; several strong places; conquered the richest part of Piedmont; you have made fifteen thousand prisoners, and killed or wounded more than ten thousand men. You had hitherto fought only for sterile rocks, rendered illustrious by your courage, but useless to the country; you have equalled by your services the victorious army of Holland and the Rhine. Deprived of everything, you have supplied everything. You have won battles without cannon; made forced marches without shoes; watched without brandy, and often without bread. The republican phalanxes, the soldiers of liberty were alone capable of suffering what you have suffered.

2. Thanks be to you, soldiers. The grateful country will, in part, be indebted to you for her prosperity; and if, when victorious at Toulon, you predicted the immortal campaign of 1794, your present victories will be the presages of more brilliant victories. The two armies

which attacked you with audacity, fly disheartened before you. Men, who smiled at your misery, and rejoiced in thought at the idea of the triumphs of your enemies, are confounded and appalled. But it must not, soldiers, be concealed from you, that you have done *nothing*, since *something* remains yet to be done. Neither Turin nor Milan are in your power. The ashes of the conquerors of the Tarquins are still disgraced by the assassins of Basseville. At the commencement of the campaign, you were destitute of everything; now you are amply provided; the magazines taken from your enemies are numerous; the artillery for the field and for besieging is arrived.

3. Soldiers, the country has a right to expect great things from you; justify her expectations. The greatest obstacles are undoubtedly overcome; but you have still battles to fight, cities to take, rivers to pass. Is there one among you whose courage is diminished? Is there one who would prefer returning to the summits of the Alps and the Appenines? No: all burn with the desire of extending the glory of the French; to humble the proud kings who dare to meditate putting us again in chains; to dictate a peace that shall be glorious, and that shall indemnify the country for the immense sacrifices which she made. All of you burn with a desire to say on your return to your home, I belonged to the victorious army of Italy.

4. Friends, I promise this conquest to you; but there is one condition which you must swear to fulfil; it is to respect the people whom you deliver; to repress the horrible pillage which some wretches, instigated by our

enemies, had practised. Unless you do this, you will no longer be the friends, but the scourges of the human race: you will no longer form the honor of the French people. They will disavow you. Your victories, your successes, the blood of your brethren who died in battle: all, even honor and glory will be lost. With respect to myself, to the generals who possess your confidence, we shall blush to command an army without discipline, and who admit no other law than that of force.

5. People of Italy, the French army comes to break your chains; the French people are the friends of all people; come with confidence to them; your property, religion, and customs shall be respected. We make war as generous enemies; and wish only to make war against the tyrants who oppress you.

PATRICK HENRY'S CELEBRATED SPEECH IN THE LEGIS-LATURE OF VIRGINIA.

1. MR. PRESIDENT :—It is natural for man to indulge in the illusions of hope. We are apt to shut our eyes against a painful truth, and listen to the song of that syren, till she transforms us into beasts. Is this the part of wise men, engaged in a great and arduous struggle for liberty? Are we disposed to be of the number of those, who, having eyes, see not, and having ears, hear not, the things which so nearly concern their temporal salvation? For my part, whatever anguish of spirit it may cost, I am willing to know the whole truth; to know the worst, and to provide for it.

2. I have but one lamp, by which my feet are guided;

and that is the lamp of experience. I know of no way
of judging of the future, but by the past. And, judging by the past, I wish to know what there has been, in
the conduct of the British ministry, for the last ten
years, to justify those hopes, with which gentlemen have
been pleased to solace themselves, and the house? Is
it that insidious smile, with which our petition has been
lately received?

3. Trust it not, sir, it will prove a snare to your feet.
Suffer not yourselves to be betrayed with a kiss. Ask
yourselves, how this gracious reception of our petition
comports with those warlike preparations, which cover
our waters, and darken our land. Are fleets and armies
necessary to a work of love and reconciliation? Have
we shown ourselves so unwilling to be reconciled, that
force must be called in to win back our love?

4. Let us not deceive ourselves, sir. These are the
implements of war and subjugation—the last arguments
to which kings resort. I ask gentlemen, sir, what
means this martial array, if its purpose be not to force
us to submission? Can gentlemen assign any other
possible motive for it? Has Great Britain any enemy,
in this quarter of the world, to call for all this accumulation of navies and armies? No, sir, she has none.
They are meant for us; they can be meant for no other.
They are sent over to bind and rivet upon us those
chains, which the British ministry have been so long
forging.

5. And what have we to oppose to them? Shall we
try argument? Sir, we have been trying that for the
last ten years. Have we anything new to offer upon

the subject? Nothing. We have held the subject up in every light of which it is capable; but it has been all in vain. Shall we resort to entreaty and humble supplication? What terms shall we find, which have not been already exhausted?

6. Let us not, I beseech you, sir, deceive ourselves longer. Sir, we have done everything that could be done, to avert the storm which is now coming on. We have petitioned; we have remonstrated; we have supplicated; we have prostrated ourselves before the throne, and have implored its interposition, to arrest the tyrannical hands of the ministry and parliament. Our petitions have been slighted; our remonstrances have produced additional violence and insult; our supplications have been disregarded, and we have been spurned, with contempt, from the foot of the throne.

7. In vain, after these things, may we indulge the fond hope of peace and reconciliation. There is no longer any room for hope. If we wish to be free; if we mean to preserve, inviolate, those inestimable privileges, for which we have been so long contending; if we mean not basely to abandon the noble struggle, in which we have been so long engaged, and which we have pledged ourselves never to abandon until the glorious object of our contest shall be obtained, we must fight! I repeat it! sir, we must fight! An appeal to arms, and to the God of hosts, is all that is left us.

8. They tell us, sir, that we are weak, unable to cope with so formidable an adversary. But when shall we be stronger? Will it be the next week, or the next year? Will it be when we are totally disarmed, and

when a British guard shall be stationed in every house?
Shall we gather strength by irresolution and inaction?
Shall we acquire the means of effectual resistance, by
lying supinely on our backs, and hugging the delusive
phantom of hope, until our enemies shall have bound
us hand and foot?

9. Sir, we are not weak, if we make a proper use of
those means which the God of nature hath placed in
our power.   Three millions of people, armed in the holy
cause of liberty, and in such a country as that which we
possess, are invincible, by any force which our enemy
can send against us.

10. Besides, sir, we shall not fight our battles alone.
There is a just God, who presides over the destinies of
nations, and who will raise up friends to fight our battles
for us.   The battle, sir, is not to the strong alone; it
is to the vigilant, the active, the brave.   Besides, sir,
we have no election.   If we were base enough to desire
it, it is now too late to retire from the contest.   There
is no retreat but in submission and slavery!   Our chains
are forged.   Their clanking n ay be heard on the plains
of Boston!   The war is inevitable, and let it come!   I
repeat it, sir, let it come!

11. It is vain, sir, to extenuate the matter.   Gentlemen may cry, peace, peace—but there is no peace.   The
war is actually begun!   The next gale that sweeps
from the north, will bring to our ears the clash of resounding arms!   Our brethren are already in the field!
Why stand we here idle?   What is it that gentlemen
wish?   What would they have?   Is life so dear, or peace
so sweet, as to be purchased at the price of chains and

slavery? Forbid it, Almighty God. I know not what course others may take, but, as for me, give me liberty, or give me death!

BURKE ON THE RIGHT TO TAX AMERICA—1781.

OH! inestimable right, oh! wonderful, transcendent right, the assertion of which has cost this country thirteen provinces, six islands, one hundred thousand lives, and seventy millions of money! Oh invaluable right! for the sake of which we have sacrificed our rank among nations, our importance abroad, and our happiness at home! Oh right! more dear to us than our existence, which has already cost us so much, and which seems likely to cost us our all. Infatuated man! (cried Mr. Burke, fixing his eyes on the minister,) miserable and undone country! not to know that the claim of right without the power of enforcing it, is nugatory and idle. We had a right to tax America, the noble lord tells us; therefore we ought to tax America. This is the profound logic which comprises the whole chain of his reasoning. Not inferior to this was the wisdom of him who resolved to shear the wolf. What! shear a wolf! Have you considered the resistance, the difficulty, the danger of the attempt? No, says the madman, I have considered nothing but the right. Man has a right of dominion over the beasts of the forest; and therefore I will shear the wolf. How wonderful that a nation could be thus deluded! But the noble lord dealt in cheats and delusions. They were the daily traffic of his invention; and he would continue to play off his cheats on this

house, so long as he thought them necessary to his pur
pose, and so long as he had money enough at command
to bribe gentlemen to pretend that they believed him.
But a black and bitter day of reckoning would surely
come; and whenever that day came, he trusted he should
be able, by a parliamentary impeachment, to bring upon
the heads of the authors of our calamities, the punish
ment they deserved.

LORD CHATHAM ON THE EMPLOYMENT OF INDIANS AGAINST AMERICA.

I AM astonished, SHOCKED to hear such principles confessed: to hear them avowed in this house, or even in
this country. My lords, I did not intend to have en-
croached again on your attention, but I cannot repress
my indignation. I feel myself IMPELLED to speak. My
lords, we are called upon as members of this house, as
men, as Christians, to protest against such horrible barbarity—"That God and Nature put into our hands!"
What ideas of God and Nature that noble lord may entertain, I know not; but I know that such detestable
principles are equally abhorrent to religion and humanity! What! to attribute the sacred sanction of God and
Nature to the massacres of the Indian scalping-knife!—
to the cannibal savage, torturing, murdering, devouring,
drinking the blood of his mangled victims! Such notions
shock every precept of morality, every feeling of humanity, every sentiment of honor. These abominable
principles, and this more abominable avowal of them,
demand the most decisive indignation. I call upon that

reverend, and this most learned bench to vindicate the religion of their God, to support the justice of their country. I call upon the bishops to interpose the unsullied sanctity of their lawn: upon the judges to interpose the purity of their ermine, to save us from this pollution. I call upon the honor of your lordships to reverence the dignity of your ancestors, and to maintain your own. I call upon the spirit and humanity of my country, to vindicate the national character, I invoke the genius of the constitution. From the tapestry that adorns these walls, the immortal ancestor of this noble lord frowns with indignation at the disgrace of his country.

UNITY OF THE CHURCH.—*Lacordaire.*

The true Church, that which from the commencement of its existence has taken the title of Catholic, which no other during eighteen centuries has even once dared to dispute—the true Church, divinely instituted to instruct the human race, has alone established an universal authority, in spite of the enormous difficulty of the thing.

2. The whole Roman empire leagued itself together against this immense authority which sprung up on all sides, and, notwithstanding the persecution with which she was assailed from the earliest times, the Catholic Church passed the bounds of the Roman empire, and penetrated into Persia, Ethiopia, the Indies, and Scythia. After she had subjugated the Roman empire and passed beyond its limits, the barbarians came to annihilate the temporal unity founded by heathen Rome, and, whilst all the nations changed and divided them-

7

selves, the Catholic Church spread its un ty and uni
versality wherever force broke up the ancient commu
nities: she also sought the barbarians even in their
forests, to lead them to the foot of the same altar and
the same episcopal throne. New worlds disclosed themselves; the Church was there as soon as the conquerors.
The Indians of the West and of the East knew Jesus
Christ, and the sun nevermore set but in the kingdom
of truth. Protestantism, in endeavoring to break up
Catholic unity and universality, has but produced, by
the spectacle of its divisions, new proof of the impossi
bility of founding an universal Church by the simple
power of man.

FOX ON THE ARRIVAL OF THE NEWS OF THE SURREN-DER OF LORD CORNWALLIS

I HAD expected, and I know it has been expected by
many others, to hear on this occasion his majesty declare
from the throne, that he had been deceived and imposed
upon by misinformation and misrepresentation; that in
consequence of his delusion, the parliament had been
deluded; but that now the deception was at an end; and
requesting of his parliament to devise the most speedy
and efficacious means of putting an end to the public
calamities; instead of which they had heard a speech
breathing little else than vengeance, misery, and blood.
Those who were ignorant of the personal character of
the Sovereign, and who imagined this speech to originate
with him, might be led to suppose that he was an unfeeling despot, rejoicing in the horrid sacrifice of the
liberty and lives of his subjects, who, when all hope of
victory was vanished, still thirsted for revenge. The

ministers, who advised this speech, are a curse to the
country, over the affairs of which they have too long
been suffered to preside. From that unrivalled pre-
eminence which we so lately possessed, they have made
us the object of ridicule and scorn to the surrounding
nations. The noble lord in the blue riband has indeed
thought fit to ascribe the American war and all its attendant calamities to the speeches of Opposition. Oh!
wretched and incapable ministry, whose measures are
framed with so little foresight, and executed with so
little firmness, that because a rash and intemperate in-
vective is uttered against them in the House of Commons,
they shall instantly crumble in pieces, and bring down
ruin upon the country! Miserable statesman! to allow
for no contingencies of fortune, no ebullition of passion,
no collision of sentiment! Could he expect the concurrence of every individual in that house? and was he so
weak or wicked, as to contrive plans of government of
such a texture, that the intervention of circumstances,
obvious and unavoidable, would occasion their total failure, and hazard the existence of the empire? Ministers
must expect to hear of the calamities in which they had
involved the empire, again and again—not merely in that
house, but at the tribunal of justice; for the time will
surely come, when an oppressed and irritated people will
firmly call for signal punishment on those whose counsels
have brought the nation so near to the brink of destruction. An indignant nation will surely in the end compel
them to make some faint atonement for the magnitude
of their offences or a public scaffold.

ROLLA'S ADDRESS.

1. My brave associates, partners of my toil, my feel
ings, and my fame! Can Rolla's words add vigor to
the virtuous energies which inspire your hearts? No—
you have judged as *I* have, the foulness of the crafty
plea by which these bold invaders would delude you.
Your generous spirit has compared, as *mine* has, the
motives, which in a war like this, can animate *their*
minds and ours.

2. *They*, by a strange frenzy driven, fight for *power*,
for *plunder*, and *extended rule*—*we,* for our *country*, our
altars, and our *homes*. *They* follow an adventurer whom
they *fear*, and obey a power which they *hate*—*we* serve
a *monarch* whom we *love*—a *God* whom we *adore*

3 Whenever they move in anger, desolation tracks
their progress! Whenever they pause in amity, affliction mourns their friendship! They boast they come
but to improve our state, enlarge our thoughts, and free
us from the yoke of error! Yes—they *will* give enlightened freedom to our minds, who are themselves the
slaves of passion, avarice, and pride.

4. They offer us their protection—Yes, such protection as vultures give to lambs—covering and devouring
them! They call on us to barter all of good we have
inherited and proved, for the desperate chance of something better, which they promise. Be our plain answer
this :—

5. The *throne we* honor, is the *people's choice* — the
laws we reverence are our brave fathers' legacy — the
faith we follow teaches us to live in bonds of charity

with all mankind, and die in hopes of bliss beyond the grave. Tell your invaders this; and tell them too, we seek no change; and least of all, such change as *they* would bring us.

THE HOPE OF THE FUTURE.—*Lacordaire.*

It is often said that the past is at war with the fu ture, and this is true. The old world is at war with the new : and what is the new world, if it is not that which has produced the Church? What is the old world, save that which was without a Church? As the Christian is the *new man*, according to the language of the Holy Scriptures, so the Catholic Church is the *new humanity.* Whoever attacks it invokes the past; whoever defends it appeals to the future.

2. I know that many wait for a new revelation more perfect than that of Christ, a new Church more perfect than that founded by Christ, a new humanity more perfect than that formed by the Church. But where is the new Christ, where is the new Church, where is the new humanity, and what do we see around us save the old passions, the ancient selfishness, so much the more hideous because it rears its head in the midst of a society which charity has founded?

3. Ah! gentlemen, when the Church appeared upon earth she did not thus announce herself. She edified without ruining anything; you ruin without edifying anything. But I trespass on your time. Be, then, men of hope and desire; and you who are more advanced, who appreciate at their just value the powerless

efforts of this age, and who know that the tomb of the Church will be the tomb of the civilized world, entertain more ardent faith and charity, devote yourselves entirely to that Church out of which there is no salvation in time or in eternity.

HOTSPUR'S SOLILOQUY ON THE CONTENTS OF A LETTER.— *Shakspeare.*

"But for mine own part, my lord, I could be well contented to be there, in respect of the love I bear your house." He could be contented to be there! Why is he not then? In respect of the love he bears your house; he shows in this, he loves his own barn better than he loves your house. Let me see some more. "The purpose you undertake is dangerous." Why that's certain; 'tis dangerous to take a cold, to sleep, to drink; but I tell you, my lord fool, out of this nettle danger, we pluck this flower safety. "The purpose you undertake is dangerous; the friends you have named uncertain; the time itself unsorted; and the whole plot too light for the counterpoise of so great an opposition." Say you so, say you so? I say unto you again, you are a shallow, cowardly hind, and you lie. What a lack-brain is this! our plot is a good plot as ever was laid; our friends true and constant; a good plot, good friends, and full of expectation; an excellent plot; very good friends. What a frosty spirited rogue is this! Why, my lord of York commends the plot, and the general course of the action. By this hand, if

I were now by this rascal, I could brain him with his lady's fan. Is there not my father, my uncle, and myself; lord Edmund Mortimer, my lord of York, and Owen Glendower? Is there not, besides, the Douglas? Have I not all their letters to meet me in arms by the ninth of the next month; and are there not some of them set forward already? What a pagan rascal is this! an infidel! Ha! you shall see now, in very sincerity of fear and cold heart, will he to the king, and lay open all our proceedings. Oh! I could divide myself and go to buffets, for moving such a dish of skimmed milk with so honorable an action. Hang him! let him tell the king. We are prepared. I will set forward to-night.

MAJESTY OF THE LAW.—*Hopkinson.*

How imposing is the majesty of the law! how calm her dignity; how vast her power; how firm and tranquil, in her reign! It is not by fleets and arms, by devastation and wrong, by oppression and blood — she maintains her sway, and executes her decrees. Sustained by justice, reason, and the great interests of man, she but speaks, and is obeyed. Even those who do not approve, hesitate not to support her; and the individual, upon whom her judgment falls, knows that submission is not only a duty he must perform, but that the security and enjoyment of all that is dear to him, depend upon it.

2. A mind accustomed to acknowledge no power but physical force, no obedience but personal fear, must view

with astonishment, a feeble individual, sitting with no
parade of strength, surrounded by no visible agents of
power, issuing his decrees with oracular authority, while
the rich and the great, the first and the meanest, await
alike to perform his will.   Still more wonderful is it, to
behold the co-ordinate officers of the same government,
yielding their pretensions to his higher influence ! the
executive, the usual depository and instrument of power,
the legislature, even the representative of the people,
yield a respectful acquiescence to the judgments of the
tribunals of the law, pronounced by the minister, and ex-
pounder of the law.   It is enough for him to say, "It is
the opinion of the court," and the farthest corner of our
republic feels and obeys the mandate.   What a sublime
spectacle !   This is, indeed, the empire of the law : and
safe and happy are all they who dwell within it.

MODERN REPUBLICS.—*Story.*

Where are the republics of modern times, which clus-
tered round immortal Italy ?   Venice and Genoa exist,
but in name.   The Alps, indeed, look down upon the
brave and peaceful Swiss, in their native fastnesses ; but
the guarantee of their freedom is in their weakness, and
not in their strength.   The mountains are not easily
crossed, and the valleys are not easily retained.   When
the invader comes, he moves like an avalanche, carrying
destruction in his path.   The peasantry sink before him.
The country is too poor for plunder, and too rough for
valuable conquest   Nature presents her eternal barriers

on every side, to check the wantonness of ambition ; and
Switzerland remains, with her simple institutions, a military road to fairer climates, scarcely worth a permanent
possession.

2. We stand the latest, and, if we fail, probably the
last experiment of self-government by the people.　We
have begun it under circumstances of the most auspicious
nature.　We are in the vigor of youth.　Our growth has
never been checked by the oppressions of tyranny.　Our
constitutions have never been enfeebled by the vices, or
luxuries of the old world.　Such as we are, we have been .
from the beginning; simple, hardy, intelligent, accustomed to self-government and self-respect.　The Atlantic
rolls between us, and any formidable foe.　Within our
own territory, stretching through many degrees of lati-
tude and longitude, we have the choice of many pro-
ducts, and many means of independence.　The government is mild.　The press is free.　Knowledge reaches,
or may reach, every home.　What fairer prospect of
success could be presented ?　What means more adequate
to accomplish the sublime end ?　What more is necessary, than for the people to preserve what they themselves have created ?

3. Already has the age caught the spirit of our institutions.　It has already ascended the Andes, and snuffed
the breezes of both oceans.　It has infused itself into
the life-blood of Europe, and warmed the sunny plains
of France, and the lowlands of Holland.　It has touched
the philosophy of Germany and the North, and, moving
onward to the South, has opened to Greece the lessons
of her better days.

4. Can it be, that America, under such circumstances, can betray herself? that she is to be added to the catalogue of republics, the inscription upon whose ruins is : " They were, but they are not ?" Forbid it, my countrymen ! forbid it, Heaven !

NOBILITY OF LABOR.—*Dewey.*

Why, in the great scale of things, is labor ordained for us ? Easily, had it so pleased the great Ordainer, might it have been dispensed with. The world itself might have been a mighty machinery, for producing all that man wants. Houses might have been risen like an exhalation,

> " With the sound
> Of dulcet symphonies, and voices sweet,
> Built like a temple."

Gorgeous furniture might have been placed in them, and soft couches, and luxurious banquets, spread by hands unseen ; and man, clothed with fabrics of nature's weaving, rather than imperial purple, might have been sent to disport himself in those Elysian palaces.

2. " Fair scene!" I imagine you are saying: " fortunate for us, had it been the scene ordained for human life?" But where, then, had been human energy, perseverance, patience, virtue, heroism? Cut off labor with one blow from the world, and mankind had sunk to a crowd of Asiatic voluptuaries.

3. No; it had not been fortunate! Better that the earth be given to man as a dark mass, whereupon to labor. Better, that rude and unsightly materials be provided in

the ore-bed, and in the forest, for him to fashion in splendor and beauty.   Better, I say, not because of that splendor and beauty, but, because the act of creating them is
better than the things themselves ; because exertion is
nobler than enjoyment ; because the laborer is greater
and more worthy of honor, than the idler.

4. I call upon those whom I address, to stand up for
the nobility of labor.   It is heaven's great ordinance for
human improvement.   Let not the great ordinance be
broken down.   What do I say?   It is broken down ;
and it has been broken down for ages.   Let it, then, be ˙
built again ; here, if anywhere, on the shores of a new
world—of a new civilization.

5. But how, it may be asked, is it broken down?   Do
not men toil? it may be said.   They do indeed, toil, but
they too generally do, because they must.   Many submit to it, as in some sort, a degrading necessity ; and
they desire nothing so much on earth, as an escape
from it.   They fulfil the great law of labor in the letter,
but break it in the spirit.   To some field of labor,
mental or manual, every idler should hasten, as a
chosen, coveted field of improvement.

6. But so he is not compelled to do, under the teach
ings of our imperfect civilization.   On the contrary, he
sits down, folds his hands, and blesses himself in idleness.
This way of thinking is the heritage of the absurd and
unjust feudal system, under which serfs labored, and
gentlemen spent their lives in fighting and feasting.   It
is time that this opprobrium of toil were done away.

7. Ashamed of toil? Ashamed of thy dingy work-shop,
ard dusty labor-field ; of thy hard hand, scarred with

service more honorable than that of war; of thy soiled and weather-stained garments, on which mother nature has embroidered mist, sun, and rain, fire, and steam, her own heraldic honors? Ashamed of those tokens and titles, and envious of the flaunting robes of imbecile idleness, and vanity? It is treason to nature, it is impiety to heaven; it is breaking heaven's great ordinance. Toil, I repeat—toil, either of the brain, of the heart, or of the hand, is the only true manhood—the only true nobility!

LIBERTY AND UNION.—*Webster.*

I profess, sir, in my career hitherto, to have kept steadily in view the prosperity and honor of the whole country, and the preservation of our federal union. It is to that union we owe our safety at home, and our consideration and dignity abroad. It is to that union that we are chiefly indebted for whatever makes us most proud of our country. That union we reached, only by the discipline of our virtues in the severe school of adversity. It had its origin in the necessities of disordered finance, prostrate commerce, and ruined credit. Under its benign influences, these great interests immediately awoke, as from the dead, and sprang forth with newness of life. Every year of its duration has teemed with fresh proofs of its utility and its blessings; and, although our territory has stretched out wider and wider, and our population spread farther and farther, they have not outrun its protection or its benefits. It has been to us all a copious fountain of national, social, and personal happiness.

2. I have not allowed myself, sir, to look beyond the union, to see what might lie hidden in the dark recess behind. I have not coolly weighed the chances of preserving liberty, when the bonds that unite us together, shall be broken asunder. I have not accustomed myself to hang over the precipice of disunion, to see whether, with my short sight, I can fathom the depth of the abyss below; nor could I regard him as a safe counsellor in the affairs of this government, whose thoughts should be mainly bent on considering, not how the union should be preserved, but, how tolerable might be the condition of the people, when it shall be broken up and destroyed.

3. While the union lasts, we have high, exciting, gratifying prospects spread out before us, for us and our children. Beyond that, I seek not to penetrate the veil. God grant, that in my day, at least, that curtain may not rise. God grant, that on my vision never may be opened what lies behind. When my eyes shall be turned to behold for the last time, the sun in heaven, may I not see him shining on the broken and dishonored fragments of a once glorious union; on states dissevered, discordant, belligerent; on a land rent with civil feuds, or drenched, it may be, in fraternal blood! Let their last feeble and lingering glance, rather, behold the gorgeous ensign of the republic, now known and honored throughout the earth, still full high advanced, its arms and trophies streaming in their original lustre; not a stripe erased or polluted, nor a single star obscured, bearing for its motto, no such miserable interrogatory as, What is all this worth? nor those other words of delusion and folly: Liberty first, and union afterwards; but every

where, spread all over in characters of living light, blazing on all its ample folds, as they float over the sea,
and over the land, and in every wind under the whole
heavens, that other sentiment, dear to every true American heart, Liberty and union, now and forever, one and
inseparable!

AGAINST THE AMERICAN WAR.—*Chatham.*

I cannot, my lords, I will not join in congratulation
on misfortune and disgrace. This, my lords, is a perilous and tremendous moment. It is not a time for adula-
tion; the smoothness of flattery cannot save us, in this
rugged and awful crisis. It is now necessary to instruct
the throne in the language of truth. We must, if possible, dispel the delusion and darkness which envelop it,
and display, in its full danger and genuine colors, the
ruin which is brought to our doors. Can ministers still
presume to expect support in their infatuation? Can
parliament be so dead to its dignity and duty, as to give
their support to measures, thus obtruded and forced upon
them? Measures, my lords, which have reduced this late
flourishing empire, to scorn and contempt! "But yesterday, and Britain might have stood against the world;
now, none so poor, as to do her reverence." The people, whom we at first despised as rebels, but whom we
now acknowledge as enemies, are abetted against us,
supplied with every military store, have their interests
consulted, and their ambassadors entertained by our in-
veterate enemy; and ministers do not, and dare not, interpose, with dignity or effect. The desperate state of

our army abroad, is in part known. No man more highly esteems and honors the British troops, than I do; I know their virtues, and their valor; I know they can achieve anything but impossibilities; and I know that the conquest of British America *is* an impossibility. You cannot, my lords, you cannot conquer America. What is your present situation there? We do not know the worst; but we know, that in three campaigns, we have done nothing, and suffered much. You may swell every expense, and accumulate every assistance, and extend your traffic to the shambles of every German despot: your attempts will be for ever vain and impotent; doubly so, indeed, from this mercenary aid, on which you rely; for it irritates, to an incurable resentment, the minds of your adversaries, to overrun them with the mercenary sons of rapine and plunder, devoting them and their possessions to the rapacity of hireling cruelty. If I were an American, as I am an Englishman, while a foreign troop was landed in my country, I never would lay down my arms. No; *never, never, never!*

SPEECH OF COL. BARRÉ, IN REPLY TO CHARLES TOWNS HEND, A MEMBER OF THE BRITISH MINISTRY.—1765.

The honorable member has asked: "And now will these Americans, children planted by our care, nour ished up by our indulgence, and protected by our arms, —will they grudge to contribute their mite?" *They planted by your care!*—No, your oppressions planted them in America! They fled from your tyranny to a then uncultivated and inhospitable country, where they exposed themselves to almost all the hardships to which human nature is liable; and, among others, to the cruelties of a savage foe the most subtle, and I will take upon me to say the most formidable, of any people upon the face of God's earth; and yet, actuated by principles of true English liberty, our American brethren met all hardships with pleasure, compared with those they suffered in their own country, from the hands of those that should have been their friends.

2. *They nourished up by your indulgence!*—They grew by your neglect of them! As soon as you began to care about them, that care was exercised in sending persons to rule them, in one department and another, who were, perhaps, the deputies of deputies to some members of this house, sent to spy out their liberties, to misrepresent their actions, and to prey upon them; men whose behavior, on many occasions, has caused the blood of those sons of liberty to recoil within them; men promoted to the highest seats of justice, some who, to my knowledge, were glad, by going to a foreign country, to escape being brought to the bar of a court of justice in their own.

3. *They protected by your arms!*—They have nobly taken up arms in your defence!—have exerted a valor, amidst their constant and laborious industry, for the defence of a country whose frontier was drenched in blood, while its interior parts yielded all its little savings to your emolument. And, believe me,—remember I this day told you so,—that same spirit of freedom which actuated that people at first will accompany them still; but pru-

dence forbids me to explain myself further. God knows
I do not at this time speak from motives of party heat.
What I deliver are the genuine sentiments of my heart.
However superior to me, in general knowledge and experience, the respectable body of this house may be, yet
I claim to know more of America than most of you, having seen and been conversant in that country. The people, I believe, are as truly loyal as any subjects the
king has; but they are a people jealous of their liberties,
and who will vindicate them to the last drop of their
blood, if they should ever be violated.

BURKE'S CELEBRATED DESCRIPTION OF MARIE ANTOI NETTE.—1790.—*Edmund Burke.*

It is now sixteen or seventeen years since I saw the
Queen of France, then the Dauphiness, at Versailles; and
surely never lighted on this orb, which she hardly seemed
to touch, a more delightful vision. I saw her just above
the horizon, decorating and cheering the elevated sphere
she just began to move in,—glittering like the morning
star, full of life, and splendor and joy. Oh! what a revolution! and what a heart must I have, to contemplate
without emotion that elevation and that fall! Little did I
dream, when she added titles of veneration to those of
enthusiastic, distant, respectful love, that she should ever
be obliged to carry the sharp antidote against disgrace
concealed in that bosom; little did I dream that I should
have lived to see such disasters fallen upon her, in a
nation of gallant men, in a nation of men of honor, and
of cavaliers! I thought ten thousand swords must have

leaped from their scabbards, to avenge even a look that
threatened her with insult.

2. But the age of chivalry is gone; that of sophisters,
economists, and calculators, has succeeded; and the
glory of Europe is extinguished forever. Never, never
more, shall we behold that generous loyalty to rank and
sex, that proud submission, that dignified obedience, that
subordination of the heart, which kept alive, even in
servitude itself, the spirit of an exalted freedom! The
unbought grace of life, the cheap defence of nations, the
nurse of manly sentiment and heroic enterprise, is gone!
It is gone, that sensibility of principle, that chastity of
honor, which felt a stain like a wound, which inspired
courage whilst it mitigated ferocity, which ennobled
whatever it touched, and under which vice itself lost
half its evil, by losing all its grossness.

MR. GRATTAN'S FAMOUS REPLY TO MR. CORRY.—1800.

A duel, in which Mr. Corry was wounded in the arm, was the sequel
to this speech. The immediate provocation of the speech was a remark from Corry, that Grattan, instead of having a voice in the coun
cils of his country, should have been standing as a culprit at her bar.

Has the gentleman done? Has he completely done?
He was unparliamentary from the beginning to the end
of his speech. There was scarce a word that he uttered
that was not a violation of the privileges of the house.
But I did not call him to order. Why? Because the
limited talents of some men render it impossible for them
to be severe without being unparliamentary. But before
I sit down I shall show him how to be severe and par-

liamentary at the same time. On any other occasion, I
should think myself justifiable in treating with silent contempt anything which might fall from that honorable
member; but there are times when the insignificance of
the accuser is lost in the magnitude of the accusation.
I know the difficulty the honorable gentleman labored
under when he attacked me, conscious that, on a com-
parative view of our characters, public and private,
there is nothing he could say which would injure me.
The public would not believe the charge. I despise the
falsehood. If such a charge were made by an honest
man, I would answer it in the manner I shall do before
I sit down. But I shall first reply to it when not made
y an honest man.

2. The right honorable gentleman has called me "an
unimpeached traitor." I ask, why not "traitor," un-
qualified by any epithet? I will tell him: it was because he dare not! It was the act of a coward, who
raises his arm to strike, but has not courage to give
the blow! I will not call him villain, because it would
be unparliamentary, and he is a privy councillor. I
will not call him fool, because he happens to be Chancellor of the Exchequer. But I say he is one who has
abused the privilege of Parliament and freedom of debate, to the uttering language, which, if spoken out of
the house, I should answer only with a blow! I care
not how high his situation, how low his character, how
contemptible his speech; whether a privy councillor or
a parasite, my answer would be a blow! He has charged
me with being connected with the rebels. The charge
is utterly, totally, and meanly false! Does the honor-

able gentleman rely on the report of the House of Lords for the foundation of his assertion? If he does, I can prove to the committee there was a physical impossibility of that report being true. But I scorn to answer any man for my conduct, whether he be a political coxcomb, or whether he brought himself into power by a false glare of courage or not.

3. I have returned, not, as the right honorable member has said, to raise another storm,—I have returned to discharge an honorable debt of gratitude to my country, that conferred a great reward for past services, which, I am proud to say, was not greater than my desert. I have returned to protect that Constitution, of which I was the parent and the founder, from the assassination of such men as the honorable gentleman and his unworthy associates. They are corrupt—they are seditious—and they, at this very moment, are in a conspiracy against their country! I have returned to refute a libel, as false as it is malicious, given to the public under the appellation of a report of the committee of the Lords. Here I stand for impeachment or trial! I dare accusation! I defy the honorable gentleman! I defy the government! I defy their whole phalanx!—let them come forth! I tell the ministers I shall neither give them quarter nor take it! I am here to lay the shattered remains of my constitution on the floor of th's house, in defence of the liberties of my country.

THE CHURCH THE KINGDOM OF PERSUASION.--- *Lacordaire*

In the midst of universal change, the Church still
persuades, and her astonished enemies, not being able
to comprehend her existence, amuse themselves by
prophesying her death. Like the dust which insults
the passing traveller, this age, in ruin, outrages the
eternity of the Church, and does not perceive that her
immobility itself is proof of her strength.

2. Elevated in the world by a persuasion of eighteen
centuries, upon an antiquity of four thousand years,
the Catholic Church is invincible, because that which
she has been able to accomplish everywhere she is able
to do always. That which is universal is perpetual, as
that which is infinite is eternal. For nothing can become universal in humanity but that which has a necessary connection with the nature of man; and as the
nature of man does not change, that which has a necessary connection with it is also unchanging. If a persuasion as long in duration and as widely spread as
that which the Catholic Church founded could perish
in the human mind, it would be the same with human
reason.

3. What would a reality be if such a reality were
only an illusion? For what say the last adversaries,
the present adversaries of the Church? They maintain
that man's reason is a continual progress in which each
new idea destroys the old, where there is nothing stable
and absolute, where everything is destined to perish
save that marvellous faculty which gives a moment's
life to that which must necessarily perish. They thus

confess the nothingness of their hopes and of their reason, which is but a passage through sepulchres in which it leaves a little ashes. But, as said Bossuet, *"this miserable lot is not assured to them;"* the Church is living even in the heart of their predictions; the human race, which has hoped so much, will never accept so much despair!

VINDICATION OF SPAIN. (PRÒNOUNCED DURING THE DE-BATE ON THE SEMINOLE WAR, IN CONGRESS, 1819.)— *Hopkinson.*

Permit me, sir, to express my regret and decided disapprobation of the terms of reproach and contempt in which this nation has been spoken of on this floor; "poor, degraded Spain," has resounded from various parts of the house. Is it becoming, sir, the dignity of a representative of the American people to utter, from his high station, invectives against a nation with whom we cultivate and maintain the most friendly relations? Is it discreet, sir, in an individual, however enlightened, to venture upon a denunciation of a whole people?

2. In this poor, degraded Spain, it must be remembered, there is a vast mass of learning, and genius, and virtue, too; and a gentleman, who passes it all under his condemnation and contempt, hardly considers what a task he has undertaken. No people has suffered more than ourselves by these exterminating, sweeping judgments. Let us not be guilty of the same injustice to others. When I see one of these scribbling travellers, or insignificant atoms, gravely take upon himself to put

down the character of my own country, I turn from
him with disgust and derision.

2. Let us be equally just to others. This at least is
not the place for the indulgence of national prejudices
or resentments. A regard for ourselves forbids it. May
I add, sir, that, in reference to the weakness of Spain,
we should characterize her, perhaps more justly, certainly more liberally, by saying exhausted, rather than
degraded Spain. Yes, sir, exhausted in a contest, for
existence with a tremendous power, under which every
other nation of Europe, save one, sunk and fell. She
bore herself through with inflexible perseverance; and,
if she came out of the conflict enfeebled and exhausted,
it is no cause of reproach or contempt.

4. We talk of a war with Spain as a matter of amuse-
ment. I do not desire to partake of it. It will not be
found a very comfortable war, not from her power to do
so much harm, but from the impossibility of gaining
anything by it, or of wearing out her patience, or sub-
duing her fortitude. The history of every Spanish war,
is a history of immovable obstinacy, that seems to be
confirmed and hardened by misfortune and trial. In
her frequent contests with England, the latter, after all
her victories, has been the first to desire peace.

5. Let gentlemen not deceive themselves about the
pleasantry of a Spanish war. May they not, sir, have some
respect for the past character of this nation? The time
has been, when a Spanish knight was the type of everything that was chivalrous in valor, generous in honor,
and pure in patriotism. A century has hardly gone by,
since the Spanish infantry was the terror of Europe,

and the pride of soldiers. But those days of her glory
are past. Where, now, is that invincible courage; that
noble devotion to honor; that exalted love of country?
Let me tell you, in a voice of warning; they are buried
in the mines of Mexico, and the mountains of Peru.
Beware, my countrymen; look not with so eager an eye
to these fatal possessions, which will also be the grave
of your strength and virtue, should you be so unfortunate as to obtain them.

THE SOUTH. EXTRACT FROM MR. HAYNE'S SPEECH IN THE SENATE OF THE UNITED STATES, 1830.

If there be one State in the Union, Mr. President,
(and I say it not in a boastful spirit,) that may challenge
comparison with any other for a uniform, zealous, ardent, and uncalculating devotion to the Union, that
State is South Carolina. Sir, from the very commencement of the revolution up to this hour, there is no sacrifice, however great, she has not cheerfully made; no
service she has ever hesitated to perform. She has ad-
hered to you in your prosperity; but in your adversity,
she has clung to you with more than filial affection. No
matter what was the condition of her domestic affairs,
though deprived of her resources, divided by parties,
or surrounded by difficulties, the call of the country has
been to her as the voice of God. Domestic discord
ceased at the sound, every man became at once reconciled to his brethren, and the sons of Carolina were all
seen crowding together to the temple, bringing their
gifts to the altar of their common country.

2. What, sir, was the conduct of the South during the revolution? Sir, I honor New England for her conduct in that glorious struggle. But great as is the praise which belongs to her, I think at least equal honor is due to the South. They espoused the quarrel of their brethren with a generous zeal, which did not suffer tnɔm to stop to calculate their interest in the dispute. Favorites of the mother country, possessed of neither ships nor seamen to create commercial rivalship, they might have found in their situation a guarantee that their trade would be for ever fostered and protected by Great Britain. But, trampling on all considerations, either of interest or of safety, they rushed into the conflict, and, fighting for principle, periled all in the sacred cause of freedom.

3. Never was there exhibited in the history of the world, higher examples of noble daring, dreadful suffering, and heroic endurance, than by the Whigs of Carolina, during the revolution. The whole State, from the mountains to the sea, was overrun by an overwhelming force of the enemy. The fruits of industry perished on the spot where they were produced, or were consumed by the foe. The "plains of Carolina" drank up the most precious blood of her citizens! Black and smoking ruins marked the places which had been the habitations of her children! Driven from their homes into the gloomy and almost impenetrable swamps, even there the spirit of liberty survived, and South Carolina, sustained by the example of her Sumpters and her Marions, proved by her conduct, that though her soil might be overrun, the spirit of her people was invincible.

MARCO BOZZARIS.—*Halleck.*

At midnight, in his guarded tent,
  The Turk was dreaming of the hour,
When Greece, her knee in suppliance bent,
  Should tremble at his power;
In dreams, through camp and court, he bore
The trophies of a conqueror;
  In dreams his song of triumph heard;
Then wore his monarch's signet ring,—
Then press'd that monarch's throne,—a king,
As wild his thoughts, and gay of wing,
  As Eden's garden bird.

2.

An hour pass'd on—the Turk awoke;
  That bright dream was his last;
He woke—to hear his sentry's shriek,
"To arms! they come! the Greek! the Greek!"
He woke—to die midst flame and smoke,
And shout, and groan, and sabre stroke,
  And death-shots falling thick and fast,
As lightnings from the mountain cloud;
And heard, with voice as trumpet loud,
  Bozzaris cheer his band;
"Strike—till the last arm'd foe expires,
Strike—for your altars and your fires,
Strike—for the green graves of your sires,
  God—and your native land!"

3.

They fought—like brave men, long and well;
  They piled that ground with Moslem slain;

They conquer'd—but Bozzaris fell,
  Bleeding at every vein.
His few surviving comrades saw
His smile, when rang their proud hurrah
  And the red field was won;
Then saw in death his eyelids close
Calmly, as to a night's repose,
  Like flowers at set of sun.

4.

Come to the bridal chamber, death!
  Come to the mother, when she feels
For the first time her first-born's breath;—
  Come when the blessed seals
Which close the pestilence are broke,
And crowded cities wail its stroke;
Come in consumption's ghastly form,
The earthquake shock, the ocean storm;—
Come when the heart beats high and warm,
  With banquet-song, and dance, and wine,
And thou art terrible: the tear,
The groan, the knell, the pall, the bier,
And all we know, or dream, or fear
  Of agony, are thine.

5.

But to the hero, when his sword
  Has won the battle for the free,
Thy voice sounds like a prophet's word,
And in its hollow tones are heard
  The thanks of millions yet to be.
Bozzaris! with the storied brave
  Greece nurtured in her glory's time,

Rest thee—there is no prouder grave,
   Even in her own proud clime.
. We tell thy doom without a sigh ;
For thou art freedom's now, and fame's—
One of the few, the immortal names,
   That were not born to die.

SPEECH OF A CHRISTIAN MARTYR.—*Croly.*

For what have these my brethren died ?   Answer me,
priests of Rome ; what temple did they force—what
altar overthrow—what insults offer to the slightest of
your public celebrations ?   Judges of Rome, what offence
did they commit against the public peace ?   Consuls,
where were they found in rebellion against the Roman
majesty ?   People ! patricians ! who among your thousands can charge one of these holy dead with extortion,
impurity, or violence ; can charge them with anything,
but the patience that bore wrong without a murmur, and
the charity that answered tortures only by prayers ?

2. Do I stand here demanding to be believed for opinions ? No; but for facts. I have seen the sick made
whole, the lame walk, the blind receive their sight, by
the mere name of Him whom you crucified. I have seen
men once ignorant of all languages but their own, speaking with the language of every nation under heaven—the
still greater wonder, of the timid defying all fear, the
unlearned instantly made wise in the mysteries of things
divine and human, putting to shame the learned, hum-
bling the proud, enlightening the darkened ; alike in the
courts of kings, before the furious people, and in the

dungeon, armed with an irrepressible spirit of knowledge, reason, and truth, that confounded their adversaries.

3. I have seen the still greater wonder of the renewed heart; the impure, suddenly abjuring vice; the covetous, the cruel, the faithless, the godless, gloriously changed into the holy, the gentle, the faithful, the worshiper of the true God in spirit and in truth; the conquest of the passions which defied your philosophers, your tribunals, your rewards, your terrors, achieved in the one mighty name. These are facts, things which I have seen; and who, that had seen them, could doubt that the finger of the eternal God was there?

4. I dared not refuse my belief to the divine mission of the Being by whom, and even in memory of whom, things, baffling the proudest human means, were brought before my eyes. Thus, irresistibly compelled by facts to believe that Christ was sent by God, I was with equal force compelled to believe in the doctrines declared by this glorious messenger of the Father, alike of quick and dead. And thus I stand before you this day, at the close of a long life of labor and hazard, a Christian.

LOCHINVAR.—*Sir W. Scott.*

O, young Lochinvar is come out of the West,
Through all the wide border his steed was the best;
And save his good broad sword he weapon had none,
He rode all unarm'd, and he rode all alone.
So faithful in love, and so dauntless in war,
There never was knight like the young Lochinvar.

He stayed not for brake, and he stopp'd not for stone,
He swam the Esk river where ford there was none ;
But, ere he alighted at Netherby gate,
The bride had consented, the gallant came late :
For a laggard in love, and a dastard in war,
Was to wed the fair Ellen of brave Lochinvar.

2.

So boldly he enter'd the Netherby hall,
Among bride's-men, and kinsmen, and brothers, and
    all
Then spoke the bride's father, his hand on his sword,
(For the poor craven bridegroom said never a word,)
" Oh come ye in peace here, or come ye in war,
Or to dance at our bridal, young Lord Lochinvar ?"

3.

" I long woo'd your daughter, my suit you denied ;—
Love swells like the Solway, but ebbs like its tide—
And now am I come with this lost love of mine,
To lead but one measure, drink one cup of wine.
There are maidens in Scotland more lovely by far,
That would gladly be bride to the young Lochinvar."

4.

The bride kiss'd the goblet ; the knight took it up,
He quaff'd off the wine, and he threw down the cup.
She look'd down to blush, and she look'd up to sigh,
With a smile on her lips, and a tear in her eye.
He took her soft hand, ere her mother could bar,—
" Now tread we a measure," said young Lochinvar.

So stately his form, and so lovely her face,
That never a hall such a galliard did grace ;
While her mother did fret, and her father did fume,

And the bridegroom stood dangling his bonnet and
plume,
And the bridemaidens whisper'd, "'Twere better by
far
To have matched our fair cousin to young Lochinvar."

One touch to her hand, and one word in her ear,
When they reach'd the hall door, and the charger
stood near ;
So light to the croupe the fair lady he swung,
So light to the saddle before her he sprung !
" She is won ! we are gone, over bank, bush, and scaur ;
They'll have fleet steeds that follow," quoth young
Lochinvar.

5.

There was mounting 'mong Græmes of the Netherby
clan ;
Forsters, Fenwicks, and Musgraves, they rode, and
they ran ;
There was racing, and chasing, on Cannobie Lee,
But the lost bride of Netherby ne'er did they see.
So daring in love, and so dauntless in war,
Have ye e'er heard of gallant like young Lochinvar ?

SUPPOSED SPEECH OF JAMES OTIS.—*Mrs. L. M. Child.*

England may as well dam up the waters of the Nile
with bulrushes as fetter the step of Freedom, more proud
and firm in this youthful land than where she treads the
sequestered glens of Scotland, or couches herself among
the magnificent mountains of Switzerland. Arbitrary
principles, like those against which we now contend,

have cost one king of England his life,--another, his
crown,—and they may yet cost a third his most flourishing colonies.

2. We are two millions,—one-fifth fighting men. We
are bold and vigorous,—and we call no man master. To
the nation from whom we are proud to derive our origin
we ever were, and we ever will be, ready to yield un-
forced assistance; but it must not, and it never *can* be,
extorted. Some have sneeringly asked, "Are the
Americans too poor to pay a few pounds on stamped
paper?" No! America, thanks to God and herself, is
rich. But the right to take ten pounds, implies the
right to take a thousand; and what must be the wealth
that avarice, aided by power, cannot exhaust? True,
the spectre is now small; but the shadow he casts before
him is huge enough to darken all this fair land. Others,
in sentimental style, talk of the immense debt of gratitude which we owe to England. And what is the amount
of this debt? Why, truly, it is the same that the young
lion owes to the dam, which has brought it forth on the
solitude of the mountain, or left it amid the winds and
storms of the desert.

3. We plunged into the wave, with the great charter
of freedom in our teeth, because the fagot and torch were
behind us. We have waked this new world from its
savage lethargy; forests have been prostrated in our
path; towns and cities have grown up suddenly as the
flowers of the tropics, and the fires in our autumnal
woods are scarcely more rapid than the increase of our
wealth and population. And do we owe all this to the
kind succor of the mother country? No! we owe it to

the tyranny that drove us from her,—to the pelting storms which invigorated our helpless infancy.

4. But perhaps others will say, "We ask no money from your gratitude,—we only demand that you should pay your own expenses." And who, I pray, is to judge of their necessity? Why, the king,—and, with all due reverence to his sacred majesty, he understands the real wants of his distant subjects as little as he does the language of the Choctaws! Who is to judge concerning the frequency of these demands? The ministry. Who is to judge whether the money is properly expended? The cabinet behind the throne. In every instance, those who take are to judge for those who pay. If this system is suffered to go into operation, we shall have reason to esteem it a great privilege that rain and dew do not depend upon Parliament; otherwise, they would soon be taxed and dried. But, thanks to God, there is freedom enough left upon earth to resist such monstrous injustice! The flame of liberty is extinguished in Greece and Rome; but the light of its glowing embers is still bright and strong on the shores of America. Actuated by its sacred influence, we will resist unto death. But we wil. not countenance anarchy and misrule. The wrongs that a desperate community have heaped upon their enemies shall be amply and speedily repaid. Still, it may be well for some proud men to remember, that a fire is lighted in these Colonies which one breath of their king may kindle into such fury that the blood of all England cannot extinguish it!

9

SPEECH OF SALATHIEL IN FAVOR OF RESISTING THE
ROMAN POWER.—*Croly.*

What! must we first mingle in the cabals of Jeru
salem, and rouse the frigid debaters and disputers of the
Sanhedrim into action?   Are we first to conciliate the
irreconcilable, to soften the furious, to purify the corrupt?   If the Romans are to be our tyrants till we can
teach patriotism to faction, we may as well build the
dungeon at once, for to the dungeon we are consigned
for the longest life among us.

2. Death or glory for me.   There is no alternative
between, not merely the half slavery that we now live in
and independence, but between the most condign suffering and the most illustrious security.   If the people
would rise, through the pressure of public injury, they
must have risen long since; if from private violence,
what town, what district, what family, has not its claims
of deadly retribution!   Yet here the people stand, after
a hundred years of those continued stimulants to resistance, as unresisting as in the day when Pompey marched
over the threshold of the temple.

3. I know your generous friendship, Eleazer, and fear
that your anxiety to save me from the chances of the
struggle may bias your better judgment.   But here I
pledge myself, by all that constitutes the honor of man,
to strike at all risks a blow upon the Roman crest that
shall echo through the land.

What! commit our holy cause into the nursing of
those pampered hypocrites, whose utter baseness of
heart you know still more deeply than I do?   Linger,

till those pestilent profligates raise their price with Florus by betraying a design, that will be the glory of every man who draws a sword in it? Vainly, madly, ask a brood that, like the serpent, engender and fatten among the ruins of their country, to discard their venom, tc cast their fangs, to feel for human feelings? As well ask the serpent itself to rise from the original curse.

4. It is the irrevocable nature of faction to be base till it can be mischievous; to lick the dust until it can sting; to creep on its belly until it can twist its folds round the victim. No! let the old pensionaries, the bloated hangers-on in the train of every governor, the open sellers of their country for filthy lucre, betray me when I leave it in their power. To the field, I say; once and for all, to the field.

THE TREASURES OF THE DEEP.—*Hemans.*

What hidest thou in thy treasure-caves and cells?
   Thou hollow-sounding and mysterious main!
Pale glistening pearls, and rainbow-color'd shells,
   Bright things which gleam unreck'd of and in vain.
Keep, keep thy riches, melancholy sea!
       We ask not such from thee.
         2.
Yet more, the depths have more!—What wealth untold,
   Far down, and shining through their stillness, lies!
Thou hast the starry gems, the burning gold,
   Won from ten thousand royal argosies.
Sweep o'er thy spoils, thou wild and wrathful main'
       Earth claims not these again!

Yet more, the depths have more!—Thy waves have roll'd
  Above the cities of a world gone by!
Sand hath fill'd up the palaces of old,
  Sea-weed o'ergrown the halls of revelry!
Dash o'er them, ocean! in thy scornful play,
          Man yields them to decay!

3.

Yet more! the billows and the depths have more!
  High hearts and brave are gather'd to thy breast!
They hear not now the booming waters roar,—
  The battle-thunders will not break their rest.
Keep thy red gold and gems, thou stormy grave!
          Give back the true and brave!

4.

Give back the lost and lovely!—Those for whom
  The place was kept at board and hearth so long;
The prayer went up through midnight's breathless gloom
And the vain yearning woke midst festal song!
Hold fast thy buried isles, thy towers o'erthrown,
          —But all is not thine own!

THE MURDERER. EXTRACT FROM MR. WEBSTER'S SPEECH ON THE TRIAL OF J. F. KNAPP.

Against the prisoner at the bar, as an individual, I cannot have the slightest prejudice. I would not do him the smallest injury or injustice. But I do not affect to be indifferent to the discovery, and the punishment of this deep guilt. I cheerfully share in the opprobrium, how much soever it may be, which is cast on those who feel and manifest an anxious concern that all who had a part in planning, or a hand in executing this deed of

midnight assassination, may be brought to answer for
their enormous crime at the bar of public justice. Gentlemen, it is a most extraordinary case. In some respects it has hardly a precedent anywhere; certainly
none in our New England history. This bloody drama
exhibited no suddenly excited, ungovernable rage. The
actors in it were not surprised by any lion-like temptation upon their virtue, overcoming it before resistance
could begin. Nor did they do the deed to glut savage
vengeance, or satiate long-settled and deadly hate. It
was a cool, calculating, money-making murder. It was
all " hire and salary, not revenge." It was the weigh-
ing of money against life; the counting out of so many
pieces of silver, against so many ounces of blood.

2. An aged man without an enemy in the world, in
his own house, and in his own bed, is made the victim of
butcherly murder for mere pay. Truly, here is a new
lesson for painters and poets. Whoever shall hereafter
draw the portrait of murder, if he will show it as it has
been exhibited in an example, where such example was
last to have been looked for, in the very bosom of our
New England society, let him not give it the grim visage
of Moloch, the brow knitted by revenge, the face black
with settled hate, and the blood-shot eye emitting livid
fires of malice; — let him draw, rather, a decorous,
smooth-faced, bloodless demon; a picture in repose,
rather than in action; not so much an example of human nature in its depravity, and in its paroxysms of
crime, as an infernal nature,—a fiend in the ordinary
display and development of his character.

3. The deed was executed with a degree of self-posses-

sion and steadiness, equal to the wickedness with which
it was planned.   The circumstances now clearly in evidence, spread out the whole scene before us.   Deep
sleep had fallen on the destined victim, and on all beneath his roof.   A healthful old man, to whom sleep
was sweet—the first sound slumbers of the night held
him in their soft but strong embrace.   The assassin
enters, through the window already prepared, into an
unoccupied apartment.   With noiseless foot he paces
the lonely hall, half lighted by the moon; he winds up
the ascent of the stairs, and reaches the door of the
chamber.   Of this he moves the lock, by soft and continued pressure, till it turns on its hinges; and he
enters, and beholds his victim before him.   The room
was uncommonly open to the admission of light.   The
face of the innocent sleeper was turned from the murderer, and the beams of the moon, resting on the gray
locks of his aged temple, showed him where to strike.
The fatal blow is given !—and the victim passes, without
a struggle or a motion, from the repose of sleep to the
repose of death !   It is the assassin's purpose to make
sure work; and he yet plies the dagger, though it was
obvious that life had been destroyed by the blow of the
bludgeon.   He even raises the aged arm, that he may
not fail in his aim at the heart; and replaces it again
over the wounds of the poniard !   To finish the picture,
he explores the wrist for the pulse ! he feels it, and
ascertains that it beats no longer !   It is accomplished.
The deed is done.   He retreats, retraces his steps to
the window, passes out through it as he came in, and
escapes.   He has done the murder — no eye has seen

him; no ear has heard him. The secret is his own, and it is safe!

4. Ah! gentlemen, that was a dreadful mistake. Such a secret can be safe nowhere. The whole creation of God has neither nook nor corner, where the guilty can bestow it, and say it is safe. Not to speak of that eye which glances through all disguises, and beholds everything as in the splendor of noon,—such secrets of guilt are never safe from detection, even by men. True it is, generally speaking, that "murder will out." True it is, that Providence hath so ordained, and doth so govern things, that those who break the great law of heaven, by shedding man's blood, seldom succeed in avoiding discovery. Especially, in a case exciting so much attention as this, discovery must come, and will come, sooner or later. A thousand eyes turn at once to explore every man, every thing, every circumstance connected with the time and place; a thousand ears catch every whisper; a thousand excited minds intensely dwell on the scene, shedding all their light, and ready to kindle the slightest circumstance into a blaze of discovery. Meantime the guilty soul cannot keep its own secret. It is false to itself; or rather it feels an irresistible impulse of conscience to be true to itself. It labors under its guilty possession, and knows not what to do with it. The human heart was not made for the residence of such an inhabitant. It finds itself preyed on by a torment, which it does not acknowledge to God or man. A vulture is devouring it, and it can ask no sympathy or assistance either from heaven or earth. The secret which the murderer possesses, soon comes to possess

him; and, like the evil spirits of which we read, it ever comes him, and leads him whithersoever it will. He feels it beating at his heart, rising to his throat, and demanding disclosure. He thinks the whole world sees it in his face, reads it in his eyes, and almost hears its workings in the very silence of his thoughts. It has become his master. It betrays his discretion, it breaks down his courage, it conquers his prudence. When suspicions from without begin to embarrass him, and the net of circumstances to entangle him, the fatal secret struggles with still greater violence to burst forth. It must be confessed, it will be confessed, there is no refuge from confession but suicide, and suicide is confession.

THE BURIAL OF SIR JOHN MOORE.—*Wolfe.*

Not a drum was heard, not a funeral note,
 As his corse to the ramparts we hurried;
Not a soldier discharged his farewell shot
 O'er the grave where our hero we buried.

2.

We buried him darkly at dead of night,
 The sods with our bayonets turning,
By the struggling moonbeam's misty light,
 And the lantern dimly burning.

3.

N) useless coffin enclosed his breast,
 Not in sheet or in shroud we wound him;
But he lay like a warrior taking his rest,
 With his martial cloak around him.

Few and short were the prayers we said,
  And we spoke not a word of sorrow ;
But we steadfastly gazed on the face that was dead,
  And we bitterly thought of the morrow
4.
We thought, as we hollow'd his narrow bed,
  And smooth'd down his lonely pillow,
That the foe and the stranger would tread o'er his
    head,
  And we far away on the billow !

Lightly they'll talk of the spirit that's gone,
  And o'er his cold ashes upbraid him,—
But little he'll reck, if they let him sleep on
  In the grave where a Briton has laid him.
5.
But half of our heavy task was done,
  When the clock struck the hour of retiring ;
And we heard the distant and random gun
  That the foe was sullenly firing.

Slowly and sadly we laid him down,
  From the field of his fame fresh and gory ;
We carved not a line, we raised not a stone—
  But we left him alone with his glory !

THE HOMES OF ENGLAND.—*Hemans.*

The stately homes of England,
  How beautiful they stand !
Amid their tall ancestral trees,
  O'er all the pleasant land !

The deer across their greensward bound
  Through shade and sunny gleam,
And the swan glides past them with the sound
  Of some rejoicing stream.

2.

The merry homes of England!
  Around their hearths by night,
What gladsome looks of household love
  Meet in the ruddy light!
There woman's voice flows forth in song
  Or childhood's tale is told;
Or lips move tunefully along
  Some glorious page of old.

3.

The blessed homes of England!
  How softly on their bowers
Is laid the holy quietness
  That breathes from Sabbath hours!
Solemn, yet sweet, the church bell's chime
  Floats through their woods at morn,
All other sounds in that still time
  Of breeze and leaf are borne.

4.

The cottage homes of England!
  By thousands on her plains,
They're smiling o'er the silvery brook,
  And round the hamlet fanes.
Through glowing orchards forth they peep,
  Each from its nook of leaves;
And fearless there the lowly sleep,
  As the bird beneath their eaves.

5.

e free fair homes of England!
ong, long in hut and hall
    hearts of native proof be rear'd,
    guard each hallow'd wall.
        een forever be the groves,
    ₋a bright their flowery sod,
, there first the child's glad spirit loves
    Its country and its God.

ADDRESS OF DANIEL WEBSTER TO THE SURVIVORS OF THE
    BATTLE OF BUNKER HILL, DELIVERED AT THE LAYING
    OF THE CORNER-STONE OF THE BUNKER HILL MONU-
    MENT.

Venerable men! you have come down to us from a
former generation. Heaven has bounteously lengthened
out your lives, that you might behold this joyous day.
You are now where you stood fifty years ago, this very
hour, with your brothers, and your neighbors, shoulder
to shoulder, in the strife for your country. Behold, how
altered! The same heavens are indeed over your heads;
the same ocean rolls at your feet; but all else, how
changed! You hear now no roar of hostile cannon, you
see no mixed volumes of smoke and flame rising from
burning Charlestown. The ground strewed with the
dead and the dying; the impetuous charge; the steady
and successful repulse; the loud call to repeated assault;
the summoning of all that is manly to repeated resistance; a thousand bosoms freely and fearlessly bared in
an instant to whatever of terror there may be in war and
death;—all these you have witnessed, but you witness

them no more. All is peace. The heights of yonder
metropolis, its towers and roofs, which you then saw
filled with wives, and children, and countrymen, in distress
and terror, and looking with unutterable emotions for
the issue of the combat, have presented you to-day with
the sight of its whole happy population, come out to welcome and greet you with an universal jubilee. Yonder
proud ships, by a felicity of position, appropriately lying
at the foot of this mount, and seeming fondly to cling
around it, are not means of annoyance to you, but your
country's own means of distinction and defence. All is
peace; and God has granted you this sight of your
country's happiness, ere you slumber in the grave forever. He has allowed you to behold and to partake the
reward of your patriotic toils; and he has allowed us,
your sons and countrymen, to meet you here, and in the
name of the present generation, in the name of your
country, in the name of liberty, to thank you!

2. But, alas! you are not all here! Time and the
sword have thinned your ranks. Prescot, Putnam, Stark,
Brooks, Read, Pomeroy, Bridge! our eyes seek for you
in vain amid this broken band. You are gathered to
your fathers, and live only to your country, in her
grateful remembrance, and your own bright example.
But let us not too much grieve, that you have met the
common fate of men. You lived, at least, long enough
to know that your work had been nobly and successfully
accomplished. You lived to see your country's independence established, and to sheathe your swords from
war. On the light of liberty you saw arise the light of
peace, like

'another morn,
Risen on midnoon ;'—

and the sky, on which you closed your eyes, was cloud
less.

3. But—ah!—him! the first great martyr in this great
cause! Him! the premature victim of his own self-de-
voting heart! Him! the head of our civil councils, and
the destined leader of our military bands; whom nothing
brought hither but the unquenchable fire of his own
spirit! Him! cut off by Providence, in the hour of overwhelming anxiety, and thick gloom; falling, ere he saw
the star of his country rise; pouring out his generous
blood, like water, before he knew whether it would fer-
tilize a land of freedom or of bondage! how shall I
struggle with the emotions that stifle the utterance of thy
name! Our poor work may perish, but 'thine shall endure! This monument may moulder away, the solid
ground it rests upon may sink down to a level with the
sea; but thy memory shall not fail! Wheresoever
among men a heart shall be found that beats to the
transports of patriotism and liberty, its aspirations shall
be to claim kindred with thy spirit.

4. But the scene amid which we stand does not permit us to confine our thoughts or our sympathies to
those fearless spirits who hazarded or lost their lives
on this consecrated spot. We have the happiness to
rejoice here in the presence of a most worthy representation of the survivors of the whole revolutionary army.

5. Veterans! you are the remnant of many a well-fought
field. You bring with you marks of honor from Tren-
ton and Monmouth, from Yorktown, Camden, Benning-

ton, and Saratoga.   Veterans of half a century! when
in your youthful days, you put everything at hazard in
your country's cause, good as that cause was, and sanguine as youth is, still your fondest hopes did not stretch
onward to an hour like this!   At a period to which you
could not reasonably have expected to arrive ; at a moment of national prosperity, such as you could never
have foreseen ; you are now met here, to enjoy the fellowship of old soldiers, and to receive the overflowings of a
universal gratitude.

6. But your agitated countenances, and your heaving
breasts, inform me that even this is not an unmixed
joy. I perceive that a tumult of contending feelings
rushes upon you.   The images of the dead, as well as
the persons of the living, throng to your embraces.   The
scene overwhelms you, and I turn from it.   May the Father of all mercies smile upon your declining years, and
bless them !   And when you shall here have exchanged
your embraces, when you shall once more have pressed
the hands which have been so often extended to give
succor in adversity, or grasped in the exultation of victory, then look abroad into this lovely land, which your
young valor defended, and mark the happiness with
which it is filled; yea, look abroad into the whole earth,
and see what a name you have contributed to give your
country, and what a praise you have added to freedom,
and then rejoice in the sympathy and gratitude which
beam upon your last days from the improved condition
of mankind.

THE AFRICAN CHIEF.—*Bryant.*

Chain'd in the market-place he stood,
   A man of giant frame,
Amid the gathering multitude
   That shrunk to hear his name—
All stern of look and strong of limb
   His dark eye on the ground:—
And silently they gazed on him,
   As on a lion bound.

2.

Vainly, but well, that chief had fought,
   He was a captive now,
Yet pride, that fortune humbles not,
   Was written on his brow.
The scars his dark broad bosom wore,
   Show'd warrior true and brave;
A prince among his tribe before,
   He could not be a slave.

3.

Then to his conqueror he spake—
   "My brother is a king;
Undo this necklace from my neck,
   And take this bracelet ring,
And send me where my brother reigns,
   And I will fill thy hands
With store of ivory from the plains,
   And gold-dust from the sands."

4.

"Not for thy ivory nor thy gold
   Will I unbind thy chain;
That bloody hand shall never hold
   The battle spear again.

A price thy nation never gave,
 Shall yet be paid for thee;
For thou shalt be the Christian's slave,
 In lands beyond the sea."

5.

Then wept the warrior chief, and bade
 To shred his locks away;
And, one by one, each heavy braid
 Before the victor lay.
Thick were the platted locks, and long
 And deftly hidden there
Shone many a wedge of gold among
 The dark and crisped hair.

6.

"Look, feast thy greedy eye with gold
 Long kept for sorest need;
Take it—thou askest sums untold,
 And say that I am freed.
Take it—my wife, the long, long day,
 Weeps by the cocoa tree,
And my young children leave their play,
 And ask in vain for me."

7.

"I take thy gold—but I have made
 Thy fetters fast and strong,
And ween that by the cocoa shade
 Thy wife will wait thee long."
Strong was the agony that shook
 The captive's frame to hear,
And the proud meaning of his look
 Was changed to mortal fear.

8.

His heart was broken—crazed his brain;
   At once his eye grew wild;
He struggled fiercely with his chain,
   Whisper'd, and wept, and smiled;
Yet wore not long those fatal bands,
   And once, at shut of day,
They drew him forth upon the sands,
   The foul hyena's prey.

THE DEATH OF ALIATAR.—*Bryant.*

'Tis not with gilded sabres
   That gleam in baldricks blue,
Nor nodding plumes in caps of Fez
   Of gay and gaudy hue—
But habited in mourning weeds,
   Come marching from afar, .
By four and four, the valiant men
   Who fought with Aliatar.
All mournfully and slowly
   The afflicted warriors come,
To the deep wail of the trumpet,
   And beat of muffled drum.

2.

The banner of the Phenix,
   The flag that loved the sky
That scarce the wind dared wanton with,
   It flew so proud and high—
Now leaves its place in battle-field,
   And sweeps the ground in grief;
The bearer drags its glorious folds
   Behind the fallen chief,

As mournfully and slowly
  The afflicted warriors come,
To the deep wail of the trumpet,
  And beat of muffled drum.

3.

Brave Aliatar led forward
  A hundred Moors to go
To where his brother held Motril
  Against the leaguering foe.
On horseback went the gallant Moor,
  That gallant band to lead;
And now his bier is at the gate,
  From whence he prick'd his steed.
While mournfully and slowly
  The afflicted warriors come,
To the deep wail of the trumpet,
  And beat of muffled drum.

4.

The knights of the Grand Master
  In crowded ambush lay;
They rush'd upon him where the reeds
  Were thick beside the way;
They smote the valiant Aliatar,
  They smote him till he died,
And broken, but not beaten, were
  The brave ones by his side.
Now mournfully and slowly
  The afflicted warriors come,
To the deep wail of the trumpet,
  And beat of muffled drum.

5.

Oh! what was Zayda's sorrow,
  How passionate her cries!
Her lover's wounds stream'd not more free
  Than that poor maiden's eyes.
Say, love—for thou didst see her tears:
  O no! he drew more tight
The blinding fillet o'er his lids,
  To spare his eyes the sight.
While mournfully and slowly
  The afflicted warriors come,
To the deep wail of the trumpet,
  And beat of muffled drum.

6.

Nor Zayda weeps him only,
  But all that dwell between
The great Alhambra's palace walls
  And springs of Albaicin.
The ladies weep the flower of knights,
  The brave the bravest here:
The people weep a champion,
  The alcaydes a noble peer.
While mournfully and slowly
  The afflicted warriors come,
To the deep wail of the trumpet,
  And beat of muffled drum.

SPEECH OF ROBERT EMMETT, AT THE CLOSE OF HIS
TRIAL FOR HIGH TREASON.

My Lords,—You ask me what I have to say, why
sentence of death should not be pronounced on me ac-

cording to law?   I have nothing to say, that can alter
your predetermination, or that it will become me to say
with any view to the mitigation of that sentence, which
you are here to pronounce, and I must abide by   But
I have that to say which interests me more than life, and
which you have labored to destroy.   I have much to say
why my reputation should be rescued from the load of
false accusation and calumny which has been heaped
upon it.

2. I am charged with being an emissary of France. An
emissary of France! And for what end? It is alleged,
that I wished to sell the independence of my country!
And for what end?   Was this the object of my ambition?   No; I am no emissary—my ambition was to hold
a place among the deliverers of my country—not in
power, not in profit, but in the glory of the achievement!   Sell my country's independence to France! and
for what?   A change of masters?   No; but for ambition!   O my country, was it personal ambition that in-
fluenced me—had it been the soul of my actions, could
I not, by my education and fortune, by the rank and
consideration of my family, have placed myself among
the proudest of your oppressors?   My country was my
idol—to it I sacrificed every selfish, every endearing
sentiment, and for it I now offer up my life.   No, my
lord, I acted as an Irishman, determined on delivering
my country from the yoke of a foreign and unrelenting
tyranny, and from the more galling yoke of a domestic
faction.

3. Connection with France was indeed intended—but
only so far as mutual interest would sanction or require

Were the French to assume any authority inconsistent with the purest independence, it would be the signal of their destruction. Were they to come as invaders, or enemies uninvited by the wishes of the people, I should oppose them to the utmost of my strength. Yes, my countrymen, I should advise you to meet them on the beach, with a sword in one hand and a torch in the other. I would meet them with all the destructive fury of war, and I would animate my countrymen to immolate them in their boats, before they had contaminated the soil of my country. If they succeeded in landing, and if forced to retire before superior discipline, I would dispute every inch of ground, raze every house, burn every blade of grass, and the last intrenchment of liberty should be my grave.

4. I have been charged with that importance, in the efforts to emancipate my country, as to be considered the keystone of the combination of Irishmen, or, as your lordship expresses it, "the life and blood of the conspiracy." You do me honor overmuch—you have given to the subaltern all the credit of a superior; there are men engaged in this conspiracy, who are not only superior to me, but even to your own conceptions of yourself, my lord—men, before the splendor of whose genius and virtues I should bow with respectful deference, and who would think themselves dishonored to be called your friends—who would not disgrace themselves by shaking your blood-stained hand. [Here he was interrupted.]

5. What, my lord, shall you tell me, on the passage to that scaffold, which that tyranny, of which you are only

the intermediate executioner, has erected for my murder, that I am accountable for all the blood that has been and will be shed in this struggle of the oppressed against the oppressor—shall you tell me this, and must I be so very a slave as not to repel it? I, who fear not to approach the Omnipotent Judge, to answer for the conduct of my whole life—am I to be appalled and falsified by a mere remnant of mortality here—by you, too, who, if it were possible to collect all the innocent blood that you have shed, in your unhallowed ministry, in one great reservoir, your lordship might swim in it?

6. My lords, you seem impatient for the sacrifice—the blood for which you thirst is not congealed by the artificial terrors which surround your victim; it circulates warmly and unruffled through the channels which God created for noble purposes, but which you are bent to destroy for purposes so grievous, that they cry to Heaven. Be yet patient! I have but a few more words to say. I am going to my cold and silent grave: my lamp of life is nearly extinguished: my race is run: the grave opens to receive me, and I sink into its bosom. I have but one request to ask at my departure from this world: it is the charity of its silence. Let no man write my epitaph; for as no man who knows my motives, dare now vindicate them, let no prejudice or ignorance asperse them. Let them and me repose in obscurity, and my tomb remain uninscribed, until other times and other men can do justice to my character. When my country takes her place among the nations of the earth, then, and not till then, let my epitaph be written. I have done!

ARNOLD WINKELRIED.—*Montgomery.*

" Make way for liberty !" he cried;
Made way for liberty, and died !—

2.

It must not be : this day, this hour,
Annihilates the oppressor's power !
All Switzerland is in the field,
She will not fly, she cannot yield—
She must not fall ; her better fate
Here gives her an immortal date.
Few were the numbers she could boast;
But every freeman was a host,
And felt as though himself were he,
On whose sole arm hung victory.

3.

It did depend on one indeed;
Behold him—Arnold Winkelried !
There sounds not to the trump of fame
The echo of a nobler name.
Unmark'd he stood amid the throng,
In rumination deep and long,
Till you might see, with sudden grace,
The very thought come o'er his face ;
And, by the motion of his form,
Anticipate the bursting storm ;
And, by the uplifting of his brow,
Tell where the bolt would strike, and how.

4.

But 'twas no sooner thought than done,
The field was in a moment won :—

"Make way for liberty :" he cried,
Then ran, with arms extended wide,
As if his dearest friend to clasp ;
Ten spears he swept within his grasp :
"Make way for liberty !" he cried,
Their keen points met from side to side ;
He bow'd amongst them like a tree,
And thus made way for liberty.

5.

Swift to the breach his comrades fly ;
"Make way for liberty !" they cry.
And through the Austrian phalanx dart,
As rush'd the spears through Arnold's heart,
While instantaneous as his fall,
Rout, ruin, panic, scattered all :
An earthquake could not overthrow
A city with a surer blow.

6.

Thus Switzerland again was free ;
Thus death made way for liberty.

THE PASSING OF THE RUBICON.—*Knowles.*

A gentleman, Mr. President, speaking of Cæsar'
benevolent disposition, and of the reluctance with which
he entered into the civil war, observes, " How long did
he pause upon the brink of the Rubicon !"   How came
he to the brink of that river !   How dared he cross it !
Shall private men respect the boundaries of private
property, and shall a man pay no respect to the boundaries of his country's rights ?   How dared he cross
that river !   Oh ! but he paused upon the brink !   He

should have perished upon the brink ere he had crossed it! Why did he pause? Why does a man's heart palpitate when he is on the point of committing an unlawful deed? Why does the very murderer, his victim sleeping before him, and his glaring eye, taking the measure of the blow, strike wide of the mortal part? Because of conscience! 'Twas that made Cæsar pause upon the brink of the Rubicon. Compassion! What compassion! The compassion of an assassin, that feels a momentary shudder, as his weapon begins to cut! Cæsar paused upon the brink of the Rubicon! What was the Rubicon? The boundary of Cæsar's province. From what did it separate his province? From his country. Was that country a desert? No; it was cultivated and fertile; rich and populous! Its sons were men of genius, spirit, and generosity! Its daughters were lovely, susceptible, and chaste · Friendship was its inhabitant! Love was its inhabitant! Domestic affection was its inhabitant! Liberty was its inhabitant! All bounded by the stream of the Rubicon! What was Cæsar, that stood upon the bank of that stream? A traitor, bringing war and pestilence into the heart of that country! No wonder that he paused—no wonder if, his imagination wrought upon by his conscience, he had beheld blood instead of water; and heard groans, instead of murmurs! No wonder, if some gorgon horror had turned him into stone upon the spot! But, no!—he cried, "The die is cast!" He plunged!—he crossed!—and Rome was free no more!

SPEECH OF LORD CHANCELLOR THURLOW IN THE HOUSE
OF LORDS, IN REPLY TO THE DUKE OF GRAFTON.*

I am amazed at the attack the noble duke has made
on me.   Yes, my lords, [considerably raising his voice,]
I am amazed at his grace's speech.   The noble duke
cannot look before him, behind him, or on either side
of him, without seeing some noble peer who owes his
seat in this house to his successful exertions in the profession to which I belong.   Does he not feel that it is
as honorable to owe it to these, as to being the accident
of an accident ?   To all these noble lords the language
of the noble duke is as applicable and as insulting as it
is to myself.   But I do not fear to meet it single and
alone.   No one venerates the peerage more than I do :
but, my lords, I must say, that the peerage solicited me,
not I the peerage.   Nay, more : I can say, and will say,
that as a peer of parliament, as speaker of this right
honorable house, as keeper of the great seal, as guardian of his majesty's conscience, as lord high chancellor

---

* The Duke of Grafton had reproached Lord Thurlow with his
plebeian extraction, and his recent admission into the peerage. "Lord
Thurlow rose from the woolsack, and advanced slowly to the place
from which the chancellor generally addresses the house : then fixing
on the duke the look of Jove when he grasps the thunder, in a level
tone of voice, he spoke as above.

"The effect of this speech, both within the walls and out of them,
was prodigious.   It gave Lord Thurlow an ascendancy in the house
which no chancellor had ever possessed ; it invested him, in public
opinion, with a character of independence and honor ; and this, though
he was ever on the unpopular side in politics, made him always popular with the people."

of England, nay, even in that character alone in which
the noble duke would think it an affront to be considered,—as A MAN, I am at this moment as respectable,—
I beg leave to add,—I am at this time as much respected, as the proudest peer I now look down upon.

THE THREE BLACK CROWS.—*Byrom.*

Two honest tradesmen meeting in the Strand,
One took the other briskly by the hand;
"Hark ye," said he, "'tis an odd story this,
About the crows!"—"I don't know what it is,"
Replied his friend.—"No! I'm surprised at that;
Where I come from it is the common chat:
But you shall hear: an odd affair indeed!
And that it happen'd, they are all agreed:
Not to detain you from a thing so strange,
A gentleman, that lives not far from 'Change,
This week, in short, as all the alley knows,
Taking a puke, has thrown up three black crows."
"Impossible!"—"Nay, but it's really true,
I had it from good hands, and so may you."
"From whose, I pray?" So having named the man,
Straight to inquire his curious comrade ran.
"Sir, did you tell"—relating the affair—
"Yes, sir, I did; and if it's worth your care,
Ask Mr. Such-a-one, he told it me;
But, by the way, 'twas two black crows, not three."
Resolved to trace so wondrous an event,
Whip to the third, the virtuoso went.

"Sir,"— and so forth—"Why, yes; the thing is **fact**,
Though in regard to number not exact;
It was not two black crows, 'twas only one;
The truth of that you may depend upon.
The gentleman himself told me the case."
"Where may I find him?" "Why,—in such a place."
Away he goes, and having found him out,—
"Sir, be so good as to resolve a doubt."
Then to his last informant he referr'd,
And begg'd to know if true what he had heard.
"Did you, sir, throw up a black crow?" "Not 1!"
"Bless me! how people propagate a lie!
Black crows have been thrown up, three, two, and one,
And here I find at last all comes to none!
Did you say nothing of a crow at all?"
"Crow—crow—perhaps I might, now I recall
The matter over." "And pray, sir, what was't?"
"Why, I was horrid sick, and at the last,
I did throw up, and told my neighbor so,
Something that was as black, sir, as a crow."

CHARACTER OF NAPOLEON BONAPARTE.—*Phillips.*

He is fallen! We may now pause before that splen-
di' prodigy, which towered amongst us like some ancient
ruin, whose frown terrified the glance its magnificence
attracted. Grand, gloomy, and peculiar, he sat upon
the throne a sceptred hermit, wrapt in the solitude of
his own originality. A mind bold, independent, and
decisive—a will despotic in its dictates—an energy that
distanced expedition, and a conscience pliable to every

touch of interest, marked the outline of this ex: 'aordinary character—the most extraordinary, perhaps, that in the annals of this world ever rose, or reigned, or fell. Flung into life, in the midst of a revolution that quickered every energy of a people who acknowledge no superior, he commenced his course, a stranger by birth, and a scholar by charity! With no friend but his sword, and no fortune but his talents, he rushed in the list where rank, and wealth, and genius had arrayed themselves, and competition fled from him as from the glance of destiny. He knew no motive but interest—he acknowledged no criterion but success — he worshipped no god but ambition, and with an eastern devotion he knelt at the shrine of his idolatry. Subsidiary to this, there was no creed that he did not profess, there was no opinion that he did not promulgate: in the hope of a dynasty, he upheld the crescent; for the sake of a divorce, he bowed before the cross: the orphan of St. Louis, he became the adopted child of the republic: and with a parricidal ingratitude, on the ruins both of the throne and tribune, he reared the throne of his despotism. A professed Catholic, he imprisoned the pope; a pretended patriot, he impoverished the country; and, in the name of Brutus, he grasped without remorse, and wore without shame, the diadem of the Cæsars! Through this pantomime of policy, fortune played the clown to his caprices. At his touch, crowns crumbled, beggars reigned, systems vanished, the wildest theories took the color of his whim, and all that was venerable, and all that was novel, changed places with the rapidity of a drama. Even apparent defeat assumed the appear

ance of victory—his flight from Egypt confirmed his
destiny—ruin itself only elevated him to empire. But
if his fortune was great, his genius was transcendent;
decision flashed upon his councils; and it was the same
to decide and to perform. To inferior intellects his
combinations appeared perfectly impossible, his plans
perfectly impracticable; but, in his hands, simplicity
marked their development, and success vindicated their
adoption. His person partook the character of his
mind—if the one never yielded in the cabinet, the other
never bent in the field. Nature had no obstacle that he
did not surmount—space no opposition that he did not
spurn; and whether amid Alpine rocks, Arabian sands,
or Polar snows, he seemed proof against peril, and em-
powered with ubiquity ! The whole continent trembled
at beholding the audacity of his designs, and the miracle of their execution. Skepticism bowed to the prodi-
gies of his performance; romance assumed the air of
history; nor was there aught too incredible for belief,
or too fanciful for expectation, when the world saw a
subaltern of Corsica waving his imperial flag over her
most ancient capitals. All the visions of antiquity became commonplaces in his contemplation; kings were
his people—nations were his outposts; and he disposed
of courts, and crowns, and camps, and churches, and
cabinets, as if they were titular dignitaries of the chess-
board !—Amid all these changes he stood immutable as
adamant.

2. It mattered little whether in the field or in the
drawing room—with the mob or the levee—wearing the
Jacobin bonnet or the iron crown—banishing a Bra

ganza, or espousing a Hapsburg—dictating peace on a
raft to the Czar of Russia, or contemplating defeat at
the gallows of Leipsig—he was still the same military
despot !

8. In this wonderful combination, his affectations of
literature must not be omitted. The jailor of the press
he affected the patronage of letters—the proscriber of
books, he encouraged philosophy—the persecutor of
authors and the murderer of printers, he yet pretended
to the protection of learning ! the assassin of Palm, the
silencer of De Stael, and the denouncer of Kotzebue,
he was the friend of David, the benefactor of De Lille,
and sent his academic prize to the philosopher of England. Such a medley of contradictions, and at the
same time such an individual consistency, were never
united in the same character. A royalist—a republican
and an emperor—a Mohammedan—a Catholic and a
patron of the synagogue—a subaltern and a sovereign
—a traitor and a tyrant—a Christian and an infidel—
he was, through all his vicissitudes, the same stern, impatient, inflexible original—the same mysterious, incomprehensible self—the man without a model, and without
a shadow.

REPLY TO LORD LYNDHURST.—*Sheil.*

There is, however, one man, of great abilities, not a
member of this house, but whose talents and whose
boldness have placed him in the topmost place in his
party—who, disdaining all imposture, and thinking it
the best course to appeal directly to the religious and

national antipathies of the people of this country.—
abandoning all reserve, and flinging off the slender
veil by which his political associates affect to cover
although they cannot hide, their motives—distinctly
and audaciously tells the Irish people that they are not
entitled to the same privileges as Englishmen; and
pronounces them, in any particular which could enter
his minute enumeration of the circumstances by which
fellow-citizenship is created, in race, identity, and religion—to be aliens—to be aliens in race—to be aliens
in country—to be aliens in religion.*

2. Aliens! good God! was Arthur, Duke of Wellington, in the House of Lords, and did he not start up
and exclaim, "Hold! I have seen the aliens do their
duty"? The Duke of Wellington is not a man of an
excitable temperament. His mind is of a cast too
martial to be easily moved; but notwithstanding his
habitual inflexibility, I cannot help thinking that when
he heard his Roman Catholic countrymen (for we are
his countrymen) designated by a phrase as offensive as
the abundant vocabulary of his eloquent confederate
could supply—I cannot help thinking that he ought to
have recollected the many fields of fight in which we
have been contributors to his renown. "The battles,
sieges, fortunes that he has passed," ought to have come
back upon him.

3. He ought to have remembered that, from the

---

* Lord Lyndhurst was sitting under the gallery during Mr. Sheil's speech. Mr.
Sheil looked and shook his head indignantly at him at this part of his speech. The
effect produced was remarkable. The whole house turned towards Lord Lyndhurst,
and the shouts of the ministerialists, encountered by the vehement outcries of the
Conservatives, continued for minutes.

earliest achievement in which he displayed that military genius which has placed him foremost in the annals of modern warfare, down to that last and surpass
ing combat which has made his name imperishable—
from Assaye to Waterloo—the Irish soldiers, with whom
your armies are filled, were the inseparable auxiliaries
to the glory with which his unparalleled successes have
been crowned. Whose were the arms that drove your
bayonets at Vimiera through the phalanxes that never
reeled in the shock of war before? What desperate
valor climbed the steeps and filled the moats at Badajos?
All his victories should have rushed and crowded back
upon his memory—Vimiera, Badajos, Salamanca, Al
buera, Toulouse, and, last of all, the greatest——.
Tell me, for you were there—I appeal to the gallant
soldier before me (Sir Henry Hardinge), from whose
opinions I differ, but who bears, I know, a generous
heart in an intrepid breast;—tell me, for you must
needs remember—on that day when the destinies of
mankind were trembling in the balance—while death
fell in showers— when the artillery of France was
levelled with a precision of the most deadly science—
when her legions, incited by the voice and inspired by
the example of their mighty leader, rushed again and
again to the onset—tell me if, for an instant, when, to
hesitate for an instant was to be lost, the "aliens"
blenched? And when at length the moment for the
last and decisive movement had arrived, and the valor
which had so long been wisely checked, was at last let
loose—when, with words familiar, but immortal, the
great captain commanded the great assault—tell me, if

Catholic Ireland, with less heroic valor than the natives
of this your own glorious country, precipitated herself
upon the foe? The blood of England, Scotland, and
of Ireland, flowed in the same stream, and drenched
the same field. When the chill morning dawned, their
dead lay cold and stark together;—in the same deep
pit their bodies were deposited—the green corn of
spring is now breaking from their commingled dust—
the dew falls from heaven upon their union in the
grave. Partakers in every peril—in the glory shall we
not be permitted to participate; and shall we be told,
as a requital, that we are estranged from the noble
country for whose salvation our life-blood was poured
out?

CORNELIA.—*Anonymous.*

Two Roman ladies sought the arbor's shade,
Where one her store of precious gems displayed.
The glittering bracelet from its case she brought,
Studded with sapphires, in fine gold inwrought.
From ivory casket, next the Carcanet
With emerald pale, and costly diamonds set.
On her white robe the ruby brooch was placed,
And amethysts and pearls her fingers graced
But her prized treasure was an opal stone
Which lay upon her brow as on a throne:
A regal gem, whose tremulous fire is bright
With rainbow hues that vary with the light;
And flashing tints, which soft each other chase,
Like joyous smiles upon a lovely face.
Then spake she to Cornelia, while her eye

Glanced on the treasure round, triumphantly,
"These are my jewels, brought from Eastern mine
And ocean caves ; fair lady, show me thine."—
Two little boys upon the floor the while
Sat by Cornelia ; with a quiet smile
She laid her hand upon each shining head,
Stroking their silky curls, and gently said,
"These are my jewels. Thine from sea and earth
Their being drew—mine are of heavenly birth."

PAUL BEFORE AGRIPPA.—*Anonymous.*

"And on the next day, when Agrippa and Bernice were come
with great pomp, and had entered into the hall of audience, with the
tribunes and principal men of the city, Festus commanding it, Paul
was brought forth."—ACTS xxv. 23. See also xxvi. 28, 29.

On gorgeous throne, in hall of state,
In regal "pomp" the monarch sate,
The rich folds of his purple vest
Girt with bright gems around his breast :
Attendant nobles throng the gate,
To learn his will, whose will is fate.
Happy in love—for tender pride
Still placed Bernice at his side ;
Happy in power, and wealth, and rank,
For proudest knees before him sank—
In all life's gifts supremely blest,
Was he of perfect peace possest ?
Before him stands a form erect,
Which even from him commands respect,

Though galling chains his limbs contro.,
The iron enters not his soul;
Captive, forsaken, doth he quail?
He has *one* friend, who cannot fail!
And is he come to swell the pride,
Glittering that sceptred form beside;
To wring the hands, and bend the knee,
And abject sue for liberty?
Which wouldst thou be—that captive lone,
Or he who fills that dazzling throne?

2.

Paul speaks—and on th' inspired tongue
That awed assemblage silent hung—
He shuns not boldly to reveal
The fire of his first sinful zeal;
Its quenching in that heavenly light
"More than the sun exceeding bright,"
Till in his breast that blessed ray
Shone onward to the perfect day.
What check'd the prisoner's purpose high?
'Twas King Agrippa's troubled sigh—
The blood forsakes his pallid cheek!
At length broke forth in accents weak,
Which well the soul's pent fear avow,
"Almost I would I were as thou!"

3.

Then loftier rose th' Apostle's head,
And firmer his elastic tread;
And his heart yearn'd o'er that crush'd thing—
So weak, so wretched, though a king;
Till, stretching forth the fetter'd hand,
As from the fire to pluck the brand!

"I would to God," he said, "that thou
And all within thy presence now,
Might both almost and wholly gain
To be as I—except this chain!"

4.

Christians—ere ye for wealth or state
On this world's power impatient wait,
Still to this scene let memory turn,
From Paul the hidden spring to learn
Whence flows the stream that ever lives,
The peace that this world never gives.

THE WIZARD.—*Miss Jewsbury.*

I.

He waved his hand !—dark Spirits knew
   That rod—yet none obeyed its call ;
And twice the mystic signs he drew,
   And twice beheld them bootless all :
Then knew the seer Jehovah's hand,
And crushed the scroll, and broke the wand

II.

"I feel him like a burning fire,—
   When I would curse, my lips are dumb ;
But from those lips, 'mid hate and ire,
   Unchecked the words of blessing come ;
They come—and on his people rest,
A people by the curser blest !

III.

" I see them from the mountain-top,—
   How fair their dwellings on the plain!
Like trees that crown the valley's slope,
   Like waves that glitter on the main!
Strong, strong the lion slumbering there—
Who first shall rouse him from his lair ?

IV.

" Crouch, Amalek—and thou, vain King!
   Crouch by thine altars—vainer still !
Hear ye the royal shouts that ring
   From Israel's camp beneath the hill ?
They have a God amidst their tents,—
Banner at once, and battlements !

V.

" A Star shall break through yonder skies,
   And beam on every nation's sight ;
From yonder ranks a Sceptre rise,
   And bow the nations to its might :
I see their glorious strength afar—
All hail, dread Sceptre ! hail, bright Star !

VI.

" And who am I, for whom is flung
   Aside the shrouding veil of Time ?
The Seer, whose rebel soul is wrung
   By wrath, and prophecy, and crime :
The future as the past I see,—
Woe, then, for Moab ! woe for me !"

VII.

On Peor's top the Wizard stood,
  Around him Moab's Princes bowed ;
He bade—and altars streamed with blood,
  And incense wrapped him like a shroud
But vain the rites of earth and hell—
He spake—a mastered Oracle !

PERPETUITY OF THE CHURCH.—*Archbishop Spalding.*

But think or say what you will of particular state-
ments * * *, quibble as you may about this or that
detail, there are two great, all-pervading FACTS of
Ecclesiastical History, which you will not—cannot
deny. No sophistry can weaken, no special pleading
can obscure, no scepticism can doubt them. We refer
to the Perpetuity of the Catholic Church, and the Immortality of the Papacy. These two facts, as indu-
bitable as they are significant, unfold the net results of
all Church History. They stand forth amidst the ruins
of the past, more solid and immovable than do the
pyramids from the sands of the desert. They are as
luminous as the sun, which, spite of darkness and
storms, still maintains his undeviating course. Your
prejudices and your passions can no more blot them
out from the record of the past, than can the mists and
the clouds blot out the sun from the heavens. There
they are firmly fixed in the firmament of history, and
you can neither deny them nor even ignore their existence. In spite of yourself, you cannot fail to be deeply

impressed with their significance in settling the prac tical and vital question: Which is the one true Church of Christ?

2. To unfold the logic of these two prominent facts, we will offer a few remarks on each of them in suc cession. They cover the whole ground of Church His tory, giving a coloring to all its parts, and knitting its facts together into one harmonious and solid whole.

3. Is the Catholic Church human, or is she divine? This is the important inquiry, the correct answer to which involves our happiness, both in this life and in eternity. If she be human, we would naturally expect to find in her history the evidences of change, decline, and dissolution, which we find in all merely human institutions. Like all these, she would have her begin- ning, her culminating point, her decline, and her fall. If she be divine, we would not be surprised to find her rudely buffeted indeed by the storms which threaten, and ultimately destroy all human institutions, but we would yet expect to see her come out of all these tem- pests, not only with the principle of life still strong in her, but even with reawakened energies and renewed vitality. The principle announced by the wise Gama- liel, when it was question in the Sanhedrim of crushing the Church in her very infancy, will be here appropriate:

4. "And now, therefore," said the sage, "I say to you, refrain from these men, and let them alone; for if this design or work be of men, it will fall to nothing; BUT IF IT BE OF GOD, YOU ARE NOT ABLE TO DESTROY IT LEST PERHAPS YOU BE FOUND TO OPPOSE GOD. (Acts v 38, 39.)

5. We are willing to rest the issue upon the application of this test, and we are, moreover, content that even the most bitter adversaries of the Church shall make the application. They dare not deny the great facts to which we shall refer, nor can they logically resist the force of their application to the matter in hand.

6. Considering the terrible struggles through which the Church has passed during her weary pilgrimage of eighteen hundred years on earth, her permanency, with her ever-increasing extension and vitality, is certainly the most remarkable fact in all history. Were she a merely human institution, according to all the lights of the past, this perpetuity would be utterly incredible —impossible. It would be a greater and more stupendous miracle even, than that of her continued preservation by special divine interposition, which we assert. In this latter hypothesis, the fact would be at least consistent and intelligible; in any other, it would be utterly incomprehensible, and would border on the impossible or absurd. Glance for a moment at the vicissitudes of the strongest human institutions which ' ɔ hand of man has ever founded. Take, for instance, the Roman Empire, whose framework was of iron, and which for centuries lorded it over the conquered nations of the earth. This huge colossus, bestriding the earth, was most strongly established upon its solid and world-wide base at the birth of Christianity. It had reached its culminating point of prosperity and power at the precise moment when the Founder of the Church was born in a stable in an obscure village of one of its

most remote conquered provinces. The golden age of Augustus had dawned upon the world, and the temple of Janus was closed in token of universal peace and prosperity. Here were then two claimants for universal empire: Augustus the Great, wielding the destinies of the most mighty empire which the world had ever seen; and JESUS OF NAZARETH, the Infant Founder of a new empire, an apparently helpless babe, born in poverty and covered with swaddling clothes, weeping in His manger, and having court paid to Him only by His poor but Immaculate Mother, His devoted foster-father, and a few peasant shepherds. Which of these two, according to all human calculation, was more likely to gain and retain the mastery of the world? Which has actually obtained the ascendency; which has survived, and which has ceased to exist?

Church History solves the problem. The issue was fairly made up between the two empires, and the Church founded by Christ gained the final victory over the splendid empire founded by Augustus. During two hundred and fifty years the contest fiercely raged, the Roman Empire, meanwhile, wielding all its immense and terrible power to crush the infant Church ere she could have time to gain a sure foothold on the earth. All the odds were clearly against her in the fearful and bloody struggle. Power, wealth, the passions, the sword, were all arrayed against her, while she could oppose to such fearful weapons nothing but poverty, weakness, and unalterable meekness and patience. The blood of her children flowed in torrents, while under her merciful guidance they repaid evil by good, and shed not a

drop of blood in return. Time and again she was
driven from the surface of the earth and the light of
day into dark caverns underground—into the now
hallowed Catacombs—where in darkness and sorrow
she offered up with trembling hands her pure prayers
and holy sacrifice. The Roman Empire, drunk with
the blood of the saints, toppled over and fell to
rise no more; while she calmly built up her temples
amidst its ruins, and erected the Rome of the Popes
from the *débris* of the Rome of the Cæsars. The
former became, in many respects, even more splendid;
it was certainly more permanent than the latter.
The Cross, which appeared surrounded with a halo
of light to the admiring eyes of Constantine, vanquished the Roman eagles which had been borne in
all-conquering triumph to the remotest corners of the
earth. Who will not say that the finger of God was
surely here?

THE SURRENDER OF CALAIS.—*Mrs. Embury.*

The king was in his tent,
    And his lofty heart beat high,
As he gazed on the city's battered walls
    With proud and flashing eye;
But darker grew his brow, and stern,
    As slowly onward came
The chiefs who long had dared to spurn
    The terror of his name.

2.

With calm and changeless cheek,
Before the king they stood,
For their native soil to offer up
The sacrifice of blood.
Like felons were they meanly clad,
But the lightning of their look,
The marble sternness of their brow,
Ev'n the monarch could not brook.

3.

With angry voice he cried,
"Haste! bear them off to death!
Let the trumpet's joyous shout be blent
With the traitor's parting breath!"
Then silently they turned away,
Nor word nor sound awoke,
Till, from the monarch's haughty train,
The voice of horror broke.

4.

And, hark! a step draws near—
Not like the heavy clang
Of the warrior's tread—and through the guards
A female figure sprang;
"A boon! a boon! my noble king!
If still thy heart can feel
The love Phillippa once could claim,
Look on me while I kneel.

5.

"'Tis for thyself I pray;
Let not the darkening cloud
Of base-born cruelty arise,
Thy glory to enshroud.

Nay, nay—I will not rise;
 For never more thy wife
Will hail thee victor, till thy soul
 Can conquer passion's strife.

6.

"Turn not away, my king!
 Look not in anger down!
I've lived so long upon thy smile,
 I cannot bear thy frown.
Oh! doom me not, dear lord, to feel
 The pang all pangs above,
To see the light I worship fade,
 And blush because I love.

7.

"Think how, for thee, I laid
 My woman's fears aside,
And dared, where charging squadrons met,
 With dauntless front to ride.
Think how, in all the matchless strength
 Of woman's love, I spread
Thy banners, till they proudly waved
 In victory o'er my head.

8.

"Thou saidst that I deserved
 To share thy glorious crown;
Oh! force me not to turn away
 In shame from thy renown.
My Edward! thou wert wont to bear
 A kind and gentle heart;
Then listen to Philippa's prayer,
 And let these men depart."

9.

Oh! what is all the pride
Of man's oft boasted power,
Compared with those sweet dreams that wake,
In love's triumphant hour!
Slowly the haughty king unbent
His stern and vengeful brow,
And the look he turned upon her face
Was full of fondness now.

10.

Ne'er yet was woman slow
To read in telltale eyes,
Such thoughts as these—a moment more
And on his breast she lies.
Then, while her slender form still clung
To his supporting arm,
He cried, "Sweet, be it as thou wilt;
They shall not meet with harm!"

11.

Then from the patriot band,
Arose one thrilling cry;
And tears rained down the iron cheek,
That turned unblenched to die.
"Now, we indeed are slaves," they cried;
"Now vain our warlike arts—
Edward has won our shattered walls,
Philippa wins our hearts."

JOSHUA COMMANDING THE SUN AND MOON TO STAND STILL.—*Van Schaick.*

The day rose clear on Gibeon.   Her high towers
Flashed the red sunbeams gloriously back,

And the wind-driven banners, and the steel
Of her ten thousand spears caught dazzlingly
The sun, and on the fortresses of rock
Played a soft glow, that as a mockery seemed
To the stern men who guarded by its light.
Beth-horon in the distance slept, and breath
Was pleasant in the vale of Ajalon,
Where armed heels trod carelessly the sweet
Wild spices, and the trees of gum were shook
By the rude armor on their branches hung.
Suddenly in the camp without the walls
Rose a deep murmur, and the men of war
Gathered around their kings, and "Joshua!
From Gilgal, Joshua!" was whispered low,
As with a secret fear, and then, at once,
With the abruptness of a dream, he stood
Upon the rock before them. Calmly then
Raised he his helm, and with his temples bare
And hands uplifted to the sky, he prayed;—
"God of this people, hear! and let the sun
Stand upon Gibeon, still; and let the moon
Rest in the vale of Ajalon!" He ceased—
And lo! the moon sits motionless, and earth
Stands on her axis indolent. The sun
Pours the unmoving column of his rays
In undiminished heat; the hours stand still;
The shade hath stopped upon the dial's face;
The clouds and vapors that at night are wont
To gather and enshroud the lower earth,
Are struggling with strange rays, breaking them up,
Scattering the misty phalanx like a wand,

Glancing o'er mountain tops, and shining down
In broken masses on the astonished plains.
The fevered cattle group in wondering herds;
The weary birds go to their leafy nests,
But find no darkness there, and wander forth
On feeble, fluttering wing, to find a rest;
The parched, baked earth, undamped by usual dews,
Has gaped and cracked, and heat, dry, mid-day heat,
Comes like a drunkard's breath upon the heart.

2.

On with thy armies, Joshua!   The Lord
God of Sabaoth is the avenger now!
His voice is in the thunder, and his wrath
Poureth the beams of the retarded sun,
With the keen strength of arrows, on their sight.
The unwearied sun rides in the zenith sky;
Nature, obedient to her Maker's voice,
Stops in full course all her mysterious wheels.
On! till avenging swords have drunk the blood
Of all Jehovah's enemies, and till
Thy banners in returning triumph wave;
Then yonder orb shall set mid golden clouds,
And, while a dewy rain falls soft on earth,
Show in the heavens the glorious bow of God,
Shining, the rainbow banner of the skies.

RESPECTABILITY.

"Pray, what do you mean by 'respectability?'
Is it wisdom, or worth, sir? or rank, or gentility

as it rough, sound sense? or a manner refined?
Is it kindness of heart? or expansion of mind?
Is it learning, or talent, or honor, or fame,
That you mean by that phrase (so expressive to name)?'
"No, no—these are not, sir, the things now in vogue;
A 'respectable man,' sir, may be a great rogue—
A respectable person may be a great fool—
Have lost even the little he picked up at school—
Be a glutton, adulterer, deep-drowned in debt—
May forfeit his honor, his best friend forget—
May be a base sycophant, tyrant, or knave—
But a livery servant, at least, he must have:
In vice he may vie with the vilest of sinners—
But he *must* keep a cook, and give capital dinners."

THE DESTROYING ANGEL.—*Miss Browne.*

"And it came to pass, at midnight the Lord slew every first-born in the land of Egypt, from the first-born of Pharao who sat on his throne unto the first-born of the captive woman that was in the prison; and all the first-born of cattle. And Pharao arose in the night, and all his servants, and all Egypt; and there arose a great cry in Egypt; for there was not a house wherein there lay not one 'dead."—EXODUS, chap. xii. verses 29, 30.

> Midnight, and the moon was high,
> Lighting Egypt's cloudless sky;
> Calmly fell her silvery smile
> On the broad and placid Nile,
> Calmly came its glory down,
> Bathing all the slumbering town;
> So the outward world might seem
> 'Neath the influence of a dream.

12

2.

Dreams as lovely, peace as deep,
Many a mother's pillow steep,—
Many a father's manly heart
In his infant's joy hath part,
As in visioned sport they rove,
By the waters—through the grove;
Now they love without love's cares;
What awakening shall be theirs!

3.

Lo! one dim and angry spot
That serenest Heaven doth blot,
Borne in solemn darkness near,
On the windless atmosphere,—
On it passes,—stately, slow,
Blighting somewhat still below,
Silent lightnings all unseen
Hide its dusky folds between.

4.

Hark! through every mother's dream
Comes an infant's stifled scream;
And the father starts to hear
Son or daughter wailing near;
And the captive hath arisen,
Startled in his gloomy prison,
By a sound that seems to come
Echoed from his lowly home.

5.

One fair mother is at rest,
With her infant at her breast,
Waking suddenly, her eye
Seeks its features eagerly;

By the dim and waning lamp,
See—its brow is white and damp,
One faint shiver—one short breath,
And it sleeps the sleep of death!

6.

Will the terror,—loud the cry
Ere the midnight hour went by,
For the king upon his throne
Waileth for his first-born son,
And the household of the slave
Hath a tenant for the grave,
Every where the woe hath sped—
Every house may mourn its dead!

7.

Even the cattle in the field
To the fatal influence yield;
There each mother stood aghast
As the deadly cloud went past,
Owning with instinctive fear
The Destroying Angel near,
As the youngling by her side,
Sudden moaned, and fell, and died.

8.

All may see that dusky cloud
Not the form its fleeces shroud;
He who bears that fearful blight,
Is an angel, proudly bright,
Nothing evil doth appear
On his forehead, broad and clear,—
He but bears that burning rod
As the messenger of God

9.

Awful is the earthquake's shock,
When the trembling mountains rock;
Dire the fear when mastering fire
Twines round kindling roof and spire;
Terrible the battle field
With the clash of sword and shield;
Wild the alarm, when o'er the land
Famine waves her blighting wand.

10.

But a terror deeper still
Now through Egypt's land may thrill;
Silent—sudden was the blow,
That hath laid these thousands low;—
Not a murmur in the air—
Peace and slumber every where;
One short hour hath done it all,—
Broken, too, a nation's thrall!

11.

Yes! though dread the judgment seem,
Touch with reverent thought the theme;
He, who rules in heaven and earth,
Thus hath brought his people forth,
Sent this lesson from His throne,
That He shieldeth still His own;
That His care is ever near
Those who serve in holy fear.

THE HEIGHT OF HONESTY.

Three friends once, in the course of conversation,
  Touched upon honesty; "no virtue better,"
Says Dick, quite lost in sweet self-admiration,
  "I'm sure I'm honest;—ay, beyond the letter;
You know the field I farm,—well, underground
  My plough stuck in the middle of a furrow,
And there a pot of silver coins I found;—
  My landlord has it, without fail, to-morrow."
So modestly his good intents he told:
  "But wait," says Bob, "we soon shall see who's best,
A stranger left with me uncounted gold;
  And I don't touch it: which is honestest?"
"Your deeds are pretty good," says Jack, "but I
  Have done much better (would that all folks learned it!)
Hear then the highest pitch of honesty,—
  I borrowed an umbrella—*and returned it ! !*"

THE DROUGHT.—*Montgomery.*

"And it shall come to pass in that day, I will hear, saith the Lord
I will hear the heavens, and they shall hear the earth, and the earth
shall hear the corn and the wine, and the oil, and these shall hear
Jezrahel."—OSEE ii. 21, 22.

What strange, what fearful thing hath come to pass?
The ground is iron, and the skies are brass:
Man, on the withering harvest, casts his eye,
"Give me your fruits in season, or I die;"
The timely fruits implore their parent—Earth,
"Where is thy strength to bring us forth to birth!"

The Earth, all prostrate, to the Clouds complains—
"Send to my heart your fertilizing rains;"
The Clouds invoke the Heavens—"Collect, dispense
Through us your healing, quickening influence;"
The Heavens to Him that rules them raise their moan—
"Command thy blessing, and it shall be done."
—The Lord is in his temple :—hushed and still,
The suppliant Universe awaits his will.

2.

He speaks ;—and to the clouds the heavens dispense
With lightning speed their genial influence :
The gathering, breaking clouds pour down the rains ,
Earth drinks the bliss thro' all her eager veins.
From teeming furrows start the fruits to birth,
And shake their riches on the lap of Earth :
Man sees the harvests grow beneath his eye,
Turns, and looks up with rapture to the sky ;
All that have breath and being then rejoice,
All Nature's voices blend in one great voice ;
"Glory to God, who thus Himself makes known !"
—When shall all tongues confess Him God alone ?
Lord, as the rain comes down from heaven—the rain
That waters Earth, and turns not thence again,
But makes the tree to bud, the corn to spring,
And feeds and gladdens every living thing ;
So come thy Gospel o'er a world destroyed,
In boundless blessings, and return not void :
So let it come, in universal showers,
To fill Earth's dreariest wilderness with flowers,
—With flowers of promise, fill the wild within
Men's heart, laid waste and desolate by sin :

Where thorns and thistles curse the infested ground,
Let the rich fruits of righteousness abound ;
And trees of life, forever fresh and green,
Flourish, where only trees of death have been ;
Let Truth look down from heaven, Hope soar above,
Justice and Mercy kiss, Faith work by Love ;
Heralds the year of jubilee proclaim ;
Bow every knee at the Redeemer's name ;
Nations new-born, their father's idols spurn :
The ransomed of the Lord with songs return ;
Through realms, with darkness, thraldom, guilt, o'er·
spread,
In light, joy, freedom, be the spirit shed.
Speak thou the word :—to Satan's power say, " Cease !"
But to a world of pardoned sinners—" Peace !"

3.
Thus, in thy grace, O God, Thyself make known,
Then shall all tongues confess Thee God alone !

THE RESTORATION OF ISRAEL.—*Croly.*

"And I heard a great voice from the throne, saying: Behold the tabernacle of God with men, and He will dwell with them. And they shall be His people; and God Himself with them shall be their God."—APOC. xxi. 3.

King of the dead ! how long shall sweep
Thy wrath ! how long thy outcasts weep !
Two thousand agonizing years
Has Israel steeped her bread in tears ;
The vial on her head been poured—
Flight, famine, shame, the scourge, the sword!

'Tis done !   Has breathed thy trumpet b.ast,
The Tribes at length have wept their last!
On rolls the host !   From land and wave
The earth sends up th' unransomed slave !
There rides no glittering chivalry,
No banner purples in the sky ;
The world within their hearts has died ;
Two thousand years have slain their pride !
The look of pale remorse.is there,
The lip, involuntary prayer ;
The form still marked with many a stain—
Brand of the soil, the scourge, the chain ;
The serf of Afric's fiery ground ;
The slave, by Indian suns embrowned ,
The weary drudges of the oar,
By the swart Arab's poisoned shore,
The gatherings of earth's wildest tract—
On bursts the living cataract !
What strength of man can check its speed ?
They come—the Nation of the Freed ;
Who leads their march ?   Beneath His wheel
Back rolls the sea, the mountains reel !
Before their tread His trump is blown,
Who speaks in thunder, and 'tis done !
King of the dead !   Oh, not in vain
Was Thy long pilgrimage of pain ;
Oh, not in vain arose Thy prayer,
When pressed the thorn Thy temples bare ;
Oh, not in vain the voice that cried,
Tc spare Thy maddened homicide

Even for this hour Thy heart's blood strᴇamed!
They come!—the Host of the Redeemed.

2.

What flames upon the distant sky?
'Tis not the comet's sanguine dye,
'Tis not the lightning's quivering spire,
'Tis not the sun's ascending fire.
And, now, as nearer speeds their march,
Expands the rainbow's mighty arch;
Though there has burst no thunder-cloud
No flash of death the soil has ploughed,
And still ascends before their gaze,
Arch upon arch, their lovely blaze;
Still, as the gorgeous clouds unfold,
Rise towers and domes, immortal mould.

3.

Scenes! that the patriarch's visioned eye
Beheld, and then rejoiced to die;—
That, like the altar's burning coal,
Touched the pale prophet's harp with soul,—
That the throned seraphs longed to see,
Now given. thou slave of slaves, to thee!
Whose city this? What potentate
Sits there the King of Time and Fate?
Whom glory covers like a robe,
Whose sceptre shakes the solid globe,
Whom shapes of fire and splendor guard?
There sits the Man, "whose face was marred,"
To whom archangels bow the knee—
The weeper in Gethsemane!

Down in the dust, aye, Israel, kneel;
For now thy withered heart can feel!
Aye, let thy wan cheek burn like flame,
There sits thy glory and thy shame!

THE CHURCH THE MISTRESS OF KNOWLEDGE.—*Lacordaire.*

We have already seen, gentlemen, or rather have faintly perceived, that the Church possesses the highest rational certainty, since she trusts for support to ideas, to history, to morals, and to society, to an extent unexercised by any other teaching body; and this assures to her here below, the empire of persuasion. It only remains, then, for us to treat of her moral certainty and infallibility.

2. The certainty or moral authority of a teaching body results from three conditions, which furnish for that body and for those whom it teaches the proof that it is in affinity with truth, and that it dispenses that truth with exactitude and reverence. These three con ditions are, knowledge, virtue, and number.

3. Knowledge is the first condition of certainty or moral authority; for how is it possible to be certain of that which we do not understand, and how can we understand that which we do not know? When men know, on the contrary, the more they know the more they possess for themselves and for others a guarantee from error. Knowledge is the eye which perceives, scrutinizes, compares, and reflects, which watches for and seizes the light, which adds to past ages the weight of new ones: it is the patient sentinel of time, and

draws one by one from the universe its eternal secrets.
If laborious and persevering knowledge merited no
credit, we should be obliged to despair of truth; and
never, gentlemen, in addressing you shall we regard
despair as a thing worthy of our attention. Knowledge
is incontestably a title, yet it is not of itself sufficient
to found the moral authority of a teaching. Now the
Church possesses knowledge, she was born in knowledge, she has saved knowledge, she has wrestled against
false knowledge, she is in every point of view a learned
body.

4. The Church understands what she teaches; she
does not act from blind faith, but from faith founded,
as we have seen in our second Conference, upon the
most elevated general ideas; upon historical records of
the highest antiquity and of the most certain authen-
ticity; upon the experience of the happy and civilizing
influence which she exercises in the world; and finally,
upon a tradition, and an accumulation of accomplished
facts of all kinds, which she unceasingly explores and
increases by her labors. If knowledge, application,
experience exists anywhere, it is assuredly in an association where the display of all the powers of the mind
play so conspicuous a part, and which has possessed,
from the commencement of time, and above all, since
Jesus Christ, an innumerable multitude of enlightened
men, who have filled the earth with their sayings and
their writings.

5. And how was it possible for the Church to be
other than learned? She was born in knowledge, in
one of the brightest epochs in history, in the Augustan

age, preceded by others which had brought literature, the arts, and philosophy even to perfection, that it might not be said that Christianity was engendered in darkness. Knowledge received us in the cradle, watched over us, studied us, contended with us, gave us defenders from amongst the philosophers whom we came to dethrone, very many of whom bore to the Crucified the triple testimony of their genius, their knowledge, and their errors.

6. Afterwards, when knowledge was in danger of being extinguished in Europe by the invasion of the barbarians, who saved it from shipwreck? Who prepared new nations, worthy of possessing truth? Was it your fathers? Ah! your fathers!—they drew the sword, the sword yesterday, the sword to-morrow, the sword continually! See what was your share in them, men now so proud of your knowledge, and we do not blame you for it. You were there, in the persons of your ancestors, forming an armed barrier against which new invasions came to their destruction—an immense European square to protect from without that which developed itself within; whilst we, peaceful and laborious, in the persons also of our ancestors—we reconstructed knowledge from its own ruins, in order that you might one day receive that heritage from us, and that truth, finding again an age worthy of it, might not command slaves, but might shine in an empire founded upon the legitimate convictions of intelligent minds. It came—that age which we prepared—it came, and Knowledge, like an ungrateful and unnatural daughter, scarcely fallen from our hands into yours, raised herself

ap against us and denounced us, who had labored fif
teen centuries for her, who received her again when
saving herself, bloody from the sword of Mahomet II.,
she threw herself all dismayed into the robes of our
popes! What did we then? Did we betray knowledge,
or did we submit to bear its yoke? Neither the one
nor the other: we resisted, we opposed ourselves like a
wall of brass, not to knowledge, but to its errors; and
now, children of knowledge, saviors of knowledge, protectors of knowledge, we arrive at an epoch not less
glorious for the Church, that in which knowledge,
recognizing the vanity of its efforts against us, will
come into our temples to seek us, and to offer to us the
kiss of reconciliation and of justice, which she owes to
us, and which she will give us.

THE NUN OF NIDAROS.—*Longfellow.*

In the convent of Drontheim,
Alone in her chamber
Knelt Astrid the Abbess,
At midnight, adoring,
Beseeching, entreating
The Virgin and Mother.

She heard in the silence
The voice of one speaking,
Without in the darkness,
In gusts of the night-wind
Now louder, now nearer,
Now lost in the distance.

The voice of a stranger
It seemed as she listened,
Of some one who answered
Beseeching, imploring,
A cry from afar off
She could not distinguish.

The voice of Saint John,
The beloved disciple
Who wandered and waited
The Master's appearance,
Alone in the darkness,
Unsheltered and friendless.

" It is accepted
The angry defiance,
The challenge of battle !
It is accepted,
But not with the weapons
Of war that thou wieldest !

" Cross against corslet,
Love against hatred,
Peace-cry for war-cry !
Patience is powerful ;
He that o'ercometh
Hath power o'er the nations !

" As torrents in summer,
Half dried in their channels,
Suddenly rise, though the
Sky is still cloudless,
For rain has been falling
Far off at their fountains ;

" So hearts that are fainting
Grow full to o'erflowing,
And they that behold it
Marvel, and know not
That God at their fountain
Far off has been raining!

" Stronger than steel
Is the sword of the Spirit;
Swifter than arrows
The light of the truth is,
Greater than anger
Is love, and subdueth!

" Thou art a phantom,
A shape of the sea-mist,
A shape of the brumal
Rain, and the darkness
Fearful and formless;
Day dawns and thou art not!

" The dawn is not distant,
Nor is the night starless;
Love is eternal!
God is still God, and
His faith shall not fail us;
Christ is eternal!"

UNION LINKED WITH LIBERTY, 1833.—*Andrew Jackson.*

Without Union, our independence and liberty would
never have been achieved; without Union, they can
never be maintained. Divided into twenty-four, or even
a smaller number of separate communities we shall see

our internal trade burdened with numberless restraints
and exactions; communication between distant points
and sections obstructed, or cut off; our sons made soldiers, to deluge with blood the fields they now till in
peace; the mass of our people borne down and impoverished by taxes to support armies and navies; and
military leaders, at the head of their victorious legions,
becoming our lawgivers and judges. The loss of liberty,
of all good government, of peace, plenty, and happiness,
must inevitably follow a dissolution of the Union. In
supporting it, therefore, we support all that is dear to
the freeman and the philanthropist.

2. The time at which I stand before you is full of interest. The eyes of all nations are fixed on our republic.
The event of the existing crisis will be decisive, in the
opinion of mankind, of the practicability of our federal
system of government. Great is the stake placed in
our hands; great is the responsibility which must rest
upon the people of the United States. Let us realize
the importance of the attitude in which we stand before
the world. Let us exercise forbearance and firmness.
Let us extricate our country from the dangers which
surround it, and learn wisdom from the lessons they
inculcate. Deeply impressed with the truth of these
observations, and under the obligation of that solemn
oath which I am about to take, I shall continue to exert
all my faculties to maintain the just powers of the constitution, and to transmit unimpaired to posterity the
blessings of our Federal Union.

3. At the same time, it will be my aim to inculcate,
by my official acts, the necessity of exercising, by the

general government, those powers only that are clearly
delegated; to encourage simplicity and economy in the
expenditures of the government; to raise no more
money from the people than may be requisite for these
objects, and in a manner that will best promote the
interests of all classes of the community, and of all por-
tions of the Union. Constantly bearing in mind that,
in entering into society, "individuals must give up a
share of liberty to preserve the rest," it will be my desire so to discharge my duties as to foster with our
brethren, in all parts of the country, a spirit of liberal
concession and compromise; and, by reconciling our
fellow-citizens to those partial sacrifices which they
must unavoidably make, for the preservation of a greater
good, to recommend our invaluable Government and
Union to the confidence and affections of the American
people. Finally, it is my most fervent prayer to that
Almighty Being before whom I now stand, and who has
kept us in his hands from the infancy of our republic to
the present day, that he will so overrule all my inten-
tions and actions, and inspire the hearts of my fellow-
citizens, that we may be preserved from dangers of all
kinds, and continue for ever a UNITED AND HAPPY
PEOPLE.

THE TORCH OF LIBERTY.—*Thomas Moore.*

I saw it all in Fancy's glass—
    Herself the fair, the wild magician,
Who bade this splendid day-dream pass,
    And named each gliding apparition.

A3

'Twas like a torch-race—such as they
  Of Greece performed, in ages gone,
When the fleet youths, in long array,
  Passed the bright torch triumphant on.

2.

I saw the expectant Nations stand,
  To catch the coming flame in turn;—
I saw, from ready hand to hand,
  The clear, though struggling, glory burn
And, Oh! their joy, as it came near,
  'Twas, in itself, a joy to see;—
While Fancy whispered in my ear,
  "That torch they pass is Liberty!"

3.

And each, as she received the flame,
  Lighted her altar with its ray;
Then, smiling, to the next who came,
  Speeded it on its sparkling way.
From Albion first, whose ancient shrine
  Was furnished with the fire already,
Columbia caught the boon divine,
  And lit a flame, like Albion's, steady.

4.

The splendid gift then Gallia took,
  And, like a wild Bacchanté, raising
The brand aloft, its sparkles shook,
  As she would set the world a-blazing!
Thus, kindling wild, so fierce and high
  Her altar blazed into the air,
That Albion, to that fire too nigh,
  Shrank back, and shuddered at its glare!

5.

Next, Spain,—so new was light to her,
  Leaped at the torch; but, ere the spark
That fell upon her shrine could stir,
  'Twas quenched, and all again was dark!
Yet, no—*not* quenched,—a treasure, worth
  So much to mortals, rarely dies:
Again her living light looked forth,
  And shone, a beacon, in all eyes!

6.

Who next received the flame? Alas!
  Unworthy Naples. Shame of shames,
That ever through such hands should pass
  That brightest of all earthly flames!
Scarce had her fingers touched the torch,
  When, frighted by the sparks it shed,
Nor waiting even to feel the scorch,
  She dropped it to the earth—and fled!

7.

And fallen it might have long remained;
  But Greece, who saw her moment now,
Caught up the prize, though prostrate, stained,
  And waved it round her beauteous brow.
And Fancy bade me mark where, o'er
  Her altar, as its flame ascended,
Fair laureled spirits seemed to soar,
  Who thus in song their voices blended:

8.

" Shine, shine forever, glorious Flame,
  Divinest gift of gods to men!
From Greece thy earliest splendor came,
  To Greece thy ray returns again.

Take, Freedom, take thy radiant round;
  When dimmed, revive,—when lost, return,
Till not a shrine through earth be found,
  On which thy glories shall not burn!"

A COLLOQUY WITH MYSELF.—*Barton.*

As I walked by myself, I talked to myself,
  And myself replied to me;
And the questions myself then put to myself,
  With their answers, I give to thee.
Put them home to thyself, and if unto thyself
  Their responses the same should be,
Oh look well to thyself, and beware of thyself,
  Or so much the worse for thee.

2.

What are Riches?   Hoarded treasures
  May, indeed, thy coffers fill;
Yet, like earth's most fleeting pleasures,
  Leave thee poor and heartless still.

3.

What are Pleasures?   When afforded,
  But by gauds which pass away,
Read their fate in lines recorded
  On the sea-sands yesterday.

4.

What is Fashion?   Ask of Folly,
  She her worth can best express.
What is moping Melancholy?
  Go and learn of idleness.

5.

What is Truth ?   Too stern a preacher
  For the prosperous and the gay ;
But a safe and wholesome teacher
  In adversity's dark day.

6.

What is Friendship ?   If well founded,
  Like some beacon's heavenward glow ;
If on false pretensions grounded,
  Like the treach'rous sands below.

7.

What is Love ?   If earthly only,
  Like a meteor of the night;
Shining, but to leave more lonely
  Hearts that hailed its transient light;

8.

But, when calm, refined, and tender,
  Purified from passion's stain,
Like the moon, in gentle splendor,
  Ruling o'er the peaceful main.

9.

What are Hopes, but gleams of brightness,
  Glancing darkest clouds between ?
Or foam-crested waves, whose whiteness
  Gladdens ocean's darksome green.

10.

What are Fears ?   Grim phantoms, throwing
  Shadows o'er the pilgrim's way,
Every moment darker growing,
  If we yield unto their sway. ·

11.

What is Mirth ?   A flush of lightning,
  Followed but by deeper gloom.—

Patience ?   More than sunshine bright'ning
  Sorrow's path, and labor's doom.

12.

What is Time ?   A river flowing
  To Eternity's vast sea,
Forward, whither all are going,
  On its bosom bearing thee.

13.

What is Life ?   A bubble floating
  On that silent, rapid stream ;
Few, too few its progress noting,
  Till it bursts, and ends the dream.

14.

What is Death, asunder rending
  Every tie we love so well ?
But the gate to life unending,
  Joy in heaven ! or woe in hell !

15.

Can these truths, by repetition,
  Lose their magnitude or weight ?
Estimate thy own condition,
  Ere thou pass that fearful gate.

16.

Hast thou heard them oft repeated ?
  Much may still be left to do :
Be not by profession cheated ;
  Live—as if thou knews't them true !

17.

As I walked by myself, I talked to myself,
  And myself replied to me ;
And the questions myself then put to myself,
  With their answers I've given to thee.

18.

Put them home to thyself, and if unto thyself
  Their responses the same should be,
Oh look well to thyself, and beware of thyself
  Or so much the worse for thee.

THE SHIPWRECKED.—*Anonymous.*

They rolled above me, the wild waves—
  The broken mast I grappled yet;
My fellow-men had found their graves,
  On me another sun had set.
But, merciless, the ocean still
  Dash'd me, then calmly round me lay,
To wake another human thrill,
  As tyrants torture ere they slay.
But when the foaming breakers rush'd,
  And passed o'er me, or bore me high,
Then into circling eddies gush'd,
  I struggled—yet I knew not why;
It was not hope that bade me cling
Still to that only earthly thing,
I knew not then His mercy gave
To keep me level with the wave.
The tempest, when the day was gone,
More fiercely with the night came on;
But, howling o'er the trackless sea,
Gave neither hope nor fear to me;
Despair had made me brave my fate,—
To die—thus lone and desolate.
I saw another morning sun,
But yet my struggles were not done:—

A passing billow wafted then
  A comrade's body to my side,
Who lately with his fellow-men,
  Had bravely stemmed the dashing **tide**
His calm cheek and half open eye
Betokened that in agony
His spirit had not left him,—he
Seemed as if slumbering on the sea.
I calmly gazed, and without dread,
Upon the dull eye of the dead;
But when his cold hand touched my **cheek,**
My voice came from me in a shriek;
At mine own voice I gazed around,
'Twas so unlike a human sound;
But on the waters none were near,
Save the corpse upon its watery bier,
And hungry birds that hovered nigh,
Screaming his sole funereal cry.

2.

My sum of human pangs to fill,
There came a calm—more deathly **still,**
Because its sullen silence brought,
A dull repose that wakened thought.
How my limbs quivered, as the sea
  By some less gentle breeze was **stirred,**
  As if I every moment heard
The ocean monsters follow me!
Then came the sun in all his might,
To mock me with his noon-day height:
When the waves lay beneath me long,
I felt his power grow fiercely strong

3.

Above me, and would often dip
My burning brow and parched lip,
To cool them in the fresh'ning wave,
Wishing the waters were my grave.
But oft the sea-bird o'er me flew,
   And once it flapped me with its wing:
That I must be its prey I knew,
   And smiled at my heart's shivering!
But yet I could not bear to see
   Its yellow beak, or hear its cry,
Telling me what I soon must be ;—
   I moaned, I wept, I feared to die.

4.

And as the chill wave grew more chill,
The evening breeze became more still,
And, breathing o'er the awful deep,
Had lulled me, and I longed to sleep :
My senses slept, my head bowed low,
   The waters splashed beneath, then broke
Suddenly o'er my aching brow,
   With a convulsive start I woke,
And, waking, felt them o'er me float,
While gurgling in my parched throat.

5.

Where'er I drifted with the tide,
My comrade's corpse was by my side.
Still to the broken mast I clung,
At times aside the waves I flung,
All day I struggled hard ; but when
Another and another came,
Weaker and weaker grew my frame,—

I deemed that I was dying then.
My head fell on the wave once more,
And reason left me,—all seemed o'er,
Yet something I remember now,—
   I knew I gazed upon the sky,
And felt the breeze pass o'er my brow,
   Along the unbroken sea to die;
And, half with faintness, half with dread,
The spirit that sustained me fled.

6.

There was an eye that watch'd me then,—
   An ear that heard my frequent prayer;
And God, who trod the unyielding wave,
   When human efforts all were vain,
Ere the death-struggle, came to save,
   And called me back to life again.

* * * * * * * * * * * * *

7.

I thought that I was yielding life,
To perish in that mortal strife,
And calmly lay along the sea,
That soon would calmly pass o'er me;
But my clenched teeth together met,
As if with death I struggled yet—
Then I was stemming it once more;
   And then again the sea-bird's cry
Was mingling with the billows' roar,
   As I laid down my head to die.

8.

Returning reason came at last,
   And bade returning hope appear:

That remnant of the broken mast,
   And my dead comrade both were near;
Not floating o'er the billows now,
   For they had drifted us to land—
And I was saved—I knew not how—
   But felt that an Almighty hand
Had chased the waters from the strand.

9.

Beside the corpse, and by the wave,
   I knelt, and murmured praise to Him,
Who, in the fearful trial, gave
   Strength to the spirit and the limb!

THE SCHOOLBOY.—*Anonymous.*

The School-boy had been rambling all the day,
A careless, thoughtless idler, till the night
Came on, and warned him homeward; then he left
The meadows where the morning had been passed,
Chasing the butterfly, and took the road
Toward the cottage where his mother dwelt:
He had her parting blessing, and she watched
Once more to breathe the welcome to her child,
Who sauntered lazily—ungrateful boy!
Till deeper darkness came o'er sky and earth,
And then he ran, till almost breathless grown,
He passed within the wicket gate which led
Into the village church-yard—then he paused,
And earnestly looked round; for o'er his head
The gloomy cypress waved, and at his feet
Lay the last bed of many a villager.

But on again he pressed with quickened step,
"Whistling aloud to keep his courage up."
The bat came flapping by, the ancient church
Threw its deep shadows o'er the path he trod,
And the boy trembled like the aspen leaf;
For now he fancied that all shapeless forms
Came flitting by him, each with bony hand,
And motion as if threatening; while a weight
Unearthly pressed the satchel and the slate
He strove to keep within his grasp. The wind
Played with the feather that adorned his cap,
And seemed to whisper something horrible.
The clouds had gathered thickly round the moon,
But now and then her light shone gloriously
Upon the sculptured tombs and humble graves,
And in a moment all was dark again.
  O'ercome with terror, the pale boy sank down,
And wildly gazed around him, till his eye
Fell on a stone, on which these warning words
Were carved:—

    "Time! thou art flying rapidly—
      But whither art thou flying?"
    "To the grave—which yours will be—
      I wait not for the dying.
    In early youth you laughed at me,
      And, laughing, passed life's morning,
    But in thy age I laugh at thee—
      Too late to give thee warning"

"Death ! thy shadowy form I see,
The steps of Time pursuing ;
Like him, thou comest rapidly—
What deed must thou be doing ?"
" Mortal, my message is for thee—
Thy chain to earth is rended ;
I bear thee to eternity—
Prepare—thy course is ended !"

Attentively the fainting boy perused
The warning lines—then grew more terrified ;
For, from the grave there seemed to rise a voice
Repeating them, and telling him of time
Misspent, of death approaching rapidly,
And of the dark eternity that followed.
His fears increased, till on the ground he lay
Almost bereft of feeling and of sense—
And there his mother found him ;
From the damp church-yard sod she bore her child,
Frightened to feel his clammy hands, and hear
The sighs and sobs that from his bosom came !

'Twas strange the influence which that fearful hour
Had o'er his future life ; for from that night
He was a thoughtful and industrious boy !
And still the memory of those warning words
Bids him reflect—now that he is a man,
And writes those feeble lines that others may.

CHRIST STILLING THE TEMPEST.—*Hemans.*

"But the boat in the midst of the sea was tossed with the waves, for the wind was contrary."—St. Matthew, chap. xiv., ver. 24.

Fear was within the tossing bark,
   When stormy winds grew loud,
And waves came rolling high and dark,
   And the tall mast was bowed.
2.
And men stood breathless in their dread,
   And baffled in their skill—
But One was there, who rose and said
   To the wild sea, Be still!
3.
And the wind ceased—it ceased—that word
   Passed through the gloomy sky;
The troubled billows knew their Lord,
   And sank beneath his eye.
4.
And slumber settled on the deep,
   And silence on the blast,
As when the righteous falls asleep,
   When death's fierce throes are past
5.
Thou that didst rule the angry hour,
   And tame the tempest's mood,—
Oh! send thy Spirit forth in power,
   O'er our dark souls to brood!
6.
Thou that didst bow the billow's pride,
   Thy mandates to fulfil,—
So speak to passion's raging tide,
   Speak, and say,—Peace, be still!

KING HENRY V. AND THE HERMIT OF DREUX.—*Southey.*

While Henry V. lay at the siege of Dreux, an honest Hermit, un-known to him, came and told him the great evils he brought on Christendom by his unjust ambition, who usurped the kingdom of France, against all manner of right, and contrary to the will of God; wherefore, in his holy name, he threatened him with a severe and sudden punishment if he desisted not from his enterprise. Henry took this exhortation either as an idle whimsy, or a suggestion of the dauphin's, and was but the more confirmed in his design. But the blow soon followed the threatening; for, within some few months after, he was smitten with a strange and incurable disease.—*Mezeray.*

He pass'd unquestion'd through the camp,
  Their heads the soldiers bent
In silent reverence, or begg'd
  A blessing as he went;
And so the Hermit pass'd along,
  And reached the royal tent.

2.

King Henry sat in his tent alone;
  The map before him lay;
Fresh conquests he was planning there
  To grace the future day.

3.

King Henry lifted up his eyes
  The intruder to behold;
With reverence he the hermit saw;
  For the holy man was old;
His look was gentle as a Saint's,
  And yet his eye was bold.

4.

" Repent thee, Henry, of the wrongs
    Which thou hast done this land !
O King, repent in time, for know
    The judgment is at hand.

5.

" I have pass'd forty years of peace
    Beside the river Blaise;
But what a weight of woe hast thou
    Laid on my latter days !

6.

" I used to see along the stream
    The white sail gliding down,
That wafted food, in better times,
    To yonder peaceful town.

7.

" Henry ! I never now behold
    The white sail gliding down ;
Famine, Disease, and Death, and Thou,
    Destroy that wretched town.

8.

" I used to hear the traveler's voice
    As here he pass'd along,
Or maiden, as she loiter'd home
    Singing her even-song.

9.

" No traveler's voice may now be heard ;
    In fear he hastens by ;
But I have heard the village maid
    In vain for succor cry.

10.

" I used to see the youths row down
    And watch the dripping oar,

As pleasantly their viol's tones
Came soften'd to the shore.

11.

"King Henry, many a blacken'd corpse
I now see floating down!
Thou man of blood! repent in time,
And leave this leaguer'd town."

12.

"I shall go on," King Henry cried,
"And conquer this good land;
Seest thou not, Hermit, that the Lord
Hath given it to my hand?"

13.

The Hermit heard King Henry speak,
And angrily look'd down;—
His face was gentle, and for that
More solemn was his frown.

14.

"What if no miracle from Heaven
The murderer's arm control;
Think you for that the weight of blood
Lies lighter on his soul?

15.

"Thou conqueror King, repent in time,
Or dread the coming woe!
For, Henry, thou hast heard the threat,
And soon shalt feel the blow!"

16.

King Henry forced a careless smile,
As the hermit went his way;
But Henry soon remember'd him
Upon his dying day

HUMOROUS DESCRIPTION OF THE VOYAGE OF THE MAYFLOWER.

[FROM I. H.'S "TRUE HISTORY OF THE COLONY OF NEW PLYMOUTH.']

[This may be divided into parts for the purpose of declamation; and some slight changes made in the phraseology, to adapt it to that purpose.]

It fell out, that when the Mayflower was ready to sail, there were but one hundred souls willing to make a third trial in her upon the waters,—these being the cullings of the rest, just as larger coals remain in the rake, while the smaller slip through the teeth of the same.

2. All things being thus ordered, and the new arrangements finished, there were sad leave-takings again, when the vessel hove anchor. But first they transferred the New England's symbol to her deck, with great pomp and circumstance, then bracing her yards, the Mayflower shook out her canvas for a sail upon the dangerous waters of eternal renown. This was in the early part of the month of September.

3. Although at a season of the year when the Atlantic is usually quiet, the Mayflower, all things being considered, made a good average passage of it, say, from ninety to one hundred days, which even now is sometimes imitated by many of our slow sailing merchant-men; although the pilgrim fathers were neither caught between icebergs, nor stranded upon Sable Island, yet this expedition was one of unusual hardship. At least we ought to believe so, and I consider it my duty to give it an extraordinary character if possible. And as conjecture

to the historian is what imagination is to the poet, I
must avail myself of the only plausible incident which
could add grandeur and solemnity to the voyage, and
enhance the perils of this narrative by attempting to
describe a storm at sea.

4. Oh, my reader! I know but little of navigation, never
having been upon the briny deep, except to play props
and catch haddock off Nahant; still less do I understand the vocabulary of nautical men. So I venture
upon this part of my true history with unusual diffi-
dence. If I do not use the proper phrases, my critics
will discover my mistakes; it will all be the same a
hundred years hence. Who cares? Here goes!

THE STORM.

5. The Mayflower had not been out of sight of land for
many weeks, before the wind, which had hitherto been
upon the leeward quarter, suddenly shifted around and
began to blow a-port. Captain Jones immediately or
dered all hands abaft, and shook a reef out of the stud-
din' sails, at the same time ordering a hauser to be rove
through the main truck, and a couple of kedges made
fast to the davits. These precautions, however, were
in vain; the wind increased in violence, a long, low
range of stratified clouds hung gloomily upon the skirts
of the horizon, and the waves rolled their shaggy tops
almost as high as the weather-cock on the mast-head.
To add to the horror of the scene, the bilge-water began
to rise in the hold, and upon taking an observation they
found they had two feet in each pump. By this time
many of the passengers had gone below to pack up, and
the jolly boat was caulked and painted, to prepare for

the worst.   But the gale, instead of subsiding, increased
in violence, the dead-heads were blown to ribbons, and
they were obliged to let go the anchor.

6. The sky had now grown fearfully dark; the ship's
lanterns were all trimmed and lighted, and a signal of
distress hoisted upon the poop.   All of a sudden, a large
wave rolled over the bows, which obliged them to open
the scuppers.   This made them lose their reckoning, and
upon heaving the log they found themselves in about
three fathoms, with shells and fine sand; whereupon the
helm was put a-beam, and an attempt made to jibe her,
but in vain.   The moon now broke through the clouds,
and showed them the helplessness of their position.
They were riding at anchor, in the midst of the ocean;
not a sail in sight; the mizen mast upon its beam ends,
and the forecastle jammed in the fetlocks.   But if this
were the state of affairs on deck, what were the condition of those below?   A chaos of misery and despair
Ham sandwiches—anchovy toast—sword and feather—
Captain Standish—basswood fiddles—Elder Brewster—
broken crockery—helpless women—tin basins—pump-
kin pies—tobacco pipes and schnapps—W. Bradford—
hard bread—E. Winslow—opera glasses—elbow chairs—
tin candlesticks—steeple-top hats—mess beef—and a
thousand articles, scattered in wild profusion, which
would have made the Historian of the United States
melt into tears, or set the late President of the Massa
chusetts Historical Society crazy with delight.

7. My reader, I do not wish to dwell upon this picture!
If I am an artist, as I trust I am a scholar and a gentleman, the likeness will be faithful to the original.   If

not, your imagination must supply my deficiency, and paint upon the retina of your fancy the miseries of a storm at sea in the year 1620.

END OF THE STORM.

8. The lowering clouds which for many days hung their ragged fringes around the Atlantic horizon, at last uplifted themselves, and were exhaled like transient sorrows to the sky   Now then came everybody upon deck, while peacefully and sweetly the Mayflower rippled upon her course, counting her progress by the number of ocean sunsets, and the stars of Pisces and of Aries, that every night sank earlier in the west.   Now did they softly sing and tune the dulcet violin to aid their voices, and so with little danger and less distress they passed over the waste of waters until they saw a low range of sand hills looming up in the distance, and after tempting perilous shoals and breakers, Pollock's Rip, Bass Rip, and Great Rip, they finally cast anchor in the harbor of Provincetown, Cape Cod.

9. Oh, my reader, what a gift is eloquence! Had I the power of a great American orator, whose communications to this truly national paper are the envy of the twopenny critics of feeble magazines, the small fry editors who earn a wretched subsistence by dogging at the heels of the public for weekly advertisements, the supernumerary corps of literateurs, whose names never appear in big letters on any bills but their own; had I that power of eloquence which he has made so envied and so eminent, then I might portray this stupendous event in language that would make the hair of New England stand on end from Eastport to New Haven!

10. Then would the very ocean become luminous under the electric flashes of my pen! Then would the storm be heard, "moaning through the tattered canvas of the Mayflower," as she creeps, almost sinking, past the rip-raps of Tucker's Terror, into the harbor of Province-town! Then would the terrible front of this dangerous coast be made ten times more frightful by the art of rhetoric! Then might you see "*the mountains of New England rising from their rocky thrones—rushing forward, and settling down as they advance, to form a bulwark,*" or breakwater, around this exceedingly popular vessel! Nay, not only this, but the Cape itself, in spite of whole regiments of Agassiz's turtles, and the geological volumes of Sir Charles Lyell, would "run out to sea, a hundred miles, on purpose to receive and encircle the precious ship"—the Pantheon of the ever-worshiped deities of New England—the Junos, Venuses, Jupiters, and Jug-gernauts, of our national mythology!

11. But this is not for me to do, I am but a plain histo-rian—the page and valet only of heroic men. To them I shall confine myself in future, not departing from the modesty of my position, trimming my habit to the sober fashion of my station, and flying my kite no higher than the limits of its string.

THE BALL AT BRUSSELS, THE NIGHT BEFORE THE BATTLE OF WATERLOO, JUNE 17, 1815.—*Lord Byron.*

There was a sound of revelry by night,
And Belgium's capital had gathered then
Her Beauty and her Chivalry, and bright
The lamps shone o'er fair women and brave men:

A thousand hearts beat happily; and when
Music arose, with its voluptuous swell,
Soft eyes looked love to eyes which spake again,
And all went merry as a marriage-bell.
But hush! hark! a deep sound strikes like a rising knell.

2.

Did ye not hear it?—No; 'twas but the wind,
Or the car rattling o'er the stony street;
On with the dance! let joy be unconfined;
No sleep till morn, when Youth and Pleasure meet
To chase the glowing Hours with flying feet!
But hark! that heavy sound breaks in once more,
As if the clouds its echo would repeat;
And nearer, clearer, deadlier, than before!
Arm! arm! it is—it is—the cannon's opening roar!

3.

Within a windowed niche of that high hall
Sat Brunswick's fated chieftain. He did hear
That sound the first amidst the festival,
And caught its tone with Death's prophetic ear;
And when they smiled because he deemed it near,
His heart more truly knew that peal too well,
Which stretched his father on a bloody bier,
And roused the vengeance blood alone could quell;
He rushed into the field, and, foremost fighting, fell.

4.

Ah! then and there was hurrying to and fro,
And gathering tears, and tremblings of distress,
And cheeks all pale, which but an hour ago
Blushed at the praise of their own loveliness;

And there were sudden partings, such as press
The life from out young hearts, and choking sighs
Which ne'er might be repeated. Who could guess
If ever more should meet those mutual eyes,
Since upon night so sweet such awful morn could rise !

5.

And there was mounting in hot haste: the steed,
The mustering squadron, and the clattering car,
Went pouring forward with impetuous speed,
And swiftly forming in the ranks of war;
And the deep thunder, peal on peal, afar;
And near, the beat of the alarming drum
Roused up the soldier ere the morning star;
While thronged the citizens, with terror dumb,
Or whispering, with white lips—"The foe! they come
        they come!"

6.

Last noon beheld them full of lusty life;
Last eve, in Beauty's circle, proudly gay;
The midnight brought the signal-sound of strife
The morn, the marshalling in arms; the day,
Battle's magnificently stern array!
The thunder-clouds close o'er it, which when rent
The earth is covered thick with other clay,
Which her own clay shall cover—heaped and pent,
Rider and horse,—friend,—foe,—in one red burial
        blent!

THE DYING GLADIATOR.--*Lord Byron.*

1 see before me the Gladiator lie:
He leans upon his hand,—his manly brow
Consents to death, but conquers agony,
And his drooped head sinks gradually low,—
And through his side the last drops, ebbing slow
From the red gash, fall heavy, one by one,
Like the first of a thunder-shower; and now
The arena swims around him—he is gone,
Ere ceased the inhuman shout which hailed the wretch
    who won.

2.

He heard it, but he heeded not: his eyes
Were with his heart, and that was far away;
He recked not of the life he lost nor prize,
But where his rude hut by the Danube lay,
There were his young barbarians all at play,
There was their Dacian mother,—he, their sire,
Butchered to make a Roman holiday,—
All this rushed with his blood.—Shall he expire,
And unavenged?—Arise, ye Goths, and glut your ire.

WILLIAM TELL ON SWITZERLAND.—*J. S. Knowles*

Once Switzerland was free! With what a pride
I used to walk these hills,—look up to Heaven,
And bless God that it was so! It was free
From end to end, from cliff to lake 't was free!
Free as our torrents are, that leap our rocks,

And plough our valleys, without asking leave,
Or as our peaks, that wear their caps of snow
In very presence of the regal sun!
How happy was I in it, then! I loved
Its very storms. Ay, often have I sat
In my boat at night, when midway o'er the lake,
The stars went out, and down the mountain gorge
The wind came roaring,—I have sat and eyed
The thunder breaking from his cloud, and smiled
To see him shake his lightnings o'er my head,
And think I had no master save his own.

   You know the jutting cliff, round which a track
Up hither winds, whose base is but the brow
To such another one, with scanty room
For two abreast to pass? O'ertaken there
By the mountain blast, I've laid me flat along,
And while gust followed gust more furiously,
As if to sweep me o'er the horrid brink,
And I have thought of other lands, whose storms
Are summer flaws to those of mine, and just
Have wished me there;—the thought that mine was free
Has checked that wish, and I have raised my head,
And cried in thraldom to that furious wind,
Blow on! This is the land of liberty!

WILLIAM TELL AMONG THE MOUNTAINS.—*J. S. Knowles.*

   Ye crags and peaks, I'm with you once again!
I hold to you the hands you first beheld,
To show they still are free. Methinks I hear
A spirit in your echoes answer me,

And bid your tenant welcome to his home
Again!—Oh! sacred forms, how proud you look!
How high you lift your heads into the sky!
How huge you are! how mighty, and how free!
Ye are the things that tower, that shine,—whose smile
Makes glad, whose frown is terrible, whose forms,
Robed or unrobed, do all the impress wear
Of awe divine. Ye guards of liberty,
I'm with you once again!—I call to you
With all my voice!—I hold my hands to you,
To show they still are free. I rush to you
As though I could embrace you!
　　——Scaling yonder peak,
I saw an eagle wheeling near its brow
O'er the abyss:—his broad-expanded wings
Lay calm and motionless upon the air,
As if he floated there without their aid,
By the sole act of his unlorded will,
That buoyed him proudly up. Instinctively
I bent my bow; yet kept he rounding still
His airy circle, as in the delight
Of measuring the ample range beneath
And round about; absorbed, he heeded not
The death that threatened him. I could not shoot!
'Twas liberty!—I turned my bow aside,
And let him soar away!

THE UNION. PERORATION OF THE REPLY TO MR. HAYNE
—*Daniel Webster.*

Mr. President, I have thus stated the reasons of my dissent to the doctrines which nave been advanced and maintained. I am conscious of having detained you, and the Senate, much too long. I was drawn into the debate, with no previous deliberation such as is suited to the discussion of so grave and important a subject But it is a subject of which my heart is full, and I have not been willing to suppress the utterance of its spontaneous sentiments.

2. I cannot, even now, persuade myself to relinquish it, without expressing once more my deep conviction, that since it respects nothing less than the Union of the States, it is of most vital and essential importance to the public happiness. I profess, sir, in my career hitherto, to have kept steadily in view the prosperity and honor of the whole country, and the preservation of our Federal Union. It is to that Union we owe our safety at home, and our consideration and dignity abroad. It is to that Union that we are chiefly indebted for whatever makes us most proud of our country. That Union we reached only by the discipline of our virtues in the severe school of adversity. It had its origin in the necessities of disordered finance, prostrate commerce, and ruined credit. Under its benign influences, these great interests immediately awoke, as from the dead, and sprang forth with newness of life. Every year of its duration has teemed with fresh proofs of its utility and its blessings; and although our territory has

stretched out wider and wider, and our population spread farther and farther, they have not outrun its protection or its benefits. It has been to us all a copious fountain of national, social, personal happiness. I have not allowed myself, sir, to look beyond the Union, to see what might lie hidden in the dark recesses behind. I have not coolly weighed the chances of preserving liberty, when the bonds that unite us together shall be broken asunder. I have not accustomed myself to hang over the precipice of disunion, to see whether, with my short sight, I can fathom the depth of the abyss below; nor could I regard him as a safe counsellor in the affairs of this government, whose thoughts should be mainly bent on considering, not how the Union should be best preserved, but how tolerable might be the condition of the people when it shall be broken up and destroyed. While the Union lasts, we have high, exciting, gratifying prospects spread out before us, for us and our chil dren. Beyond that I seek not to penetrate the veil God grant that, in my day at least, that curtain may not rise. God grant that on my vision never may be opened what lies behind. When my eyes shall be turned to behold, for the last time, the sun in heaven, may I not see him shining on the broken and dishonored fragments of a once-glorious Union; on States dissevered, discordant, belligerent; on a land rent with civil feuds, or drenched, it may be, in fraternal blood! Let their last feeble and lingering glance, rather, behold the gorgeous ensign of the Republic, now known and honored throughout the earth, still full high advanced, its arms and trophies streaming in their original lustre, not

a stripe erased or polluted, nor a single star obscured--
bearing for its motto no such miserable interrogatory as,
What is all this worth? nor those other words of delu
sion and folly, *Liberty first, and Union afterwards;* but
everywhere, spread all over in characters of living light,
blazing on all its ample folds, as they float over the sea
and over the land, and in every wind under the whole
heavens, that other sentiment, dear to every true
American heart,—Liberty *and* Union, now and forever,
one and inseparable!

BEAUTY, WIT, AND GOLD.—*Anonymus.*

In her bower a widow dwelt;
At her feet, three suitors knelt;
Each adored the widow much,
Each essayed her heart to touch;
One had wit, and one had gold,
And one was cast in beauty's mould;
Guess which was it won the prize,
Purse, or tongue, or handsome eyes?
First appeared the handsome man,
Proudly peeping o'er her fan;
Red his lips, and white his skin;
Could such beauty fail to win?
Then stepped forth the man of gold,
Cash he counted, coin he told,
Wealth the burden of his tale;
Could such golden projects fail?
Then the man of wit and sense,
Moved her with his eloquence;

Now she heard him with a sigh ;
Now she blushed, she knew not why ;
Then she smiled to hear him speak,
Then the tear was on her cheek ;
Beauty, vanish ! gold, depart !
Wit has won the widow's heart.

ADVICE.—*Shakespeare.*

　　　Give thy thoughts no tongue,
Nor any unproportioned thought his act.
Be thou familiar ; but by no means vulgar.
The friends thou hast, and their adoption tried,
Grapple them to thy soul, with hooks of steel ;
But do not dull thy palm with entertainment
Of ev'ry new-hatch'd, unfledged comrade.　Beware
Of entrance into quarrel ! but, being in,
Bear it, that the opposer may beware of thee.
Give every man thine ear, but few thy voice.
Take each man's censure, but reserve thy judgment.
Costly thy habit, as thy purse can buy,
But not expressed in fancy ; rich, not gaudy.
For the apparel oft proclaims the man.
Neither a borrower, nor a lender be ;
For loan oft loses both itself and friend,
And borrowing dulls the edge of husbandry.
This above all—to thine own self be true,
And it must follow, as the night the day,
Thou canst not then be false to any man.

SATAN'S SUPPOSED SPEECH TO HIS LEGIONS.—*Milton.*

Princes, Potentates,
Warriors, the flower of Heaven! once yours, now lost,
If such astonishment as this can seize
Eternal spirits; or have ye chosen this place,
After the toil of battle, to repose
Your wearied virtue, for the ease you find
To slumber here, as in the vales of Heaven?

Or, in this abject posture have ye sworn
To adore the conqueror? who now beholds
Cherub, and seraph, rolling in the flood,
With scatter'd arms and ensigns; till anon
His swift pursuers, from Heaven's gates discern
The advantage, and descending, tread us down
Thus drooping, or with linked thunderbolts,
Transfix us to the bottom of this gulf?
Awake, arise, or be forever fallen!

TERROR.—*Moliere.*

Ah! mercy on my soul. What is that? My old
friend's ghost? They say none but wicked folks walk;
I wish I were at the bottom of a coal-pit. See! how
.ong and pale his face has grown since his death; he never
was handsome; and death has improved him very much
the wrong way. Pray do not come near me! I wished
you very well when you were alive, but I could never
abide a dead man, cheek by jowl with me. Ah, ah,
mercy on us! No nearer, pray; if it be only to take

leave of me, that you are come back, I could have excused you the ceremony with all my heart; or, if you—mercy on us! no nearer, pray, or, if you have wronged anybody, as you always loved money a little, I give you the word of a frightened christian; I will pray as long as you please for the deliverance, or repose of your departed soul. My good, worthy, noble friend, do, pray disappear, as eve. you would wish your old friend to come to his senses again.

NATIONAL UNION.—*Morris.*

Do not, gentlemen, suffer the rage of passion to drive reason from her seat. If this law be indeed bad, let us join to remedy its defects. Has it been passed in a manner which wounded your pride, or roused your re sentment? Have, I conjure you, the magnanimity to pardon that offence. I entreat, I implore you, to sacrifice those angry passions to the interests of our country. Pour out this pride of opinion on the altar of patriotism. Let it be an expiatory libation for the weal of America. Do not suffer that pride to plunge us all into the abyss of ruin. Indeed, indeed, it will be but of little, very little avail, whether one opinion or the other be right or wrong; it will heal no wounds, it will pay no debts, it will rebuild no ravaged towns. Do not rely on that popular will, which has brought us frail beings into political existence. That opinion is but a changeable thing. It will soon change. This very measure will change it. You will be deceived. Do not, I beseech you, in reliance on a foundation so frail, commit the

15

dignity, the harmony, the existence of our nation to the
wild wind. Trust not your treasure to the waves.
Throw not your compass and your charts into the ocean.
Do not believe that its billows will waft you into port.
Indeed, indeed, you will be deceived. Cast not away
this only anchor of our safety. I have seen its progress.
I know the difficulties through which it was obtained. I
stand in the presence of Almighty God and of the world.
I declare to you, that if you lose this charter, never, no
never, will you get another. We are now perhaps arrived at the parting point. Here, even here, we stand
on the brink of fate. Pause, then—pause. For Heaven's sake, pause.

SUBLIMITY OF MOUNTAIN SCENERY.—*Croly.*

Of all the sights that nature offers to the eye and mind
of man, mountains have always stirred my strongest feelings. I have seen the ocean, when it was turned up
from the bottom by tempest, and noon was like night,
with the conflict of the billows, and the storm, that tore
and scattered them in mist and foam across the sky. I
have seen the desert rise around me, and calmly, in the
midst of thousands, uttering cries of horror, and par-
alyzed by fear, have contemplated the sandy pillars,
coming like the advance of some gigantic city of conflagration flying across the wilderness, every column glowing with intense fire, and every blast death; the sky
vaulted with gloom, the earth a furnace. But with me,
the mountain, in tempest or in calm, the throne of the
thunder, or with the evening sun painting its dells and

declivities in colors dipped in heaven, has been the source
of the most absorbing sensations.   There stands magnitude, giving the instant impression of a power above
man, grandeur that defies decay, antiquity that tells of
ages unnumbered, beauty that the touch of time makes
only more beautiful, use exhaustless for the service of
man, strength imperishable as the globe; the monument
of eternity,—the truest earthly emblem of that ever-
living, unchangeable, irresistible Majesty, by whom and
for whom all things were made!

ODE ON THE PASSIONS.—*Collins.*

When Music, heavenly maid, was young,
While yet, in early Greece, she sung,
The Passions oft, to hear her shell,
Throng'd around her magic cell;
Exulting, trembling, raging, fainting,
Possess'd beyond the Muse's painting.
By turns, they felt the glowing mind
Disturb'd, delighted, raised, refined:
Till once, 'tis said, when all were fired,
Fill'd with fury, rapt, inspired,
From the supporting myrtles round,
They snatch'd her instruments of sound;
And, as they oft had heard apart,
Sweet lessons of her forceful art,
Each—for madness ruled the hour—
Would prove his own expressive power.

2.

First, Fear, his hand its skill to try,
    Amid the chords, bewilder'd laid;
And back recoil'd, he knew not why,
    Even at the sound himself had made.

3.

Next, Anger rush'd, his eyes on fire,
    In lightnings, own'd his secret stings:
In one rude clash he struck the lyre,
    And swept, with hurried hands, the strings.

4.

With woful measures, wan Despair—
    Low, sullen sounds! his grief beguiled;
A solemn, strange, and mingled air;
    'Twas sad, by fits—by starts, 'twas wild.

5.

But thou, O Hope, with eyes so fair,
    What was thy delighted measure!
    Still it whisper'd—promised pleasure,
And bade the lovely scenes at distance hail,
    Still would her touch the strain prolong;
And from the rocks, the woods, the vale,
    She call'd on Echo still, through all her song.
And, where her sweetest theme she chose,
A soft, responsive voice was heard at every close;
And Hope, enchanted, smiled and wav'd her golden hair.

6.

And longer had she sung—but, with a frown,
    Revenge—impatient rose,
He threw his blood-stained sword in thunder down
    And, with a withering look,
    The war-denouncing trumpet took,

And blew a blast, so loud and dread,
Were ne'er prophetic sounds so full of woe;
   And, ever and anon, he beat
   The doubling drum with furious heat.
And though, sometimes, each dreary pause between,
   Dejected Pity, at his side,
   Her soul-subduing voice applied,
 Yet still, he kept his wild unalter'd mien;
While each strain'd ball of sight seem'd bursting from his
   head.

7.

Thy numbers, Jealousy, to nought were fix'd;
 Sad proof of thy distressful state!
Of differing themes the veering song was mix'd:
 And, now, it courted Love; now, raving, call'd on Hate.

8.

   With eyes upraised, as one inspired,
   Pale Melancholy sat, retired;
   And, from her wild sequester'd seat,
   In notes, by distance made more sweet,
Pour'd thro' the mellow horn her pensive soul:
   And, dashing soft, from rocks around,
   Bubbling runnels joined the sound.
  Thro' glades and glooms, the mingled measure stole;
   Or o'er some haunted streams, with fond delay,
   Round—a holy calm diffusing,
   Love of peace, and lonely musing—
  In hollow murmurs—died away.

9.

  But, oh! how alter'd was its sprightlier tone!
   When Cheerfulness, a nymph of healthiest hue,
   Her bow across her shoulders flung,

Her buskins gemm'd with morning dew,
    Blew an inspiring air, that dale and thicket rung,
The hunter's call, to Faun and Dryad known!

10.

  The oak-crown'd sisters, and their chaste eyed queen,
Satyrs, and sylvan boys, were seen,
Peeping from forth their alleys green;
Brown Exercise rejoiced to hear;
And Sport leap'd up, and seiz'd his beechen spear.

11.

    Last came Joy's ecstatic trial.
He, with viny crown advancing,
First to the lively pipe his hand address'd;
    But soon he saw the brisk awakening viol,
Whose sweet, entrancing voice he lov'd the best.
They would have thought, who heard the strain,
    They saw, in Tempe's vale, her native maids,
    Amid the festal-sounding shades,
To some unwearied minstrel dancing;
    While, as his flying fingers kiss'd the strings,
Love fram'd, with Mirth, a gay fantastic round—
Loose were her tresses seen, her zone unbound;
    And he, amid his frolic play,
    As if he would the charming air repay,
Shook thousand odors—from his dewy wings.

THE HOLY ALLIANCE.—*Daniel Webster.*

It is not a little remarkable, that a writer of reputation upon the Public Law, described, many years ago, not inaccurately, the character of the Holy Alliance.

I allude to Puffendorff. "It seems useless," says he, "to frame any pacts or leagues barely for the defence and support of universal peace; for, by such a league, nothing is superadded to the obligation of natural law, and no agreement is made for the performance of anything, which the parties were not previously bound to perform; nor is the original obligation rendered firmer or stronger by such an addition. Men of any tolerable culture and civilization might well be ashamed of entering into any such compact, the conditions of which imply only that the parties concerned shall not offend in any clear point of duty. Besides, we should be guilty of great irreverence toward God, should we suppose that his injunctions had not already laid a sufficient obligation upon us to act justly, unless we ourselves voluntarily consented to the same engagement: as if our obligation to obey his will depended upon our own pleasure.

2. "If one engage to serve another, he does not set it down expressly and particularly among the terms and conditions of the bargain, that he will not betray nor murder him, nor pillage nor burn his house. For the same reason, that would be a dishonorable engagement in which men should bind themselves to act properly and decently, and not break the peace."*

3. Such were the sentiments of that eminent writer. How nearly he had anticipated the case of the Holy Alliance, will appear from comparing his observations with the preamble to that alliance, which is as follows:

---

* Book 2, chap. ii.

4. "In the name of the most Holy and Indivisible
Trinity, their Majesties the Emperor of Austria, the
King of Prussia, and the Emperor of Russia,"—" solemnly declare, that the present act has no other object
than to publish, in the face of the whole world, their
fixed resolution, both in the administration of their respective States, and in their political relations with every
other Government, to take for their sole guide the precepts of that holy religion,—namely: the precepts of
justice, Christian charity, and peace, which, far from
being applicable only to private concerns, must have an
immediate influence on the councils of princes, and
guide all their steps, as being the only means of conso-
lidating human institutions, and remedying their imper-
fections."

5. This measure, however, appears principally import
ant, as it was the first of a series, and was followed afterward by others of a more marked and practical nature.
These measures, taken together, profess to establish
two principles, which the Allied Powers would enforce,
as a part of the law of the civilized world; and the
establishment of which is menaced by a million and a
half of bayonets.

6. The first of these principles is, that all popular, or
constitutional rights, are holden no otherwise than as
grants from the crown. Society, upon this principle,
has no rights of its own; it takes good government,
when it gets it, as a boon and a concession, but can demand nothing. It is to live in that favor which ema-
nates from royal authority, and if it have the misfortune
to lose that favor, there is nothing to protect it against

any degree of injustice and oppression. It can right-
fully make no endeavor for a change, by itself; its
whole privilege is to receive the favors that may be dispensed by the sovereign power, and all its duty is described in the single word *submission*. This is the plain
result of the principal continental state papers; indeed,
it is nearly the identical text of some of them.

7. The Laybach circular of May, 1821, alleges, "that
useful and necessary changes in legislation and administration ought only to emanate from the free will and
intelligent conviction of those whom God has rendered
responsible for power; all that deviates from this line
necessarily leads to disorder, commotions, and evils, far
more insufferable than those which they pretend to
remedy." * Now, sir, this principle would carry Europe
back again, at once, into the middle of the dark ages.
It is the old doctrine of the divine right of kings, advanced now by new advocates, and sustained by a formidable array of power. That the people hold their
fundamental privileges, as matter of concession or indulgence, from the sovereign power, is a sentiment not easy
to be diffused in this age, any further than it is enforced
by the direct operation of military means. It is true,
certainly, that some six centuries ago, the early founders
of English liberty called the instrument which secured
their rights a *Charter;* it was, indeed, a concession;
they had obtained it, sword in hand, from the king;
and, in many other cases, whatever was obtained, favorable to human rights, from the tyranny and despotism

---

* Annual Register, for 1821.

of the feudal sovereigns, was called by the names of *privileges* and *liberties,* as being matters of special favor. And, though we retain this *language* at the present time, the principle itself belongs to ages that have long passed by us. The civilized world has done with the enormous faith, of many made for one. Society asserts its own rights, and alleges them to be original, sacred, and unalienable. It is not satisfied with having kind masters; it demands a participation in its own government: and, in states much advanced in civilization, it urges this demand with a constancy and an energy, that cannot well, nor long, be resisted. There are, happily, enough of regulated Governments in the world, and those among the most distinguished, to operate as constant examples, and to keep alive an unceasing panting in the bosoms of men for the enjoyment of similar free institutions.

8. When the English Revolution of 1688 took place, the English people did not content themselves with the example of Runnymede; they did not build their hopes upon royal charters; they did not, like the Laybach circular, suppose that all useful changes in constitutions and laws must proceed from those only whom God has rendered responsible for power. They were somewhat better instructed in the principles of civil liberty, or at least they were better lovers of those principles, than the sovereigns of Laybach. Instead of petitioning for charters, they *declared* their rights, and, while they offered to the family of Orange the crown with one hand, they held in the other an enumeration of those privileges which they did not profess to hold as favors,

but which they *demanded* and *insisted upon*, as their undoubted rights.

9. I need not stop to observe, Mr. Chairman, how totally hostile are these doctrines of Laybach to the fundamental principles of our Government. They are in direct contradiction: the principles of good and evil are hardly more opposite. If these principles of the sovereigns be true, we are but in a state of rebellion or of anarchy, and are only tolerated among civilized states because it has not yet been convenient to conform us to the true standard.

10. But the second, and if possible, the still more objectionable principle, avowed in these papers, is the right of forcible interference in the affairs of other states. A right to control nations in their desire to change their own Government, wherever it may be conjectured or pretended that such change might furnish an example to the subjects of other states, is plainly and distinctly asserted. The same Congress that made the declaration at Laybach had declared, before its removal from Troppau, "That the powers have an undoubted right to take a hostile attitude in regard to those states in which the overthrow of the Government may operate as an example."

11. There cannot, as I think, be conceived a more flagrant violation of public law, or national independence, than is contained in this short declaration.

12. No matter what be the character of the Government resisted; no matter with what weight the foot of the oppressor bears on the neck of the oppressed; if he struggle, or if he complain, he sets a dangerous exam

ple of resistance,—and from that moment he becomes
an object of hostility to the most powerful potentates
of the earth.   I want words to express my abhorrence
of this abominable principle.   I trust every enlightened
man throughout the world will oppose it, and that, especially, those who, like ourselves, are fortunately out of
the reach of the bayonets that enforce it, will proclaim
their detestation of it, in a tone both loud and decisive.
The avowed object of such declarations is to preserve
the peace of the world.   But by what means is it proposed to preserve this peace ?   Simply, by bringing the
power of all the Governments to bear against all subjects.   Here is to be established a sort of double, or
treble, or quadruple, or, for aught I know, a quintuple
allegiance.   An offence against one king is to be an
offence against all kings, and the power of all is to be
put forth for the punishment of the offender.   A right
to interfere in extreme cases, in the case of contiguous
states, and where imminent danger is threatened to one
by what is transpiring in another, is not without precedent in modern times, upon what has been called the
law of vicinage ; and when confined to extreme cases,
and limited to a certain extent, it may perhaps be defended upon principles of necessity and self-defence.
But to maintain that sovereigns may go to war upon the
subjects of another state to *repress an example*, is monstrous indeed.   What is to be the limit to such a principle, or to the practice growing out of it ?   What, in
any case, but sovereign pleasure, is to decide whether
the example be good or bad ?   And what, under the
operation of such rule, may be thought of OUR *example !*

Why are we not as fair objects for the operation of the new principle, as any of those who may attempt to reform the condition of their Government, on the other side of the Atlantic?

13. The ultimate effect of this alliance of sovereigns, for objects personal to themselves, or respecting only the permanence of their own power, must be the destruction of all just feeling, and all natural sympathy, between those who exercise the power of government and those who are subject to it. The old channels of mutual regard and confidence are to be dried up, or cut off. Obedience can now be expected no longer than it is enforced. Instead of relying on the affections of the governed, sovereigns are to rely on the affections and friendship of other sovereigns. There are, in short, no longer to be nations. Princes and people no longer are to unite for interests common to them both. There is to be an end of all patriotism, as a distinct national feeling. Society is to be divided horizontally; all sovereigns above, and all subjects below; the former coalescing for their own security, and for the more certain subjection of the undistinguished multitude beneath.

OUR COUNTRY.— *Webster.*

Let the sacred obligations which have devolved upon this generation, and on us, sink deep into our hearts. Those are daily dropping from among us, who established our liberty and our government. The great trust now descends to new hands. Let us apply ourselves to that which is presented to us, as our appropriate object. We can win no laurels in a war for independence. Earlier and worthier hands have gathered them all. Nor are there places for us by the side of Solon, and Alfred, and other founders of states. Our fathers have filled them. But there remains to us a great duty of defence and preservation; and there is opened to us, also, a noble pursuit, to which the spirit of the times strongly invites us. Our proper business is improvement. Let our age be the age of improvement. In a day of peace, let us advance the arts of peace, and the works of peace; let us develop the resources of our land; call forth its powers, build up its institutions, promote all its great interests, and see whether we also, in our day and generation, may not perform something worthy to be remembered. Let us cultivate a true spirit of union and harmony. In pursuing the great objects which our condition points out to us, let us act under a settled conviction, and an habitual feeling, that these twenty-six states are one country. Let our conceptions be enlarged to the circle of our duties. Let us extend our ideas over the whole of the vast field in which we are called to act. Let our object be, our country, our whole country, and nothing but our country. And, by the blessing of God, may that country itself become a vast and splendid monument, not of oppression and terror, but of wisdom, of peace, and of liberty, upon which the world may gaze with admiration forever.

THE DESTRUCTION OF SENNACHERIB. —*Byron.*

The Assyrian came down, like a wolf on the fold,
And his cohorts were gleaming in purple and gold;
And the sheen of his spears was like stars on the sea,
When the blue wave rolls nightly, on deep Galilee.
2.
Like the leaves of the forest, when summer is green,
That host with their banners at sunset were seen;
Like the leaves of the forest, when autumn hath blown,
That host, on the morrow, lay withered and strewn.
3.
For the angel of death spread his wings on the blast,
And breathed in the face of the foe as he passed;
And the eyes of the sleepers waxed deadly and chill,
And their hearts but once heaved, and forever were
  still.
4.
And there lay the steed, with his nostrils all wide,
But through them there rolled not the breath of his
  pride;
And the foam of his gasping lay white on the turf,
And cold as the spray of the rock-beating surf.
5.
And there lay the rider, distorted and pale,
With the dew on his brow, and the rust on his mail;
And the tents were all silent, the banners alone,
The lances unlifted, the trumpets unblown.
6.
And the widows of Ashur are loud in their wail,
And the idols are broke in the temple of Baal;
And the might of the Gentile, unsmote by the sword,
Hath melted, like snow, in the glance of the Lord '

RIGHT OF FREE DISCUSSION.—*Webster.*

Important as I deem it, to discuss, on all proper occa
sions, the policy of the measures at present pursued, it
is still more important to maintain the right of such discussion in its full and just extent.   Sentiments, lately
sprung up, and now growing fashionable, make it necessary to be explicit on this point.   The more I perceive
a disposition to check the freedom of inquiry, by extra-
vagant and unconstitutional pretences, the firmer shall
be the tone in which I shall assert, and the freer the
manner in which I shall exercise it.

2. It is the ancient and undoubted prerogative of this
people, to canvass public measures, and the merits of public men.   Is is a " home-bred right," a fireside privilege.
It hath ever been enjoyed in every house, cottage, and
cabin in the nation.   It is not to be drawn into controversy.   It is as undoubted, as the right of breathing the
air, or walking on the earth.   Belonging to private life,
as a right, it belongs to public life, as a duty ; and it is
the last duty which those, whose representative I am,
shall find me to abandon.   Aiming, at all times, to be
courteous and temperate in its use, except when the
right itself shall be questioned, I shall then carry it to
its extent.   I shall place myself on the extreme boundary of my right, and bid defiance to any arm that would
move me from my ground.

3. This high constitutional privilege I shall defend,
and exercise within this house, and without this house, and
in all places ; in time of peace, and in all times. Living, I

shall assert it; and, should I leave no other inheritance
so my children, by the blessing of God, I will leave them
the inheritance of free principles, and the example of a
manly, independent, and constitutional defence of them.

SUPPOSED SPEECH OF JOHN ADAMS, ON ADOPTING THE
DECLARATION OF INDEPENDENCE.— *Webster*.

It is true, indeed, that in the beginning, we aimed
not at independence. But there's a Divinity which
shapes our ends. The injustice of England has driven
us to arms; and, blinded to her own interest, for our
good, she has obstinately persisted, till independence is
now within our grasp. We have but to reach forth to
it, and it is ours. Why, then, should we defer the declaration? Is any man so weak, as now to hope for a
reconciliation with England, which shall leave either
safety to the country and its liberties, or safety to his
own life and his own honor?

2. Are not you, sir, who sit in that chair; is not he, our
venerable colleague near you; are you not both, already,
the proscribed and predestined objects of punishment,
and of vengeance? Cut off from all hope of royal
clemency, what are you, what can you be, while the
power of England remains, but outlaws? If we post-
pone independence, do we mean to carry on, or to give
up the war? Do we mean to submit to the measures of
Parliament, Boston port-bill and all? Do we mean to
submit, and consent that we ourselves shall be ground
to powder, and our country and its rights trodden down
in the dust?

16

3. I know we do not mean to submit. We never shall submit. Do we intend to violate that most solemn obligation ever entered into by men, that plighting, before God, of our sacred honor to Washington, when, putting him forth to incur the dangers of war, as well as the political hazards of the times, we promised to adhere to him, in every extremity, with our fortunes and our lives?

4. I know there is not a man here, who would not rather see a general conflagration sweep over the land, or an earthquake sink it, than one jot or tittle of that plighted faith to fall to the ground. For myself, having twelve months ago, in this place, moved you, that George Washington be appointed commander of the forces raised or to be raised, for defence of American liberty, may my right hand forget her cunning, and my tongue cleave to the roof of my mouth, if I hesitate or waver in the support I give him.

5. The war, then, must go on. We must fight it through. And, if the war must go on, why put off longer the declaration of independence? That measure will strengthen us. It will give us character abroad. The nations will then treat with us, which they never can do while we acknowledge ourselves subjects, in arms against our sovereign. Nay, I maintain that England herself will sooner treat for peace with us, on the footing of independence, than consent, by repealing her acts, to acknowledge that her whole conduct toward us has been a course of injustice and oppression.

6. Her pride will be less wounded, by submitting to that course of things which now predestinates our inde-

pendence, than by yielding the points in controversy to her rebellious subjects. The former she would regard as the result of fortune; the latter she would feel as her own deep disgrace. Why then, sir, do we not, as soon as possible, change this from a civil to a national war? And, since we must fight it through, why not put ourselves in a state to enjoy all the benefits of victory, if we gain the victory?

7. If we fail, it can be no worse for us. But we shall not fail. The cause will raise up armies; the cause will create navies. The people, if we are true to them, will carry us, and will carry themselves, gloriously through this struggle. I care not how fickle other people have been found. I know the people of these colonies; and I know that resistance to British aggression is deep and settled in their hearts, and cannot be eradicated. Every colony, indeed, has expressed its willingness to follow, if we but take the lead.

8. Sir, the declaration will inspire the people with increased courage. Instead of a long and bloody war for restoration of privileges, for redress of grievances, for chartered immunities, held under a British king, set before them the glorious object of entire independence, and it will breathe into them anew the breath of life. Read this declaration at the head of the army; every sword will be drawn from its scabbard, and the solemn vow uttered, to maintain it, or to perish on the bed of honor. Publish it from the pulpit; religion will approve it, and the love of religious liberty will cling around it, resolved to stand with it or fall with it. Send it to the public halls; proclaim it there; let them hear it, who

heard the first roar of the enemy's cannon; let them see
it, who saw their brothers and their sons fall on the field
of Bunker Hill, and in the streets of Lexington and
Concord,—and the very walls will cry out in its support.

9. Sir, I know the uncertainty of human affairs, but
I see clearly through this day's business. You and I,
indeed, may rue it. We may not live to the time when
this declaration shall be made good. We may die—die
colonists, die slaves, die, it may be, ignominiously, and
on the scaffold. Be it so. If it be the pleasure of
Heaven, that my country shall require the poor offering
of my life, the victim shall be ready at the appointed
hour of sacrifice, come when that hour may.

10. But, whatever may be our fate, be assured that this
declaration will stand. It may cost treasure, and it may
cost blood; but it will stand, and it will richly compen-
sate for both. Through the thick gloom of the present,
I see the brightness of the future as the sun in heaven.
We shall make this a glorious, an immortal day. When
we are in our graves, our children will honor it. They
will celebrate it with thanksgiving, with festivity, with
bonfires, and illuminations. On its annual return, they
will shed tears, copious, gushing tears, not of subjection
and slavery, not of agony and distress, but of exultation, of gratitude, and of joy. Sir, before God I believe
the hour is come. My judgment approves this measure,
and my whole heart is in it. All that I am, all that I
have, and all that I hope for, in this life, I am now ready
here to stake upon it; and I leave off as I began: sink
or swim, live or die, survive or perish, I am for the de-

daration. It is my living sentiment, and by the blessing of God it shall be my dying sentiment—Independence now! and independence FOREVER!

THANATOPSIS.—*Bryant.*

To him who, in the love of nature, holds
Communion with her visible forms, she speaks
· A various language; for his gayer hours,
She has a voice of gladness, and a smile,
And eloquence of beauty, and she glides
Into his dark musings, with a mild
And gentle sympathy, that steals away
Their sharpness, ere he is aware.

2.

When thoughts—
Of the last bitter hour, come like a blight
Over thy spirit, and sad images
Of the stern agony, and shroud, and pall,
And breathless darkness, and the narrow house,
Make thee to shudder, and grow sick at heart;
Go forth into the open sky, and list
To nature's teaching, while, from all around.
Comes a still voice—

3.

"Yet a few days, and thee
The all-beholding sun shall see no more,
In all his course; nor yet, in the cold ground,
Where thy pale form was laid, with many tears,
Nor in the embrace of ocean, shall exist
Thy image. Earth, that nourished thee, shall claim
Thy growth, to be resolved to earth again,

An I, lost each human trace, surrendering **up**
Thine individual being, shalt thou go,
To mix forever with the elements,
To be a brother—to th' insensible rock,
And to the sluggish clod, which the rude swain
Turns with his share, and treads upon.

4.

The oak—
Shall send his roots abroad, and pierce thy mold,
Yet not, to thy eternal resting place,
Shalt thou retire alone—nor could'st thou wish
Couch more magnificent. Thou shalt lie down
With patriarchs of the infant world, with kings,
The powerful of the earth, the wise, the good,
Fair forms, and hoary seers of ages past,
All—in one—mighty sepulchre.

5.

The hills,
Rock-ribbed, and ancient as the sun; the vales,
Stretching in pensive quietness between;
The venerable woods; rivers, that move
In majesty, and the complaining brooks
That make the meadows green; and, poured round all,
Old ocean's gray and melancholy waste,
Are but the solemn decorations all—
Of the great tomb of man. The golden sun,
The planets, all the infinite host of heaven,
Are shining on the sad abodes of death,
Through the still lapse of ages.

6.

All that tread
The globe are but a handfull, to the tribes

That slumber in its bosom. Take the wings
Of morning, and the Barcan desert pierce,
Or lose thyself in the continuous woods,
Where rolls the Oregon, and hears no sound,
Save its own dashings—yet the dead are there;
And millions in those solitudes, since first
The flight of years began, have laid them down
In their last sleep: the dead reign there alone.

7.

So shalt thou rest; and what, if thou shalt fall
Unnoticed by the living, and no friend
Take note of thy departure? All that breathe
Will share thy destiny. The gay will laugh
When thou art gone; the solemn brood of care
Plod on; and each one, as before, will chase
His favorite phantom; yet all these shall leave
Their mirth and their enjoyments, and shall come,
And make their bed with thee. As the long train
Of ages glide away, the sons of men,
The youth, in life's green spring, and he who goes
In the full strength of years, matron, and maid,
The bowed with age, the infant, in the smiles
And beauty of its innocent age, cut off,—
Shall, one by one, be gathered to thy side,
By those who, in their turn, shall follow them.

8.

So live, that when thy summons comes to join
The innumerable caravan that moves
To the pale realms of shade, where each shall take
His chamber in the silent halls of death,
Thou go not, like the quarry-slave at night,

Scourged to his dungeon, but unstained and soothed
By an unfaltering trust, approach thy grave,
Like one who wraps the drapery of his couch
About him, and lies down to pleasant dreams.

PASSAGE OF THE RED SEA.—*Heber*.

'Mid the light spray, their snorting camels stood,
Nor bath'd a fetlock, in the nauseous flood:
He comes—their leader comes! the man of God,
O'er the wide waters, lifts his mighty rod,
And onward treads.   The circling waves retreat
In hoarse, deep murmurs, from his holy feet;
And the chas'd surges, inly roaring, show
The hard, wet sand, and coral hills below.
2.
With limbs that falter, and with hearts that swell,
Down, *down* they pass—a steep, and slippery dell;
Around them rise, in pristine chaos hurl'd,
The ancient rocks, the secrets of the world;
And flowers, that blush beneath the ocean green,
And caves, the sea-calves' low-roof'd haunts, are seen
Down, *safely* down the narrow pass they tread;
The beetling waters—storm above their head;
While far behind, retires the sinking day,
And fades on Edom's hills, its latest ray.
3.
Yet not from Israel—fled the friendly light,
Or dark to them, or cheerless came the night;
Still, in their van, along that dreadful road,
Blaz'd broad and fierce, the brandish'd torch of God.

Its meteor glare—a tenfold lustre gave,
On the long mirror—of the rosy wave:
While its blest beams—a sunlike heat supply,
Warm every cheek, and dance in every eye.
To them alone—for Misraim's wizard train
Invoke, for light, their monster-gods in vain:
Clouds heap'd on clouds, their struggling sight confine,
And tenfold darkness broods above their line.

4.

Yet on they press, by reckless vengeance led,
And range, unconscious, through the ocean's bed,
Till midway now—that strange, and fiery form,
Show'd his dread visage, lightning through the storm;
With withering splendor, blasted all their might,
And brake their chariot-wheels, and marred their cour-
    sers' flight.
"Fly, Misraim, fly!" The ravenous floods they see,
And, *fiercer* than the floods, the *Deity.*

5.

"Fly, Misraim, fly!" From Edom's coral strand,
Again the prophet stretch'd his dreadful wand:
With one wild crash, the thundering waters sweep,
And all—is waves—a dark, and lonely deep:—
Yet, o'er these lonely waves, such murmurs past,
As mortal wailing swell'd the nightly blast:
And strange, and sad, the whispering breezes bore
The groans of Egypt—to Arabia's shore.

TALENTS.— *Wirt.*

Talents, whenever they have had a suitable theatre,
have never failed to emerge from obscurity, and assume

their proper rank in the estimation of the world. The jealous pride of power may attempt to repress and crush them; the base and malignant rancor of impotent spleen, and envy—may strive to embarrass and retard their flight: but these efforts, so far from achieving their ignoble purpose, so far from producing a discernible obliquity, in the ascent of genuine, and vigorous talents, will serve only to increase their momentum, and mark their transit, with an additional stream of glory.

2. When the great earl of Chatham first made his appearance in the House of Commons, and began to astonish and transport the British parliament, and the British nation, by the boldness, the force, and range of his thoughts, and the celestial fire and pathos of his eloquence, it is well known that the minister, Walpole, and his brother Horace, from motives very easily understood, exerted all their wit, all their oratory, all their acquirements of every description, sustained and enforced by the unfeeling "insolence of office," to heave a mountain on his gigantic genius, and hide it from the world. Poor and powerless attempt! The tables were turned. He rose upon them, in the might and irresistible energy of his genius, and, in spite of all their convulsions, frantic agonies, and spasms, he strangled them, and their whole faction, with as much ease as Hercules did the serpent Python.

3. Who can turn over the debates of the day, and read the account of this conflict between youthful ardor and hoary-headed cunning and power, without kindling in the cause of the tyro, and shouting at his victory? That they should have attempted to pass off the grand,

yet solid and judicious operations of a mind like his, as
being mere theatrical start and emotion; the giddy,
hair-brained eccentricities of a romantic boy! That
they should have had the presumption to suppose themselves capable of chaining down to the floor of the parliament, a genius so etherial, towering, and sublime,
seems unaccountable! Why did they not, in the next
breath, by way of crowning the climax of vanity, bid
the magnificent fire-ball to descend from its exalted and
appropriate region, and perform its splendid tour along
the surface of the earth?

4. Talents, which are before the public, have nothing
to dread, either from the jealous pride of power, or from
the transient misrepresentations of party, spleen, or
envy. In spite of opposition from any cause, their
buoyant spirit will lift them to their proper grade. The
man who comes fairly before the world, and who possesses the great and vigorous stamina which entitle him
to a niche in the temple of glory, has no reason to dread
the ultimate result; however slow his progress may be,
he will, in the end, most indubitably receive that distinction. While the rest, "the swallows of science,"
the butterflies of genius, may flutter for their spring;
but they will soon pass away, and be remembered no
more. No enterprising man, therefore, and, least of
all, the truly great man, has reason to droop, or repine,
at any efforts which he may suppose to be made with
the view to depress him. Let, then, the tempest of
envy or of malice howl around him. His genius will
consecrate him; and any attempt to extinguish that

will be as unavailing as would a human effort "to
quench the stars.'

GENIUS.—*Dewey.*

The favorite idea of a genius among us, is of one who
never studies, or who studies nobody can tell when; at
midnight, or at odd times and intervals, and now and
then strikes out, "at a heat," as the phrase is, some
wonderful production.　This is a character that has figured largely in the history of our literature, in the person of our Fieldings, our Savages, and our Steeles;
"loose fellows about town, or loungers in the country,"
who slept in ale-houses, and wrote in bar-rooms; who
took up the pen, as a magician's wand, to supply their
wants, and, when the pressure of necessity was relieved,
resorted again to their carousals.　Your real genius is
an idle, irregular, vagabond sort of personage: who
muses in the fields, or dreams by the fireside: whose
strong impulses—that is the cant of it—must needs
hurry him into wild irregularities, or foolish eccentricity:
who abhors order, and can bear no restraint, and eschews
all labor; such a one as Newton or Milton?　What?
they must have been irregular, else they were no geni-
uses.　"The young man," it is often said, "has genius
enough, if he would only study."　Now, the truth is, as
I shall take the liberty to state it, that the genius will
study; it is that in the mind which does study; that is
the very nature of it.　I care not to say, that it will
always use books.　All study is not reading, any more
than all reading is study.

2. Attention it is, though other qualities belong to this transcendent power ; attention it is, that is the very soul of genius ; not the fixed eye, not the poring over a book, but the fixed thought.   It is, in fact, an action of the mind, which is steadily concentrated upon one idea, or one series of ideas, which collects in one point the rays of the soul, till they search, penetrate, and fire the whole train of its thoughts.   And while the fire burns within, the outside may be indeed cold, indifferent, negligent, absent, in appearance ; he may be an idler, or a wanderer, apparently without aim or intent ; but still the fire burns within.   And what though "it bursts forth " at length, as has been said, " like volcanic fires, with spontaneous, original, native force ?"   It only shows the intense action of the elements beneath.   What, though it breaks forth like lightning from the cloud ?   The electric fire had been collecting in the firmament, through many a silent, clear, and calm day.   What, though the might of genius appears in one decisive blow, struck in some moment of high debate, or at the crisis of a nation's peril !   That mighty energy, though it may have heaved in the breast of Demosthenes, was once a feeble infant thought.   A mother's eye watched over its dawnings. A father's care guarded its early youth.   It soon trod, with youthful steps, the halls of learning, and found other fathers to wake, and to watch for it, even as it finds them here.   It went on ; but silence was upon its path, and the deep strugglings of the inward soul silently ministered to it.   The elements around breathed upon it, and " touched it to finer issues."   The golden ray of heaven fell upon it, and ripened its expanding faculties.

The slow revolutions of years slowly added to its collected energies and treasures ; till, in its hour of glory, it stood forth embodied in the form of living, commanding, irresistible eloquence. The world wonders at the manifestation, and says, " Strange, strange that it should come thus unsought, unpremeditated, unprepared." But the truth is, there is no more a miracle in it, than there is in the towering of the pre-eminent forest-tree, or in the flowing of the mighty, and irresistible river, or in the wealth and waving of the boundless harvest.

THE OCEAN.—*Byron.*

Oh ! that the desert were my dwelling-place,
With one fair spirit for my minister,
That I might all forget the human race,
And hating no one, love but only her !
Ye elements ! in whose ennobling stir
I feel myself exalted, can ye not
Accord me such a being ? Do I err
In deeming such inhabit many a spot ?
Though with them to converse can rarely be my lot.

2.

There is a pleasure in the pathless woods,
There is a rapture on the lonely shore,
There is society where none intrudes,
By the deep sea, and music in its roar ;
I love not man the less, but nature more,
From these our interviews, in which I steal
From all I may be, or have been before,

To mingle with the Universe, and feel
What I can ne'er express, yet cannot all conceal
3.
Roll on, thou deep and dark blue ocean, roll!
Ten thousand fleets sweep over thee in vain;
Man marks the earth with ruin; his control •
Stops with the shore; upon the watery plain
The wrecks are all thy deed, nor doth remain
A shadow of man's ravage, save his own;
When for a moment, like a drop of rain,
He sinks into thy depths with bubbling groan,
Without a grave, unknelled, uncoffined, and unknown.
4.
The armaments which thunderstrike the walls •
Of rock-built cities, bidding nations quake,
And monarchs tremble in their capitals—
The oak leviathans, whose huge ribs make
Their clay creator, the vain title take
Of lord of thee, and arbiter of war!
These are thy toys, and, as the snowy flake,
They melt into thy yeast of waves, which mar
Alike the Armada's pride, or spoils of Trafalgar.
5.
Thy shores are empires, changed in all save thee.
Assyria, Greece, Rome, Carthage, what are they?
Thy waters wasted them while they were free,
And many a tyrant since; their shores obey
The stranger, slave, or savage; their decay
Has dried up realms to deserts: not so thou
Unchangeable, save to thy wild waves' play.
Time writes no wrinkle on thine azure brow—
Such as creation's dawn beheld, thou rollest now.

6.

Thou glorious mirror, where the Almighty's form
Glasses itself in tempests ; in all time,
(Calm or convulsed, in breeze, or gale, or storm,
Icing the pole, or in the torrid clime,
Dark heaving,) boundless, endless, and sublime,
The image of Eternity—the throne
Of the Invisible ; even from out thy slime
The monsters of the deep are made ! each zone
Obeys thee ; thou goest forth, dread, fathomless, alone.

7.

And I have loved thee, Ocean ! and my joy
Of youthful sports was on thy breast to be
Borne like the bubbles, onward ; from a boy,
I wantoned with thy breakers—they to me
Were a delight ; and if the freshening sea
Made them a terror, 'twas a pleasing fear,
For I was, as it were, a child of thee,
And trusted to thy billows far and near,
And laid my hand upon thy mane, as I do here

IMMORTALITY OF THE CHURCH.—*Archbishop Spalding.*

Amidst all this Babel-like confusion of dissent, and
this rapid tendency to dissolution among the sects, what
of the Catholic Church? Is she waning in her fortunes,
diminishing in her numbers, or losing her influence?
Is her dissolution threatened? Is her vitality even
imperilled? The answer rises instinctively to the lips
of every candid man: she was never stronger, never
more thoroughly alive, than she is at this very day.
Her terrible conflicts of eighteen centuries—conflicts

which may continue for eighteen centuries more, should the world last so long—have left her more vigorous than ever. Her bishops were never before so numerous or devoted ; her priests never more active or influential ; her spirits never more buoyant; her face never more radiant. She sends her missionaries to the most remote confines of the earth and to the farthest off islands of the sea, with the same exuberant and hopeful zeal which marked the apostolic age ; and her modern apostles still pant for, win, and wear the crown of martyrdom, with the same burning charity and the same abounding joy, as did their predecessors in the race of spiritual conquest in the halcyon days of her early history. In the often quoted language of Lord Macaulay :—

2. " Nor do we see any sign which indicates that the term of her long duration is approaching. She saw the commencement of all the governments, and of all the ecclesiastical establishments that now exist in the world ; and we feel no assurance that she is not destined to see the end of them all. She was great and respected before the Saxon set foot on Britain—before the Frank had crossed the Rhine—when Grecian elo quence still flourished at Antioch—when idols were still worshipped in the Temple of Mecca. * * * When we reflect on the tremendous assaults which she has survived, we find it difficult to conceive in what way she is to perish."

3. Yes ; it is more than difficult, it is simply impossible that she should perish. He who said, " Heaven and earth may pass away, but My word shall not pass

away," built her securely upon a Rock, and He pledged His solemn word that "the gates of hell should not prevail against her." History shows the faithful fulfilment of this divine prophecy and promise. Its verdict was already foreshadowed in other prophetic words of the inspired Record: "And the rain fell, and the floods came, and they beat upon that House; AND IT FELL NOT, FOR IT WAS FOUNDED ON A ROCK." (See Matt. vii. 25.) This is the clue to the difficulty, the key of the position; with it all is clear, without it history were an inextricable labyrinth.

> "Strong as the rock of the ocean, which stems
> A thousand wild waves on the shore,"

she will stand unshaken amidst all the storms of the future, as she has nobly withstood all the storms of the past.

THE IMMORTALITY OF THE PAPACY.—*Archbishop Spalding.*

Even from a human point of view, there is, perhaps, no more remarkable or magnificent spectacle in history than that presented by the long line of Roman Pontiffs. The golden chain of the succession stretches across the broad historic field, from St. Peter in the first century, to Pius IX. in the nineteenth; and not a link of it has been broken by the changes of time and the rude shocks of events, during more than eighteen centuries! Compared with this venerable line of bishops, the oldest ancestral and royal houses of Europe are but of yesterday. These have all undergone the changes incident to human things; that has proved itself superior to all vicissitudes, and has come triumphant out of every fiery ordeal. Through sunshine and tempest, through whirlwinds and revolutions, through the wreck of empires and the changes of dynasties, through ruins cumbering its pathway during long ages, the Papacy has survived, and it still lives, with undiminished vigor and ever-renewed vitality.

2. The imperial line of the Roman Cæsars began the race with the Papacy; it was strong and the Papacy was weak; but the line of the Cæsars, which was inaugurated under auspices so promising and so splendid by Augustus, after a period of less than five centuries terminated disastrously and ingloriously in Augustulus (or the little Augustus); while the Papacy was still young, and had hardly yet gained a firm foothold on the earth. The line of the Eastern Cæsars began with Constantine in the fourth century, and closed with Constantine Paleologus in the fifteenth; still the Papacy remained, more firmly seated than ever on the Chair of Peter. The old French monarchy began in the fifth century, and after having undergone manifold vicissitudes, and passed through the various dynasties of the Merovingian, the Carlovingian, and the Capetian houses, it was extinguished for a time at the close of the last century, in the blood of Louis XVI., and though subsequently revived for a brief period, it seems that its sun has now set forever; still the Papacy exhibits no signs of decay. The English monarchy has undergone similar changes, and has passed through the successive

dynasties of the British, Saxon, Danish, Norman, Plan-
tagenet, Tudor, Stuart, and Brunswick houses; but the
Papacy, which was already four centuries old when
Hengist, the Saxon, first set foot on British soil, has
outlived the past, and it bids fair to survive the present
and future royal lines. The same may be said of the
imperial line of Germany, and of the royal line of
Spain—not to speak of the smaller principalities of
Europe, or the comparatively modern line of the Rus-
sian Czars. They are all of the earth, earthly; they
have all in turn bowed to the decree of instability, and
to the doom of dissolution, inscribed on all merely human institutions; while the Papacy has plainly risen
above this law of change, has exhibited no signs of decay which would indicate approaching dissolution, and,
after having bravely battled with events for eighteen
centuries, has immortality still engraved on its triple
crown.

This wonderful tenacity of life becomes still more
astonishing when we reflect upon the terrible conflicts
through which the Papacy, like the Church, has passed
during its long pilgrimage on earth. For three centuries the sword of persecution, wielded by the mightiest empire which the world ever saw, was seldom
returned to the scabbard, and to be a Roman Pontiff
was to be a candidate for martyrdom. More than thirty
of the early Pontiffs were made to pass from an earthly
to a heavenly crown, under the axe of the pagan executioner. At each successive decapitation, the cruel instruments of imperial despotism no doubt boasted that
the line was extinct, and that no priest would be found

bold enough to step into the dangerous post stained with the blood of the previous incumbent. No doubt the certain downfall of popery was then a hundred times predicted, with at least as much earnestness, and with more seeming probability, than it has been foretold on less plausible grounds by many in modern times, who so loudly vaunt their zeal for Christianity. But as the pagan prophecies were falsified by the event, so we may reasonably hope and confidently expect that those of their *Christian* imitators will not be realized. If history convey any certain lesson, we may safely derive this steadfast conclusion from its faithful and constant verdict of eighteen centuries.

THUNDER STORM ON THE ALPS.—*Byron.*

It is the hush of night; and all between
Thy margin and the mountains, dusk, yet clear,
Mellow'd and mingling, yet distinctly seen,
Save darkened Jura, whose capped heights appear
Precipitously steep; and drawing near,
There breathes a living fragrance from the shore,
Of flowers, yet fresh with childhood; on the ear
Drops the light drip of the suspended oar,
Or chirps the grasshopper one good-night carol more.

2.

He is an evening reveler, who makes
His life an infancy, and sings his fill!
At intervals, some bird from out the brakes,
Starts into voice, a moment, then is still.

There seems a floating whisper on the hill,
But that is fancy, for the starlight dews
All silently their tears of love instill,
Weeping themselves away, till they infuse
Deep into Nature's breast, the spirit of her hues.

3.

The sky is changed! and such a change! O night,
And storm, and darkness, ye are wondrous strong!
Yet lovely in your strength, as is the light
Of a dark eye in woman! Far along,
From peak to peak, the rattling crags among,
Leaps the live thunder! not from one lone cloud,
But every mountain now hath found a tongue,
And Jura answers through her misty shroud,
Back to the joyous Alps, who call to her aloud!

4.

And this is in the night: most glorious night!
Thou wert not sent for slumber! Let me be
A sharer in thy fierce and far delight,
A portion of the tempest, and of thee!
How the lit lake shines! a phosphoric sea!
And the big rain comes dancing to the earth!
And now again 'tis black, and now the glee
Of the loud hills shakes with its mountain mirth,
As if they did rejoice o'er a young earthquake's birth

5.

Now, where the swift Rhone cleaves his way between
Heights, which appear as lovers who have parted
In hate, whose mining depths so intervene,
That they can meet no more, though broken hearted!

Though in their souls, which thus each other thwarted,
Love was the very root of the fond rage,
Which blighted their life's bloom, and then departed!
Itself expired, but leaving them an age
Of years, all winters! war within themselves to wage!

6.

Now, where the quick Rhone thus hath cleft his way,
The mightiest of the storms hath taken his stand;
For here, not one, but many, make their play,
And fling their thunderbolts from hand to hand,
Flashing and cast around! of all the band,
The brightest through these parted hills hath forked
His lightnings, as if he did understand,
That in such gaps as desolation worked,
There the hot shaft should blast whatever therein lurked.

ADAMS AND JEFFERSON.—*Everett.*

They have gone to the companions of their cares, of their toils. It is well with them. The treasures of America are now in Heaven. How long the list of our good, and wise, and brave, assembled there! how few remain with us! There is our Washington, and those who followed him in their country's confidence, are now met together with him, and all that illustrious company.

2. The faithful marble may preserve their image; the engraven brass may proclaim their worth; but the humblest sod of independent America, with nothing but the dew-drops of the morning to gild it, is a prouder mausoleum than kings or conquerors can boast. The coun-

try is their monument. Its independence is their epitaph.

3. But not to their country is their praise limited. The whole earth is the monument of illustrious men. Wherever an agonizing people shall perish, in a generous convulsion, for want of a valiant arm and a fearless heart, they will cry, in the last accents of despair, Oh, for a Washington, an Adams, a Jefferson! Wherever a regenerated nation, starting up in its might, shall burst the links of steel that enchain it, the praise of our fathers shall be the prelude of their triumphal song.

4. The contemporary and successive generations of men will disappear. In the long lapse of ages, the tribes of America, like those of Greece and Rome, may pass away. The fabric of American freedom, like all things human, however firm and fair, may crumble into dust. But the cause in which these our fathers shone is immortal. They did that, to which no age, no people of reasoning men, can be indifferent.

5. Their eulogy will be uttered in other languages, when those we speak, like us who speak them, shall all be forgotten. And when the great account of humanity shall be closed at the throne of God, in the bright list of his children, who best adorned and served it, shall be found the names of our Adams and our Jefferson.

DUTIES OF AMERICAN CITIZENS.— *Webster*.

FELLOW CITIZENS :—Let us not retire from this occasion, without a deep and solemn conviction of the duties which have devolved upon us. This lovely land, this

glorious liberty, these benign institutions, the dear purchase of our fathers, are ours; ours to enjoy, ours to
preserve, ours to transmit. Generations past, and generations to come, hold us responsible for this sacred
trust. Our fathers from behind admonish us with their
anxious, paternal voices; posterity calls out to us from
the bosom of the future; the world turns hither its solicitous eyes; all, all conjure us to act wisely, and faith-
fully, in the relation which we sustain. We can never,
indeed, pay the debt which is upon us; but, by virtue,
by morality, by religion, by the cultivation of every good
principle, and every good habit, we may hope to enjoy
the blessing, through our day, and leave it, unimpaired,
to our children.

2. Let us feel deeply how much of what we are, and
what we possess, we owe to this liberty, and to these institutions of government. Nature has, indeed, given us
a soil, which yields bounteously to the hands of industry;
the mighty and fruitful ocean is before us, and the skies
over our heads shed health and vigor. But what are
lands, and seas, and skies, to civilized man, without society, without knowledge, without morals, without religious culture; and how can these be enjoyed in all their
extent, and all their excellence, but under the protection
of wise institutions and a free government? Fellow-citizens, there is not one of us here present, who does not
at this moment, and at every moment, experience in his
own condition, and in the condition of those most near
and dear to him, the influence and the benefits of this
liberty, and these institutions. Let us, then, acknow-
edge the blessing; let us feel it deeply and powerfully;

let us cherish a strong affection for it, and resolve to maintain and perpetuate it. The blood of our fathers, let it not have been shed in vain; the great hope of posterity, let it not be blasted.

3. The striking attitude, too, in which we stand to the world around us, cannot be altogether omitted here. Neither individuals nor nations can perform their part well, until they understand and feel its importance, and comprehend and justly appreciate all the duties belonging to it. It is not to inflate national vanity, nor to swell a light and empty feeling of self-importance ; but it is, that we may judge justly of our situation and of our duties, that I earnestly urge this consideration of our position, and our character among the nations of the earth.

4. It cannot be denied, but by those who would dispute against the sun, that with America, and in America, a new era commences in human affairs. This era is distinguished by free representative governments, by entire religious liberty, by improved systems of national inter-course, by a newly awakened and an unquenchable spirit of free inquiry, and by a diffusion of knowledge through the community, such as has been before altogether unknown and unheard of. America, America, our country, fellow-citizens, our own dear and native land, is inseparably connected, fast bound up, in fortune and by fate, with these great interests. If they fall, we fall with them ; if they stand, it will be because we have upholden them.

5. Let us contemplate, then, this connection which binds the posterity of others to our own; and let us manfully

discharge all the duties it imposes. If we cherish tne virtues and the principles of our fathers, Heaven will assist us to carry on the work of human liberty and human happiness. Auspicious omens cheer us. Great examples are before us. Our firmament now shines brightly upon our path. Washington is in the clear, upper sky. Adams, Jefferson, and other stars have joined the American constellation; they circle round their center, and the heavens beam with new light. Beneath this illumination let us walk the course of life; and, at its close, devoutly commend our beloved country, the common parent of us all, to the divine benignity.

THE CHURCH AND CÆSAR.—*Lacordaire.*

The Church reaches two orders, the one internal, the other external. By the first, the interior order, she is in contact with that which is higher than man; she derives her strength from grace. By the second, the exterior order, she is in contact with that which is human, she derives her strength from freedom of action. And thus, when we are asked by what right the Church has taken away a part of the power of the Cæsars, it is as if we were asked by what right Christian liberty is established. For the Church has not taken from the Cæsars the internal and div'ne power of grace—they did not possess it; her only quarrels with them have been about the external power, which is that of liberty. Consequently, between Cæsar and the Church the question is reduced to this: "By what right is Christian liberty established?"

2. I answer, first, by divine right. It is not, in fact,
by a grant of princes that it has been given to us to
teach the world. It was not the Cæsars, but Jesus
Christ, who said to us, "*Go, and teach all nations.*" It
was not the Cæsars, but Jesus Christ, who said to us,
"*Remit sins; whatever ye shall bind on earth shall be
bound in heaven.*" It was not the Cæsars, but Jesus
Christ, who said to us, "*Crucify your flesh, with its affections and lusts.*" It was not the Cæsars, but Jesus
Christ, who said to us, "*Receive the Holy Ghost.*" Consequently, we do not derive our liberty from the Cæsars,
we derive it from God, and we shall keep it because it
comes from Him. Princes might combine together to
combat the prerogatives of the Church, call them by
opprobrious names in order to make them odious, say
that it is an exorbitant power, which ruins states; we
shall let them do so, and we shall continue to preach
truth, to remit sins, to combat vice, to communicate the
spirit of God. If they drive us into exile, we shall do
so in exile; if they cast us into prisons, we shall do so
in prisons; if they enchain us in mines, we shall do so
there; if they drive us from one kingdom, we shall pass
into another. It was said to us that, even to the day
when each will be called to give an account of his
deeds, we shall not exhaust the kingdoms of the earth.
But if we are pursued on all sides, if the power of
Antichrist should spread itself over the whole surface of the world, then, as at the commencement of
the Church, we shall fly into tombs and catacombs.
And if at last we are pursued even there, if they make
us mount their scaffolds, in every noble heart of man

we shall find a last asylum, because we shall not have despaired of the truth, the justice, and the liberty of mankind.

NO EXCELLENCE WITHOUT LABOR.— *Wirt.*

The education, moral and intellectual, of every individual, must be chiefly his own work. Rely upon it, that the ancients were right—*Quisque suæ fortunæ faber* —both in morals and intellect, we give their final shape to our own characters, and thus become, emphatically, the architects of our own fortunes. How else could it happen, that young men who have had precisely the same opportunities, should be continually presenting us with such different results, and rushing to such opposite destinies? Difference of talent will not solve it, because that difference very often is in favor of the disappointed candidate. You shall see, issuing from the walls of the same college—nay, sometimes from the bosom of the same family—two young men, of whom the one shall be admitted to be a genius of high order—the other scarcely above the point of mediocrity; yet you shall see the genius sinking and perishing in poverty, obscurity, and wretchedness; while, on the other hand, you shall observe the mediocre, plodding his slow but sure way, up the hill of life, gaining steadfast footing at every step, and mounting, at length, to eminence and distinction, an ornament to his family, a blessing to his country. Now, whose work is this? Manifestly their own. They are the architects of their respective fortunes. The best seminary of learning that can open its portals to you, can do no more than to afford you the opportunity of instruction; but it must depend, at last, on yourselves, whether you will be instructed or not, or to what point you will push your instruction. And of this be assured —I speak from observation a certain truth: there is no excellence without great labor. It is the fiat of fate, from which no power of genius can absolve you. Genius, unexerted, is like the poor moth that flutters around a candle, till it scorches itself to death. If genius be desirable at all, it is only of that great and magnanimous kind, which, like the condor of South America, pitches from the summit of Chimborazo, above the clouds, and sustains itself at pleasure, in that empyreal region, with an energy rather invigorated than weakened by the effort. It is this capacity for high and long-continued exertion—this vigorous power of profound and searching investigation—this careering and wide-spreading comprehension of mind, and those long reaches of thought, that

" —Pluck bright honor from the pale-faced-moon,
Or dive into the bottom of the deep,
Where fathom line could never touch the ground,
And drag up drowned honor by the locks.-- "

This is the prowess, and these the hardy achievements, which are to enroll your names among the great men of the earth.

PUBLIC FAITH.—*Fisher Ames.*

To expatiate on the value of public faith, may pass with some men, for declamation. To such men I have

nothing to say. To others, I will urge—can any circumstance mark upon a people more turpitude and
debasement? Can anything tend more to make men
think themselves mean, or degrade to a lower point,
their estimation of virtue, and their standard of action?

2. It would not merely demoralize mankind, it tends
to break all the ligaments of society, to dissolve that
mysterious charm which attracts individuals to the
nation, and to inspire, in its stead, a repulsive sense of
shame and disgust.

3. What is patriotism? Is it a narrow affection for
the spot where a man was born? Are the very clods
where we tread entitled to this ardent preference,
because they are greener? No, this is not the character of the virtue, and it soars higher for its object.
It is an extended self-love, mingling with all the enjoyments of life, and twisting itself with the minutest
filaments of the heart.

4. It is thus: we obey the laws of society, because
they are the laws of virtue. In their authority we see,
not the array of force and terror, but the venerable
image of our country's honor. Every good citizen
makes that honor his own, and cherishes it, not only as
precious but as sacred. He is willing to risk his life in its
defence, and is conscious that he gains protection while
he gives it. For, what rights of a citizen will be deemed
inviolable, when a state renounces the principles that
constitute their security?

5. Or, if this life should not be invaded, what would
its enjoyments be, in a country odious in the eyes of

strangers, and dishonored in his own? Could he look
with affection and veneration to such a country as his
parent? The sense of having one would die within him;
he would blush for his patriotism, if he retained any, and
justly, for it would be a vice. He would be a banished
man in his native land.

THE RAINY DAY.

LONGFELLOW.

THE day is cold, and dark, and dreary;
It rains, and the wind is never weary;
The vine still clings to the mouldering wall,
But at every gust the dead leaves fall,
   And the day is dark and dreary.

My life is cold, and dark, and dreary;
It rains, and the wind is never weary;
My thoughts still cling to the mouldering Past,
But the hopes of youth fall thick in the blast,
   And the days are dark and dreary.

Be still, sad heart! and cease repining;
Behind the clouds is the sun still shining;
Thy fate is the common fate of all,
Into each life some rain must fall,
   Some days must be dark and dreary

CATILINE DENOUNCED.—*Cicero.*

Cicero, the greatest of Roman orators, was born at Arpīnum, 106 B.C., two hundred and sixteen years after the death of Demosthenes. Having taken part against Antony, after the assassination of Cæsar, Cicero was proscribed. He was murdered by a party of soldiers, headed by Popilius Lænas, whose life he had formerly saved by his eloquence; and his head and hands were publicly exhibited on the rostrum at Rome. He perished in his sixty-fourth year, 43 B.C. His writings are voluminous. As an orator, Cicero ranks next to Demosthenes; and his orations against Catiline and Verres are masterpieces of denunciatory eloquence.

How far, O Catîline, wilt thou abuse our patience? How long shalt thou baffle justice in thy mad career? To what extreme wilt thou carry thy audacity? Art thou nothing daunted by the nightly watch, posted to secure the Palātium? Nothing, by the city guards? Nothing, by the rally of all good citizens? Nothing, by the assembling of the Senate in this fortified place? Nothing, by the averted looks of all here present? Seest thou not that all thy plots are exposed?—that thy wretched conspiracy is laid bare to every man's knowledge, here in the Senate?—that we are well aware of thy proceedings of last night; of the night before;—the place of meeting, the company convoked, the measures concerted? Alas, the times! Alas, the public morals! The Senate understands all this. The Consul sees it. Yet the traitor lives! Lives? Ay, truly, and confronts us here in council,—takes part in our deliberations,—and, with his measuring eye, marks out each man of us for slaughter! And we, all this while, strenuous that we are, think we have amply dis-

charged our duty to the State, if we but *shun* this madman's sword and fury!

2. Long since, O Catiline, ought the Consul to have
ordered thee to execution, and brought upon thy own
head the ruin thou hast been meditating against others!
There was that virtue once in Rome, that a wicked
citizen was held more execrable than the deadliest foe.
We have a law still, Catiline, for thee. Think not that
we are powerless, because forbearing. We have a decree,—though it rests among our archives like a sword
in its scabbard,—a decree, by which thy life would be
made to pay the forfeit of thy crimes. And, should I
order thee to be instantly seized and put to death, I
make just doubt whether all good men would not think
t done rather too late than any man too cruelly. But,
for good reasons, I will yet defer the blow long since
deserved. *Then* will I doom thee, when no man is
found, so lost, so wicked, nay, so like thyself, but shall
confess that it was justly dealt. While there is one
man that dares defend thee, live! But thou shalt live
so beset, so surrounded, so scrutinized, by the vigilant
guards that I have placed around thee, that thou shalt
not stir a foot against the Republic, without my knowledge. There shall be eyes to detect thy slightest movement, and ears to catch thy wariest whisper, of which
thou shalt not dream. The darkness of night shall not
cover thy treason—the walls of privacy shall not stifle
its voice. Baffled on all sides, thy most secret counsels
clear as noon-day, what canst thou now have in view!
Proceed, plot, conspire, as thou wilt; there is nothing
you can contrive, nothing you can propose, nothing you

can attempt, which I shall not know, hear, and prompt-
ly understand. Thou shalt soon be made aware that
I am even more active in providing for the preservation
of the State than thou in plotting its destruction !

CATILINE EXPELLED.—*Cicero.*

At length, Romans, we are rid of Catiline! We
have driven him forth, drunk with fury, breathing mis-
chief, threatening to revisit us with fire and sword.
He is gone; he is fled; he has escaped; he has broken
away. No longer, within the very walls of the city, shall
he plot her ruin. We have forced him from secret plots
into open rebellion. The bad citizen is now the avowed
traitor. His flight is the confession of his treason !
Would that his attendants had not been so few ! Be
speedy, ye companions of his dissolute pleasures ; be
speedy, and you may overtake him before night, on the
Aurelian road. Let him not languish, deprived of
your society. Haste to join the congenial crew that
compose his army; *his* army, I say,—for who doubts
that the army under Manlius expect Catiline for their
leader? And such an army ! Outcasts from honor,
and fugitives from debt; gamblers and felons ; mis-
creants, whose dreams are of rapine, murder, and conflagration.

2. Against these gallant troops of your adversary, prepare, O Romans, your garrisons and armies ; and first
to that maimed and battered gladiator oppose your
Consuls and Generals ; next, against that miserable out-

cast horde, lead forth the strength and flower of all
Italy!　On the one side chastity contends; on the
other, wantonness; here purity, there pollution; here
integrity, there treachery; here piety, there profane-
ness; here constancy, there rage; here honesty, there
baseness; here continence, there lust; in short, equity,
temperance, fortitude, prudence, struggle with iniquity, luxury, cowardice, rashness; every virtue with
every vice; and, lastly, the contest lies between well-
grounded hope and absolute despair.　In such a conflict, were even human aid to fail, would not the immortal gods empower such conspicuous virtue to triumph over such complicated vice?

VERRES DENOUNCED.—*Cicero.*

An opinion has long prevailed, Fathers, that, in public prosecutions, men of wealth, however clearly convicted, are always safe.　This opinion, so injurious to
your order, so detrimental to the State, it is now in your
power to refute.　A man is on trial before you who is
rich, and who hopes his riches will compass his acquittal; but whose life and actions are his sufficient
condemnation in the eyes of all candid men.　I speak
of Caius Verres, who, if he now receive not the sentence his crimes deserve, it shall not be through the
lack of a criminal, or of a prosecutor; but through the
failure of the ministers of justice to do their duty.
Passing over the shameful irregularities of his youth,
what does the quæstorship of Verres exhibit but one
continued scene of villanies?　The public treasure

squandered, a Consul stripped and betrayed, an army
deserted and reduced to want, a province robbed, the
civil and religious rights of a people trampled on! But
his prætorship in Sicily has crowned his career of
wickedness, and completed the lasting monument of
his infamy. His decisions have violated all law, all
precedent, all right. His extortions from the industrious poor have been beyond computation. Our most
faithful allies have been treated as enemies. Roman
citizens have, like slaves, been put to death with tortures. Men the most worthy have been condemned
and banished without a hearing, while the most atrocious criminals have, with money, purchased exemption
from the punishment due to their guilt.

2. I ask now, Verres, what have you to advance against
these charges? Art thou not the tyrant prætor, who,
at no greater distance than Sicily, within sight of the
Italian coast, dared to put to an infamous death, on the
cross, that ill-fated and innocent citizen, Publius Ga-
vius Cosānus? And what was his offence? He had
declared his intention of appealing to the justice of his
country against your brutal persecutions! For this,
when about to embark for home, he was seized, brought
before you, charged with being a spy, scourged and
tortured. In vain did he exclaim: "I am a Roman
citizen! I have served under Lucius Pretius, who is
now at Panormus, and who will attest my innocence!"
Deaf to all remonstrance, remorseless, thirsting for innocent blood, you ordered the savage punishment to be
inflicted! While the sacred words, "I am a Roman
citizen," were on his lips,—words which, in the remot-

est regions, are a passport to protection,—you ordered
him to death, to a death upon the cross!

3. O liberty! O sound once delightful to every
Roman ear! O sacred privilege of Roman citizenship!
once sacred,—now trampled on! Is it come to this!
Shall an inferior magistrate, a governor, who holds his
whole power of the Roman people, in a Roman province,
within sight of Italy, bind, scourge, torture, and put to
an infamous death, a Roman citizen! Shall neither
the cries of innocence expiring in agony, the tears of
pitying spectators, the majesty of the Roman Commonwealth, nor the fear of the justice of his country,
restrain the merciless monster, who, in the confidence
of his riches, strikes at the very root of. liberty, and
sets mankind at defiance! And shall this man escape!
Fathers, it must not be! It must not be, unless you
would undermine the very foundations of social safety,
strangle justice, and call down anarchy, massacre, and
ruin on the Commonwealth!

NECKER'S FINANCIAL PLAN, SEPT. 26, 1789.—*Mirabeau*.

Necker, the minister of finance, having proposed an income tax of twenty-five per cent., with other measures, in view of the desperate state of the financial affairs of France, the proposition was advocated by Mirabeau, who did not, however, profess to comprehend or endorse all its details. Although a known enemy to the minister, he magnanimously made two speeches in behalf of his measure; without, however, inducing the Assembly to pass it, until, on the eve of its being rejected, Mirabeau rushed to the Tribune, and poured forth a last appeal, an abridgment of which is here given. This speech proved effectual. The Assembly received it with shouts of enthusiasm; and Necker's plan was adopted. Madame de Staël (Necker's daughter), who was near Mirabeau at the time of the delivery of this speech, says that "its effect was prodigious."

The minister of finance has presented a most alarming picture of the state of our affairs. He has assured us that delay must aggravate the peril; and that a day, an hour, an instant, may render it fatal. We have no plan that can be substituted for that which he proposes. On this plan, therefore, we must fall back. But, have we time, gentlemen ask, to examine it, to probe it thoroughly, and verify its calculations? No, no! a thousand times no! Hap-hazard conjectures, insignificant inquiries, gropings that can but mislead,—these are all that we can give to it now. Shall we therefore miss the decisive moment? Do gentlemen hope to escape sacrifices and taxation by a plunge into national bankruptcy? What, then, is bankruptcy, but the most cruel, the most iniquitous, most unequal, and disastrous of imposts? Listen to me for one moment!

2. Two centuries of plunder and abuse have dug th abyss which threatens to engulf the Nation. It must be filled up—this terrible chasm. But how? Here is a list of proprietors. Choose from the wealthiest, in order that the smallest number of citizens may be sacrificed. But choose! Shall not a few perish, that the mass of the people may be saved? Come, then! Here are two thousand Notables, whose property will supply the deficit. Restore order to your finances, peace and prosperity to the Kingdom! Strike! Immolate, without mercy, these unfortunate victims! Hurl them into the abyss!—It closes!

3. You recoil with dismay from the contemplation. Inconsistent and pusillanimous! What! Do you not perceive that, in decreeing a public bankruptcy, or, what is worse, in rendering it inevitable without decreeing it, you disgrace yourselves by an act a thousand times more criminal, and—folly inconceivable!—gratuitously criminal? For, in the shocking alternative I have supposed, at least the deficit would be wiped off. But do you imagine that, in refusing to pay, you shall cease to owe? Think you that the thousands, the millions of men, who will lose in an instant, by the terrible explosion of a bankruptcy, or its revulsion, all that formed the consolation of their lives, and perhaps their sole means of subsistence,—think you that they will leave you to the peaceable fruition of your crime? Stoical spectators of the incalculable evils which this catastrophe would disgorge upon France; impenetrable egotists, who fancy that these convulsions of despair and of misery will pass, as other calamities have passed,

—and all the more rapidly because of their intense violence,—are you, indeed, certain that so many men without bread will leave you tranquilly to the enjoyment of those savory viands, the number and delicacy of which you are so loath to diminish? No! you will perish; and, in the universal conflagration, which you do not shrink from kindling, you will not, in losing your honor, save a single one of your detestable indulgences. This is the way we are going. And I say to you, that the men who, above all others, are interested in the enforcement of these sacrifices which the Government demands, are you yourselves! Vote, then, this subsidy extraordinary; and may it prove sufficient! Vote it, inasmuch as whatever doubts you may entertain as to the means,—doubts vague and unenlightened, —you can have none as to the necessity, or as to our inability to provide—immediately, at least—a substitute. Vote it, because the circumstances of the country admit of no evasion, and we shall be responsible for all delays. Beware of demanding more time! Misfortune accords it never. Why, gentlemen, it was but the other day, that, in reference to a ridiculous commotion at the Palais-Royal,*—a Quixotic insurrection, which never had any importance save in the feeble imaginations or perverse designs of certain faithless men,—you heard these wild words: " *Catiline is at the gates of Rome, and yet you deliberate!* " And

* The *s* in *Palais* is mute, and the diphthong *ai* has the sound of *ai* in *air*, before the *r* is reached. The French pronunciation of *Royal* may be expressed in English thus: *Roh-ah-ee-ahl;* but the syllables must be fused rapidly in the utterance.

verily there was neither a Catiline nor a Rome, neither
perils nor factions around you.   But, to-day, bankruptcy, hideous bankruptcy, is there before you, and
threatens to consume you, yourselves, your property,
your honor,—and yet you deliberate!

IN REPLY TO THOSE WHO DENIED THE NATIONAL ASSEMBLY THE LEGITIMATE POWERS OF A NATIONAL CONVENTION, APRIL 19, 1790.--*Mirabeau.*

It is with difficulty, gentlemen, that I can repress
an emotion of indignation, when I hear hostile rhetori-
cians continually oppose the Nation to the National
Assembly, and endeavor to excite a sort of rivalry between them.   As if it were not through the National
Assembly that the Nation had recognized, recovered,
reconquered its rights!   As if it were not through the
National Assembly that the French had, in truth, become a Nation!   As if, surrounded by the monuments
of our labors, our dangers, our services, we could be
come suspected by the People—formidable to the liberties of the People!   As if the regards of two worlds
upon you fixed, as if the spectacle of your glory, as if
the gratitude of so many millions, as if the very pride
of a generous conscience, which would have to blush
too deeply to belie itself,—were not a sufficient guarantee of your fidelity, of your patriotism, of your virtue!
  2. Commissioned to form a Constitution for France, I
will not ask whether, with that authority, we did not
receive also the power to do all that was necessary to

&..mplete, establish, and confirm that Constitution. I will not ask, ought we to have lost in pusillanimous consultations the time of action, while nascent Liberty would have received her death-blow? But if gentlemen insist on demanding when and how, from simple deputies of bailiwicks, we became all at once transformed into a National Convention, I reply, It was on that day, when, finding the hall where we were to assemble closed, and bristling and polluted with bayonets, we resorted to the first place where we could reunite, to swear to perish rather than submit to such an order of things! That day, if we were not a National Convention, we became one; became one for the destruction of arbitrary power, and for the defence of the rights of the Nation from all violence. The strivings of Despotism which we have quelled, the perils which we have averted, the violence which we have repressed, — these are our titles! Our successes have consecrated them; the adhesion, so often renewed, of all parts of the Empire, has legitimized and sanctified them. Summoned to its task by the irresistible tocsin of necessity, our National Convention is above all imitation, as it is above all authority. It is accountable only to itself, and can be judged only by posterity.

3. Gentlemen, you all remember the instance of that Roman, who, to save his country from a dangerous conspiracy, had been constrained to overstep the powers conferred on him by the laws. A captious Tribune exacted of him the oath that he had respected those laws; hoping, by this insidious demand, to drive the Consul to the alternative of perjury or of an embar

rassing avowal. "Swear," said the Tribune, "that you have observed the laws." "I swear," replied the great man,—"I swear that I have saved the Republic." Gentlemen, I swear that you have saved France!

.

ON BEING SUSPECTED OF RECEIVING OVERTURES FROM THE COURT, MAY 22, 1790.—*Mirabeau.*

It would be an important step towards the reconciliation of political opponents, if they would clearly signify on what points they agree, and. on what they differ. To this end, friendly discussions avail more, far more, than calumnious insinuations, furious invectives, the acerbities of partisan rivalry, the machinations of intrigue and malevolence. For eight days, now, it has been given out that those members of the National Assembly in favor of the provision requiring the concurrence of the royal will for the exercise of the right of peace and war are parricides of the public liberty. Rumors of perfidy, of corruption, have been bruited. Popular vengeance has been invoked to enforce the tyranny of opinion; and denunciations have been uttered, as if, on a subject involving one of the most delicate and difficult questions affecting the organization of society, persons could not dissent without a crime. What strange madness, what deplorable infatuation, is this, which thus incites against one another men whom—let debate run never so high—one common object, one indestructible sentiment of patriotism, ought always to bring together, always to reunite; but

who thus substitute, alas! the irascibility of self-love
for devotion to the public good, and give one another
over, without compunction, to the hatred and distrust
of the People!

And *me*, too—*me*, but the other day, they would
have borne in triumph;—and *now* they cry in the
streets, THE GREAT TREASON OF THE COUNT OF MIRA-
BEAU! I needed not this lesson to teach me, *how short
the distance from the Capitol to the Tarpeian Rock!*
But the man who battles for reason, for country, does
not so easily admit that he is vanquished. He who
has the consciousness that he deserves well of that
country, and above all, that he is still able to serve her;
who disdains a vain celebrity, and prizes veritable glory
above the successes of the day; who would speak the
truth, and labor for the public weal, independently of
the fluctuations of popular opinion,—such a man carries in his own breast the recompense of his services,
the solace of his pains, the reward of his dangers.
The harvest *he* looks for—the destiny, the only destiny,
to which *he* aspires—is that of his good name; and
for that he is content to trust to time,—to time, that
incorruptible judge, who dispenses justice to all!

Let those who, for these eight days past, have been
ignorantly predicting my opinion,—who, at this moment, calumniate my discourse without comprehending
it,—let them charge me, if they will, with beginning
to offer incense to the impotent idols I have overturned
—with being the vile stipendiary of men whom I have
never ceased to combat; let them denounce as an ene
my of the Revolution *him*, who at least has contributed

so much to its cause, that his safety, if not his glory, lies in its support;—let them deliver over to the rage of a deceived People *him*, who, for twenty years, has warred against oppression in all its forms;—who spoke to Frenchmen of Liberty, of a Constitution, of Resistance, at a time when his vile calumniators were sucking the milk of Courts, —living on those dominant abuses which he denounced :—what matters it? These underhand attacks shall not stop me in my career. I will say to my traducers, Answer if you can, and then calumniate to your hearts' content! And now I re-enter the lists, armed only with my principles and a steadfast conscience.

TO THE FRENCH PEOPLE, 1792.—*Vergniaud.*

Vergniaud, the most eloquent orator of the celebrated party known as the Girondists, during the French Revolution, was born at Limoges, in 1759. He was executed in 1793. As an orator, his renown is second only to that of Mirabeau, in France. His speeches were always carefully prepared beforehand.

Preparations for war are manifest on our frontiers; and we hear of renewed plots against liberty. Our armies reassemble; mighty movements agitate the Empire. Martial law having become necessary, it has seemed to us just. But we have succeeded only in brandishing for a moment the thunderbolt in the eyes of rebellion. The sanction of the King has been refused to our decrees. The princes of Germany make their territory a retreat for the conspirators against you. They favor the plots of the emigrants. They furnish them an asylum—they furnish them gold, arms, horses, and munitions. Is not the patience suicidal which tolerates all this? Doubtless you have renounced all projects of conquest; but you have not promised to endure such insolent provocations. You have shaken off the yoke of your tyrants; but it was not to bend the knee to foreign despots.

2. But, beware! You are environed by snares. They seek to drive you, by disgust or lassitude, to a state of languor fatal to your courage,—or fatal to its right direction. They seek to separate you from us; they pursue a system of calumny against the National Assembly; they incriminate your Revolution in your eyes. O! beware of these attempts at panic! Repel, indignantly, these impostors, who, while they affect a hypocritical zeal for the Constitution, cease not to urge upon you the monarchy! The *monarchy!* With them it is the counter-revolution! The monarchy? It is the *nobility!* The counter-revolution—what is it but taxation, feudality, the Bastile, chains and executioners, to punish the sublime aspirations of liberty? What is it but foreign satellites in the midst of the State? What, but bankruptcy, engulfing, with your assignats, your private fortunes and the national wealth; what, but the furies of fanaticism and of vengeance,— assassinations, pillage, and incendiarism,—in short, despotism and death, disputing, over rivers of blood and heaps of carcasses, the dominion of your wretched country? The *nobility!* That is to say, two classes of men; the one for grandeur, the other for debase-

ment!—the one for tyranny, the other for servitude!
The nobility! Ah! *the very word is an insult to the
human race!*

And yet, it is in order to secure the success of those
conspiracies that Europe is now put in motion against
you! Be it so! By a solemn declaration must these
guilty hopes be crushed. Yes, the free representatives
of France, unshaken in their attachment to the Constitution, will be buried beneath its ruins, before they consent to a capitulation at once unworthy of them and of
you. Rally! Be reassured! They would raise the
Nations against you:—they will raise only princes.
The heart of every People is with you. It is *their*
cause which you embrace, in defending *your own.*
Ever abhorred be war! It is the greatest of the crimes
of men;—it is the most terrible scourge of humanity!
But, since you are irresistibly forced to it, yield to the
course of your destinies. Who can foresee where will
end the punishment of the tyrants who will have driven
you to take up arms?

AGAINST THE TERRORISM OF THE JACOBINS, 1792.—*Id.
Trans.*

The blinded Parisians presume to call themselves
free. Alas! it is true they are no longer the slaves of
crowned tyrants; but they are the slaves of men the
most vile, and of wretches the most detestable; men
who continue to imagine that the Revolution has been
made for themselves alone, and who have sent Louis

XVI. to the Temple, in order that *they* may be enthroned at the Tuileries! * It is time to break these disgraceful chains—to crush this new despotism. It is time that those who have made honest men tremble should be made to tremble in their turn. I am not ignorant that they have poniards at their service. On the night of the second of September—that night of proscription!—did they not seek to turn them against several deputies, and myself among the number? Were we not denounced to the People as traitors? Fortunately, it was the People into whose hands we fell. The assassins were elsewhere occupied. The voice of calumny failed of its effect. If *my* voice may yet make itself heard from this place, I call you all to witness, it shall not cease to thunder, with all its energy, against tyrants, whether of high or low degree. What to me their ruffians and their poniards? What his own life to the representative of the People, while the safety of the country is at stake?

When William Tell adjusted the arrow which was to pierce the fatal apple that a tyrant had placed on his son's head, he exclaimed, " Perish my name, and perish my memory, provided Switzerland may be free!" And we, also,—*we* will say, " Perish the National Assembly and its memory, provided France may be free!"† Ay, perish the National Assembly. and its

---

* Pronounced *Tweedree.*

† The deputies here rose, as by an unanimous impulse, and repeated, with enthusiasm, the oath of Vergniaud. The audience, who occupied the galleries, also mingled their voices with those of the deputies. To appreciate fully the intrepid eloquence of this speech, it should be remembered that France was at that moment

memory, so by its death it may save the Nation from a course of crime that would affix an eternal stigma to the French name; so, by its action, it may show the Nations of Europe that, despite the calumnies by which it is sought to dishonor France, there is still in the very bosom of that momentary anarchy where the brigands have plunged us—there is still in our country some public virtue, some respect for humanity left! Perish the National Assembly and its memory, if upon on. ashes our more fortunate successors may establish the edifice of a Constitution, which shall assure the happiness of France, and consolidate the reign of liberty and equality!

THE SPIRIT OF DEMOCRACY IN AMERICA AND IN EUROPE

The American who respects the law of God respects also the law of man; and if he believes it unjust, he reserves himself to obtain the repeal of it some day, not by violence, but in making for himself a peaceful and sure arm of all those means of persuasion which intelligence gives a man, and by the still more powerful means which he is able to possess from a tried devotion to the cause of justice.

2. To the European democrat I may say still, with necessary exceptions, the law is only a decree rendered by force, and which force has the right to overthrow.

---

virtually under the sanguinary dictatorship of the Jacobin Club; and that their proscriptions and massacres threatened to involve all who did not acquiesce in their measures. Vergniaud soon afterward paid the penalty of his courage; and justified his bold words by a bold death on the scaffold.

Was it an entire people who had given their assent and their sanction, he pretends that a minority, or even a single man, has the right to oppose to it the protestation of the sword, and to tear in blood a paper which has no other value than the want of power to replace it by another.

3. The American, come from a land where the aristocracy of birth always enjoyed a considerable part in public affairs, has cast away from his institutions the hereditary nobility, and reserved to personal merit the honor of governing.

4. But at the same time that he is passionately devoted to the equality of conditions, whether he considers it in a point of view derived from God, or in the point of view of a man, he does not estimate liberty at a less price, and, if the occasion presented itself for choosing between one and the other, he would do as the mother did in the judgment of Solomon : he would say to God and the world, "Do not separate them, because they have but one life in my soul; and I wil die the day that one dies."

5. The European democrat does not understand it thus. In his eyes equality is the grand and supreme law, that which prevails over all others, and to which all should be sacrificed. Equality in servitude appears preferable to him to liberty sustained by a hierarchy of ranks. He likes much better Tiberius ruling a multitude which no longer possess either rights or a name, to the Roman people governed by a patrician class, and receiving from it the impulse which makes them free with the reign which makes them strong.

6. The American leaves nothing to the mercy of an arbitrary power. He understands that, commencing with his soul, all that belongs to and surrounds him should be free—family, commerce, province, association for letters or science, for the worship of his God or the well-being of his body.

7. The European democrat, idolater of what he calls the State, takes the man from his infancy to offer him as a holocaust to public omnipotence.

8. He pretends that the infant, before seeing the property of the family, is the property of the city, and the city—that is, the people represented by those who govern it—has the right to form his intellect on a uniform and equal model. He pretends that the commune, the province, and every association, even the most indifferent, depend on the State, and can neither act, speak, sell, buy, nor, in fine, exist without the intervention of the State, and only within the bonds determined by it, making thus the most absolute civil servitude the vestibule and foundation of political liberty.

9. The American gives to the unity of the country only just what is necessary to make it a body; the European democrat oppresses every man in order to create for him, under the name of country, a narrow prison.

10. If, finally, gentlemen, we compare the results, American democracy has founded a great people—religious, powerful, respected; free, in fine, although not without trials and perils. European democracy has broken the ties that connect the present with the past, buried abuses in ruins, raised up here and there a pre-

carious liberty, agitated the world by events much more than it has renewed it by institutions; and, incontestable master of the future, it prepares for us, if not instructed, the frightful alternative of a demagogy without foundations, or a despotism without curb.

LECORDAIRE.

THE DEATH OF O'CONNELL.

There is sad news from Genoa. An aged and weary pilgrim, who can travel no further, passes beneath the gate of one of her ancient palaces, saying with pious resignation as he enters its silent chambers, "Well, it is God's will that I shall never see Rome. I am disappointed. But I am ready to die. It is all right." The superb though fading queen of the Mediterranean holds anxious watch, through ten long days, over that majestic stranger's wasting frame. And now death is there—the Liberator of Ireland has sunk to rest in the Cradle of Columbus.

2. Coincidence beautiful and most sublime! It was the very day set apart by the elder daughter of the Church for prayer and sacrifice throughout the world, for the children of the sacred island, perishing by famine and pestilence in their homes and in their native fields, and on their crowded paths of exile, on the sea and in the havens, and on the lakes, and along the rivers of this far-distant land. The chimes rung out by pity for his countrymen were O'Connell's fitting knell; his soul went forth on clouds of incense that rose from altars of Christian charity; and the mourn-

ful anthems which recited the faith, and the virtue, and the endurance of Ireland, were his becoming requiem.

3. It is a holy sight to see the obsequies of a soldier, not only of civil liberty, but of the liberty of conscience —of a soldier, not only of freedom, but of the Cross of Christ—of a benefactor, not merely of a race of people, but of mankind. The vault lighted by suspended worlds is the temple within which the great solemnities are celebrated. The nations of the earth are mourners; and the spirits of the just made perfect, descending from their golden thrones on high, break forth into songs.

4. Behold now a nation which needeth not to speak its melancholy precedence. The lament of Ireland comes forth from palaces deserted, and from shrines restored; from Boyne's dark water, witness of her desolation, and from Tara's lofty hill, ever echoing her renown. But louder and deeper yet that wailing comes from the lonely huts on mountain and on moor, where the people of the greenest island of all the seas are expiring in the midst of insufficient though world-wide charities. Well indeed may they deplore O'Connell, for they were his children; and he bore them

> " A love so vehement, so strong, so pure,
> That neither age could change nor art could cure."

W. H. SEWARD.

DECLARATION OF IRISH RIGHTS, 1780.—*Henry Grattan.*

Henry Grattan, one of the most renowned of Irish orators, was born in Dublin, on the 3d of July, 1746, and died in 1820. In December, 1775, he took his seat in the Irish House of Commons; and from that time till 1800, he figured politically in that body chiefly. The Irish Revolution of 1782 was carried mainly by his efforts. Although a Protestant, he was a most earnest advocate of the entire emancipation of the Catholics from all invidious distinctions and disabilities. In 1805 Grattan took his seat in the British Parliament, where he became the leading Champion of Catholic rights. The passages from his speeches in this collection bearing date anterior to 1805, were pronounced in the Irish Parliament; those of a subsequent date, were delivered before the popular branch of the Imperial Parliament. Of Grattan we may add, in the words of the Rev. Sydney Smith :—"No Government ever dismayed him; the world could not bribe him : he thought only of Ireland; lived for no other object; dedicated to her his beautiful fancy, his manly courage, and all the splendor of his astonishing eloquence."

Sir, I have entreated an attendance on this day, that you might, in the most public manner, deny the claim of the British Parliament to make law for Ireland, and with one voice lift up your hands against it. England now smarts under the lesson of the American war; her enemies are a host, pouring upon her from all quarters of the earth; her armies are dispersed; the sea is not hers; she has no minister, no ally, no admiral, none in whom she long confides, and no general whom she has not disgraced; the balance of her fate is in the hands of Ireland; you are not only her last connection,—you are the only nation in Europe that is not her enemy. Let corruption tremble; but let the friends of liberty rejoice at these means of safety, and this hour of redemption. You have done too much not to do more; you have gone too far not to go on; you have brought yourselves into that situation in which you must silently abdicate the rights of your country, or publicly restore them. Where is the freedom of trade? Where is the security of property? Where is the liberty of the People? I therefore say, nothing is safe, satisfactory, or honorable, nothing except a declaration of rights. What! are you, with three hundred thousand men at your back, with charters in one hand and arms in the other, afraid to say you are a free People? If England is a tyrant, it is you have made her so; it is the slave that makes the tyrant, and then murmurs at the master whom he himself has constituted.

The British minister mistakes the Irish character; had he intended to make Ireland a slave, he should have kept her a beggar. There is no middle policy: win her heart by the restoration of her rights, or cut off the Nation's right hand; greatly emancipate, or fundamentally destroy. We may talk plausibly to England, but so long as she exercises a power to bind this country, so long are the Nations in a state of war; the claims of the one go against the liberty of the other, and the sentiments of the latter go to oppose those claims to the last drop of her blood. The English opposition, therefore, are right; mere trade will not satisfy Ireland. They judge of us by other great Nations; by the Nation whose political life has been a struggle for liberty,—America! They judge of us with a true knowledge and just deference for our character; that a country enlightened as Ireland, chartered as treland, armed as Ireland, and injured as Ireland, will be satisfied with nothing less than liberty.

I might, as a constituent, come to your bar and demand my liberty.

REPLY TO MR. FLOOD, 1783.—*Henry Grattan.*

At the time of this speech in the Irish Parliament, Flood and Grattan, although previously friends, stood before the Irish people as rival leaders. A bitter animosity had arisen between them; and Grattan having unfortunately led the way in personality, by speaking of his opponent's "affectation of infirmity," Flood replied with great asperity, denouncing Grattan as "a mendicant patriot," who, "bought by his country for a sum of money, then sold his country for prompt payment." He also sneered at Grattan's "aping the style of Lord Chatham." To these taunts Grattan replied in a speech, an abridgment of which we here give. An arrangement for a hostile meeting between the parties was the consequence of this speech; but Flood was arrested, and the crime of a duel was not added to the offence of vindictive personality, of which both had been guilty. Grattan lived to regret his harshness, and speak in generous terms of his rival.

It is not the slander of an evil tongue that can defame me. I maintain my reputation in public and in private life. No man, who has not a bad character, can ever say that I deceived. No country can call me a cheat. But I will suppose such a public character. I will suppose such a man to have existence. I will begin with his character in his political cradle, and I will follow him to the last stage of political dissolution. I will suppose him, in the first stage of his life, to have been intemperate; in the second, to have been corrupt; and in the last, seditious;—that, after an envenomed

attack on the persons and measures of a succession of
viceroys, and after much declamation against their ille-
galities and their profusion, he took office, and became
a supporter of Government, when the profusion of ministers had greatly increased, and their crimes multiplied
beyond example.

With regard to the liberties of America, which were
inseparable from ours, I will suppose this gentleman to
have been an enemy decided and unreserved; that he
voted against her liberty, and voted, moreover, for an
address to send four thousand Irish troops to cut the
throats of the Americans; that he called these butchers
" armed negotiators," and stood with a metaphor in his
mouth and a bribe in his pocket, a champion against
the rights of America,—of America, the only hope of
Ireland, and the only refuge of the liberties of mankind. Thus defective in every relationship, whether to
constitution, commerce, and toleration, I will suppose
this man to have added much private improbity to
public crimes; that his probity was like his patriotism,
and his honor on a level with his oath. He loves to
deliver panegyrics on himself. I will interrupt him,
and say:

Sir, you are much mistaken if you think that your
talents have been as great as your life has been repre-
hensible. You began your parliamentary career with
an acrimony and personality which could have been
justified only by a supposition of virtue; after a rank
and clamorous opposition you became, on a sudden,
silent; you were silent for seven years; you were silent on the greater questions, and you were silent for

money! You supported the unparalleled profusion and jobbing of Lord Harcourt's scandalous ministry. You, sir, who manufacture stage thunder against Mr. Eden for his anti-American principles,—you, sir, whom it pleases to chant a hymn to the immortal Hampden,— you, sir, approved of the tyranny exercised against America,—and you, sir, voted four thousand Irish troops to cut the throats of the Americans fighting for their freedom, fighting for your freedom, fighting for the great principle, *liberty!* But you found, at last, that the Court had bought, but would not trust you. Mortified at the discovery, you try the sorry game of a trimmer in your progress to the acts of an incendiary; and observing, with regard to Prince and People, the most impartial treachery and desertion, you justify the suspicion of your Sovereign by betraying the Government, as you had sold the People. Such has been your conduct, and at such conduct every order of your fellow-subjects have a right to exclaim! The merchant may say to you, the constitutionalist may say to you, the American may say to you,—and I, I now say, and say to your beard—Sir, you are not an honest man.

NATIONAL GRATITUDE, 1780.—*Henry Grattan.*

I shall hear of ingratitude. I name the argument to despise it, and the men who make use of it. I know the men who use it are not grateful: they are insatiate; they are public extortioners, who would stop the tide of public prosperity, and turn it to the channel of their own emolument. I know of no species of gratitude

which should.prevent my country from being free; no
gratitude which should oblige Ireland to be the slave
of England. In cases of robbery and usurpation,
nothing is an object of gratitude except the thing
stolen, the charter spoliated. A nation's liberty cannot, like her treasure, be meted and parcelled out in
gratitude. No man can be grateful or liberal of his
conscience, nor woman of her honor, nor nation of her
liberty. There are certain unimpartable, inherent, invaluable properties, not to be alienated from the person, whether body politic or body natural. With the
same contempt do I treat that charge which says that
Ireland is insatiable; saying that Ireland asks nothing
but that which Great Britain has robbed her of,—her
rights and privileges. To say that Ireland will not be
satisfied with liberty, because she is not satisfied with
slavery, is folly. I laugh at that man who supposes
that Ireland will not be content with a free trade and
a free constitution; and would any man advise her to
be content with less?

DISQUALIFICATION OF ROMAN CATHOLICS, 1793.—*Henry
Grattan.*

You are struggling with difficulties, you imagine;
you are mistaken,—you are struggling with impossibilities. In making laws on the subject of religion,
legislators forget mankind, until their own distraction
admonishes them of two truths,—the one that there is
a God; the other, that there is a people! Never was
it permitted to any nation,—they may perplex their

understandings with various apologies,—but 1 ever was it long permitted to exclude from essential—from what they themselves have pronounced essential blessings— a great portion of themselves for a period of time; and for no reason, or, what is worse, for such reasons as you have advanced.

Conquerors, or tyrants proceeding from conquerors, have scarcely ever for any length of time governed by those partial disabilities; but a people so to govern itself, or, rather, under the name of government, so to exclude itself—the industrious, the opulent, the useful —that part that feeds you with its industry, and supplies you with its taxes, weaves that you may wear, and ploughs that you may eat,—to exclude a body so useful, so numerous, and that forever!—and in the mean time to tax them *ad libitum*, and occasionally to pledge their lives and fortunes!--for what?—for their disfranchisement?—it cannot be done! Continue it, and you expect from your laws what it were blasphemy to ask of your Maker. Such a policy always turns on the inventor, and bruises him under the stroke of the sceptre or the sword, or sinks him under accumulations of debt and loss of dominion. Need I go to instances? What was the case of Ireland, enslaved for a century, and withered and blasted with her Protestant ascendency, like a shattered oak scathed on its hill by the fires of its own intolerance? What lost England America, but such a policy? An attempt to bind men by a parliament wherein they are not represented! Such an attempt as some would now continue to practise on the Catholics. Has your pity traversed leagues of sea

to sit down by the black boy on the coast of Guinea,—
and have you forgot the man at home by your side,
your brother?

HEAVEN FIGHTS ON THE SIDE OF A GREAT PRINCIPLE.—
Grattan.

The Kingdom of Ireland, with her imperial crown,
stands at your Bar. She applies for the civil liberty of
three-fourths of her children. Will you dismiss her
without a hearing? You cannot do it! I say you cannot finally do it! The interest of your country would
not support you; the feelings of your country would
not support you: it is a proceeding that cannot long
be persisted in. No courtier so devoted, no politician
so hardened, no conscience so capacious! I am not
afraid of occasional majorities. A majority cannot
overlay a great principle. God will guard his own
cause against rank majorities. In vain shall men appeal to a church-cry, or to a mock thunder; the pro
prietor of the bolt is on the side of the people.

It was the expectation of the repeal of Catholic dis-
ability which carried the Union. Should you wish to
support the minister of the crown against the People
of Ireland, retain the Union, and perpetuate the disqualification, the consequence must be something more
than alienation. When you finally decide against the
Catholic question, you abandon the idea of governing
Ireland by affection, and you adopt the idea of coercion
in its place. You are pronouncing the doom of England. If you ask how the People of Ireland feel
towards you, ask yourselves how you would feel towards

us, if we disqualified three-fourths of the People of England forever. The day you finally ascertain the disqualification of the Catholic, you pronounce the doom of Great Britain. It is just it should be so. The King who takes away the liberty of his subjects loses his Crown; the People who take away the liberty of their fellow-subjects lose their empire. The scales of your own destinies are in your own hands; and if you throw out the civil liberty of the Irish Catholic, depend on it, Old England will be weighed in the balance, and found wanting: you will then have dug your own grave, and you may write your own epitaph thus:—
" ENGLAND DIED, BECAUSE SHE TAXED AMERICA AND DIS-QUALIFIED IRELAND."

UNION WITH GREAT BRITAIN, 1800.—*Henry Grattan.*

The minister misrepresents the sentiments of the People, as he has before traduced their reputation. He asserts, that after a calm and mature consideration, they have pronounced their judgment in favor of an Union. Of this assertion not one syllable has any existence in fact, or in the appearance of fact. I appeal to the petitions of twenty-one counties in evidence. To affirm that the judgment of a Nation *against* is *for;* to assert that she has said *ay* when she has pronounced *no;* to make the falsification of her sentiments the foundation of her ruin and the ground of the Union ‧ to affirm that her Parliament, Constitution, liberty, honor, property, are taken away by her own authority

—there is, in such artifice, an effrontery, a hardi
hood, an insensibility, that can best be answered by
sensations of astonishment and disgust.

The Constitution may be *for a time* so lost. The
character of the country cannot be so lost.   The min
isters of the Crown will, or may, perhaps, at length
find that it is not so easy, by abilities however great,
and by power and corruption however irresistible, to
put down forever an ancient and respectable Nation.
Liberty may repair her golden beams, and with re-
doubled heat animate the country.   The cry of loyalty
will not long continue against the principles of liberty.
Loyalty is a noble, a judicious, and a capacious principle ; but in these countries loyalty, distinct from liberty, is corruption, not loyalty.

The cry of disaffection will not, in the end, avail
against the principle of liberty.   I do not give up the
country.   I see her in a swoon, but she is not dead.
Though in her tomb she lies helpless and motionless,
still there is on her lips a spirit of life, and on her
cheek a glow of beauty :—

> " Thou art not conquered ; beauty's ensign yet
> Is crimson in thy lips, and in thy cheeks,
> And Death's pale flag is not advanced there."

While a plank of the vessel sticks together, I will not
leave her.   Let the courtier present his flimsy sail, and
carry the light bark of his faith with every new breath
of wind ; I will remain anchored here, with fidelity to
the fortunes of my country, faithful to her freedom,
faithful to her fall !

THE CATHOLIC QUESTION, 1805.—*Henry Grattan.*

The Parliament of Ireland!—of that assembly I have a parental recollection. I sat by her cradle,—I followed her hearse. ·In fourteen years she acquired for Ireland what you did not acquire for England in a century,—freedom of trade, independency of the Legislature, independency of the judges, restoration of the final judicature, repeal of a perpetual mutiny bill, habeas corpus act, nullum tempus act—a great work! You will exceed it, and I shall rejoice. I call my countrymen to witness, if in that business I compromised the claims of my country, or temporized with the power of England; but there was one thing which baffled the effort of the patriot, and defeated the wisdom of the Senate,—it was the folly of the theologian! When the Parliament of Ireland rejected the Catholic petition, and assented to the calumnies then uttered against the Catholic body, on that day she voted the Union: if you should adopt a similar conduct, on that day you will vote the separation. Many good and pious reasons you may give; many good and pious reasons *she* gave; and she lies THERE, with her many good and pious reasons! That the Parliament of Ireland should have entertained prejudices, I am not astonished; but that you,—that you, who have as individuals and as conquerors, visited a great part of the globe, and have seen men in all their modifications, and Providence in all her ways,—that you, now, at this time of day, should throw up dikes against the Pope, and barriers against the Catholic, instead of uniting with that Catholic to throw up barriers against the French, this surprises; and, in addition to this, that you should have set up the Pope in Italy to tremble at him in Ireland; and further, that you should have professed to have placed yourself at the head of a Christian, not a Protestant league, to defend the civil and religious liberty of Europe, and should deprive of their civil liberty one-fifth of yourselves, on account of their religion, —this— this surprises me !

This prescriptive system you may now remove. What the best men in Ireland wished to do, but could not do, you may accomplish. Were it not wise to come to a good understanding with the Irish now ? The franchises of the Constitution !—your ancestors were nursed in that cradle. The ancestors of the petitioners were less fortunate. The posterity of both, born to new and strange dangers,—let them agree to renounce jealousies and proscriptions, in order to oppose what, without that agreement, will overpower both. Half Europe is in battalion against us, and we are devoting one another to perdition on account of mysteries,— when we should form against the enemy, and march !

RELIGION INDEPENDENT OF GOVERNMENT, 1811.—*Henry Grattan.*

Let us reflect on the necessary limits of all human legislation. No Legislature has a right to make partial laws ; it has no right to make arbitrary laws—I mean laws contrary to reason; because that is beyond the power of the Deity   Neither has it a right to institute any inquisition into men's thoughts, nor to punish any man merely for his religion. It can have no power to make a religion for men, since that would be to dethrone the Almighty. I presume it will not be arrogated, on the part of the British Legislature, that his Majesty, by and with the advice of the Lords spiritual and temporal, etc., can enact that he will appoint and constitute a new religion for the People of this empire; or that, by an order in Council, the consciences and creeds of his subjects might be suspended. Nor will it be contended, I apprehend, that any authoritative or legislative measure could alter the law of the hypothenuse. Whatever belongs to the authority of God, or to the laws of nature, is necessarily beyond the province and sphere of human institution and government. The Roman Catholic, when you disqualify him on the ground of his religion, may, with great justice, tell you that you are not his God, that he cannot mould or fashion his faith by your decrees. When once man goes out of his sphere, and says he will legislate for God, he would, in fact, make himself God.

But this I do not charge upon the Parliament, because, in none of the penal acts, has the Parliament imposed a religious creed. The qualifying oath, as to the great number of offices, and as to seats in Parliaments, scrupulously evades religious distinctions. A Dissenter of any class may take it. A Deist, an Atheist, may likewise take it. The Catholics are alone excepted; and for what reason? If a Deist be fit to sit in Parliament, it can hardly be urged that a Christian is unfit! If an Atheist be competent to legislate

for his country, surely this privilege cannot in denied
to the believer in the divinity of our Saviour! If it be
contended that, to support the Church, it is expedient
to continue these disabilities, I dissent from that opin
ion. If it could, indeed, be proved, I should say that
you had acted in defiance of all the principles of
human justice and freedom, in having taken away their
Church from the Irish, in order to establish your own;
and in afterwards attempting to secure that establishment by disqualifying the People, and compelling them
at the same time to pay for its support. This is to fly
directly in the face of the plainest canons of the Almighty. For the benefit of eleven hundred, to disqualify four or five millions, is the insolent effort of
bigotry, not the benignant precept of Christianity;
and all this, not for the preservation of their property,
—for that was secured,—but for bigotry, for intolerance, for avarice, for a vile, abominable, illegitimate,
and atrocious usurpation. The laws of God cry out
against it; the spirit of Christianity cries out against
it; the laws of England, and the spirit and principles
of its Constitution, cry out against such a system.

SECTARIAN TYRANNY, 1812.--*Henry Grattan.*

Whenever one sect degrades another on account of
religion, such degradation is the tyranny of a sect.
When you enact that, on account of his religion, no
Catholic shall sit in Parliament, you do what amounts
to the tyranny of a sect. When you enact that no
Catholic shall be a sheriff, you do what amounts to the

tyranny of a sect. When you enact that no Catholic shall be a general, you do what amounts to the tyranny of a sect. There are two descriptions of laws—the municipal law, which binds the People, and the law of God, which binds the Parliament and the People. Whenever you do an act which is contrary to His laws, as expressed in His work, which is the world, or in His book, the Bible, you exceed your right; whenever you rest any of your establishments on that excess, you rest it on a foundation which is weak and fallacious; whenever you attempt to establish your government, or your property, or your church, on religious restrictions, you establish them on that false foundation, and you oppose the Almighty; and though you had a host of mitres on your side, you banish God from your ecclesiastical constitution, and freedom from your political. In vain shall men endeavor to make this the cause of the Church; they aggravate the crime by the endeavor to make their God their fellow in the injustice. Such rights are the rights of ambition; they are the rights of conquest; and in your case, they have been the rights of suicide. They begin by attacking liberty; they end by the loss of empire!

MAGNANIMITY IN POLITICS, 1775.—*Edmund Burke.* *Born,* 1730; *died,* 1797.

A revenue from America, transmitted hither? Do not delude yourselves! You never can receive it—no, not a shilling! Let the Colonies always keep the idea of their civil rights associated with your government,

and they will cling and grapple to you. These are ties
which, though light as air, are strong as links of iron.
But let it once be understood that your government
may be one thing and their privileges another, the ce-
ment is gone, the cohesion is loosened. Do not entertain so weak an imagination as that your registers and
your bonds, your affidavits and your sufferances, your
cockets and your clearances, are wl.at form the great
securities of your commerce. These things do not
make your government. Dead instruments, passive
tools, as they are, it is the spirit of the English communion that gives all their life and efficacy to them.
It is the spirit of the English Constitution which, in
fused through the mighty mass, pervades, feeds, unites,
invigorates, vivifies, every part of the Empire, even
down to the minutest member.

Do you imagine that it is the land-tax which raises
your revenue? that it is the annual vote in the committee of supply which gives you your army? or that
it is the mutiny bill which inspires it with bravery and
discipline? No! Surely no! It is the love of the
People; it is their attachment to their Government,
from the sense of the deep stake they have in such a
glorious institution, which gives you your army and
your navy, and infuses into both that liberal obedience,
without which your army would be a base rabble, and
your navy nothing but rotten timber.

All this, I know well enough, will sound wild and
chimerical to the profane herd of those vulgar and
mechanical politicians, who have no place among us;
a sort of people who think that nothing exists but what

is gross and material; and who, therefore, far from
being qualified to be directors of the great movement
of empire, are not fit to turn a wheel in the machine.
But to men truly initiated and rightly taught, these
ruling and master principles which, in the opinion of
such men as I have mentioned, have no substantial ex
istence, are, in truth, everything, and all in all. Magnanimity in politics is not seldom the truest wisdom;
and a great empire and little minds go ill together.
Let us get an American revenue as we have got an
American empire. English privileges have made it
all that it is; English privileges alone will make it all
it can be!

ENTERPRISE OF AMERICAN COLONISTS, 1775.—*Edmund Burke.*

Burke, the greatest of Irish statesmen, and unsurpassed as a writer
of English prose, impaired his immediate success as a speaker by a
badly-regulated voice and an infelicitous delivery. Grattan, his
countryman and contemporary, wrote of him: "Burke is unques-
tionably the first orator of the Commons of England, notwithstanding the want of energy, the want of grace, and the want of elegance,
in his manner." "He was a prodigy of nature and of acquisition.
He read everything—he saw everything. His knowlege of history
amounted to a power of foretelling; and when he perceived the
wild work that was doing in France, that great political physician,
cognizant of symptoms, distinguished between the access of fever
and the force of health, and what others conceived to be the vigor
of her constitution he knew to be the paroxysm of her madness;
and then, prophet-like, he pronounced the destinies of France, and
in his prophetic fury admonished nations."

For some time past, Mr. Speaker, has the Old World
been fed from the New. The scarcity which you have

felt would have been a desolating famine, if this child of your old age—if America—with a true filial piety, with a Roman charity, had not put the full breast of its youthful exuberance to the mouth of its exhausted parent. Turning from the agricultural resources of the Colonies, consider the wealth which they have drawn from the sea by their fisheries. The spirit in which that enterprising employment has been exercised ought to raise your esteem and admiration. Pray, sir, what in the world is equal to it? Pass by the other parts, and look at the manner in which the people of New England have of late carried on the whale fishery. Whilst we follow them among the tumbling mountains of ice, and behold them penetrating into the deepest frozen recesses of Hudson's Bay and Davis' Straits, whilst we are looking for them beneath the Arctic Circle, we hear that they have pierced into the opposite region of Polar cold, that they are at the antipodes, and engaged under the frozen serpent of the South. Falkland Island, which seemed too remote and romantic an object for the grasp of national ambition, is but a stage and resting-place in the progress of their victorious industry. Nor is the equinoctial heat more discouraging to them than the accumulated winter of both the poles. We know that whilst some of them draw the line and strike the harpoon on the coast of Africa, others run the longitude, and pursue their gigantic game along the coast of Brazil. No sea but what is vexed by their fisheries. No climate that is not witness to their toils. Neither the perseverance of Holland, nor the activity of France, nor the dexterous and firm sagacity of English enterprise, ever carried this most perilous mode of hardy industry to the extent to which it has been pushed by this recent people: a people who are still, as it were, but in the gristle, and not yet hardened into the bone of manhood.

When I contemplate these things,—when I know that the colonies in general owe little or nothing to any care of ours, and that they are not squeezed into this happy form by the constraints of a watchful and suspicious government, but that; through a wise and salutary neglect, a generous nature has been suffered to take her own way to perfection,—when I reflect upon these effects, when I see how profitable they have been to us, I feel all the pride of power sink, and all presumption in the wisdom of human contrivances melt and die away within me. My rigor relents. I pardon something to the spirit of liberty.

DESPOTISM INCOMPATIBLE WITH RIGHTS, 1788.—*Id.*

My Lords, you have now heard the principles on which Mr. Hastings governs the part of Asia subjected to the British empire. Here he has declared his opinion, that he is a despotic prince ; that he is to use arbitrary power ; and, of course, all his acts are covered with that shield. "I know," says he, "the Constitution of Asia only from its practice." Will your Lordships submit to hear the corrupt practices of mankind made the principles of Government ? *He* have arbitrary power !—My Lords, the East India Company have

not arbitrary power to give him; the King has no ar
bitrary power to give him; your Lordships have not;
nor the Commons; nor the whole Legislature. We
have no arbitrary power to give, because arbitrary
power is a thing which neither any man can hold nor
any man can give. No man can lawfully govern himself according to his own will,—much less can one person be governed by the will of another. We are all
born in subjection,—all born equally, high and low,
governors and governed, in subjection to one great,
immutable, pre-existent law, prior to all our devices,
and prior to all our contrivances, paramount to all our
ideas and to all our sensations, antecedent to our very
existence, by which we are knit and connected in the
eternal frame of the universe, out of which we cannot
stir.

This great law does not arise from our convention
or compacts; on the contrary, it gives to our conven-
tions and compacts all the force and sanction they can
have;—it does not arise from our vain institutions.
Every good gift is of God; all power is of God;—and
He who has given the power, and from whom alone it
originates, will never suffer the exercise of it to be
practised upon any less solid foundation than the power
itself. If, then, all dominion of man over man is the
effect of the divine disposition, it is bound by the eternal laws of Him that gave it, with which no human
authority can dispense; neither he that exercises it,
nor even those who are subject to it; and, if they were
mad enough to make an express compact, that should
release their magistrate from his duty, and should de-

clare their lives, liberties, and properties dependent upon, not rules and laws, but his mere capricious will, that covenant would be void.

This arbitrary power is not to be had by conquest. Nor can any sovereign have it by succession; for no man can succeed to fraud, rapine, and violence. Those who give and those who receive arbitrary power are alike criminal; and there is no man but is bound to resist it to the best of his power, wherever it shall show its face to the world.

Law and arbitrary power are in eternal enmity. Name me a magistrate, and I will name property; name me power, and I will name protection. It is a contradiction in terms, it is blasphemy in religion, it is wickedness in politics, to say that any man can have arbitrary power. In every patent of office the duty is included. For what else does a magistrate exist? To suppose for power, is an absurdity in idea. Judges are guided and governed by the eternal laws of justice, to which we are all subject. We may bite our chains, if we will; but we shall be made to know ourselves, and be taught that man is born to be governed by *law;* and he that will substitute *will* in the place of it is an enemy to God.

IMPEACHMENT OF WARREN HASTINGS, 1788.—*Id.*

The unremitting energy of Burke's appeals, in the prosecution of
Hastings, was a subject of wonder at the time, and is a lasting me-
morial of his zeal in what he believed an honest cause, for the admiration of posterity.   Hastings himself has said of Burke's eloquence
against him,—" For the first half hour, I looked up to the orator in
a revery of wonder; and, during that time, I felt myself the most
culpable man on earth."   The trial of Warren Hastings commenced
in Westminster Hall, Feb. 18, 1788.   The whole process occupied
ten years, from 1785 to 1795.   On the 23d of April, 1790, Hastings
was acquitted by a large majority of the Peers.

My Lords, I do not mean now to go further than
just to remind your Lordships of this,—that Mr. Hastings' government was one whole system of oppression,
of robbery of individuals, of spoliation of the public,
and of supersession of the whole system of the English
Government, in order to vest in the worst of the natives
all the power that could possibly exist in any Govern
ment; in order to defeat the ends which all govern
ments ought, in common, to have in view.   In the
name of the Commons of England, I charge all this
villany upon Warren Hastings, in this last moment of
my application to you.

My Lords, what is it that we want here, to a great
act of national justice?   Do we want a cause, my
Lords?   You have the cause of oppressed princes, of
undone women of the first rank, of desolated Provinces,
and of wasted Kingdoms.

Do you want a criminal, my Lords?   When was
there so much iniquity ever laid to the charge of any
one?   No, my Lords, you must not look to punish any

other such delinquent from India. Warren Hastings has not left substance enough in India to nourish such another delinquent.

My Lords, is it a prosecutor you want? You have before you the Commons of Great Britain as prosecutors; and I believe, my Lords, that the sun, in his bene - ficent progress round the world, does not behold a more glorious sight than that of men, separated from a re- mote people by the material bounds and barriers of na ture, united by the bond of a social and moral com- munity; all the Commons of England resenting, as their own, the indignities and cruelties that are offered to all the people of India.

Do we want a tribunal? My Lords, no example of antiquity, nothing in the modern world, nothing in the range of human imagination, can supply us with a tribunal like this. We commit safely the interests of India and humanity into your hands. Therefore, it is with confidence that, ordered by the Commons,

I impeach Warren Hastings, Esquire, of high crimes and misdemeanors.

I impeach him in the name of the Commons of Great Britain in Parliament assembled, whose Parliamentary trust he has betrayed.

I impeach him in the name of all the Commons of Great Britain, whose national character he has dis- honored.

I impeach him in the name of the people in India, whose laws, rights, and liberties, he has subverted: whose properties he has destroyed; whose country he has laid waste and desolate.

I impeach him in the name and by virtue of those eternal laws of justice which he has violated.

I impeach him in the name of human nature itself, which he has cruelly outraged, injured, and oppressed, in both sexes, in every age, rank, situation, and condition of life.

PERORATION AGAINST WARREN HASTINGS.—*Edmund Burke.*

My Lords, at this awful close, in the name of the Commons, and surrounded by them, I attest the retiring, I attest the advancing generations, between which, as a link in the great chain of eternal order, we stand.

We call this Nation, we call the world to witness, that the Commons have shrunk from no labor; that we have been guilty of no prevarication, that we have made no compromise with crime; that we have not feared any odium whatsoever, in the long warfare which we have carried on with the crimes, with the vices, with the exorbitant wealth, with the enormous and overpowering influence of Eastern corruption.

My Lords, it has pleased Providence to place us in such a state that we appear every moment to be upon the verge of some great mutations. There is one thing, and one thing only, which defies all mutation: that which existed before the world, and will survive the fabric of the world itself,—I mean justice; that justice which, emanating from the Divinity, has a place in the breast of every one of us, given us for our guide with regard to ourselves and with regard to others, and which will stand, after this globe is burned to ashes, our advocate or our accuser, before the great Judge, when He comes to call upon us for the tenor of a well-spent life.

My Lords, the Commons will share in every fate with your Lordships; there is nothing sinister which can happen to you, in which we shall not all be involved; and, if it should so happen that we shall be subjected to some of those frightful changes which we have seen, —if it should happen that your Lordships, stripped of all the decorous distinctions of human society, should, by hands at once base and cruel, be led to those scaffolds and machines of murder upon which great kings and glorious queens have shed their blood, amidst the prelates, amidst the nobles, amidst the magistrates, who supported their thrones,—may you in those moments feel that consolation which I am persuaded they felt in the critical moments of their dreadful agony!

My Lords, if you must fall, may you so fall! but, if you stand,—and stand I trust you will,—together with the fortune of this ancient monarchy, together with the ancient laws and liberties of this great and illustrious Kingdom, may you stand as unimpeached in honor as in power; may you stand, not as a substitute for virtue, but as an ornament of virtue, as a security for virtue; may you stand long, and long stand the terror of tyrants; may you stand the refuge of afflicted Nations; may you stand a sacred temple, for the perpetual residence of an inviolable justice!

SATIRE ON THE PENSION SYSTEM, 1786.—*Curran.*

John Philpot Curran was born in Newcastle, Ireland, July 24th, 1750. "There never lived a greater advocate," says Charles Phillips; "certainly never one more suited to the country in which his lot was cast. His eloquence was copious, rapid, and ornate, and his powers of mimicry beyond all description." In his boyhood he had a confusion in his utterance, from which he was called by his school-fellows "stuttering Jack Curran." He employed every means to correct his elocution, and render it perfect. "He accustomed himself," says one of his biographers, "to speak very slowly, to correct his precipitate utterance. He practised before a glass, to make his gestures graceful. He spoke aloud the most celebrated orations. One piece,—the speech of Antony over the dead body of Cæsar,—he was never weary of repeating. This he recommended to his young friends at the bar, as a model of eloquence. And while he thus used art to smooth a channel for his thoughts to flow in, no man's eloquence ever issued more freshly and spontaneously from the heart. It was always the heart of the man that spoke." Curran died October 14th, 1817.

This polyglot of wealth, this museum of curiosities, the Pension List, embraces every link in the human chain, every description of men, women, and children, from the exalted excellence of a Hawke or a Rodney, to the debased situation of the lady who humbleth herself that she may be exalted. But the lessons it inculcates form its greatest perfection: It teacheth, that Sloth and Vice may eat that bread which Virtue and Honesty may starve for after they have earned it. It teaches the idle and dissolute to look up for that support which they are too proud to stoop and earn. It directs the minds of men to an entire reliance on the ruling Power of the State, who feeds the ravens of the Royal aviary, that cry continually for food. It teaches them to imitate those Saints on the Pension List, that are like the lilies of the field ; they toil not, neither do they spin, and yet are arrayed like Solomon in his glory. In fine, it teaches a lesson, which, indeed, they might have learned from Epictētus, that it is sometimes good not to be over-virtuous; it shows, that, in propor tion as our distresses increase, the munificence of the Crown increases also ; in proportion as our clothes are rent, the royal mantle is extended over us.

Notwithstanding that the Pension List, like charity, covers a 'multitude of sins, give me leave to consider it as coming home to the members of this House ;—give me leave to say, that the Crown, in extending its charity, its liberality, its profusion, is laying a foundation for the independence of Parliament; for, hereafter, instead of orators or patriots accounting for their con duct to such mean and unworthy persons as freehold ers, they will learn to despise them, and look to the first man in the State ; and they will, by so doing, have this security for their independence,—that while any man in the Kingdom has a shilling, they will not want one !

REPLY TO THREATS OF VIOLENCE, 1790.—*Curran.*

We have been told this night, in express words, that the man who dares to do his duty to his country in this House may expect to be attacked without these walls by the military gentlemen of the Castle. If the army had been directly or indirectly mentioned in the course of the debate, this extraordinary declaration might be
14*

attributable to the confusion of a mistaken charge, or an absurd vindication; but, without connection with the subject, a new principle of government is advanced, and that is—the bayonet! And this is stated in the fullest house, and the most crowded audience, I ever saw. We are to be silenced by corruption within, or quelled by force of arms without. If the strength of numbers or corruption should fail against the cause of the public, it is to be backed by assassination. Nor is it necessary that those avowed principles of bribery and arms should come from any high personal authority; they have been delivered by the known retainers of Administration, in the face of that bench, and heard even without a murmur of dissent or disapprobation.

For my part, I do not know how it may be my destiny to fall;—it may be by chance, or malady, or violence; but, should it be my fate to perish the victim of a bold and honest discharge of my duty, I will not shun it. I will do that duty; and, if it should expose me to sink under the blow of the assassin, and become a victim to the public cause, the most sensible of my regrets would be, that on such an altar there should not be immolated a more illustrious sacrifice. As to myself, while I live, I shall despise the peril. I feel in my own spirit the safety of my honor, and in my own and the spirit of the People do I feel strength enough to hold that Administration, which can give a sanction to menaces like these, responsible for their consequences to the Nation and the individual.

AGAINST RELIGIOUS DISTINCTIONS, 1796.—*Curran.*

Gentlemen say the Catholics have got everything but seats in Parliament. Are we really afraid of giving them that privilege? Are we seriously afraid that Catholic venality might pollute the immaculate integrity of the House of Commons?—that a Catholic member would be more accessible to a promise, or a pension, or a bribe, than a Protestant? Lay your hands upon your hearts, look in one another's faces, and say Yes, and 1 will vote against this amendment! But is it the fact that they have everything? Is it the fact that they have the common benefit of the Constitution, or the common protection of the law?

Another gentleman has said, the Catholics have got much, and ought to be content. Why have they got that much? Is it from the minister? Is it from the Parliament, which threw their petition over its bar? No,—they got it by the great revolution of human affairs; by the astonishing march of the human mind; a march that has collected too much momentum, in its advance, to be now stopped in its progress. The bark is still afloat; it is freighted with the hopes and liberties of millions of men; she is already under way; the rower may faint, or the wind may sleep, but, rely upon it, she has already acquired an energy of advancement that will support her course, and bring her to her destination; rely upon it, whether much or little remains, it is now vain to withhold it; rely upon it, you may as well stamp your foot upon the earth, in order to prevent its revolution. You cannot stop it! You will only remain a silly gnômon upon its surface, to meas ure the rapidity of rotation, until you are forced round and buried in the shade of that body whose irresistible course you would endeavor to oppose !

THE LIBERTY OF THE PRESS, 1794.—*John Philpot Curran.*

What, then, remains ? The liberty of the Press, *only,* —that sacred palladium, which no influence, no power, no minister, no Government, which nothing but the depravity or folly or corruption of a jury, can ever destroy. And what calamities are the People saved from, by having public communication left open to them ? I will tell you, Gentlemen, what they are saved from, and what the Government is saved from ; I will tell you, also, to what both are exposed by shutting up that communication. In one case, sedition speaks aloud, and walks abroad ; the demagogue goes forth,— the public eye is upon him,—he frets his busy hour upon the stage ; but soon either weariness, or bribe, or punishment, or disappointment, bears him down, or drives him off, and he appears no more. In the other case, how does the work of sedition go forward ? Night after night, the muffled rebel steals forth in the dark, and casts another and another brand upon the pile, to which, when the hour of fatal maturity shall arrive, he will apply the torch.

In that awful moment of a Nation's travail, of the last gasp of tyranny, and the first breath of freedom, how pregnant is the example ! The Press extinguished, the People enslaved, and the Prince undone! As the advocate of society, therefore, of peace, of domestic liberty, and the lasting union of the two countries, I conjure you to guard the liberty of the Press, that great sentinel of the State, that grand detector of public imposture! Guard it, because, when it sinks, there sinks with it, in one common grave, the liberty of the subject, and the security of the Crown!

DESCRIPTION OF MR. ROWAN, 1794.—*John Philpot Curran.*

Gentlemen, if you still have any doubt as to the guilt or innocence of the defendant, give me leave to suggest to you what circumstances you ought to consider, in order to found your verdict. You should consider the character of the person accused; and in this your task is easy. I will venture to say there is not a man in this Nation more known than the gentleman who is the subject of this prosecution; not only by the part he has taken in public concerns, and which he has taken in common with many, but still more so by that extraordinary sympathy for human affliction, which, I am sorry to think, he shares with so small a number. There is not a day that you hear the cries of your starving manufacturers in your streets, that you do not also see the advocate of their sufferings,—that you do not see his honest and manly figure, with uncovered head, soliciting for their relief,—searching the frozen heart of charity for every string that can be touched by compassion, and urging the force of every argument

and every motive, save that which his modesty sup-
presses, the authority of his own generous example.

Or, if you see him not there, you may trace his steps
to the private abodes of disease, and famine, and
despair,—the messenger of Heaven, bringing with him
food, and medicine, and consolation. Are these the
materials of which you suppose anarchy and public
rapine to be formed? Is this the man on whom to
fasten the abominable charge of goading on a frantic
populace to mutiny and bloodshed? Is this the man
likely to apostatize from every principle that can bind
him to the State—his birth, his property, his education,
his character, and his children? Let me tell you, gentlemen of the jury, if you agree with his prosecutors,
in thinking that there ought to be a sacrifice of such a
man on such an occasion. and upon the credit of such
evidence you are to convict him, never did you, never
can you give a sentence, consigning any man to public
punishment, with less danger to his person or to his
fame ; for where, to fling contumely or ingratitude at
his head, could the hireling be found, whose private
distresses he had not endeavored to alleviate, or whose
public condition he had not labored to improve?

I will not relinquish the confidence that this day will
be the period of my client's sufferings ; and that, however mercilessly he has been hitherto pursued, your
verdict will send him home to the arms of his family
and the wishes of his country. But if (which Heaven
forbid!) it hath still been unfortunately determined,
that, because he has not bent to power and authority,—
because he would not bow down before the golden calf,

and worship it,—he is to be bound and cast into the furnace, I do trust in God that there is a redeeming spirit in the Constitution, which will be seen to walk with the sufferer through the flames, and to preserve him unhurt by the conflagration !

THE HABEAS CORPUS ACT.—*John Philpot Curran, in the case of the King against Mr. Justice Johnson, Feb. 4th, 1805, before Chief Baron Lord Avonmore and the other Barons, in the Court of Exchequer.*

I now address you on a question the most vitally connected with the liberty and well-being of every man within the limits of the British empire ;—which being decided one way, he may be a freeman ; which being decided the other, he must be a slave. I refer to the maintenance of that sacred security for the freedom of Englishmen,—so justly called the second Magna Charta of British liberty,—the Habeas Corpus Act; the spirit and letter of which is, that the party arrested shall without a moment's delay, be bailed, if the offence be bailable. What was the occasion of the law? The arbitrary transportation of the subject beyond the, realm ; the base and malignant war which the odious and despicable minions of power are forever ready to wage against all those who are honest and bold enough to despise, to expose, and to resist them.

Such is the oscitancy of man, that he lies torpid for ages under these aggressions, until, at last, some signal abuse—the violation of Lucretia, the death of Virginia, the oppression of William Tell—shakes him from his

slumber. For years had those drunken gambols of
power been played in England; for years had the waters of bitterness been rising to the brim; at last, a
single drop caused them to overflow—the oppression of
a single individual raised the people of England from
their sleep. And what does that great statute do? It
defines and asserts the right, it points out the abuse;
and it endeavors to secure the right, and to guard
against the abuse, by giving redress to the suf
ferer, and by punishing the offender. For years had
it been the practice to transport obnoxious persons out
of the realm into distant parts, under the pretext of
punishment or of safe custody. Well might they
have been said to be sent "to that undiscovered country from whose bourne. no traveller returns:" for of
these wretched travellers how few ever did return?

But of that flagrant abuse this statute has laid the
axe to the root. It prohibits the abuse; it declares
such detention or removal illegal; it gives an action
against all persons concerned in the offence, by contriv-
ing, writing, signing, countersigning, such warrant, or
advising or assisting therein. Are bulwarks like these
ever constructed to repel the incursions of a contemptible enemy? Was it a trivial and ordinary occasion
which raised this storm of indignation in the Parliament of that day? Is the ocean ever lashed by the
tempest to waft a feather or to drown a fly? By this
act you have a solemn legislative declaration, "that it
is incompatible with liberty to send any subject out
of the realm, under pretence of any crime supposed
or alleged to be committed in a foreign jurisdiction,

except that crime be capital." Such were the bulwarks which our ancestors placed about the sacred temple of liberty, such the ramparts by which they sought to bar out the ever-toiling ocean of arbitrary power; and thought (generous credulity!) that they had barred it out from their posterity for ever. Little did they foresee the future race of vermin that would work their way through those mounds, and let back the in undation!

CURRAN'S APPEAL TO LORD AVONMORE.—*From the last-named Speech.*

I am not ignorant, my Lords, that the extraordinary construction of law against which I contend has received the sanction of another court, nor of the surprise and dismay with which it smote upon the general heart of the bar. I am aware that I may have the' mortification of being told, in another country, of that unhappy decision; and I foresee in what confusion I shall hang down my head when I am told it.

But I cherish, too, the consolatory hope, that I shall be able to tell them that I had an old and learned friend, whom I would put above all the sweepings of their hall, who was of a different opinion; who had derived his ideas of civil liberty from the purest fountains of Athens and of Rome; who had fed the youthful vigor of his studious mind with the theoretic knowledge of their wisest philosophers and statesmen, and who had refined that theory into the quick and ex quisite sensibility of moral instinct, by contemplating the practice of their most illustrious examples—by dwelling on the sweet-souled piety of Cimon, on the anticipated Christianity of Socrates, on the gallant and pathetic patriotism of Epaminondas, on that pure austerity of Fabricius, whom to move from his integrity would have been more difficult than to have pushed the sun from his course.

I would add, that, if he had seemed to hesitate, it was but for a moment; that his hesitation was like the passing cloud that floats across the morning sun and hides it from the view, and does so for a moment hide it, by involving the spectator, without even approaching the face of the luminary. And this soothing hope I draw from the dearest and tenderest recollections of my life; from the remembrance of those attic nights and those refections of the gods which we have partaken with those admired, and respected, and beloved companions, who have gone before us—over whose ashes the most precious tears of Ireland have been shed.*

---

* Here, according to the original report, Lord Avonmore could not refrain from bursting into tears. In the midst of Curran's legal argument, "this most beautiful episode," says Charles Phillips, "bloomed like a green spot amid the desert. Mr. Curran told me himself, that when the court rose, the tip-staff informed him he was wanted immediately in chamber by one of the judges of the exchequer. He, of course, obeyed the judicial mandate; and the moment he entered, poor Lord Avonmore, whose cheeks were still wet with the tears extorted by this heart-touching appeal, clasped him to his bosom." A coolness caused by political differences, which had for some time existed between them, gave place to a renewal of friendship, which was not again interrupted.

Yes, my good lord, I see you do not forget them; I see their sacred forms passing in sad review before your memory; I see your pained and softened fancy recalling those happy meetings, where the innocent enjoyment of social mirth became expanded into the nobler warmth of social virtue, and the horizon of the board became enlarged into the horizon of man; where the swelling heart conceived and communicated the pure and generous purpose; where my slenderer and younger taper imbibed its borrowed light from the more matured and redundant fountain of yours. Yes, my lord, we can remember those nights, without any other regret than that they can never more return; for,

> "We spent them not in toys, or lust, or wine;
>   But search of deep philosophy,
>   Wit, eloquence, and poesy;
> Arts which I loved, for they, my friend, were thine."

SONG OF MAC MURROUGH.—*Scott.*

Mist darkens the mountains, night darkens the vale,
But more dark is the sleep of the sons of the Gael:
A stranger commanded—it sunk on the land,
It has frozen each heart, and benumbed every hand!

The dirk and the targe lie sordid with dust,
The bloodless claymore is but reddened with rust;
On the hill, or the glen, if a gun should appear,
It is only to war with the heath-cock or deer.

The deeds of our sires, if our bards should rehearse,
Let a blush or a blow be the meed of their verse!
Be mute every string, and be hushed every tone,
That shall bid us remember the fame that is flown.

But the dark hours of night and of slumber are past,
The morn on our mountains is dawning at last;
Glenaladale's peaks are illumed with the rays,
And the streams of Glenfinnan leap bright in the blaze.

Oh high-minded Moray!—the exiled!—the dear!—
In the blush of the dawning the standard uprear;
Wide, wide, on the winds of the north let it fly,
Like the sun's latest flash when the tempest is nigh!

Ye sons of the strong, when the dawning shall break,
Need the harp of the aged remind you to wake?
That dawn never beamed on your forefathers' eye,
But it roused each high chieftain to vanquish or die.

Awake on your hills, on your islands awake,
Brave sons of the mountain, the frith, and the lake!
'Tis the bugle—but not for the chase is the call;
'Tis the pibroch's shrill summons—but not to the hall!

'Tis the summons of heroes to conquest or death,
When the banners are blazing on mountain and heath;
They call to the dirk, the claymore, the targe,
To the march and the muster, the line and the charge.

Be the brand of each chieftain like Fin's in his ire!
May the blood through his veins flow like currents of
    fire!
Burst the base foreign yoke as your sires did of yore,
Or die like your sires and endure it no more!

AMBITION.—*Neal.*

I loved to hear the war-horn cry,
    And panted at the drum's deep roll;
And held my breath, when flaming high
I saw our starry banners fly,
As challenging the haughty sky,
    They went like battle o'er my soul:
For I was so ambitious then,
I burned to be the slave—of men.

I stood and saw the morning light,
    A standard swaying far and free:
And loved it, like the conquering flight
Of angels, floating wide and bright,
Above the stars, above the fight,
    Where nations warred for liberty;
And thought I heard the battle-cry
Of trumpets in the hollow sky.

I sailed upon the dark blue deep,
    And shouted to the eaglet soaring;
And hung me from a rocky steep,
When all but spirits were asleep;

And oh! my very soul would leap
  To hear the gallant water's roari :g:
For every sound and shape of strife,
To me, was but the breath of life

But I am strangely altered now—
  I love no more the bugle's voice—
The rushing wave—the plunging prow—
The mountain with its clouded brow,
The thunder when the blue skies bow
  And all the sons of God rejoice.
I love to dream of tears, and sighs,
And shadowy hair, and half-shut eyes.

THE TITHE BILLS.—*O'Connell.*

The following estimate of O'Connell is said to have been written by Bulwer:—

"O'Connell was successful alike at the bar, in the senate, and before assembled thousands of his fellow-citizens and fellow-countrymen, exhibiting an almost solitary instance of eminence in the various modifications of style necessary for his different audiences. O'Connell occupies one of the highest stations among modern orators. The whole course of his eloquence, as well in Parliament as out of doors, is rapid and sonorous, and whenever he speaks he bends, or sways, or alarms, or soothes, at pleasure, the passions of his hearers. He was master of the eloquence which sometimes tears up all before it like a whirlwind, or at other times steals imperceptibly upon the senses and probes to the bottom of the heart—eloquence which engrafts opinions that are new, and eradicates the old. In graphic and heart-rending descriptions of scenes, whether of weal or of woe, O'Connell surpassed all competitors. Most soul-stirring was the debate on the Irish tithe bill, when he thus depicted the scenes of blood that had been perpetrated in Ireland, 1835."

The tithe bills were continued; laws passed, with some cessation from time to time, but the innate sense of injustice, the conviction of wrong, arising from the payment of a sinecure Protestant clergy by a Catholic population, overturned the boundaries of law; broke asunder the parchment chains of the acts of Parliament; the dungeons were filled, the convict-ship was crowded, even the scaffold was reared, and blood has been shed in oceans, but shed in vain.

2. Is it not time to put an end to such scenes of atrocity? Blood is flowing still; even now, is not Rathcormac red with human gore? I do not mean to canvass the merits of this melancholy event, which is under progress of legal inquiry; but two magistrates, who are implicated in the matter, have presided over the investigation.

3. A poor woman has been examined. Have honorable members read her statement? The mother was with her child in the morning. After the affray, she went out to look for her son. The first body she turned over she shouted for joy. Why? Because human blood had been spilled? Because the life of a human being had been sacrificed? Ah! no; but because it happened not to have been her son.

4. She had a similar shout of joy looking in the countenance of the second murdered man; but the third was her son; from that moment her eyeballs became as coals of fire, and she did not shed a single tear. That woman's tears have not yet begun to flow. When is she to have redress? She is to have no re-

dress, and the cause of her woe, the grand evil, is still to remain in Ireland.

5. We are still to follow up the old cause, giving new acts of Parliament, but no new principle, no new spirit unknown to our predecessors, and leaving all the evils of the tithe system substantially untouched and in full operation. What does it signify whether the designation be tithe or tithe composition, or land tax, or rent charge; magical as names are supposed to be will that verbal magic do away with the intolerab terminable injustice o the impost, so obnoxious itself?

UNIVERSAL RELIGIOUS LIBERTY.—*Daniel O'Connell.*

Can anything be more absurd and untenable than the argument of the learned gentleman, when you see it stripped of the false coloring he has given to it? First, he alleges that the Catholics are attached to their religion with a bigoted zeal. I admit the zeal, but I utterly deny the bigotry. He proceeds to insist that these feelings, on our part, justify the apprehensions of Protestants. The Catholics, he says, are alarmed for their Church; why should not the Protestants be alarmed, also, for theirs? The Catholic desires safety for his religion: why should not the Protestant require security for his? Hence he concludes, that, merely because the Catholic desires to keep his religion free, the Protestant is thereby justified in seeking to enslave it. He says that our anxiety for the preservation of our Church vindicates those who deem the proposed arrangement necessary for the protection of *theirs*;— a mode of reasoning perfectly true, and perfectly applicable, if we sought any interference with, or control over, the Protestant Church,—if we asked or required that a single Catholic should be consulted upon the management of the Protestant Church, or of its revenues or privileges.

But the fact does not bear him out ; for we do not seek nor desire, nor would we accept of, any kind of interference with the Protestant Church. We disclaim and disavow any kind of control over it. We ask not, nor would we allow, any Catholic authority over the mode of appointment of their clergy. Nay, we are quite content to be excluded forever from even advising his Majesty with respect to any matter relating to or concerning the Protestant Church,—its rights, its properties, or its privileges. I will, for my own part, go much further, and I do declare, most solemnly, that I would feel and express equal, if not stronger repugnance, to the interference of a Catholic with the Protestant Church, than that I have expressed and do feel to any Protestant interference with ours. In opposing their interference with us, I content myself with the mere war of words. But, if the case were reversed,— if the Catholic sought this control over the religion of the Protestant,—the Protestant should command my heart, my tongue, my arm, in opposition to so unjust and insulting a measure. So help me God! I would, in that case, not only feel for the Protestant, and speak for him, but I would fight for him, and cheerfully sacrifice my life in defence of the great principle for
15

which I have ever contended,—the principle of unuver
sal and complete religious liberty!

ON THE IRISH DISTURBANCE BILL.—*Daniel O'Connell.*

I do not rise to fawn or cringe to this House;—I do
not rise to supplicate you to be merciful toward the
Nation to which I belong,—toward a Nation which,
though subject to England, yet is distinct from it.   It
is a distinct Nation : it has been treated as such by this
country, as may be proved by history, and by seven
hundred years of tyranny.   I call upon this House, as
you value the liberty of England, not to allow the present nefarious bill to pass.   In it are involved the liberties of England, the liberty of the Press, and of every
other institution dear to Englishmen.   Against the bill
I protest, in the name of the Irish People, and in the
face of Heaven.   I treat with scorn the puny and piti-
ful assertions, that grievances are not to be complained
of,—that our redress is not to be agitated; for, in such
cases, remonstrances cannot be too strong, agitation
cannot be too violent, to show to the world with what
injustice our fair claims are met, and under what tyranny the People suffer.

The clause which does away with trial by jury,—
what, in the name of Heaven, is it, if it is not the
establishment of a revolutionary tribunal?   It drives
the judge from his bench; it does away with that
which is more sacred than the Throne itself,—that for
which your king reigns, your lords deliberate, your
commons assemble.   If ever I doubted, before, of the

success of our agitation for repeal, this bill,—this ir.-famous bill,—the way in which it has been received by the House; the manner in which its opponents have been treated; the personalities to which they have been subjected; the yells with which one of them has this night been greeted,—all these things dissipate my doubts, and tell me of its complete and early triumph. Do you think those yells will be forgotten? Do you suppose their echo will not reach the plains of my injured and insulted country; that they will not be whispered in her green valleys, and heard from her lofty hills? O, they will be heard there!—yes; and they will not be forgotten. The youth of Ireland will bound with indignation,—they will say, "We are eight millions; and you treat us thus, as though we were no more to your country than the isle of Guernsey or of Jersey!"

I have done my duty. I stand acquitted to my conscience and my country. I have opposed this measure throughout; and I now protest against it, as harsh, oppressive, uncalled for, unjust;—as establishing an infamous precedent, by retaliating crime against crime —as tyrannous,—cruelly and vindictively tyrannous!

THE ESTABLISHED CHURCH OF IRELAND, 1845.—*T. B. Macaulay.*

The English Church in Ireland was at length disestablished, and its iniquity acknowledged by the English Government in 1869.

Of all the institutions now existing in the civilized world, the Established Church of Ireland seems to me

the most absurd. Is there anything else like it? Was
there ever anything else like it? The world is full of
ecclesiastical establishments. But such a portent as this
Church of Ireland is nowhere to be found. Look round
the continent of Europe. Ecclesiastical establishments
from the White Sea to the Mediterranean; ecclesiastical establishments from the Wolga to the Atlantic; but
nowhere the church of a small minority enjoying exclu-
sive establishment. Look at America. There you have
all forms of Christianity, from Mormonism—if you call
Mormonism Christianity—to Romanism. In some
places you have the voluntary system. In some you
have several religions connected with the State. In
some you have the solitary ascendency of a single
Church. But nowhere, from the Arctic Circle to Cape
Horn, do you find the Church of a small minority ex-
clusively established. In one country alone—in Ireland
alone—is to be seen the spectacle of a community of
eight millions of human beings, with a Church which
is the Church of only eight hundred thousand!

Two hundred and eighty-five years has this Church
been at work. What could have been done for it in
the way of authority, privileges, endowments, which
has not been done? Did any other set of bishops and
priests in the world ever receive so much for doing so
little? Nay, did any other set of bishops and priests
'n the world ever receive half as much for doing twice
as much? And what have we to show for all this lavish expenditure? What, but the most zealous Roman
Catholic population on the face of the earth? On the
great solid mass of the Roman Catholic population you

have made no impression whatever. There they are, as they were ages ago, ten to one against the members of your Established Church. Explain this to me. I speak to you, the zealous Protestants on the other side of the House. Explain this to me on Protestant principles. If I were a Roman Catholic, I could easily account for the phenomenon. If I were a Roman Catholic, I should content myself with saying that the mighty hand and the outstretched arm had been put forth according to the promise, in defence of the unchangeable Church; that He, who, in the old time, turned into blessings the curses of Balaam, and smote the host of Sennacherib, had signally confounded the arts and the power of heretic statesmen. But what is the Protestant to say? Is this a miracle that we should stand aghast at it? Not at all. It is a result which human prudence ought to have long ago foreseen, and long ago averted. It is the natural succession of effect to cause. A Church exists for moral ends. A Church exists to be loved, to be reverenced, to be heard with docility, to reign in the understandings and hearts of men. A Church which is abhorred is useless, or worse than useless, and to quarter a hostile Church on a conquered People, as you would quarter a soldiery, is, therefore, the most absurd of mistakes.

ON LIMITING THE HOURS OF LABOR, 1846.—*T. B. Macaulay.*

If we consider man simply in a commercial point of view, simply as a machine for productive labor, let us

not forget what a piece of mechanism he is,—how
"fearfully and wonderfully made." If we have a fine
horse, we do not use him exactly as a steam-engine;
and still less should we treat man so, more especially
in his earlier years. The depressing labor that begins
early in life, and is continued too long every day, en-
feebles his body, enervates his mind, weakens his
spirits, overpowers his understanding, and is incompatible with any good or useful degree of education. A
state of society in which such a system prevails will
inevitably, and in no long space, feel its baneful effects.
What is it which makes one community prosperous and
flourishing, more than another? You will not say that
it is the soil; you will not say that it is its climate;
you will not say that it is its mineral wealth, or its
natural advantages,—its ports, or its great rivers. Is it
anything in the earth, or in the air, that makes Scotland
a richer country than Egypt; or, Batavia, with its
marshes, more prosperous than Sicily? No; but
Scotchmen made Scotland what she is, and Dutchmen
raised their marshes to such eminence. Look to Amer
ica. Two centuries ago, it was a wilderness of buffa-
loes and wolves. What has caused the change? Is it
her rich mould? Is it her mighty rivers? Is it her
broad waters? No; her plains were then as fertile as
they are now,—her rivers were as numerous. Nor was
it any great amount of capital that the emigrants carried out with them. They took a mere pittance. What
is it then, that has effected the change? It is simply
this,—you placed the Englishman, instead of the red
man, upon the soil; and the Englishman, intelligent

and energetic, cut down the forests, turned them into cities and fleets, and covered the land with harvests and orchards in their place.

I am convinced, sir, that this question of limiting the hours of labor, being a question connected, for the most part, with persons of tender years,—a question in which public health is concerned, and a question relating to public morality,—it is one with which the State may properly interfere. Sir, as law-givers, we have errors of two different kinds to repair. We have done that which we ought not to have done; we have left undone that which we ought to have done. We have regulated that which we ought to have left to regulate itself; we have left unregulated that which it was our especial business to have regulated. We have given to certain branches of industry a protection which was their bane. We have withheld from public health and from public morality a protection which it was our duty to have given. We have prevented the laborer from getting his loaf where he could get it cheapest, but we have not prevented him from prematurely destroying the health of his body and mind, by inordinate toil. I hope and believe that we are approaching the end of a vicious system of interference, and of a vicious system of non-interference.

REFORM, THAT YOU MAY PRESERVE. MARCH 2, 1831.—
T. B. Macaulay.

Turn where we may,—within, around,—the voice of great events is proclaiming to us, "Reform, that you

may preserve!" Now, therefore, while everything at
home and abroad forebodes ruin to those who persist
in a hopeless struggle against the spirit of the age;
now, while the crash of the proudest Throne of the
Continent is still resounding in our ears; now, while
the roof of a British palace affords an ignominious
shelter to the exiled heir of forty Kings;* now, while
we see on every side ancient institutions subverted, and
great societies dissolved; now, while the heart of England is still sound; now, while the old feelings and the
old associations retain a power and a charm which may
too soon pass away; now, in this your accepted time,—
now, in this your day of salvation,—take counsel, not
of prejudice, not of party spirit, not of the ignominious pride of a fatal consistency, but of history, of
reason, of the ages which are past, of the signs of this
most portentous time. Pronounce in a manner worthy
of the expectation with which this great debate has
been anticipated, and of the long remembrance which
it will leave behind. Renew the youth of the State.
Save property, divided against itself. Save the multitude, endangered by their own ungovernable passions.
Save the aristocracy, endangered by its own unpopular
power. Save the greatest, and fairest, and most highly
civilized community that ever existed, from calamities
which may in a few days sweep away all the rich heritage of so many ages of wisdom and glory. The
danger is terrible. The time is short. If this bill
should be rejected, I pray to God that none of those
who concur in rejecting it may ever remember their

---

* Charles the Tenth, of France.

votes with unavailing regret, amidst the wreck of laws, the confusion of ranks, the spoliation of property, and the dissolution of social order.

ALFRED THE GREAT TO HIS MEN.—*Knowles.*

1. My friends, our country must be free! The land
   Is never lost that has a son to right her—
   And here are troops of sons, and loyal ones!
   Strong in her children should a mother be.
   Shall ours be helpless, that has sons like us?
   God save our native land, whoever pays
   The ransom that redeems her! Now, what wait
      we?
2. For Alfred's word to move upon the foe?
   Upon him then! Now think ye on the things
   You most do love! Husbands and fathers, on
   Their wives and children; lovers, on their beloved;
   And *all*, upon their COUNTRY! When you use
   Your weapons, think on the beseeching eyes,
   To whet them, could have lent you tears for water!
   O, now be men, or never! From your hearths
   Thrust the unbidden feet, that from their nooks
   Drove forth your agèd sires—your wives and babes!
3. The couches your fair-handed daughters used
   To spread, let not the vaunting stranger press,
   Weary from spoiling you! Your roofs, that hear
   The wanton riot of the intruding guest
   That mocks their masters—clear them for the sake
   Of the manhood to which all that's precious clings,
      15*

Else perishes. The land that bore you—O!
Do honor to her! Let her glory in
Your breeding! Rescue her! Revenge her—or
Ne'er call her mother more! Come on, my friends!
'4. And where you take your stand upon the field,
However you advance, resolve on this—
That you will ne'er recede, while from the tongues
Of age, and womanhood, and infancy,
The helplessness whose safety in you lies,
Invokes you to be strong! Come on! Come on!
I'll bring you to the foe! And when you meet
     him,
Strike hard! Strike home! Strike while a dying
     blow
Is in an arm! Strike till you're free, or fall!

THE BATTLE.—*Schiller*.

II.

Heavy and solemn,
A cloudy column,
Thro' the green plain they marching came!
Measureless spread, like a table dread,
For the wild grim dice of the iron game.
The looks are bent on the shaking ground,
And the heart beats loud with a knelling sound;
Swift by the breasts that must bear the brunt
Gallops the Major along the front,—
          " Halt ! "
And fettered they stand at the stark command,
And the warriors, silent, halt!

II.

Proud in the blush of morning glowing,
What on the hill-top shines in flowing !
"See you the foeman's banners waving ? "
" We see the foeman's banners waving ! "

III.

God be with ye—children and wife !
Hark to the music—the trump and. the fife,
How they ring through the ranks which they rouse to
    the strife !
Thrilling they sound with their glorious tone,
Thrilling they go through the marrow and bone !
Brothers, God grant, when this life is o'er,
In the life to come that we meet once more !

IV.

See the smoke, how the lightning is clearing asunder !
Hark the guns, peal on peal, how they boom in their
    thunder !
From host to host, with kindling sound,
The shouting signals circle round ;
Ay, shout it forth to life or death—
Freer already breathes the breath !
The war is waging, slaughter raging,
And heavy through the reeking pall
The iron death-dice fall !

V.

Nearer they close—foes upon foes—
" Ready ! "--from square to square it goes.

Down on the knee they sank,
And the fire comes sharp on the foremost rank;
Many a man to the earth is sent,
Many a gap by the balls is rent—
O'er the corpse before springs the hinder man,
That the line may not fail to the fearless van.
To the right, to the left, and around and around,
Death whirls in its dance on the bloody ground
God's sunlight is quenched in the fiery fight,
Over the host falls a brooding night!
Brothers, God grant when this life is o'er,
In the life to come that we meet once more!

VI.

The dead men lie bathed in the weltering blood,
And the living are blent in the slippery flood,
And the feet, as they reeling and sliding go,
Stumble still on the corpses that sleep below.
"What, Francis!   Give Charlotte my last farewell."
As the dying man murmurs the thunders swell—
"I'll give—O God! are the guns so near?
Ho! comrades!—yon volley!—look sharp to the rear!—
I'll give thy Charlotte thy last farewell.
Sleep soft! where death thickest descendeth in rain,
The friend thou forsakest thy side shall regain!"
Hitherward—thitherward reels the fight,
Dark and more darkly day glooms into night!
Brothers, God grant when this life is o'er,
In the life to come that we meet once more!

VII.

Hark to the hoofs that galloping go!
The adjutants flying—
The horsemen press hard on the panting foe,
'Their thunder booms in dying— .
          Victory!
The terror has seized on the dastards all,
And their colors fall!
          Victory!
Closed in the brunt of the glorious fight,
And the day, like a conqueror, burst on the **night**.
Trumpet and fife swelling choral along,
The triumph already sweeps marching in song.'
Farewell, fallen brothers, though this life be o'er,
There's another in which we shall meet you once more

THE DEATH PENALTY FOR NEW OFFENCES, 1812.—*Lord*
    Byron. B. 1788; *d.* 1824.

Setting aside the palpable injustice and the certain
inefficiency of this Bill, are there not capital punishments sufficient in your statutes? Is there not blood
enough upon your penal code, that more must be
poured forth, to ascend to Heaven and testify against
you? How will you carry this Bill into effect? Can
you commit a whole country to their own prison? Will
you erect a gibbet in every field, and hang up men like
scarecrows? or will you proceed (as you must to bring
this measure into effect) by decimation; place the
country under martial law; depopulate and lay waste
all around you; and restore Sherwood Forest as an
acceptable gift to the Crown, in its former condition

of a royal chase, and an asylum for outlaws? Are these the remedies for a starving and desperate populace? Will the famished wretch who has braved your bayonets be appalled by your gibbets? When death is a relief, and the only relief, it appears, that you will afford him, will he be dragooned into tranquillity? Will that which could not be effected by your grenadiers be accomplished by your executioners?

If you proceed by the forms of law, where is your evidence? Those who have refused to impeach their accomplices when transportation only was the punishment, will hardly be tempted to witness against them when death is the penalty. With all deference to the noble Lords opposite, I think a little investigation-- some previous inquiry—would induce even *them* to change their purpose. That most favorite State measure, so marvellously efficacious in many and recent instances,—*temporizing*,—would not be without its advantage in this. When a proposal is made to emancipate or relieve, you hesitate, you deliberate for years, —you temporize and tamper with the minds of men; but a death-bill must be passed off-hand, without a thought of the consequences. Sure I am, from what I have heard, and from what I have seen, that to pass the Bill, under all the existing circumstances, without inquiry, without deliberation, would only be to add in justice to irritation, and barbarity to neglect.

The framers of such a Bill must be content to inherit the honors of the Athenian lawgiver,* whose edicts were said to be written not in ink, but in blood. But

* Dracon the author of the first written code of laws for Athens.

suppose it passed,—suppose one of these men, as I have seen them, meagre with famine, sullen with despair, careless of a life which your Lordships are, perhaps, about to value at something less than the price of a stocking-frame,—suppose this man surrounded by those children, for whom he is unable to procure bread at the hazard of his existence, about to be torn forever from a family which he lately supported in peaceful industry, and which it is not his fault that he can no longer so support;—suppose this man,—and there are ten thousand such, from whom you may select your victims, —dragged into Court, to be tried, for this new offence, by this new law,—still, there are two things wanting to convict and condemn him ; and these are, in my opinion, twelve butchers for a Jury, and a Jeffries for a Judge !

ON CHARGES AGAINST ROMAN CATHOLICS, 1828.—*Sheil.*

Richard Lalor Sheil was born in Dublin, Ireland, August 16th, 1791, and died at Florence, Italy, where he held the post of British Minister, May 25th, 1851. He was returned to the Imperial Parliament in 1829, and for twenty years was a prominent member of the House of Commons. A contemporary says of him : " His great earnestness and apparent sincerity, his unrivalled felicity of illustration, his extraordinary power of pushing the meaning of words to the utmost extent, and wringing from them a force beyond the range of ordinary expression, were such, that, when he rose to speak, members took their places, and the hum of private conversation was hushed, in order that the House might enjoy the performances of an accomplished artist." His style of speaking was peculiar ; his gesticulation rapid, fierce, and incessant ; his enunciation remarkably quick and impetuous. His matter was uniformly well arranged and logical. He carefully prepared himself before speaking.

Calumniators of Catholicism, have you read the history of your country ? Of the charges against the reli

gion of Ireland, the annals of England afford the con
futation. The body of your common law was given by
the Catholic Alfred. He gave you your judges, your
magistrates, your high-sheriffs, your courts of justice,
your elective system, and, the great bulwark of your
liberties, the trial by jury. Who conferred upon the
People the right of self-taxation, and fixed, if he did
not create, their representation ? The Catholic Edward
the First; while, in the reign of Edward the Third,
perfection was given to the representative system, Par
liaments were annually called, and the statute against
constructive treason was enacted. It is false,—foully,
infamously false,—that the Catholic religion, the religion of your forefathers, the religion of seven millions
of your fellow-subjects, has been the auxiliary of debasement, and that to its influence the suppression of
British freedom can, in a single instance, be referred.
I am loath to say that which can give you cause to take
offence ; but, when the faith of my country is made
the object of imputation, I cannot help, I cannot refrain,
from breaking into a retaliatory interrogation, and from
asking whether the overthrow of the old religion of Eng
land was not effected by a tyrant, with a hand of iron and
a heart of stone ;—whether Henry did not trample upon
freedom, while upon Catholicism he set his foot ; and
whether Elizabeth herself, the virgin of the Reformation,
did not inherit her despotism with her creed ; whether in
her reign the most barbarous atrocities were not ccm-
mitted ;—whether torture, in violation of the Catholic
common law of England, was not politically inflicted,
and with the shrieks of agony the Towers of Julius, in
the dead of night, did not re-echo ?

You may suggest to me that in the larger portion of Catholic Europe freedom does not exist; but you should bear in mind that, at a period when the Catholic religion was in its most palmy state, freedom flourished in the countries in which it is now extinct. False,—I repeat it, with all the vehemence of indignant asseveration,—utterly false is the charge habitually preferred against the religion which Englishmen have laden with penalties, and have marked with degradation. I can bear with any other charge but this—to any other charge I can listen with endurance. Tell me that I prostrate myself before a sculptured marble; tell me that to a canvas glowing with the imagery of Heaven I bend my knee; tell me that my faith is my perdition; —and, as you traverse the church-yards in which your forefathers are buried, pronounce upon those who have lain there for many hundred years a fearful and appalling sentence,—yes, call what I regard as the truth not only an error, but a sin, to which mercy shall not be extended,—all this I will bear,—to all this I will submit,—nay, at all this I will but smile,—but do not tell me that I am in heart and creed a slave!—*That*, my countrymen cannot brook! In their own bosoms they carry the high consciousness that never was imputation more foully false, or more detestably calumnious!

THE ESTABLISHED CHURCH OF IRELAND.—*Id.*

I lay down a very plain proposition, and it is this,— however harsh the truth, it must be told,—it is this:— Whatever may be your inclination, you have not the ability to maintain the Irish establishment. At first view, the subject seems to be a wretched dispute between Catholic and Protestant—a miserable sectarian controversy. It is no such thing; it is the struggle for complete political equality on the part of the overwhelming majority upon the one hand, and for political ascendency on the part of the minority on the other. Can that ascendency be maintained? Taught so long, but uninstructed still, wherefore, in the same fatal policy, with an infatuated pertinacity, do you disastrously persevere? Can you wish, and, if you wish, can you hope, that this unnatural, galling, exasperating ascendency should be maintained? Things cannot remain as they are. To what expedient will you fly? Would you drive the country into insurrection, cut down the people, and bid the yeomanry draw forth the swords clotted with the blood of 1798, that they may be brandished in massacre, and sheathed in the nation's heart? For what, into these terrific possibilities, are we madly, desperately, impiously, to plunge? For the Irish Church!—the church of the minority, long the church of the State, never the church of the people; the church on which a faction fattens, by which a nation starves; the church from which no imaginable good can flow, but evil after evil, in such black and continuous abundance, has been for centuries, and is to this day, poured out; the church by which religion has been retarded, morality has been vitiated, atrocity has been engendered; which standing armies are requisite to sustain, which has cost England millions of her treasure, and Ireland torrents of her blood!

To distinctions between Catholic and Protestant let

nere be an end. Let there be an end to national ani-
mosities, as well as to sectarian detestations. Perish
the bad theology, which, with an impious converse,
makes God according to man's image, and with infernal passions fills the heart of man! Perish the bad,
the narrow, the pernicious sentiment, which, for the
genuine love of country, institutes a feeling of despotic
domination upon your part, and of provincial turbu-
lence upon ours!

THE REPEAL OF THE UNION, 1834.—*Id.*

The population of Ireland has doubled since the
Union. What is the condition of the mass of the people? Has her capital increased in the same proportion? Behold the famine, the wretchedness, and pestilence of the Irish hovel, and, if you have the heart to
do so, mock at the calamities of the country, and proceed in your demonstrations of the prosperity of Ire
land. The mass of the people are in a condition more
wretched than that of any nation in Europe ; they are
worse housed, worse covered, worse fed, than the basest
boors in the provinces of Russia ; they dwell in habitations to which your swine would not be committed ;
they are covered with rags which your beggars would
disdain to wear, and not only do they never taste the
flesh of the animals which crowd into your markets,
but while the sweat drops from their brows, they never
touch the bread into which their harvests are converted.
For you they toil, for you they delve ; they reclaim the
bog, and drive the plough to the mountain's top, for

you. And where does all this misery exist? In a
country teeming with fertility, and stamped with the
beneficent intents of God! When the famine of Ireland prevailed,—when her cries crossed the Channel,
and pierced your ears, and reached your hearts,—the
granaries of Ireland were bursting with their contents,
and, while a people knelt down and stretched out their
hands for food, the business of deportation, the absen-
tee tribute, was going on! Talk of the prosperity of
Ireland! Talk of the external magnificence of a poor-
house gorged with misery within!

But the Secretary for the Treasury exclaims: "If
the agitators would but let us alone, and allow Ireland
to be tranquil!" The agitators, forsooth! Does he
venture—has he the intrepidity—to speak thus? Agitators! Against deep potations let the drunkard rail;
at Crockford's let there be homilies against the dice-
box; let every libertine lament the progress of licen-
tiousness, when his Majesty's ministers deplore the influence of demagogues, and Whigs complain of agitation! How did you carry the Reform? Was it not
by impelling the people almost to the verge of revolution? Was there a stimulant for their passions, was
there a provocative for their excitement, to which you did
not resort? If you have forgotten, do you think that we
shall fail to remember your meetings at Edinburgh, at
Paisley, at Manchester, at Birmingham? Did not three
hundred thousand men assemble? Did they not pass
resolutions against taxes? Did they not threaten to
march on London? Did not two of the cabinet ministers indite to them epistles of gratitude and of ad

miration? and do they now dare—have they the audacity—to speak of agitation? Have we not as good
a title to demand the restitution of our Parliament, as
the ministers to insist on the reform of this House?

ENGLAND'S MISRULE OF IRELAND.—*Id.*

If in Ireland, a country that ought to teem with
abundance, there prevails wretchedness without example,—if millions of paupers are there without employment, and often without food or raiment,—where is
the fault? Is it in the sky, which showers verdure?
—is it in the soil, which is surprisingly fertile?—or is
it in the fatal course which you, the arbiters of her destiny, have adopted? She has for centuries belonged
.o England. England has used her for centuries as she
has pleased. *How* has she used her, and *what* has been
the result? A code of laws was in the first place established, to which, in the annals of legislative atrocity,
there is not a parallel; and of that code—those institutes of unnatural ascendency—the Irish Church is a
remnant. In Heaven's name, what useful purpose has
your gorgeous establishment ever promoted? You cannot hope to proselytize us through its means. You
have put the experiment to the test of three centuries.
You have tried everything. If the truth be with you,
it may be great; but in this instance it does not sustain
the aphorism—for it does not prevail. If, in a religious point of view, the Establishment cannot conduce
to the interests of religion, what purpose does it answer?
It is said that it cements the Union—cements the

Union ! It furnishes the great argument against the Union ; it is the most degrading incident of all the in cidents of degradation by which that measure was accompanied ; it is the yoke, the brand, the shame, and the exasperation of Ireland !

Public opinion and public feeling have been created in Ireland. Men of all classes have been instructed in the principles on which the rights of Nations depend. The humblest peasant, amidst destitution the most abject, has learned to respect himself. I remember when, if you struck him, he cowered beneath the blow; but now, lift up your hand, the spirit of insulted man hood will start up in a bosom covered with rags—his Celtic blood will boil as yours would do—and he will feel, and he will act, as if he had been born where the person of every citizen is sacred from affronts, and from his birth had breathed the moral atmosphere which you are accustomed to inhale. In the name of millions of my countrymen, assimilated to yourselves, I demand the reduction of a great abuse—the retrenchment of a monstrous sinecure—I demand justice at your hands ! "Justice to Ireland " is a phrase which has been, I am well aware, treated as a topic for derision ; but the time will come—nor is it, perhaps, remote—when you will not be able to extract much matter for ridicule from those trite but not trivial words. "Do justice to America," exclaimed the father of that man by whom the Irish Union was accomplished ; "do it to-night—do it before you sleep." In your National Gallery is a picture on which Lord Lyndhurst should look: it was painted by Copley, and represents the

death of Chatham, who did not live long after the celebrated invocation was pronounced. "Do justice to
America—do it to-night—do it before you sleep."
There were men by whom that warning was heard
who laughed when it was uttered. Have a care lest
injustice to Ireland and to America may not be followed by the same results—lest mournfulness may not
succeed to mirth, and another page in the history of
England may not be writ in her heart's blood!

THE DRONES OF THE COMMUNITY.—*Percy Bysshe
Shelley.*

Those gilded flies
That, basking in the sunshine of a Court,
Fatten on its corruption—what are they?
The drones of the community! they feed
On the mechanic's labor; the starved hind
For them compels the stubborn glebe to yield
Its unshared harvests; and yon squalid form,
Leaner than fleshless misery, that wastes
A sunless life in the unwholesome mine,
Drags out in labor a protracted death,
To glut *their* grandeur. Many faint with toil,
That few may know the cares and woe of sloth.
Whence, think'st thou, kings and parasites arose
Whence that unnatural line of drones, who heap
Toil and unvanquishable penury
On those who build their palaces, and bring
Their daily bread?—From vice, black, loathsome vice;
From rapine, madness, treachery, and wrong;

From all that genders misery, and makes
Of earth this thorny wilderness; from lust
Revenge, and murder.—And, when Reason's voice,
Loud as the voice of nature, shall have waked
The Nations; and mankind perceive that vice
Is discord, war, and misery—that virtue
Is peace, and happiness, and harmony;
When man's maturer nature shall disdain
The playthings of its childhood;—kingly glare
Will lose its power to dazzle; its authority
Will silently pass by; the gorgeous throne
Shall stand unnoticed in the regal hall,
Fast falling to decay, whilst falsehood's trade
Shall be as hateful and unprofitable
As that of truth is now.

                       Where is the fame
Which the vain-glorious mighty of the earth
Seek to eternize? O! the faintest sound
From time's light foot-fall, the minutest wave
That swells the flood of ages, whelms in nothing
The unsubstantial bubble. Ay! to-day
Stern is the tyrant's mandate—red the gaze
That scatters multitudes. To-morrow comes,
That mandate is a thunder-peal that died
In ages past; that gaze, a transient flash
On which the midnight closed; and on that arm
The worm has made his meal.

CÆSAR'S PASSAGE OF THE RUBICON.—*James Sheridan Knowles.*

A gentleman, Mr. Chairman, speaking of Cæsar's benevolent disposition, and of the reluctance with which he entered into the civil war, observes, " How long did he pause upon the brink of the Rubicon!" How came he to the brink of that river? How dared he cross it? Shall private men respect the boundaries of private property, and shall a man pay no respect to the boundaries of his country's rights? How dared he cross that river? O! but he paused upon the brink. He should have perished upon the brink ere he had crossed it! Why did he pause? Why does a man's heart palpitate when he is on the point of committing an unlawful deed? Why does the very murderer, his victim sleeping before him, and his glaring eye taking the measure of the blow, strike wide of the mortal part? Because of conscience! 'Twas that made Cæsar pause upon the brink of the Rubicon. Compassion! What compassion? The compassion of an assassin, that feels a momentary shudder, as his weapon begins to cut! Cæsar paused upon the brink of the Rubicon! What was the Rubicon? The boundary of Cæsar's province. From what did it separate his province? From his country. Was that country a desert? No; it was cultivated and fertile, rich and populous! Its sons were men of genius, spirit, and generosity! Its daughters were lovely, susceptible, and chaste! Friendship was its inhabitant! Love was its inhabitant! Domestic affection was its inhabitant! Liberty was its inhabi-

16

tant! All bounded by the stream of the Rubicon!
What was Cæsar, that stood upon the bank of that
stream? A traitor, bringing war and pestilence into
the heart of that country! No wonder that he paused,—
no wonder if, his imagination wrought upon by his
conscience, he had beheld blood instead of water, and
heard groans instead of murmurs! No wonder, if
some gorgon horror had turned him into stone upon
the spot! But no!—he cried, " The die is cast!" He
plunged!—he crossed!—and Rome was free no more!

RICHELIEU AND FRANCE.—*Sir E. Bulwer Lytton.*

My liege, your anger can recall your trust,
Annul my office, spoil me of my lands,
Rifle my coffers; but my name,—my deeds,—
Are royal in a land beyond your sceptre.
Pass sentence on me, if you will;—from Kings,
Lo, I appeal to time! Be just, my liege.
I found your Kingdom rent with heresies,
And bristling with rebellion;—lawless nobles
And breadless serfs; England fomenting discord,
Austria, her clutch on your dominion; Spain
Forging the prodigal gold of either Ind
To armèd thunderbolts. The arts lay dead;
Trade rotted in your marts; your Armies mutinous
Your Treasury bankrupt. Would you now revoke
Your trust, so be it! and I leave you, sole,
Supremest Monarch of the mightiest realm,
From Ganges to the Icebergs. Look without,—
No foe not humbl:d! Look within,—the Arts

Quit, for our schools, their old Hesperìdes,
The golden Italy ! while throughout the veins
Of your vast empire flows in strengthening tides
Trade, the calm health of Nations! Sire, I know
That men have called me cruel ;—
I am not ;—I am *just !* I found France rent asunder,
The rich men despots, and the poor banditti ;
Sloth in the mart, and schism within the temple,
Brawls festering to rebellion ; and weak laws
Rotting away with rust in antique sheaths.
I have recreated France ; and, from the ashes
Of the old feudal and decrepit carcass,
Civilization, on her luminous wings,
Soars, phœnix-like, to Jove ! What was my art ?
Genius, some say ;—some, Fortune ;—Witchcraft, some.
Not so; -my art was JUSTICE!

AN APPEAL TO THE JURY.—*Phillips.*

1. Oh ! gentlemen, am I this day only the counsel of
my client ? No, no ; I am the advocate of humanity—
of yourselves, your homes, your wives, your families,
your little children. I am glad that this case exhibits
such atrocity ; unmarked as it is by any mitigatory fea-
ture, it may stop the frightful advance of this calamity ;
it will be met now, and marked with vengeance.

2. If it be not, farewell to the virtues of your country ; farewell to all confidence between man and man;
farewell to that unsuspicious and reciprocal tenderness
without which marriage is but a consecrated curse. If
oaths are to be violated, laws disregarded, friendship

betrayed, humility trampled, national and individual honor stained, and if a jury of fathers and husbands will give such miscreancy a passport to their homes, and wives, and daughters, farewell to all that yet remains of Ireland !

3. But I will not cast such a doubt upon the character of my country. Against the sneer of the foe and the skepticism of the foreigner, I will stand and point to the domestic virtues, that no perfidy could barter, and no bribery can purchase; that with a Roman usage at once embellish and consecrate households, giving to the society of the hearth all the purity of the altar; that, lingering alike in the palace and the cottage, are still to be found scattered over this land—the relic of what she was—the source, perhaps, of what she may be—the lone, the stately, and the magnificent memorials that, rearing their majesty amidst surrounding ruins, serve at once as the landmarks of departed glory, and the models by which the future may be erected.

4. Preserve those virtues with a vestal fidelity; mark this day, by your verdict, your horror of their profanation; and, believe me, when the hand which records that verdict shall be dust, and the tongue which asks it traceless in the grave, many a happy home will bless its consequences, and many a mother teach her little child to hate the impious treason of adultery.

IRELAND.—*Meagher.*

1. I do not despair of my poor old country, her peace, her liberty, her glory. For that country I can do no more than bid her hope. To lift this island up,

to make her a benefactor instead of being the meanest beggar in the world, to restore to her her native powers and her ancient constitution, this has been my ambition, and this ambition has been my crime.

2. Judged by the law of England, I know this crime entails the penalty of death; but the history of Ireland explains this crime, and justifies it. Judged by that history I am no criminal; you are no criminal; I deserve no punishment; we deserve no punishment. Judged by that history, the treason of which I stand convicted loses all its guilt, is sanctified as a duty, will be ennobled as a sacrifice.

3. With these sentiments, my lord, I await the sentence of the court, having done what I felt to be my duty, having spoken what I felt to be the truth, as I have done on every other occasion of my short career. I now bid farewell to the country of my birth, my passion, and my death—the country whose misfortunes have invoked my sympathies, whose factions I have sought to still, whose intellect I have prompted to a lofty aim, whose freedom has been my fatal dream.

4. I offer to that country, as a proof of the love I bear her, and the sincerity with which I thought and spoke and struggled for her freedom, the life of a young heart; and with that life, all the hopes, the honors, the endearments of an honorable home.

5. Pronounce, then, my lords, the sentence which the law directs, and I will be prepared to hear it. I trust I shall be prepared to meet its execution. I hope to be able, with a pure heart and a perfect composure, to appear before a higher tribunal—a tribunal where a

Judge of infinite goodness, as well as of justice, will preside, and where, my lords, many, many of the judgments of this world will be reversed.

WAR SOMETIMES A MORAL DUTY.—*Meagher.*

Sir, I dissent from the resolutions before us. I dissent because they would pledge me to the utter repudiation of physical force—at all times, in all countries, and under every circumstance. This I cannot do; for, sir, when national rights are to be vindicated, I do not repudiate the resort to physical force—I do not abhor the use of arms. There are occasions when arms alone will suffice;—when political ameliorations call for a drop of blood—ay, for many thousand drops of blood.

Opinion, I admit, sir, may be left to operate against opinion. But force must be used against force. The soldier is proof against an argument, but not against a bullet. The man that will listen to reason, let him be reasoned with. But it is only the weaponed arm of the patriot that can prevail against battalioned despotism. Therefore, sir, I do not condemn the use of arms as immoral, nor do I conceive it profane to say, that the King of Heaven, the Lord of Hosts, the God of Battles, bestows his benediction upon those who unsheathe the sword in the hour of a nation's peril.

Be it in the defence, or be it in the assertion of a people's liberty, I hail the sword as a sacred weapon; and if it has sometimes taken the shape of the serpent, and reddened the shroud of the oppressor with too deep a dye, yet, sir, like the anointed rod of the High Priest, it has at other times, and as often, blossomed into celestial flowers to deck the freeman's brow.

Abhor the sword? Stigmatize the sword? No!— for in the passes of the Tyrol it cut to pieces the banner of the Bavarian, and through those craggy defiles struck a path to fame for the peasant insurrectionist * of Innsbruck!

Abhor the sword? Stigmatize the sword? No!— for it swept the Dutch marauders out of the fine old towns of Belgium—scourged them back to their own phlegmatic swamps, and knocked their flag and sceptre, their laws and bayonets, into the sluggish waters of the Scheldt.

Abhor the sword? Stigmatize the sword? No!— for at its blow a giant nation started from the waters of the Atlantic, and by the redeeming magic of the sword, and in the quivering of its crimson light, the crippled colony sprang into the attitude of a proud republic—prosperous, limitless, and invincible!

---

* Andrew Hofer. a gallant leader of the Tyrolese. Tried by court-martial, he was shot by his country's oppressors, Feb. 20, 1810.

THE STRENGTH OF PAGANISM.—*Lacordaire*.

Nothing, save Christianity, has possessed more extent and solidity than idolatry. This is because it
fully satisfied the three great passions of man. What
are these three passions ? The first, and perhaps it will
surprise you, the first is the religious passion, the want
of intercourse with God. Yes, gentlemen, the religious
passion precedes all others, even the passion of sensuality. For sensuality touches only the senses which are
fragile, which soon become exhausted, which tire of
themselves ; whilst the religious want, a sort of divine
hunger, has its source in the most profound depths of
our being, and gathers nourishment there from all
those miseries which excite in us a continuous distaste
for the present life. Even pride comes but after it ;
however active it may be, it is subject here below to
too many humiliations not to second and bear before
itself in our soul a better and a gentler sentiment, that
which draws us near to God, and causes us to seek our
own dignity in his greatness. Religion is the first and
oldest friend of man ; even when he wounds it, he still
respects and cultivates secret intimacies with it.

2. Let not the state of our country, gentlemen, deceive us on this point ; do not think because there are
some millions of men around us who are besotted in
practical atheism, that this is the natural condition of
the human race. It is the result of extraordinary circumstances, and notwithstanding the irreligion of some
of her children, this same France has never, for a single day, ceased to bear in her glorious womb a multi-

tude of souls who serve God ardently, and honor their faith by works known throughout the world.

3. Now, idolatry, in spite of its slight doctrinal character, gave satisfaction to the religious want; it had temples, altars, a priesthood, sacrifices, prayers, public and pompous ceremonies, a very great station in the world, and the shreds of its mythology still contained sufficient remembrance of God to keep the soul from fasting and without food.

4. But it must not be forgotten that idolatry, in giving satisfaction to the elevated inclinations of our nature, did not disdain the most abject and abundantly dispensed sacred nourishment to them. A most profound and subtle art had blended together God and matter, religion and sensuality, causing grave thoughts and shameful solicitations to descend from the same altars.

5. The idolater had all in his gods; whatever he willed, heaven obeyed his desires. What a masterpiece, had heaven in its turn been obeyed! In addition, the third passion of man, the pride of domination, found also in this worship, which was erudite by its very degradation, an ample satisfaction. Idolatry was not distinct from the empire; the prince, the senate, or the people, conferred the sacerdotal magistracy, named the pontiffs, regulated the ceremonies, took pleasure in covering the robe of their consuls with the mantle of their gods. Religion was country also. The fasces and the altars were seen advancing together before the republic; the fasces, the symbol of its justice and power; the altars, the symbol of that mysterious alliance which united the destinies of the state to the very destinies of the gods

6. No, you will never adequately represent to your selves the force of that institution. Ah! if a pagan ceremony were to rise up again before you; if you could see all Rome mounting to the temple of Jupiter Capitolinus, that concourse of people, those legions, that senate, all those patriotic memorials mounting with them, and all together bearing to the gods the new victory of Rome! If you could hear the silence and the sound of unanimity, that hum of all the passions convinced of their rights and satisfied with their triumph, pride as well as sensuality, sensuality as well as religion, the elevated and the abject, heaven and earth, all at once, all in a single day and in a single action: if you had seen and heard this, you, perhaps, yielding to that total intoxication of the human faculties, would for a moment have bowed the head, and adored in the hands of Rome the antique gods of the world!

7. However, they were not to be adored, they were to be destroyed, such was the order of Jesus Christ. They were to be destroyed throughout the world, since the whole world was subject to idolatry. And what was to replace it? A man, humbled even to the punishment of slaves; a man, come from a country upon which the Romans showered floods of ridicule with oppression; a Jew, and a Jew crucified! This is what the fishermen of Judea brought to Rome, to the Capitol, to replace the statue of Jupiter Capitolinus! Judge, then! Here was ignominy instead of greatness, penance and mortification instead of sensuality. Penance and mortification; what words! After eighteen centuries of naturalization, I hardly dare to

pronounce them before you, without disguising them
to your ears, which have nevertheless been nourished
by the language of the Gospel; and it was necessary
to reveal these to the Romans! It was necessary to
say to them: We bring you a religion all pure and
holy, founded upon the immolation of the body by
chastity, and not only by chastity, which is only a simple retrenchment, but by the direct hatred of the senses.
We come, with the scourge in our hands, to teach you
to treat your body as a slave, because it is the slave of
the most vile inclinations, and because you can only
deliver your souls from it by keeping it in the respect
and chastisement of obedience. It was necessary to
say these things to a people puffed up by seven centuries of arrogance and domination, plunged in sensuality
as well as in pride, and accustomed to find in their
gods, which were to be destroyed, the justification of
their pompous ignominy. But Jesus Christ had so
ordered it; all that was said, believed, adopted, and
the reign of idols fell before the reign of the cross, in
spite of the Roman empire.

TIME VANQUISHED BY JESUS CHRIST.—*Ibid.*

What is more difficult and more necessary for the
confirmation of victory is to resist victory itself. A
celebrated diplomatist has said: "Time is the great
enemy." Has Jesus Christ then overcome the great
enemy? After idolatry, after the Roman empire, has
he overcome that other power, which is but eternity dis-
guised, the power of time? At the end of a more or

less prosperous career, has he not, like all the rest, felt that icy hand, which sooner or later dishonors the greatest events, and hurls the most stable dynasties from their throne? Is he not visibly struck by that slowly advancing thunderbolt which spares nothing? Such is the question which now claims our attention. In a word, I am about to lay before you the balance-sheet of Jesus Christ, and I invite you to examine it.

2. Why is time the great enemy? Because, gentlemen, it is endowed with a double power, the power of destroying and of building up. What was it that overthrew those primitive empires of Assyria and Chaldea? It was time. What overthrew that empire of Cyrus, vainly raised up again by Alexander? It was time. What overthrew that empire, increased by the ruins of all the others, and which we should rather call the world than an empire, the Roman world? It was time. What overthrew all those republics of the middle ages whose vestiges, surviving in marbles and paintings, we so much admire? It was time. And, on another hand, what has built up those new kingdoms whose sons we are, the kingdoms of the Franks, the Germans, the Anglo-Saxons, and the rest? It is the same hand, skilful in creating after having destroyed, and which, from the very dust where it has revelled with so much pride, draws forth substance, order, and solidity. Time destroys with one hand and rebuilds with the other, enemy alike to bo'h, since the edifice it raises up does but sink deeper the edifice it overthrows, for, with time, to found is also to destroy.

3. Nevertheless, gentlemen, let us not halt at those

splendid images, which only reveal to us the inimical
power of time by outward appearances. Let us endeavor
to unveil its secret by analysis, in order that, having
learned whence time derives its double power of destruction and edification, we may consider whether Jesus
Christ has not been subject to the exercise of that formidable action, and why he alone has been able to escape from it, should we at length prove that he has
escaped from it.

4. The action of time results from five causes, the
first of which is novelty. Time is always young, and
yet it ages all things. Each of its steps is the advance
of dawn, but it leaves darkness and night behind.
Restless child of eternity, it borrows unfading youth
there, but has no power to communicate it, save but for
a moment, to the things measured by its course. It
passes, it sheds life ; but that life of to-day soon becomes
that of yesterday, of the day before, of bygone times, a
remembrance, a relic of the past, and yet time is not
impoverished ; it is ever fertile and young, causing the
new to follow the old. Now, the new possesses a charm
which seduces the mind as well as the senses, and which
enables doctrines bearing its impress easily to prevail
against doctrines become superannuated by the simple
fact of their duration. Remark what happens around
us. As soon as a man is able to give a new form to
ideas, and appropriate them to the course of time, he
irevitably has disciples. Why? Because he has said
something which had not been said before, or had been
forgotten. We have the passion for novelty in ideas as
in all the rest, and it is not difficult to understand why

it is so. Predestinated as we are to enjoy the infinite, the infinite is our want, and we pursue it everywhere. Now, novelty is the only thing here below which gives us some sensation of the infinite. As soon as we have considered an object, we say: It is enough. Who will turn the page? Novelty turns it, and in turning it, disguises its feebleness to our intelligence by a false gleam of progress, which enchants us.

Above all others, gentlemen, Jesus Christ had to fear this inclination of our souls, which arms time with a power so dangerous to doctrinal sterility. However merciful the Gospel may be, it was not to bend to the inconstancy of our mind; "Heaven and earth shall pass away," said Jesus Christ, "but my words shall not pass away." * It was to traverse all ages, losing daily the force of its novelty without losing any of its precept, or rather, like God, who, said Saint Augustin, is beauty ever ancient and ever new, the evangelic word was to infuse into its progressive antiquity a youthfulness which should charm the heart of all new generations.

TIME VANQUISHED BY JESUS CHRIST.—*Ibid.*

This first advantage obtained over time, a second remained to be gained. The second power of time is in experience, that is to say, in the revelation that results from the application of doctrines to the positive life of mankind. Every doctrine is a body of laws, which is of value only in so much as it is considered to

---

* St. Matt. xxiv. 35.

contain true relations of beings; it is like the creation
of a world. As long as that creation remains in the
mind in the state of pure conception, we may be deceived
as to its real merits, because it is difficult to judge a
great assemblage of ideas; but it is no longer so when,
entering into the domain of reality, they are required
to found or to maintain a positive order; experience
infallibly manifests their weakness or their falsity; for
a false or powerless law is incapable of establishing
durable relations, and as a house based upon false
mathematical principles falls to the ground, so no order
whatever could subsist based upon ideas wanting the
equilibrium of truth.

2. Now, who had ever more reason to fear this terri-
ole test of experience than Jesus Christ? For, with
the Gospel, he had not placed in the world a society
confined within the narrow limits of a race and a country, but a universal society, wherein every soul, wheresoever born, could claim the rights of citizenship; and
consequently, if the Gospel were false, its ruin should
have been as great as the universe, and as rapid as time,
acting at once upon numberless places and minds.

3. The third power of time is in corruption. Everything, having reached a certain point of prosperity,
decays, because as soon as man is master he wills to
enjoy, and because the inevitable result of enjoyment is
that decomposition of the soul and body which we call
corruption. The history of all successes is the history
of Hannibal at Capua. Men grow listless and forgetful, they think themselves secure, they become intox
icated with success; the slow poison of ease relaxes all

the springs of their activity; and the being who is nothing save by activity, falls little by little into the shame of slumbering effeminacy. Nimrod begins, Sardanapalus ends. It is the high road of great fortunes; labor and virtue form them, enjoyments annihilate even their last traces. Religion, even more than any other empire, is subject to this great law, and above all the Church, or the religion of Jesus Christ, was firmly chained to it. For the blood of the cross had given her life; having sprung from the crucifixion of a God, she could not fail, in the days of her prosperity, to remember the cruel humiliations of her cradle. And, on another hand, the temptations which her triumph pre pared for her were far to surpass any temptations until then known. She was to see the kings of the earth at her feet, to issue orders from one end of the world to the other, to behold ages bending before her teaching and her action, to cover the earth with sumptuous monuments, and see it become a tributary to all the wants of unlimited power and glory; and under the weight of such success, reaching even to heaven, to preserve upon her brow, as in her heart, the sign of penance and humility. Or, if in one of the long days of her life she was about to yield, and to feel the attack of corruption, from that very corruption she was to resuscitate her life, not another life—as we see in nature—but her own life; and, like the eagle of Scripture, recovering the charm of her youth, soar aloft with outstretched wings, invigorated and renewed by her very poverty and by the shedding of her own blood.

TIME VANQUISHED BY JESUS CHRIST.-- *Ibid.*

The fourth power of time is chance, that is to say
certain conjunctures which do not blend with anything
that genius is able to combine and foresee, and which
suddenly overthrow the most ably concerted designs.
History is full of these. Human prudence makes shipwreck upon shoals imperceptible to the keenest eye. It
is the grain of sand of which Pascal speaks, which one
morning threw Cromwell into disorder, and destroyed
plans destined to change the face of Europe.

2. You sometimes wonder, perhaps, at a certain
equilibrium visible in the world, and which keeps the
strong from destroying the weak at will. Why have
those great empires not yet crushed the small neigh-
boring states ? It is because those great empires have
Cromwell's grain of sand against them. At the very
moment when their combinations are ready to succeed
and bring about the destruction of all rights upon
earth, the obscure son of some peasant, in the corner of
a hut, sharpens his knife on a broken millstone; at the
noise of war he dons his cap, slips his knife into his
girdle, and goes out to see something of what is passing
between Providence and the kings of the earth. The
smoke of powder opens his eyes; the sight of blood
elates him; God makes him the instrument of a brilliant action; behold him a great captain; empires
recede a step before him; that knife, that peasant, is
chance.

3. Judge now how much of this Jesus Christ has
had to encounter in the course of a reign of eighteer

hundred years. Consult simply the history of the papacy, and see what a slender thread has held the destinies of that throne, always surrounded by enemies, yet always enduring. It has constantly had to contend against the most skilful combinations; but what is still more terrible is that conspiracy of chance, that enemy which might at any time have destroyed it, and which, strange to say, has always respected it.

4. The fifth power of time is war. No earthly power can avoid combat; it necessarily has enemies, not only on account of its faults and abuses, but by the simple fact of its existence. To exist is to combat, because to exist is to take from the common seat of life a part of the substance destined for all; and if this be true of the most feeble being, how much more so must it be of an assemblage of beings raised to the state of power! Therefore Jesus Christ declared " that he came not to send peace, but war,"* a terrible war, and upon a scale so vast as to astound our imagination. For it is the war of the spirit against the flesh and of the flesh against the spirit, that is to say, of the two elements which constitute man, neither of which can ever completely vanquish the other. When the body is victorious the soul struggles against it, and when the soul is the stronger the body watches for the moment when its yoke may be broken. But this internal struggle does not cease here, it necessarily produces a war as general as it is deeply seated. Souls unite with souls, and bodies with bodies; it is the union of bodies

---

* St. Matt. x. 34.

against the union of souls which forms the great war of mankind. Jesus Christ at the head of one army, and Satan at the head of the other; the army of the passions, pride, sensuality, hatred, on one side; the army of the spirit, humility, chastity, obedience, mortification, charity, on the other. All these are in action in the formidable regions of the finite and the infinite, in the depths of God, of the soul, and of the senses, amidst a thousand secondary causes which add to the gloom and the chances of the struggle; and if Jesus Christ be God, he must in the end be victorious, his form remaining unchangeable, although continually insulted, upon the venerable summit of time and things.

5. Has it been so, gentlemen? Can we testify of Jesus Christ that he has been more powerful than novelty, than experience, than corruption, than chance, than war, than all these causes banded together against him during a course of eighteen centuries? Can we do this?

6. Yes, gentlemen, I can do this; I can even show you three degrees in this triumph of Jesus Christ over time. For, in the first place, he lives, his work is before you; although it has undergone more or less of attack in that long pilgrimage under the rebel hand of time, it is nevertheless still before you. It remains surrounded by sufficient glory to attract all eyes, and to be still the object of veneration to which there is no rival, as nothing is comparable to the hatred of the enemies who have not accepted in its temporal duration the proof of its origin in the very bosom of eternity. But this is not all. Not only is Jesus Christ living in

his Church and his Church in him, but, since the Christian era, no religious establishment has been founded in the world, of which Jesus Christ has not been the basis and the bond of union.

EXILE OF ERIN.—*Campbell.*

There came to the beach a poor Exile of Erin,
  The dew on his thin robe was heavy and chill:
For his country he sigh'd, when at twilight repairing
  To wander alone by the wind-beaten hill:
But the day-star attracted his eye's sad devotion,
For it rose o'er his own native isle of the ocean,
Where once, in the fire of his youthful emotion,
  He sang the bold anthem of Erin go bragh.

Sad is my fate! said the heart-broken stranger:
  The wild deer and wolf to a covert can flee,
But I have no refuge from famine and danger,
  A home and a country remain not to me.
Never again, in the green sunny bowers,
Where my forefathers lived, shall I spend the sweet
    hours,
Or cover my harp with the wild-woven flowers,
  And strike to the numbers of Erin go bragh!

Erin, my country! though sad and forsaken,
  In dreams I revisit thy sea-beaten shore;
But, alas! in a far foreign land I awaken,
  And sigh for the friends who can meet me no more!

Oh cruel fate! wilt thou never replace me
In a mansion of peace—where no perils can chase me
Never again shall my brothers embrace me?
   They died to defend me, or live to deplore!

Where is my cabin-door, fast by the wild wood?
   Sisters and sire! did ye weep for its fall?
Where is the mother that look'd on my childhood?
   And where is the bosom friend, dearer than all?
Oh! my sad heart! long abandon'd by pleasure,
Why did it dote on a fast-fading treasure?
Tears, like the rain-drop, may fall without measure,
   But rapture and beauty they cannot recall.

Yet all its sad recollections suppressing,
   One dying wish my lone bosom can draw:
Erin! an exile bequeaths thee his blessing!
   Land of my forefathers! Erin go bragh!
Buried and cold, when my heart stills her motion,
Green be thy fields,—sweetest isle of the ocean!
And thy harp-striking bards sing aloud with devo-
   tion,—
   Erin mavournin—Erin go bragh! *

WHAT MAKES A HERO?—*Henry Taylor.*

What makes a hero?—not success, not fame,
Inebriate merchants, and the loud acclaim
   Of glutted Avarice,—caps tossed up in air,
   Or pen of journalist with flourish fair;

---

* Ireland, my darling, Ireland for ever.

Bells pealed, stars, ribbons, and a titular name—
   These, though his rightful tribute, he can spare ;
His rightful tribute, not his end or aim,
   Or true reward ; for never yet did these
   Refresh the soul, or set the heart at ease.
What makes a hero ?—An heroic mind,
Expressed in action, in endurance proved.
   And if there be pre-eminence of right,
   Derived through pain well suffered, to the height
Of rank heroic, 't is to bear unmoved,
Not toil, not risk, not rage of sea or wind,
Not the brute fury of barbarians blind,
   But worse—ingratitude and poisonous darts,
   Launched by the country he had served and loved;
This, with a free, unclouded spirit pure,
This, in the strength of silence to endure,
   A dignity to noble deeds imparts,
   Beyond the gauds and trappings of renown
   This is the hero's complement and crown ;
This missed, one struggle had been wanting still,—
One glorious triumph of the heroic will,
   One self-approval in his heart of hearts.

THE BIBLE.

[Donoso Cortes is the author of several remarkably able and brilliant essays. The following extract is from a speech delivered in Madrid on the occasion of his reception as a member of the Royal Spanish Academy of Languages.]

There is a book, the treasure of a nation, which has now become the fable and the reproach of the world, though in former days the star of the East, to whose pages all the great poets of the Western world have gone to drink in divine inspiration, and from which they have learned the secret of elevating our hearts and transporting our souls with superhuman and mysterious harmonies. This book is the Bible— the Book of books. In it Dante saw his terrific vi sions; from it Petrarch learned to modulate the voice of his complainings; from that burning forge the poet of Sorrentum drew for the splendid brightness of his songs.

2. In the Bible are written the annals of heaven, of earth, and of the human race. In it, as in the Divinity itself, is contained that which was, which is, and which is to come. In its first page is recorded the beginning of time and of all things—in its last, the end of all things, and of time. It begins with Genesis, which is an idyl; it finishes with the Apocalypse of St. John, which is a funeral hymn.

3. Genesis is beautiful as the first breeze which refreshed the world, as the first flower which budded forth in the fields, as the first tender word which humanity pronounced, as the first sun that rose in the East. The Apocalypse is sad, like the last throb of nature, like the last ray of light, like the last glance of the dying; and between that funeral hymn and that idyl we behold all generations pass, one after another, before the sight of God, and one after another, all nations.

4. There all catastrophes are related or predicted, and therefore immortal models for all tragedies are to

be found there. There we find the narration of all human griefs, and therefore the Biblical harps resound mournfully, giving the tone to all lamentations and to all elegies. Who will again moan like Job, when, driven to the earth by the mighty hand that afflicted him, he fills with his groanings and waters with his tears the valleys of Idumea?

5. Who will again lament as Jeremiah lamented, wandering around Jerusalem, and abandoned of God and men? Who will be mournful and gloomy, with the gloom and mournfulness of Ezekiel, the poet of great woes and tremendous punishments, when he gave to the winds his impetuous inspiration, the terror of Babylon? Who shall again sing like Moses, when, after crossing the Red Sea, he chanted the victory of Jehovah, the defeat of Pharaoh, the liberty of his people?

6. Who shall again chant a hymn of victory like that which was sung by Deborah, the sybil of Israel, the amazon of the Hebrews, the strong woman of the Bible? And if from hymns of victory you pass to hymns of praise, what temple shall ever resound like that of Israel, when those sweet harmonious voices arose to heaven, mingled with the soft perfume of the roses of Jericho, and with the aroma of Oriental incense?

7. If you seek for models of lyric poetry, what lyre shall we find comparable to the harp of David, the friend of God, who listened to the sweet harmonies and caught the soft tones of the harps of angels? or to that of Solomon, the wisest and most fortunate

of monarchs, the inspired writer of the Song of Songs; he who put his wisdom into sentences and proverbs, and finished by pronouncing that all was vanity?

8. If you seek for models of bucolic poetry, where will you find them so fresh and so pure as in the Scriptural era of the patriarchate, when the woman and the fountain and the flower were friends, because they were all united—each one by itself the symbol of primitive simplicity and of candid innocence?

9. A prodigious book that, gentlemen, in which the human race began to read thirty-three centuries ago, and although reading it every day, every night, and every hour, have not yet finished its perusal. A prodigious book that, in which all is computed, before the science of calculation was invented; in which, without the study of the languages, we are informed of the origin of languages; in which, without astronomical studies, the revolutions of the stars are computed; in which, without historical documents, we are instructed in history; in which, without physical studies, the laws of nature are revealed.

10. A prodigious book that, which sees all and knows all; which knows the thoughts that arise in the heart of man, and those which are present to the mind of God; which views that which passes in the abysses of the sea, and that which takes place in the bosom of the earth; which relates or predicts all the catastrophes of nations, and in which are contained and heaped together all the treasures of mercy, all the treasures of justice, and all the treasures of vengeance.

11. A book, in short, gentlemen, which, when the

heavens shall fold together like a gigantic scroll, and the earth shall faint away, and the sun withdraw its light, and the stars grow pale, will remain alone with God, because it is his eternal word, and shall res ur l eternally in the heavens.

CATO ON THE SOUL'S IMMORTALITY.—*Addison*

It must be so!　Plato, thou reasonest well:
Else whence this fond desire, this pleasing hope,
This longing after immortality?
Or whence this secret dread, and inward horror
Of falling into naught?　Why shrinks the soul
Back on herself, and shudders at destruction?
'Tis the divinity that stirs within us;
'Tis heaven itself that points out a hereafter,
And intimates eternity to man!—
Eternity! thou pleasing, dreadful thought!--
Through what variety of untried being,
Through what new forms and changes must we pass?
The wide, the unbounded prospect lies before me:
But shadows, clouds, and darkness rest upon it.
Here will I hold:—If there's a Power above,—
And that there is all Nature cries aloud
Through all her works,—He must delight in, virtue;
And that which He delights in must be happy:
But when? or how?　This world was made for Cæsar
I'm weary of conjectures; this must end 'em!
　　　　　　　　　　　　[*Taking up the sword.*]
Thus am 1 doubly arm'd: my life and death,
My bane and antidote, are both before me.

This, in a moment, brings me to an end;
But this assures me I shall never die !
The soul, secure in her existence, smiles
At the drawn dagger, and defies its point
The stars shall fade away, the Sun himself
Grow dim with age, and Nature sink in years,—
Thou still shalt flourish in eternal youth,
Unhurt amidst the war of elements,
The wreck of matter and the crush of worlds !

CATO'S SPEECH OVER HIS DEAD SON.—*Addison*

Thanks to the gods ! my boy has done his duty.—
Welcome, my son ! Here set him down, my friends,
Full in my sight; that I may view at leisure
The bloody corse, and count those glorious wounds.
How beautiful is death, when earn'd by virtue !
Who would not be that youth ?—what pity is it
That we can die but once to serve our country !
Why sits this sadness on your brow, my friends ?
I should have blush'd if Cato's house had stood
Secure, and flourish'd in a civil war.—
Porcius, behold thy brother ! and remember,
Thy life is not thy own when Rome demands it !
When Rome demands !—but Rome is now no more !
The Roman empire's fall'n !—(Oh ! curs'd ambition !)
Fall'n into Cæsar's hands ! Our great forefathers
Had left him naught to conquer but his country. —
Porcius, come hither to me !—Ah ! my son,
Despairing of success,
Let me advise thee to withdraw, betimes,

To our paternal seat, the Sabine field,
Where the great censor toil'd with his own hands,
And all our frugal ancestors were bless'd
In humble virtues and a rural life.
There live retired : content thyself to be
Obscurely good.
When vice prevails, and impious men bear sway,
The post of honor is a private station!
Farewell, my friends! If there be any of you
Who dare not trust the victor's clemency,
Know, there are ships prepared by my command—
Their sails already op'ning to the winds,—
That shall convey you to the wish'd-for port.
The conqueror draws near—once more, farewell!
If e'er we meet hereafter, we shall meet
In happier climes, and on a safer shore,
Where Cæsar never shall approach us more!
There, the brave youth with love of virtue fired,
Who greatly in his country's cause expired,
Shall know he conquer'd! The firm patriot there,
Who made the welfare of mankind his care,
Tho' still by faction, vice and fortune cross'd,
Shall find the generous labor was not lost.

ENGLAND'S DOOM.—*Apb. Spalding.*

On that great and dreadful Day of the Lord, when
nations as well as individuals shall be placed at the
bar of God to be judged according to their works,
England will have an awful account to render of her
stewardship. Her impoverished and down-trodden

population withi_ her own borders, the crushed and degraded millions whom she has enslaved in India, and the widows and orphans whom she has made throughout the world, in her reckless career of ambition, wil. all rise up in judgment against her.

2. The nations of the civilized earth will stand up too, and will bear evidence to her hard-hearted and re lentless avarice, to her utter disregard of the most solemn promises and treaties, to her all-grasping spirit of aggrandizement, and to her entire recklessness as to the means by which her ends were to be attained.

3. And on that awful day of final reckoning, the voice of poor crushed and bleeding Ireland shall be heard pleading, with all the earnest eloquence of truth, that justice, swift and terrible, may at length fall on the head of that unnatural step-dame, to whose wanton cruelty, griping avarice, and iron policy she owes most of the wrongs which have weighed her down for centuries.

4. What will England say, when all these terrible witnesses shall appear against her, and when the ghosts of her countless murdered victims shall glare at her "with their fiery eye-balls?" What answer shall she give when the long and dark roll of her iniquities towards Ireland shall be unfolded before the judgment-seat of the most just, omnipotent, and all-seeing God of heaven and earth? Will her diplomacy then profit her anything?

5. Will those cunning devices and that political *legerdemain* by which, on this earth, she has so often succeeded in making "the worse appear the better cause,"

then avail her aught? No, no. The Lord will then tear from her brow the veil of hypocrisy which has so long concealed her hideous deformities; He will strip her of all disguise, and exhibit her as she is before the assembled world; for on that day " He will reveal the hidden things of darkness, and manifest the counsels of hearts."

6. And then shall proud England be humbled even unto the dust, and poor bleeding Ireland, which has been down-trodden by her for nearly seven centuries, be raised up from her lowliness to the lofty eminence to which her noble virtues and her long sufferings have entitled her. This is no mere flight of elevated fancy; it is a solemn and sober religious view of a subject invested with an all-absorbing interest.

THE MARTYRS OF FATHERLAND.—*De Vere.*

Woe, woe to tyrants!   Who are they?
    Whence come they?   Whither are they sent?
Who gave them first their baleful sway
    O'er ocean, isle, and continent?
Wild beasts they are, ravening for aye;
Vultures that make the world their prey;
Pests ambushed in the noontide day;
Ill stars of ruin and dismay.
We heard them coming from afar;
Heard, and rushed into the war:
We kissed our fathers' graves,
And rushed to meet our Country's foes.

2. I trembled when the strife began—
    Woman (was I), my clasp'd hands-trembled
    With ill-timed weakness ill dissembled;
But now beyond the strength of man,
    My strength has in a moment grown,
And I no more my griefs deplore
    Than doth a shape of stone.
And dost thou (tyrant) make thy boast then, of their
    lying
    All cold upon the mountain and the plain,
    My sons whom thou hast slain?
And that no tears nor sighing
    Can raise their heads again?

3. My sons not vainly have died,
For ye your country glorified!
Each moment as in death ye bowed,
    On high your martyred souls ascended;
Yea, soaring in perpetual cloud,
    This earth with heaven ye blended.
A living chain in death ye wove;
And, rising, raised our world more near those worlds
    above!

4. They perish idly? they in vain?
When not a sparrow to the plain
Drops uncared for! Tyrant! they
Are radiant with eternal day!
And if, unseen, on us they turn
Those looks that make us inly burn,
And swifter through our pulses flow
The bounding blood, their blood below!

5. How little cause have those for fear
   Whose outward forms alone are here!
   How nigh are they to heaven, who there
   Have stored their earliest tenderest care!
   Whate'er was ours of erring pride,
   This agony hath sanctified.
   Our destined flower thy blasts but tear
   Its sacred seed o'er earth to bear!
   O'er us the storm hath passed, and we
   Are standing here immovably
   Upon the platform of the Right.

THE FIRE-WORSHIPPERS.—(*From "Lalla Rookh."*)

MOORE.

But see—he starts—what heard he then?
That dreadful shout!—across the glen
From the land side it comes, and loud
Rings through the chasm; as if the crowd
Of fearful things that haunt that dell,
Its ghouls and dives, and shapes of hell,
Had all in one dread howl broke out,
So loud, so terrible that shout!
"They come—the Moslems come!"—he cries,
His proud soul mounting to his eyes:—
"Now, spirits of the brave, who roam
Enfranchised through yon starry dome,
Rejoice—for souls of kindred fire
Are on the wing to join your choir!"

He said—and, light as bridegrooms bound
   To their young loves, re-climb'd the steep
And gain'd the shrine—his chiefs stood round—
   Their swords, as with instinctive leap,
Together, at that cry accurst,
Had from their sheaths, like sunbeams, burst
And hark!—again—again it rings;
Near and more near its echoings
Peal through the chasm.   Oh! who that then
Had seen those listening warrior-men,
With their swords grasped, their eyes of flame
Turn'd on their chief—could doubt the shame,
Th' indignant shame with which they thrill
To hear those shouts, and yet stand still?

2. He read their thoughts—they were his own—
   "What! while our arms can wield these blades,
Shall we die tamely—die alone?
   Without one victim to our shades,
One Moslem heart where, buried deep,
The sabre from its toil may sleep?
No—God of Iran's burning skies!
Thou scorn'st th' inglorious sacrifice.
No—though of all earth's hope bereft,
Life, swords, and vengeance still are left.
We'll make yon valley's reeking caves
   Live in the awe-struck minds of men,
Till tyrants shudder when their slaves
   Tell of the Ghebers' bloody glen.

Follow, brave hea.ts !—this pile remains
Our refuge still from life and chains;
But his the best, the holiest bed,
Who sinks entomb'd in Moslem dead!"

TITUS BEFORE JERUSALEM.—*Milman.*

[From a dramatic poem entitled the "Fall of Jerusalem," by Rev. H. H. Milman.]

Titus. It must be—
And yet it moves me, Romans! It confounds
The counsel of my firm philosophy,
That Ruin's merciless ploughshare must pass o'er,
And barren salt be sown on yon proud city.
As on our olive-crowned hill we stand,
Where Kedron at our feet its scanty waters
Distils from stone to stone with gentle motion,
As through a valley sacred to sweet peace,
How boldly doth it front us, how majestically,
Like a luxurious vineyard, the hill-side
Is hung with marble fabrics, line o'er line,
Terrace o'er terrace, nearer still, and nearer
To the blue heavens. There bright and sumptuous
    palaces,
With cool and verdant gardens interspersed;
There towers of war that frown in massy strength;
While over all hangs the rich purple eve,
As conscious of its being her last farewell
Of light ard glory to that fated city.

And, as our clouds of battle, dust and smoke,
Are melted into air, behold the temple,
In undisturbed and lone serenity,
Finding itself a solemn sanctuary
In the profound of heaven! It stands before us
A mount of snow, fretted with golden pinnacles!
The very sun, as though he worshipped there,
Lingers upon the gilded cedar roofs.

THE WONDERFUL "ONE-HOSS SHAY."—*A Logical Poem.*
HOLMES.

[This witty and humorous poem is illustrative of certain New England characteristics. The words italicised are spelt in such a way as to indicate peculiarities of pronunciation sometimes heard among the uneducated in New England.]

Have you heard of the wonderful one-*hoss shay*,
That was built in such a logical way
It ran a hundred years to a day,
And then, of a sudden, it—Ah, but stay,
I'll tell you what happened, without delay;
Scaring the parson into fits,
Frightening people out of their wits—
Have you ever heard of that, I say?

2. Seventeen Hundred and Fifty-five,
Georgius Secundus was then alive—
Snuffy old drone from the German hive!
That was the year when Lisbon town
Saw the earth open and gulp her down;
And Braddock's army was done so brown
Left without a scalp to its crown.

It was on the terrible Earthquake-day
That the Deacon finished the one-*hoss shay.*

3. Now, in building of chaises, I tell you what,
There is always, somewhere, a weakest spot—
In hub, tire, felloe, in spring or thill,
In panel or crossbar, or floor or sill,
In screw, bolt, thoroughbrace—lurking still,
Find it somewhere you must and will—
Above or below, or within or without—
And that's the reason, beyond a doubt,
A chaise breaks down, but doesn't wear out.

4. But the Deacon swore—(as Deacons do,
With an "*I dew vum*" or an "I tell *yecu* ')—
He would build one *shay* to beat the *taown*
'*N' the keounty 'n' all the kentry raoun'* ;
It should be so built that it *couldn'* break *dacwn;*
"*Fur,*" said the Deacon, "'*t's* mighty plain
That the *weakes' place mus' stan'* the strain ;
'*N' the way t' fix it, uz,* I maintain,
　　　Is only *jest*
T' make that place *uz* strong *uz* the rest.

5. So the Deacon inquired of the village folk
Where he could find the strongest oak,
That couldn't be split, nor bent, nor broke—
That was for spokes, and floor, and sills:
He sent for lancewood to make the thills ;

The crossbars were ash, from the straightest trees;
The panels of white-wood, that cuts like cheese.
But lasts like iron for things like these ;
The hubs of logs from the " Settler's *ellum* "—·
Last of its timber—they couldn't sell 'em ;

6. Never an ax had seen their chips,
   And the wedges flew from between their lips,
   Their blunt ends frizzled like celery tips ;
   Step and prop-iron, bolt and screw,
   Spring, tire, axle, and linchpin too,
   Steel of the finest, bright and blue ;
   Thoroughbrace, bison-skin, thick and wide ;
   Boot, top, dasher, from tough old hide,
   Found in the pit where the tanner died.
   That was the way he "put her through."
   " There ! " said the Deacon, " *naow she'll dew !* "

7. Do ! I tell you, I rather guess
   She was a wonder, and nothing less !
   Colts grew horses, beards turned gray,
   Deacon and deaconess dropped away ;
   Children and grandchildren—where were they
   But there stood the stout old one-*hoss shay*,
   As fresh as on Lisbon-earthquake day !

8. Eighteen Hundred—it came, and found
   The Deacon's masterpiece strong and sound.
   Eighteen hundred, increased by ten—
   " *Hahnsum kerridye* " they called it then.

Eighteen hundred and twenty came;—
Running as usual—much the same.
Thirty and forty at last arrive ;
And then came Fifty—and Fifty-five.

9   Little of all we value here
Wakes on the morn of its hundredth year,
Without both feeling and looking queer.
In fact, there's nothing that keeps its youth,
So far as I know, but a tree and truth.
(This is a moral that runs at large :
Take it.—You're welcome.—No extra charge.)

10   First of November—the Earthquake-day ;
There are traces of age in the one-*hoss shay*,
A general flavor of mild decay,
But nothing local, as one may say.
There couldn't be--for the Deacon's art
Had made it so like in every part
That there wasn't a chance for one to start.
For the wheels were just as strong as the thills,
And the floor was just as strong as the sills,
And the panels just as strong as the floor,
And the whipple-tree neither less nor more,
And the back crossbar as strong as the fore,
And spring, and axle, and hub encore.
And yet, as a whole, it is past a doubt
In another hour it will be worn out !

11.   First of November, 'Fifty-five !
This morning the parson takes a drive.

Now, small boys, get out of the way!
Here comes the wonderful one-*hoss shay*,
Drawn by a rat-tailed, ewe-necked bay.
" *Huddup!* " said the parson.—Off went they!

12. The parson was working his Sunday text,—
Had got to *fifthly*, and stopped perplexed
At what the—Moses—was coming next.
All at once the horse stood still,
Close by the *meet'n'-house* on the hill.
—First a shiver, and then a thrill,
Then something decidedly like a spill—
And the parson was sitting upon a rock,
At half-past nine by the *meet'n'-house clock*—
Just the hour of the Earthquake shock!

13. What do you think the parson found,
When he got up and stared around?
The poor old chaise in a heap or mound,
As if it had been to the mill and ground!
You see, of course, if you're not a dunce,
How it went to pieces all at once—
All at once, and nothing first—
Just as bubbles do when they burst.
End of the wonderful one-*hoss shay*,
Logic *is* Logic. That's all I say.

THE RISING OF THE VENDÉE. — *Croly.*

[The Rev. George Croly was born in Dublin in 1780, and died in
1860. He was for many years rector of St. Stephens, Walbrook, in
London. He was a well-known writer in prose and verse. Among
his productions were "Catiline," a tragedy; "Salathiel," a romance; a biography of Burke; and the novel of "Marston, or Me-
moirs of a Statesman," from which the following spirited poem is
taken.

La Vendée,* or the Vendée, is a district on the western coast of
France, the inhabitants of which were royalists, and broke out into
open rebellion against the revolutionary government of France in
1793. The insurrection was suppressed after a few months, during
which the Vendeans displayed the most heroic courage. An Ange-
vine is an inhabitant of the district of Anjou. The Oriflamme was
the ancient royal standard of France.]

It was a Sabbath morning, and sweet the summer air,
And brightly shone the summer sun upon the day of
    prayer,
And silver sweet the village-bells o'er mount and val-
    ley tolled,
And in the church of St. Florent† were gathered
    young and old,—
When, rushing down the woodland hill, in fiery haste,
    was seen,
With panting steed and bloody spur, a noble Ange-
    vine;
And bounding on the sacred floor, he gave his fearful
    cry:
"Up! up for France! the time is come for France to
    live or die!

---

* Vendée. văn (g)-dā.   † St. Florent, săn(g) flŏ-răn(g)

"Your queen is in the dungeon; your king is in his
  gore;
O'er Paris waves the flag of death, the fiery Tricolor;
Your nobles in their ancient halls are hunted down
  and slain;
In convent cells and holy shrines the blood is poured
  like rain;
The peasant's vine is rooted up, his cottage given to
  flame;
His son is to the scaffold sent, his daughter sent to
  shame.
With torch in hand and hate in heart, the rebel host is
  nigh.
Up! up for France! the time is come for France to
  live or die!"

That live-long night the horn was heard from Orleans*
  to Anjou,†
And poured from all their quiet fields our shepherds
  bold and true.
Along the pleasant banks of Loire shot up the beacon-
  fires,
And many a torch was blazing bright on Luçon's‡
  stately spires;
The midnight cloud was flushed with flame, that hung
  o'er Parthenay; §
The blaze that shone o'er proud Brissac ‖ was like the
  breaking day,

---

* Orléans, ör-lā-ān(g).　　　§ Parthenay, pär-te-nā.
† Anjou, än(g)-zhô.　　　　　‖ Brissac, bris-säu.
‡ Luçon, lu-sân(g).

Till east, and west, and north, and south, the loyal bea
    cons shone

Like shooting-stars from haughty Nantes * to sea-begirt
    Olonne.†

And through the night, on horse and foot, the sleepless
    summons flew,

And morning saw the Lily-flag wide-waving o'er Poi-
    tou.‡

And many an ancient musketoon was taken from the
    wall,

And many a jovial hunter's steed was harnessed in the
    stall,

And many a noble's armory gave up the sword and
    spear,

And many a bride, and many a babe, was left with
    kiss and tear,

And many a homely peasant bade farewell to his old
    dame,

As in the days when France's king unfurled the Ori-
    flamme.

There, leading his bold marksmen, rode the eagle-eyed
    Lescure,§

And dark Stofflet,∥ who flies to fight as an eagle to
    his lure;

And fearless as the lion roused, but gentle as the lamb,

Came marching at his people's head the great and good
    Bonchamp;¶

---

* Nantes, năn(g)t.   § Lescure, lĕs-cure.
† Olonne, ŏl-lŏn.   ∥ Stofflet, stŏf-flā.
‡ Poitou, pwä-tô.   ¶ Bonchamp, băn(g)-shän(g)

Charette,* where honor was the prize, the hero sure
    to win;
And there, with Henri Quatre's plume, young la
    Rochejacquelein ; †
And there, in peasant garb and speech,—the terror of
    the foe,—
A noble, made by Heaven's own hand, the great Ca-
    thelineau.‡

We marched by tens of thousands, we marched by day
    and night,
The Lily-standard in our front, like Israel's holy light
Around us rushed the rebels, as the wolf upon the
    sheep,—
We burst upon their columns as a lion roused from
    sleep;
We tore their bayonets from their hands, we slew them
    at their guns ;
Their boasted horsemen fled like chaff before our for-
    est sons.
That night we heaped their baggage high, their lines of
    dead between,
And in the centre blazed to heaven their blood-dyed
    guillotine !

In vain they hid their heads in walls ; we rushed on
    stout Thouar ;§
What cared we for shot or shell, for battlement or
    bar ?

---

* Charette, sha-rĕt.
† la Rochejacquelein, lah-rōsh-
   shāk-lăn(g).
‡ Cathelineau, căt-eh-lĭ nō.
§ Thouar, tō-är.

We burst its gates; then like a wind we rushed on
　　Fontenay;*
We saw its flag with morning light—'twas ours by set-
　　ting day;
We crushed like ripened grapes Montreuil,† we bore
　　down old Vihiers;‡
We charged them with our naked breasts, and took
　　them with a cheer.
We'll hunt the robbers through the land, from Seine §
　　to sparkling Rhone;
Now, "Here's a health to all we love, our king shall
　　have his own."

---

* Fontenay, fân(g)-teh-uä.　　‡ Vihiers, vi-yä.
† Montreuil, mân(g)-trärl.　　§ Seine, sin.

DIALOGUES.

SELF INTEREST;

OR, WHERE THERE'S A WILL, THERE'S A WAY.

Derby. Good morning, neighbor Scrapewell. I have half a dozen miles to ride to-day, and should be extremely obliged if you would lend me your gray mare.

Scrapewell. I should be happy, friend Derby, to oblige you; but am under the necessity of going immediately to the mill with three bags of corn. My wife wants the meal this very morning.

D. Then she must want it still, for I can assure you the mill does not go to-day. I heard the miller tell Will Davis that the water was too low.

S. You don't say so? That is bad indeed; for in that case I shall be obliged to gallop off to town for the meal. My wife would comb my head for me, if I should neglect it.

D. I can save you this journey, for I have plenty of meal at home, and will lend your wife as much as she wants.

S. Ah! neighbor Derby, I am sure your meal will never suit my wife. You can't conceive how whimsical she is.

D. If she were ten times more whimsical than she is, I am certain she would like it; for you sold it to me yourself, and you assured me it was the best you ever had.

S. Yes, yes, that's true, indeed; I always have the best of everything. You know, neighbor Derby, that no one is more ready to oblige a friend than I am; but I must tell you, the mare this morning refused to eat hay; and, truly, I am afraid she will not carry you.

D. Oh, never fear! I will feed her well with oats on the road.

S. Oats! neighbor; oats are very dear.

D. Never mind that. When I have a good job in view, I never stand for trifles.

S. But it is very slippery; and I am really afraid she will fall and break your neck.

D. Give yourself no uneasiness about that. The mare is certainly sure-footed; and, besides, you were just now talking of galloping her to town.

S. Well, then, to tell you the plain truth, though I wish to oblige you with all my heart, my saddle is torn quite in pieces, and I have just sent my bridle to be mended.

D. Luckily, I have both a bridle and a saddle hang-
ing up at home.

S. Ah! that may be; but I am sure your saddle will
never fit my mare.

D. Why, then I'll borrow neighbor Clodpole's.

S. Clodpole's! his will no more fit than yours will.

D. At the worst, then, I will go to my good friend
'Squire Jones. He has half a score of them; and I
am sure he will lend me one that will fit her.

S. You know, friend Derby, that no one is more willing to oblige his neighbors than I am. I do assure
you, the beast should be at your service, with all my
heart; but she has not been curried, I believe, for three
weeks past. Her foretop and mane want combing and
cutting very much. If any one should see her in her
present plight, it would ruin the sale of her.

D. Oh! a horse is soon curried, and my son Sam shall
despatch her at once.

S. Yes, very likely; but I this moment recollect the
creature has no shoes on.

D. Well, is there not a blacksmith hard by?

S. What! that tinker of a Dobson? I would not
trust such a bungler to shoe a goat. No, no; none but
uncle Tom Thumper is capable of shoeing my mare.

D. As good luck will have it, then, I shall pass right
by his door.

S. (*calling to his son.*) Timothy, Timothy. Here's
neighbor Derby, who wants the loan of the gray mare,
to ride to town to-day. You know the skin was rubbed
off her back last week a hand's breadth or more. (*He
gives Tim a wink.*) However, I believe she is well

enough by this time. You know, Tim, how ready I am
to oblige my neighbors. And, indeed, we ought to do
all the good we can in this world. We must certainly
let neighbor Derby have her, if she will possibly answer
his purpose. Yes, yes; I see plainly, by Tim's countenance, neighbor Derby, that he's disposed to oblige
you. I would not have refused you the mare for the
worth of her. If I had, I should have expected you
would have refused me in your turn. None of my
neighbors can accuse me of being backward in doing
them a kindness. Come, Timothy, what do you say?

T. What do I say, father? Why, I say, sir, that I
am no less ready than you are to do a neighborly kindness. But the mare is by no means capable of performing the journey. About a hand's breadth did you say,
sir? Why, the skin is torn from the poor creature's
back, of the bigness of your broad-brimmed hat. And,
besides, I have promised her, as soon as she is able to
travel, to Ned Saunders, to carry a load of apples to the
market.

S. Do you hear that, neighbor? I am very sorry
matters turn out thus. I would not have disobliged you
for the price of two such mares. Believe me, neighbor
Derby, I am really sorry, for your sake, that matters
turn out thus.

D. And I as much for yours, neighbor Scrapewell;
for, to tell you the truth, I received a letter this morning
from Mr. Griffin, who tells me, if I will be in town this
day, he will give me the refusal of all that lot of timber
which he is about cutting down upon the back of cobble-
hill; and I intended you should have shared half of it,

which would have been not less than fifty dollars in your pocket. But, as your——

S. Fifty dollars, did you say?

D. Ay, truly did I; but as your mare is out of order, I'll go and see if I can get old Roan, the blacksmith's horse.

S. Old Roan! My mare is at your service, neighbor. Here, Tim, tell Ned Saunders he can't have the mare. Neighbor Derby wants her; and I won't refuse so good a friend anything he asks for.

D. But what are you to do for the meal?

S. My wife can do without it this fortnight, if you want the mare so long.

D. But then your saddle is all in pieces.

S. I meant the old one. I have bought a new one since, and you shall have the first use of it.

D. And you would have me call at Thumper's, and get her shod?

S. No, no; I had forgotten to tell you, that I let neighbor Dobson shoe her last week by way of trial, and, to do him justice, I must own, he shoes extremely well.

D. But if the poor creature has lost so much skin from off her back——

S. Poh, poh! That is just one of our Tim's large stories. I do assure you, it was not at first bigger than my thumb-nail; and I am certain it has not grown any since.

D. At least, however, let her have something she will eat, since she refuses hay.

S. She did, indeed, refuse hay this morning; but

the only reason was that she was crammed full of oats.
You have nothing to fear, neighbor; the mare is in
perfect trim; and she will skim you over the ground
like a bird. I wish you a good journey and a profitable
job.

THE BATTLE OF LIFE

● LONGFELLOW.

LET our unceasing, earnest prayer
Be, too, for light,—for strength to bear
Our portion of the weight of care
That crushes into dumb despair
    One half the human race.

O suffering, sad humanity!
O ye afflicted ones, who lie
Steeped to the lips in misery,
Longing, and yet afraid to die,
    Patient, though sorely tried!

I pledge you in this cup of grief,
Where floats the fennel's bitter leaf!
The Battle of our Life is brief,
The alarm,—the struggle,—the relief,
    Then sleep we side by side.

VANOC AND VALENS, IN THE TRAGEDY OF THE BRITON.—
Philips.

Van. Now, tribune!—

Val. Health to Vanoc.

Van. Speak your business.

Val. I come not as a herald, but a friend:
And I rejoice that Didius chose out me
To greet a prince in my esteem the foremost.

Van. So much for words.—Now to your purpose, tribune.

Val. Sent by our new lieutenant, who in Rome
And since from me has heard of your renown,
I come to offer peace ; to reconcile
Past enmities ; to strike perpetual league
With Vanoc ; whom our emperor invites
To terms of friendship ; strictest bonds of union.

Van. We must not hold a friendship with the Romans.

Val. Why must you not?

Van. Virtue forbids it.

Val. Once
You thought our friendship was your greatest glory.

Van. I thought you honest.—I have been deceived.—
Would you deceive me twice? No, tribune, no !
You sought for war,—maintain it as you may.

Val. Believe me, prince, your vehemence of spirit,
Prone ever to extremes, betrays your judgment.
Would you once coolly reason on our conduct—

Van. Oh, I have scanned it thoroughly. Night and day
I think it over, and I think it base ;
Most infamous ! let who will judge—but Romans.

Did not my wife, did not my menial servant,
Seducing each the other, both conspire
Against my crown, against my fame, my life?
Did they not levy war and wage rebellion?
And when I would assert my right and power
As king and husband, when I would chastise
Two most abandoned wretches—who but Romans
Opposed my justice and maintained their crimes?

 Val. At first the Romans did not interpose,
But grieved to see their best allies at variance.
Indeed, when you turned justice into rigor,
And even that rigor was pursued with fury,
We undertook to mediate for the queen,
And hoped to moderate—

 Van. To moderate!—
What would you moderate?—my indignation,
The just resentment of a virtuous mind?
To mediate for the queen!—you undertook?
Wherein concerned it you, but as you love
To exercise your insolence?   Are you
To arbitrate my wrongs?   Must I ask leave
Must I be taught to govern my own household?
Am I then void of reason and of justice?
When in my family offences rise,
Shall strangers, saucy intermeddlers, say,
Thus far, and thus you are allowed to punish?
When I submit to such indignities—
When I am tamed to that degree of slavery—
Make me a citizen, a senator of Rome,
To watch, to live upon the smile of Claudius;

To give my wife and children to his pleasures,
To sell my country with my voice for bread.

Val. Prince, you insult upon this day's success;
You may provoke too far—but I am cool—
I give your answer scope.

Van. Who shall confine it ?—
The Romans ?—Let them rule their slaves—I blush
That, dazzled in my youth with ostentation,
The trappings of the men seduced my virtue.

Val. Blush, rather, that you are a slave to passion;
Subservient to the wildness of your will ;
Which, like a whirlwind, tears up all your virtues,
And gives you not the leisure to consider.
Did not the Romans civilize you ?—

Van. No. They brought new customs and new vices
over
Taught us more arts than honest men require,
And gave us wants that nature never knew.

Val. We found you naked—

Van. And you found us free.

Val. Would you be temperate once, and hear me out—

Van. Speak things that honest men may hear with
temper,
Speak the plain truth, and varnish not your crimes.
Say, that you once were virtuous—long ago
A frugal, hardy people, like the Britons,
Before you grew thus elegant in vice,
And gave your luxuries the name of virtues.
The civilizers !—the disturbers, say ;—
The robbers, the corrupters of mankind,
Proud vagabonds !—who make the world your home,

And lord it where you have no right.
What virtue have you taught ?
   Val. Humanity.
   Van. Oh ! Patience !
   Val. Can you disown a truth confessed by all ?
A praise, a glory, known in barbarous climes ?
Far as our legions march, they carry knowledge,
The arts, the laws, the discipline of life.
Our conquests are indulgences, and we
Not masters, but protectors of mankind.
   Van. Prevaricating, false—most courteous tyrants ;
Romans ! Rare patterns of humanity !
Came you then thus far through the waves to conquer,
To waste, to plunder out of mere compassion ?
Is it humanity that prompts you on
To ravage the whole earth, to burn, destroy ?
To raise the cry of widows and of orphans ?
To lead in bonds the generous free-born princes,
Who spurn, who fight against your tyranny ?
Happy for us, and happy for you spoilers,
Had your humanity ne'er reached our world—
It is a virtue—(so it seems you call it)
A Roman virtue that has cost you dear :
And dearer shall it cost if Vanoc lives,—
Or if we die, we shall leave those behind us
Who know the worth of British liberty.

THE QUARREL BETWEEN BRUTUS AND CASSIUS.—*Shakespeare.*

Cas. That you have wronged me, doth appear in this :
You have condemned and noted Lucius Pella,
For taking bribes here of the Sardians ;
Wherein my letters, praying on his side,
Because I knew the man, were slighted of.
  Bru. You wronged yourself, to write in such a case.
  Cas. In such a time as this, it is not meet
That every nice offence should bear its comment.
  Bru. Yet let me tell you, Cassius, you yourself
Are much condemned to have an itching palm ;
To sell and mart your offices for gold
To undeservers.
  Cas. I an itching palm ?
You know that you are Brutus that speak this,
Or, by the gods, this speech were else your last.
  Bru. The name of Cassius honors this corruption,
And chastisement doth therefore hide its head.
  Cas. Chastisement !
  Bru. Remember March, the Ides of March remember
Did not great Julius bleed for justice' sake ?
What villain touched his body, that did stab,
And not for justice ?   What, shall one of us,
That struck the foremost man in all this world,
But for supporting robbers ; shall we now
Contaminate our fingers with base bribes ?
And sell the mighty space of our large honors,
For so much trash as may be grasped thus ?—

I had rather be a dog, and bay the moon,
Than such a Roman.

   Cas. Brutus, bay not me,
I'll not endure it; you forget yourself,
To hedge me in; I am a soldier, I,
Older in practice, abler than yourself
To make conditions.

   Bru. Go to; you're not, Cassius.

   Cas. I am.

   Bru. I say you are not.

   Cas. Urge me no more, I shall forget myself;
Have mind upon your health, tempt me no farther

   Bru. Away, slight man!

   Cas. Is't possible?

   Bru. Hear me, for I will speak.
Must I give way and room to your rash choler?
Shall I be frighted when a madman stares?

   Cas. O ye gods! ye gods! must I endure all this?

   Bru. All this? ay, more; Fret till your proud heart
    break;
Go, show your slaves how choleric you are,
And make your bondmen tremble. Must I budge?
Must I observe you? Must I stand and crouch
Under your testy humor? By the gods,
You shall digest the venom of your spleen,
Though it do split you; for, from this day forth,
I'll use you for my mirth, yea, for my laughter,
When you are waspish.

   Cas. Is it come to this?

   Bru. You say you are a better soldier:
Let it appear so; make your vaunting true,

And it shall please me well : For mine own part,
I shall be glad to learn of noble men.

Cas. You wrong me every way, you wrong me, Brutus;
I said an elder soldier, not a better.   Did I say better ?

Bru. If you did, I care not.

Cas. When Cæsar lived, he durst not thus have moved
me.

Bru. Peace, peace ; you durst not so have tempted
him.

Cas. I durst not !

Bru. No.

Cas. What ! durst not tempt him ?

Bru. For your life you durst not.

Cas. Do not presume too much upon my love ;
I may do that I shall be sorry for.

Bru. You have done that you should be sorry for.
There is no terror, Cassius, in your threats ;
For I am armed so strong in honesty,
That they pass by me as the idle wind,
Which I respect not.   I did send to you
For certain sums of gold, which you denied me ;—
For I can raise no money by vile means ;
By Heaven, I had rather coin my heart,
And drop my blood for drachmas, than to wring
From the hard hands of peasants their vile trash
By any indirection.   I did send
To you for gold to pay my legions,
Which you denied me : was that done like Cassius !
Should I have answered Caius Cassius so ?
When Marcus Brutus grows so covetous,
To lock such rascal counters from his friends

Be ready, gods, with all your thunderbolts,
Dash him to pieces.

 Cas. I denied you not.

 Bru. You did.

 Cas. I did not ;—he was but a fool
That brought my answer back.—Brutus hath rived my
  heart ;
A friend should bear his friend's infirmities,
But Brutus makes mine greater than they are.

 Bru. I do not, till you practice them on me.

 Cas. You love me not.

 Bru. I do not like your faults.

 Cas. A friendly eye could never see such faults.

 Bru. A flatterer's would not, though they do appear
As huge as high Olympus.

 Cas. Come, Antony, and young Octavius, come,
Revenge yourselves alone on Cassius,
For Cassius is aweary of the world :
Hated by one he loves ; braved by his brother ;
Checked like a bondman ; all his faults observed,
Set in a note-book, learned and conned by rote,
To cast into my teeth. Oh, I could weep
My spirit from mine eyes !—There is my dagger
And here my naked breast ; within, a heart
Dearer than Plutus' mine, richer than gold :
If that thou be'st a Roman, take it forth ;
I, that denied thee gold, will give my heart :
Strike as thou didst at Cæsar : for I know,
When thou didst hate him worst, thou lovedst him better
Than ever thou lovedst Cassius.

 Bru. Sheathe your dagger :

Be angry when you will, it shall have scope ;
Do what you will, dishonor shall be humor.
O Cassius, you are yoked with a lamb,
That carries anger, as the flint bears fire ;
Who, much enforced, shows a hasty spark,
And straight is cold again.

Cas. Hath Cassius lived
To be but mirth and laughter to his Brutus,
When grief, or blood ill-tempered vexeth him ?

Bru. When I spoke that, I was ill-tempered too.

Cas. Do you confess so much ?   Give me your hand.

Bru. And my heart too.

Cas. O Brutus !—

Bru. What's the matter ?

Cas. Have you not love enough to bear with me,
When that rash humor which my mother gave me,
Makes me forgetful ?

Bru. Yes, Cassius ; and from henceforth,
When you are over-earnest with your Brutus,
He'll think your mother chides, and leave you so.

THE SOFT ANSWER.—*T. S. Arthur.*

(*Lawyer Trueman and Mr. Singleton.*)

Mr. Singleton. I'll give him law to his heart's content, the scoundrel !

Lawyer Trueman. Don't call harsh names, Mr. Singleton.

S. Every man should be known by his true name. Williams is a scoundrel, and so he ought to be called.

T. My young friend, did you ever do a reasonable thing in your life when you were angry?

S. I can't say that I ever did, Mr. Trueman; but now I have good reason for being angry, and the language I use, in reference to Williams, is but the expression of a sober and rational conviction.

T. Did you pronounce him a scoundrel before you received this reply to your last letter?

S. No, I did not; but that letter confirmed my previously formed impressions of his character.

T. But I cannot find, in that letter, any evidence proving your late partner to be a dishonest man. He will not agree to your proposed mode of settlement, because he does not see it to be the most proper way.

S. (*excited.*) He won't agree to it, because it is an honest and equitable mode of settlement, that is all! He wants to overreach me, and is determined to do so, if he can!

T. There you are decidedly wrong. You have both allowed yourselves to become angry, and are both unreasonable; and, if I must speak plainly, I think you are the most unreasonable, in the present case. Two angry men can never settle any business properly. You have unnecessarily increased the difficulties in the way of a speedy settlement, by writing Mr. Williams an angry letter, which he has responded to in the like unhappy temper. Now, if I am to settle this business for you, I must write all letters that pass to Mr. Williams in future.

S. But how can you properly express my views and feelings?

T. That I do not wish to do, if your views and feel ings are to remain as they now are—for anything like an adjustment of the difficulties, under such circumstances, I should consider hopeless.

S. Well, let me answer this letter, and after that I promise that you shall have your own way.

T. No; I shall consent to no such thing. It is the reply to that letter which is to modify the negotiation for a settlement in such a way as to bring success or failure; and I have no idea of allowing you, in the present state of your mind, to write such an one as will most assuredly defeat an amicable adjustment.

S. (after a long pause, to consider.) Indeed, I must write this letter, Mr. Trueman. There are some things that I want to say to him, which I know you won't write. You don't seem to consider the position in which he has placed me by that letter, nor what is obligatory upon me as a man of honor. I never allow any man to reflect upon me, directly or indirectly, without a prompt response.

T. There is, in the Bible, a passage that is peculiarly applicable in the present case. It is this :— "A soft answer turneth away wrath, but grievous words stir up anger." I have found this precept, in a life that has numbered more than double your years, to be one that may be safely and honorably adopted, in all cases. You blame Mr. Williams for writing you an angry letter, and are indignant at certain expressions contained therein. Now, is it any more right for you to write an angry letter, with cutting epithets, than it is for him ?

S. But, Mr. Trueman——

T. I do assure you, my young friend, that I am acting in this case for your benefit, and not for my own; and, as your legal adviser, you must submit to my judgment, or I cannot consent to go on.

S. If I will promise not to use any harsh language, will you not consent to let me write the letter?

T. You and I, in the present state of your mind, could not possibly come at the same conclusion in reference to what is harsh and what is mild; therefore I cannot consent that you shall write one word of the proposed reply. I must write it.

S. Well, I suppose, then, I shall have to submit. Write, if you please, and let me see what sort of a letter you propose.

T. (*Writes a while, and then reads the draft of a letter*) "Dear Sir,—I regret that my proposition did not meet your approbation. The mode of settlement which I suggested was the result of a careful consideration of our mutual interests. Be kind enough to suggest to Mr. Trueman, my lawyer, any plan which you think will lead to an early and amicable adjustment of our business. You may rely upon my consent to it, if it meets his approbation."

S. (*throwing the paper from him, with contempt.*) Is it possible, Mr. Trueman, that you expect me to sign such a cringing letter as that?

T. (*very mildly.*) Well, sir, what is your objection to it?

S. Objection! How can you ask such a question? Am I to go on my knees to him, and beg him to do me justice? No! I'll sacrifice every cent I've got in the world first—the scoundrel!

T. (*looking him steadily in the face.*) Mr. Singleton, you wish to have your business settled, do you not?

S. Of course I do—honorably settled.

T. Well, what do you mean by an honorable settlement?

S. Why, I mean,—I mean,—(*hesitating.*)

T. You mean a settlement in which your interests shall be equally considered with those of Mr. Williams?

S. Yes, certainly; and that—

T. And that Mr. Williams, in the settlement, shall consider and treat you as a gentleman?

S. Certainly I do; but this is more than he ever has done.

T. Well, never mind. Let what is past go for as much as it is worth. The principal point of action is in the present.

S. But I'll never send this mean, cringing letter, I can tell you.

T. You mistake its whole tenor, I do assure you, Mr. Singleton. You have allowed your angry feelings to blind you. You, doubtless, carefully considered, before you adopted it, the proposed basis of a settlement, did you not?

S. Of course I did.

T. So the letter which I have prepared for you states. Now, as an honest and honorable man, you are, I am sure, willing to grant to him the same privilege which you asked for yourself, viz., that of proposing a plan of settlement. Your proposition does not seem to please him; now it is but fair that he should be invited to state how he wishes the settlement to be made; and in giving such an invitation, a gentleman should use gentlemanly language.

S. But he don't deserve to be treated like a gentleman. In fact, he has no claim to the title.

T. If he has none, as you say, you profess to be a gentleman; and all gentlemen should prove, by their actions and words, that they are gentlemen.

S. (*changing his tone.*) I can't say that I am convinced by what you say; but as you seem so bent on having it your own way, why, here, let me copy the thing and sign it. (*Sits and writes.*) There, now, I suppose he'll think me a low-spirited fellow, after he gets that; but he's mistaken. After it's all over, I'll take good care to tell him that it didn't contain my sentiments.

T. (*folding the letter and smiling.*) Come to-morrow afternoon, and I think we'll have things in a pretty fair way.

SCENE II.—*The next day. Trueman's office. Enter Singleton.*

T. Good afternoon, Mr. Singleton.

S. Well, sir, have you heard from that milk-and-water letter of yours? I can't call it mine.

T. Yes, here is the answer. Take a seat, and I will read it to you.

S. Well, let's hear it.

T. (*takes out a letter and reads.*) "Dear George,—I have your kind and gentlemanly note of yesterday, in reply to my harsh, unreasonable, and ungentlemanly one of the day before. We have both been playing the fool; but you are ahead of me in becoming sane. I have examined, since I got your note, more carefully the tenor of your proposition for a settlement, and it meets my views precisely. My foolish anger kept me from seeing it before. Let our mutual friend, Mr. Trueman, arrange the matter, according to the plan mentioned, and I shall most heartily acquiesce.

"Yours, &c.,   THOMAS WILLIAMS."

S. (*rising from his seat.*) He never wrote that letter in the world.

T. (*handing him the letter.*) You know his writing, I presume.

S. (*with emotion.*) It's Thomas Williams' own hand, as I live! My old friend, Thomas Williams, the best-natured fellow in the world! What a fool I have been!

Enter Williams.

W. (*advancing, and extending his hand to Singleton.*) And what a fool I have been, my friend!

S. (*grasping his hand.*) God bless you, my dear friend! Why, what has been the matter with us both?

T. (*advancing, and taking both by the hands*) My young friends, I have known you long, and have always esteemed you both. This pleasant meeting and reconciliation, you perceive, is of my arrangement. Now let me give you a precept that will make friends and keep friends. It has been my motto through life, and I don't know that I have an enemy in the world. It is,—"A

soft answer turneth away wrath, but grievous words stir
up anger."

CORIOLANUS AND AUFIDIUS.—*Shakespeare.*

Cor. I plainly, Tullus, by your looks perceive
You disapprove my conduct.

Auf. I mean not to assail thee with the clamor
Of loud reproaches and the war of words ;
But, pride apart, and all that can pervert
The light of steady reason, here to make
A candid, fair proposal.

Cor. Speak, I hear thee.

Auf. I need not tell thee, that I have performed
My utmost promise.   Thou hast been protected ;
Hast had thy amplest, most ambitious wish ;
Thy wounded pride is healed, thy dear revenge
Completely sated ; and to crown thy fortune,
At the same time, thy peace with Rome restored.
Thou art no more a Volscian, but a Roman :
Return, return ; thy duty calls upon thee
Still to protect the city thou hast saved ;
It still may be in danger from our arms ;
Retire ; I will take care thou may'st with safety.

Cor. With safety—Heavens! and thinkest thou Cori-
    olanus
Will stoop to thee for safety ?—No ; my safeguard
Is in myself, a bosom void of fear.—
Oh, 'tis an act of cowardice and baseness,
To seize the very time my hands are fettered
By the strong chain of former obligation,

The safe, sure moment to insult me.—Gods!
Were I now free, as on that day I was
When at Corioli I tamed thy pride,
This had not been.

Auf. Thou speakest the truth : it had not.
Oh, for that time again! Propitious gods,
If you will bless me, grant it! Know, for that,
For that dear purpose, I have now proposed
Thou should'st return : I pray thee, Marcius, do it;
And we shall meet again on nobler terms.

Cor. Till I have cleared my honor in your council,
And proved before them all, to thy confusion,
The falsehood of thy charge ; as soon in battle
I would before thee fly, and howl for mercy,
As quit the station they've assigned me here.

Auf. Thou canst not hope acquittal from the Vol
scians.

Cor. I do :—Nay, more, expect their approbation,
Their thanks. I will obtain them such a peace
As thou durst never ask ; a perfect union
Of their whole nation with imperial Rome,
In all her privileges, all her rights ;
By the just gods, I will.—What wouldst thou more?

Auf. What would I more, proud Roman? This I
would—
Fire the cursed forest, where these Roman wolves
Haunt and infest their nobler neighbors round them;
Extirpate from the bosom of this land
A false, perfidious people, who, beneath
The mask of freedom, are a combination

Against the liberty of human kind ;—
The genuine seed of outlaws and of robbers.
 Cor. The seed of gods. — 'Tis not for thee, vain
  boaster,—
'Tis not for such as thou,—so often spared
By her victorious sword, to speak of Rome,
But with respect, and awful veneration.—
Whate'er her blots, whate'er her giddy factions,
There is more virtue in one single year
Of Roman story, than your Volscian annals
Can boast through all their creeping, dark duration.
 Auf. I thank thy rage : This full displays the traitor.
 Cor. Traitor! How now ?
 Auf. Ay, traitor, Marcius.
 Cor. Marcius !
 Auf. Ay, Marcius, Caius Marcius : Dost thou think
I'll grace thee with that robbery, thy stolen name,
Coriolanus, in Corioli ?
You lords, and heads of the state, perfidiously
He has betrayed your business, and given up,
For certain drops of salt, your city Rome,—
I say, your city,—to his wife and mother ;
Breaking his oath and resolution like
A twist of rotten silk ; never admitting
Counsel of the war ; but at his nurse's tears
He whined and roared away your victory ;
That pages blushed at him, and men of heart
Looked wondering at each other.
 Cor. Hearest thou, Mars ?
 Auf. Name not the god, thou boy of tears.
 Cor. Measureless liar, thou hast made my heart

Too great for what contains it.—Boy !—
Cut me to pieces, Volscians ; men and lads,
Stain all your edges on me.—Boy !—
If you have writ your annals true, 'tis there,
That, like an eagle in a dovecot, I
Fluttered your Volscians in Corioli ;
Alone I did it :—Boy !—But let us part,
Lest my rash hand should do a hasty deed
My cooler thought forbids.

   Auf. I court
The worst thy sword can do ; while thou from me
Hast nothing to expect but sore destruction ;
Quit then this hostile camp ; once more I tell thee,
Thou art not here one single hour in safety.

   Cor. Oh, that I had thee in the field,
With six Aufidiuses, or more, thy tribe,
To use my lawful sword !—

CATO'S SENATE.—*Addison.*

   Cato. Fathers, we once again are met in council.
Cæsar's approach has summoned us together,
And Rome attends her fate from our resolves.
How shall we treat this bold, aspiring man ?
Success still follows him, and backs his crimes.
Pharsalia gave him Rome : Egypt has since
Received his yoke, and the whole Nile is Cæsar's.
Why should I mention Juba's overthrow,
And Scipio's death ? Numidia's burning sands
Still smoke with blood. 'Tis time we should decree
What course to take. Our foe advances on us,

And envies us even Libya's sultry deserts.
Fathers, pronounce your thoughts : are they still fixed
To hold it out and fight it to the last?
Or are your hearts subdued at length, and wrought
By time and ill success, to a submission?
Sempronius, speak.—

Sempronius. My voice is still for war.
Gods! can a Roman senate long debate
Which of the two to choose, slavery or death?
No; let us rise at once, gird on our swords,
And at the head of our remaining troops,
Attack the foe, break through the thick array
Of his thronged legions, and charge home upon him.
Perhaps some arm, more lucky than the rest,
May reach his heart, and free the world from bondage.
Rise, fathers, rise! 'tis Rome demands your help;
Rise, and revenge her slaughtered citizens,
Or share their fate! the corpse of half her senate
Manure the fields of Thessaly, while we
Sit here deliberating in cold debates
If we should sacrifice our lives to honor,
Or wear them out in servitude and chains.
Rouse up, for shame! our brothers of Pharsalia
Point at their wounds, and cry aloud—To battle!
Great Pompey's shade complains that we are slow,
And Scipio's ghost walks unrevenged amongst us!

Cato. Let not a torrent of impetuous zeal
Transport thee thus beyond the bounds of reason:
True fortitude is seen in great exploits
That justice warrants, and that wisdom guides:
Al' else is towering frenzy and distraction.

Are not the lives of those who draw the sword
In Rome's defence entrusted to our care?
Should we thus lead them to a field of slaughter,
Might not the impartial world with reason say,
We lavished at our deaths the blood of thousands,
To grace our fall, and make our ruin glorious?
Lucius, we next would know what's your opinion.

Lucius. My thoughts, I must confess, are turned on
    peace.
Already have our quarrels filled the world
With widows and with orphans; Scythia mourns
Our guilty wars, and earth's remotest regions
Lie half-unpeopled by the feuds of Rome:
'Tis time to sheathe the sword, and spare mankind.
It is not Cæsar, but the gods, my fathers,
The gods declare against us, and repel
Our vain attempts. To urge the foe to battle,
(Prompted by blind revenge and wild despair,)
Were to refuse the awards of Providence,
And not to rest in Heaven's determination.
Already have we shown our love to Rome;
Now let us show submission to the gods.
We took up arms, not to revenge ourselves,
But free the commonwealth; when this end fails,
Arms have no further use; our country's cause,
That drew our swords, now wrests 'em from our hands,
And bids us not delight in Roman blood.
Unprofitably shed; what men could do
Is done already: heaven and earth will witness,
If Rome must fall, that we are innocent.

Semp. This smooth discourse and mild behavior, oft

Conceal a traitor—Something whispers me
All is not right—Cato, beware of Lucius.

   Cato. Let us appear nor rash nor diffident :
Immoderate valor swells into a fault ;
And fear, admitted into public councils,
Betrays like treason. Let us shun 'em both.
Fathers, I cannot see that our affairs
Are grown thus desperate ; we have bulwarks round us,
Within our walls are troops inured to toil
In Afric's heats, and seasoned to the sun :
Numidia's spacious kingdom lies behind us,
Ready to rise at its young prince's call.
While there is hope, do not distrust the gods ;
But wait at least till Cæsar's near approach
Force us to yield. 'Twill never be too late
To sue for chains, and own a conqueror.
Why should Rome fall a moment ere her time ?
No, let us draw her term of freedom out
In its full length, and spin it to the last.
So shall we gain still one day's liberty ;
And let me perish, but in Cato's judgment,
A day, an hour of virtuous liberty,
Is worth a whole eternity in bondage.

HAMLET AND HORATIO.—*Shakespeare.*

   Horatio. Hail to your lordship !
   Hamlet. I am glad to see you well : (*approaches*)
Horatio,—or I do forget myself.
   Hor. The same, my lord, and your poor servant ever.
   Ham. Sir, my good friend ; I'll change that name
     with you.

And what make you from Wittenberg, Horatio?

Hor. A truant disposition, good my lord.   ·

Ham. I would not hear your enemy say so;
Nor shall you do mine ear that violence,
To make it truster of your own report
Against yourself: I know you are no truant.
But what is your affair in Elsinore?
We'll teach you to drink deep ere you depart.

Hor. My lord, I came to see your father's funeral.

Ham. I pray thee do not mock me, fellow-student:
I think it was to see my mother's wedding.

Hor. Indeed, my lord, it followed hard upon.

Ham. Thrift, thrift, Horatio! the funeral baked meats
Did coldly furnish forth the marriage tables.
Would I had met my dearest foe in heaven,
Or ever I had seen that day, Horatio!
My father,——methinks I see my father.

Hor. Where, my lord?

Ham. In my mind's eye, Horatio.

Hor. I saw him once; he was a goodly king.

Ham. He was a man, take him for all in all:
I shall not look upon his like again.

Hor. My lord, I think I saw him yesternight.

Ham. Saw! who?

Hor. My lord, the king, your father.

Ham. The king, my father?

Hor. Season your admiration for a while,
With an attent ear; till I may deliver,
Upon the witness of these gentlemen,
This marvel to you.

Ham. For Heaven's love, let me hear.

Hor. Two nights together had these gentlemen,
Marcellus and Bernardo, on their watch,
In the dead waste and middle of the night,
Been thus encountered : A figure like your father
Armed at all points, exactly, cap-à-pie,
Appears before them, and, with solemn march,
Goes slow and stately by them. Thrice he walked
By their oppressed and fear-surprised eyes,
Within his truncheon's length ; whilst they, distilled
Almost to jelly with the act of fear,
Stand dumb, and speak not to him.

Ham. But where was this ?

· *Hor.* My lord, upon the platform where we watched.

Ham. Did you not speak to it ?

Hor. My lord, I did ;
But answer made it none. Yet once, methought,
It lifted up its head, and did address
Itself to motion, like as it would speak ;
But, even then, the morning cock crew loud ;
And at the sound it shrunk in haste away,
And vanished from our sight.

Ham. 'Tis very strange !

Hor. As I do live, my honored lord, 'tis true ;
And we did think it writ down in our duty,
To let you know of it.

Ham. Indeed, indeed, sir, but this troubles me.
Hold you the watch to-night ?

Hor. We do, my lord.

Ham. Armed, say you ?

Hor. Armed, my lord.

Ham From top to toe ?

Hor. My lord, from head to foot.

Ham. Then saw you not his face?

Hor. O yes, my lord: he wore his beaver up.

Ham. What, looked he frowningly?

Hor. A countenance more in sorrow than in anger.

Ham. Pale, or red?

Hor. Nay, very pale.

Ham. And fixed his eyes upon you?

Hor. Most constantly.

Ham. I would I had been there.

Hor. It would have much amazed you.

Ham. Very like, very like; stayed it long?

Hor. While one with moderate haste might tell a
hundred.

Ham. His beard was grizzled?—no?—

Hor. It was as I have seen it in his life,
A sable silvered.

Ham. I'll watch to-night; perchance 'twill walk again.

Hor. I warrant you it will.

Ham. If it assume my noble father's person,
I'll speak to it, though hell itself should gape,
And bid me hold my peace.   I pray you, sir,
If you have hitherto concealed this sight,
Let it be tenable in your silence still;
And whatsoever else shall hap to-night,
Give it an understanding, but no tongue;
I will requite your love: so, fare you well.
Upon the platform, 'twixt eleven and twelve,
I'll visit you.

ALCESTIS AND PHERES.—*Translated by Mrs. Hemans.*

[The following scene is from "Alcestis," one of the last tragedies
of Alfieri. The plot is founded upon a Greek legend. Alcestis is the
wife of Admetus, the son of Pheres. Admetus has died, and an
oracle had declared that he might be restored to life if another
person would consent to die in his place. Alcestis, in this dialogue,
announces her purpose of devoting herself to death, in order that
her husband might return to life.]

ALCESTIS. Weep thou no more. O monarch, dry thy
    tears,
For know, he shall not die; not now shall Fate
Bereave thee of thy son.
    PHERES.   What mean thy words?
Hath then Apollo—is there then a hope?
    ALCESTIS.   Yes, hope for *thee*, hope, by the voice pro-
    nounced
From the prophetic cave. Nor would I yield
To other lips the tidings, meet alone
For thee to hear from mine.
    PHERES.   But say, oh! say,
Shall, then, my son be spared?
    ALCESTIS.   He shall, to *thee*.
Thus hath Apollo said,—Alcestis thus
Confirms the oracle; be thou secure.
    PHERES. O sounds of joy! He lives!
    ALCESTIS.   But not for this;
Think not that e'en for *this* the stranger, joy,
Shall yet revisit these devoted walls.

PHERES. Can there be grief when, from his bed of
    death,
Admetus rises? What deep mystery lurks
Within thy words? What mean'st thou? Gracious
    heaven!
Thou, whose deep love is all his own, who hearest
The tidings of his safety, and dost bear
Transport and life in that glad oracle
To his despairing sire; thy cheek is tinged
With death, and on thy pure, ingenuous brow
To the brief lightning of a sudden joy
Shades dark as night succeed, and thou art wrapt
In troubled silence. Speak! oh! speak!
    ALCESTIS. The gods
Themselves have limitations to their power,
Impassable, eternal; and their will
Resists not the tremendous laws of fate:
Nor small the boon they grant thee in the life
Of thy restored Admetus.
    PHERES. In thy looks
There is expression more than in thy words,
Which thrills my shuddering heart. Declare what
    terms
Can render fatal to thyself and us
The rescued life of him thy soul adores?
    ALCESTIS. O, father! could my silence aught avail
To keep that fearful secret from thine ear,.
Still should it rest unheard till all fulfilled
Were the dread sacrifice. But vain the wish;
And since too soon, too well, it must be known,
Hear it from me.

PHERES.   Through all my curdling veins
Runs a cold, death-like horror; and I feel
I am not all a father. In my heart
Strive many deep affections. Thee I love,
O fair and high-souled consort of my son!
More than a daughter; and thine infant race,
The cherished hope and glory of my age;
And, unimpaired by time, within my breast,
High, holy, and unalterable love
For her, the partner of my cares and joys,
Dwells pure and perfect yet. Bethink thee, then,
In what suspense, what agony of fear,
I wait thy words; for well, too well, I see
Thy lips are fraught with fatal auguries
To some one of my race.

ALCESTIS.   Death hath his rights,
Of which not e'en the great Supernal Powers
May hope to rob him. By his ruthless hand,
Already seized, the noble victim lay,
The heir of empire, in his glowing prime
And noon-day struck;—Admetus, the revered,
The blessed, the loved, by all who owned his sway,
By his illustrious parents, by the realms
Surrounding his,—and oh! what need to add,
How much by his Alcestis? Such was he,
Already in the unsparing grasp of death,
Withering, a certain prey. Apollo thence
Hath snatched him, and another in his stead,
Although not an equal,—(who can equal him?)—
Must fall a voluntary sacrifice.
Another of his lineage, or to him

By closest bonds united, must descend
To the dark realm of Orcus* in *his* place,
Who thus alone is saved.

PHERES. What do I hear?
Woe to us, woe!—what victim?—who shall be
Accepted in his stead?

ALCESTIS. The dread exchange
E'en now, O father! hath been made; the prey
Is ready, nor is wholly worthless him
For whom 'tis freely offered. Nor wilt thou,
O mighty goddess of the infernal shades!
Whose image sanctifies this threshold floor,
Disdain the victim.

PHERES. All prepared the prey!
And to our blood allied! O heaven!—and yet
Thou bad'st me weep no more!

ALCESTIS. Yes, thus I said,
And thus again I say,—thou shalt not weep
Thy son's, nor I deplore my husband's doom.
Let him be saved, and other sounds of woe,
Less deep, less mournful far, shall here be heard,
Than those *his* death had caused. With some few tears
But brief, and mingled with a gleam of joy,
E'en while the involuntary tribute lasts,
The victim shall be honored, who resigned
Life for Admetus. Wouldst thou know the prey,—
The vowed, the willing, the devoted one,
Offered and hallowed to the infernal gods?
Father! 'tis L

---

* Orcus, the god of the lower world.

Pʜᴇʀᴇs.   What hast thou done? O heaven!
What hast thou done? And think'st thou he is saved
By such a compact?   Think'st thou he can live
Bereft of thee? Of thee, his light of life,
His very soul!—Of thee, beloved far more
Than his loved parents,—than his children more,
More than himself!—Oh! no, it shall not be!
Thou perish, O Alcestis! in the flower
Of thy young beauty ;—perish, and destroy
Not him, not *him* alone, but us, but all,
Who as a child adore thee!   Desolate
Would be the throne, the kingdom, reft of thee.
And think'st thou not of those, whose tender years
Demand thy care?—thy children! think of them!
O thou, the source of each domestic joy,—
Thou in whose life alone Admetus lives,—
His glory, his delight,—thou shalt not die,
While I can die for thee!—Me, me alone,
The oracle demands,—a withered stem,
Whose task, whose duty is, for him to die.
35 My race is run ;—the fulness of my years,
The faded hopes of age, and all the love
Which hath its dwelling in a father's heart,
And the fond pity, half with wonder blent,
Inspired by thee, whose youth with heavenly gifts
So richly is endowed,—all, all unite
To grave in adamant the just decree,
That I must die.   But thou—I bid thee live!
Pheres commands thee, O Alcestis! live!
Ne'er, ne'er shall woman's youthful love surpass
An aged sire's devotedness.

ALCESTIS.   I know
Thy lofty soul, thy fond paternal love;
Pheres, I know them well, and not in vain
Strove to anticipate their high resolves.
But if in silence I have heard thy words,
Now calmly list to mine, and thou shalt own
They may not be withstood.
    PHERES.   What canst thou say
Which I should hear? I go, resolved to save
Him who, with thee, would perish :—to the shrine
E'en now I fly.
    ALCESTIS.   Stay, stay thee! 't is too late.
Already hath consenting Proserpine,
From the remote abysses of her realms,
Heard and accepted the terrific vow
Which binds me, with indissoluble ties,
To death. And I am firm, and well I know
None can deprive me of the awful right
That vow hath won.
Yes! thou mayst weep my fate,
Mourn for me, father! but thou canst not blame
My lofty purpose. Oh! the more endeared
My life by every tie, the more I feel
Death's bitterness, the more my sacrifice
Is worthy of Admetus. I descend
To the dim, shadowy regions of the dead,
A guest more honored.
        In thy presence here
Again I utter the tremendous vow,
Now more than half fulfilled. I feel, I know
Its dread effects. Through all my burning veins
    19*

The insatiate fever revels. Doubt is o'er.
The Monarch of the Dead hath heard;—he calls,
He summons me away, and thou art saved,
O my Admetus!

.———

INTROITUS.—*From Longfellow's Divine Tragedy.*

The Angel bearing the Prophet Habakkuk through the air.

PROPHET.

WHY dost thou bear me aloft,
O Angel of God, on thy pinions
O'er realms and dominions?
Softly I float as a cloud
In air, for thy right hand upholds me,
Thy garment enfolds me.

ANGEL.

Lo! as I passed on my way
In the harvest-field I beheld thee,
When no man compelled thee,
Bearing with thine own hands
This food to the famishing reapers,
A flock without keepers!

The fragrant sheaves of the wheat
Made the air above them sweet;
Sweeter and more divine
Was the scent of the scattered grain,

That the reaper's hand let fall
To be gathered again
By the hand of the gleaner!
Sweetest, divinest of all,
Was the humble deed of thine,
And the meekness of thy demeanor!

PROPHET.

Angel of Light,
I cannot gainsay thee,
I can but obey thee!

ANGEL.

Beautiful was it in the Lord's sight,
To behold his Prophet
Feeding those that toil,
The tillers of the soil.
But why should the reapers eat of it
And not the Prophet of Zion
In the den of the lion?
The Prophet should feed the Prophet!
Therefore I thee have uplifted,
And bear thee aloft by the hair
Of thy head, like a cloud that is drifted
Through the vast unknown of the air!

Five days hath the Prophet been lying
In Babylon, in the den
Of the lions, death-defying,
Defying hunger and thirst;

But the worst
Is the mockery of men!
Alas! how full of fear
Is the fate of Prophet and Seer!
Forevermore, forevermore,
It shall be as it hath been heretofore;
The age in which they live
Will not forgive
The splendor of the everlasting light,
That makes their foreheads bright,
Nor the sublime
Fore-running of their time!

PROPHET.

O tell me, for thou knowest,
Wherefore and by what grace,
Have I, who am least and lowest,
Been chosen to this place,
To this exalted part?

ANGEL.

Because thou art
The Struggler; and from thy youth
Thy humble and patient life
Hath been a strife
And battle for the Truth;
Nor hast thou paused nor halted,
Nor ever in thy pride
Turned from the poor aside,

But with deed and word and pen
Hast served thy fellow-men;
Therefore art thou exalted!

PROPHET.

By thine arrow's light
Thou goest onward through the night,
And by the clear
Sheen of thy glittering spear!
When will our journey end?

ANGEL.

Lo, it is ended!
Yon silver gleam
Is the Euphrates stream.
Let us descend
Into the city splendid,
Into the City of Gold!

PROPHET.

Behold!
As if the stars had fallen from their places
Into the firmament below,
The streets, the gardens, and the vacant spaces
With light are all aglow;
And hark!
As we draw near,
What sound is it I hear
Ascending through the dark?

ANGEL.

The tumultuous noise of the nations,
Their rejoicings and lamentations,
The pleadings of their prayer,
The groans of their despair,
The cry of their imprecations,
Their wrath, their love, their hate!

PROPHET.

Surely the world doth wait
The coming of its Redeemer!

ANGEL.

Awake from thy sleep, O dreamer!
The hour is near, though late;
Awake! write the vision sublime,
The vision, that is for a time,
Though it tarry, wait; it is nigh;
In the end it will speak and not lie.

VOX CLAMANTIS.—*From Longfellow's Divine Tragedy.*

JOHN THE BAPTIST.

REPENT! repent! repent!
For the kingdom of God is at hand,
And all the land
Full of the knowledge of the Lord shall be
As the waters cover the sea,
And encircle the continent.

Repent! repent! repent!
For lo, the hour appointed,
The hour so long foretold
By the Prophets of old,
Of the coming of the Anointed,
The Messiah, the Paraclete,
The Desire of the Nations, is nigh!
He shall not strive nor cry,
Nor his voice be heard in the street;
Nor the bruised reed shall he break,
Nor quench the smoking flax:
And many of them that sleep
In the dust of earth shall awake,
On that great and terrible day,
And the wicked shall wail and weep,
And be blown like a smoke away,
And be melted away like wax.
Repent! repent! repent!

O Priest, and Pharisee,
Who hath warned you to flee
From the wrath that is to be?
From the coming anguish and ire?
The axe is laid at the root
Of the trees, and every tree
That bringeth not forth good fruit
Is hewn down and cast into the fire!

Ye Scribes, why come ye hither?
In the hour that is uncertain,
In the day of anguish and trouble,

He that stretcheth the heavens as a curtain
And spreadeth them out as a tent,
Shall blow upon you, and ye shall wither,
And the whirlwind shall take you away as stubble!
Repent! repent! repent!

PRIEST.

Who art thou, O man of prayer!
In raiment of camel's hair,
Begirt with leathern thong,
That here in the wilderness,
With a cry as of one in distress,
Preachest unto this throng?
Art thou the Christ?

JOHN.

Priest of Jerusalem,
In meekness and humbleness,
I deny not, I confess
I am not the Christ!

PRIEST.

What shall we say unto them
That sent us here? Reveal
Thy name, and naught conceal!
Art thou Elias?

JOHN.

No!

PRIEST.

Art thou that Prophet, then,
Of lamentation and woe,
Who, as a symbol and sign
Of impending wrath divine
Upon unbelieving men,
Shattered the vessel of clay
In the Valley of Slaughter?

JOHN.

Nay.

I am not he thou namest!

PRIEST.

Who art thou, and what is the **word**
That here thou proclaimest?

JOHN.

I am the voice of one
Crying in the wilderness alone:
Prepare ye the way of the Lord;
Make his paths straight
In the land that is desolate!

PRIEST.

If thou be not the Christ,
Nor yet Elias, nor he
That, in sign of the things to be,
Shattered the vessel of clay
In the Valley of Slaughter,

Then declare unto us, and say
By what authority now
Baptizest thou?

JOHN.

I indeed baptize you with water
Unto repentance; but He,
That cometh after me,
Is mightier than I and higher;
The latchet of whose shoes
I am not worthy to unloose;
He shall baptize you with fire,
And with the Holy Ghost!
Whose fan is in his hand;
He will purge to the uttermost
His floor, and garner his wheat,
But will burn the chaff in the brand
And fire of unquenchable heat!
Repent! repent! repent!

———

MOUNT QUARANTANIA.—*From Longfellow's Divine Tragedy.*

I.

LUCIFER.

Nor in the lightning's flash, nor in the thunder,
Not in the tempest, nor the cloudy storm,
    Will I array my form;

But part invisible these boughs asunder,
And move and murmur, as the wind upheaves
 And whispers in the leaves.

Not as a terror and a desolation,
Not in my natural shape, inspiring fear
 And dread, will I appear;
But in soft tones of sweetness and persuasion,
A sound as of the fall of mountain streams,
 Or voices heard in dreams.

He sitteth there in silence, worn and wasted
With famine, and uplifts his hollow eyes
 To the unpitying skies;
For forty days and nights he hath not tasted
Of food or drink, his parted lips are pale,
 Surely his strength must fail.

Wherefore dost thou in penitential fasting
Waste and consume the beauty of thy youth?
 Ah, if thou be in truth
The Son of the Unnamed, the Everlasting,
Command these stones beneath thy feet to be
 Changed into bread for thee!

CHRISTUS.

'T is written: Man shall not live by bread alone,
But by each word that from God's mouth pro-
 ceedeth!

II.

LUCIFER.

Too weak, alas! too weak is the temptation
For one whose soul to nobler things aspires
    Than sensual desires!
Ah, could I, by some sudden aberration,
Lead and delude to suicidal death
    This Christ of Nazareth!

Unto the holy Temple on Moriah,
With its resplendent domes, and manifold
    Bright pinnacles of gold,
Where they await thy coming, O Messiah!
Lo, I have brought thee! Let thy glory here
    Be manifest and clear.

Reveal thyself by royal act and gesture,
Descending with the bright triumphant host
    Of all the highermost
Archangels, and about thee as a vesture
The shining clouds, and all thy splendors show
    Unto the world below!

Cast thyself down, it is the hour appointed;
And God hath given his angels charge and care
    To keep thee and upbear
Upon their hands his only Son, the Anointed,
Lest he should dash his foot against a stone
    And die, and be unknown.

CHRISTUS.

'T is written : Thou shalt not tempt the Lord thy
God !

III.

LUCIFER.

I cannot thus delude him to perdition !
But one temptation still remains untried,
   The trial of his pride,
The thirst of power, the fever of ambition !
Surely by these a humble peasant's son
   At last may be undone !

Above the yawning chasms and deep abysses,
Across the headlong torrents, I have brought
   Thy footsteps, swift as thought ;
And from the highest of these precipices,
The Kingdoms of the world thine eyes behold,
   Life a great map unrolled.

From far-off Lebanon, with cedars crested,
To where the waters of the Asphalt Lake
   On its white pebbles break,
And the vast desert, silent, sand-invested,
These kingdoms all are mine, and thine shall be,
   If thou wilt worship me !

CHRISTUS.

Get thee behind me, Satan ! thou shalt worship
The Lord thy God ; Him only shalt thou serve !

ANGELS MINISTRANT.

The sun goes down; the evening shadows lengthen,
The fever and the struggle of the day
    Abate and pass away;
Thine Angels Ministrant, we come to strengthen
And comfort thee, and crown thee with the palm,
    The silence and the calm.

THE DREAM OF GERONTIUS.—*Dr. Newman.*

I.

SOUL OF GERONTIUS.

I went to sleep; and now I am refresh'd,
A strange refreshment; for I feel in me
An inexpressive lightness, and a sense
Of freedom, as I were at length myself,
And ne'er had been before. How still it is!
I hear no more the busy beat of time,
No, nor my fluttering breath, nor struggling pulse,
Nor does one moment differ from the next.
I had a dream; yes:—some one softly said
"He's gone;" and then a sigh went round the room.
And then I surely heard a priestly voice
Cry "Subvenite;" and they knelt in prayer.
I seem to hear him still; but thin and low,
And fainter and more faint the accents come,
As at an ever-widening interval.
Ah! whence is this? What is this severance!
This silence pours a solitariness
Into the very essence of my soul;

And the deep rest, so soothing and so sweet,
Hath something too of sternness and of pain.
For it drives back my thoughts upon their spring
By a strange introversion, and perforce
I now begin to feed upon myself,
Because I have nought else to feed upon.

Am I alive or dead? I am not dead,
But in the body still; for I possess
A sort of confidence, which clings to me,
That each particular organ holds its place
As heretofore, combining with the rest
Into one symmetry, that wraps me round,
And makes me man; and surely I could move,
Did I but will it, every part of me.
And yet I cannot to my sense bring home,
By very trial, that I have the power.
'Tis strange; I cannot stir a hand or foot,
I cannot make my fingers or my lips
By mutual pressure witness each to each,
Nor by the eyelid's instantaneous stroke
Assure myself I have a body still.
Nor do I know my very attitude,
Nor if I stand, or lie, or sit, or kneel.

So much I know, not knowing how I know,
That the vast universe, where I have dwelt,
Is quitting me, or I am quitting it.
Or I or it is rushing on the wings
Of light or lightning on an onward course,
And we e'en now are million miles apart.

Yet . . . is this peremptory severance
Wrought out in lengthening measurements of space,
Which grow and multiply by speed and time?
Or am I traversing infinity
By endless subdivision, hurrying back
From finite towards infinitesimal,
Thus dying out of the expanded world?

Another marvel: some one has me fast
Within his ample palm; 'tis not a grasp
Such as they use on earth, but all around
Over the surface of my subtle being,
As though I were a sphere, and capable
To be accosted thus, a uniform
And gentle pressure tells me I am not
Self-moving, but borne forward on my way.
And hark! I hear a singing; yet in sooth
I cannot of that music rightly say
Whether I hear, or touch, or taste the tones.
Oh, what a heart-subduing melody!

ANGEL.

My work is done,
My task is o'er,
And so I come,
Taking it home,
For the crown is won,
Alleluia,
For evermore.

My Father gave
In charge to me
This child of earth
E'en from its birth,
To serve and save,
Alleluia,
And saved is he.

This child of clay
To me was given,
To rear and train
By sorrow and pain
In the narrow way,
Alleluia,
From earth to heaven.

SOUL.

It is a member of that family
Of wondrous beings, who, ere the worlds were made,
Millions of ages back, have stood around
The throne of God :—he never has known sin ;
But through those cycles all but infinite,
Has had a strong and pure celestial life,
And bore to gaze on the unveil'd face of God,
And drank from the eternal Fount of truth,
And served Him with a keen ecstatic love.
Hark ! he begins again.

ANGEL.

O Lord, how wonderful in depth and height,
    But most in man, how wonderful Thou art !
20

With what a love, what soft persuasive might
    Victorious o'er the stubborn fleshly heart,
Thy tale complete of saints Thou dost provide,
    To fill the throne which Angels lost through pride!

He lay a grovelling babe upon the ground,
    Polluted in the blood of his first sire,
With his whole essence shatter'd and unsound,
    And coiled around his heart a demon dire,
Which was not of his nature, but had skill
To bind and form his op'ning mind to ill.

Then was I sent from heaven to set right
    The balance in his soul of truth and sin,
And I have waged a long relentless fight,
    Resolved that death-environ'd spirit to win,
Which from its fallen state, when all was lost,
Had been repurchased at so dread a cost.

O what a shifting parti-color'd scene
    Of hope and fear, of triumph and dismay,
Of recklessness and penitence, has been
    The history of that dreary, life-long fray!
And O the grace to nerve him and to lead,
How patient, prompt, and lavish at his need!

O man, strange composite of heaven and earth!
    Majesty dwarf'd to baseness! fragrant flower
Running to poisonous seed! and seeming worth
    Cloaking corruption! weakness mastering power
Who never art so near to crime and shame,
As when thou hast achieved some deed of name;—

How should ethereal natures comprehend
    A thing made up of spirit and of clay,
Were we not tasked to nurse it and to tend,
    Link'd one to one throughout its mortal day?
More than the Seraph in his height of place,
The Angel-guardian knows and loves the ransom'd
    race.

SOUL.

Now know I surely that I am at length
Out of the body; had I part with earth,
I never could have drunk those accents in,
And not have worshipp'd as a god the voice
That was so musical; but now I am
So whole of heart, so calm, so self-possess'd,
With such a full content, and with a sense
So apprehensive and discriminant,
As no temptation can intoxicate.
Nor have I even terror at the thought
That I am clasped by such a saintliness.

ANGEL.

All praise to Him, at whose sublime decree
    The last are first, the first become the last;
By whom the suppliant prisoner is set free,
    By whom proud first-borns from their thrones are
        cast;
Who raises Mary to be Queen of heaven,
While Lucifer is left, condemn'd and unforgiven.

II.

SOUL.

I will address him. Mighty one, my Lord,
My Guardian Spirit, all hail!

ANGEL.

All hail, my child!
My child and brother, hail! what wouldest thou?

SOUL.

I would have nothing but to speak with thee
For speaking's sake. I wish to hold with thee
Conscious communion; though I fain would know
A maze of things, were it but meet to ask,
And not a curiousness.

ANGEL.

You cannot now
Cherish a wish which ought not to be wish'd.

SOUL.

Then I will speak. I ever had believed
That on the moment when the struggling soul
Quitted its mortal case, forthwith it fell
Under the awful Presence of its God,
There to be judged and sent to its own place.
What lets me now from going to my Lord?

ANGEL.

Thou art not let; but with the extremest speed
Art hurrying to the Just and Holy Judge:
For scarcely art thou disembodied yet.
Divide a moment, as men measure time,
Into its million-million-millionth part,
Yet even less than that the interval
Since thou didst leave the body; and the priest
Cried " Subvenite," and they fell to prayer;
Nay, scarcely yet have they begun to pray.

For spirits and men by different standards mete
The less and greater in the flow of time.
By sun and moon, primeval ordinances—
By stars which rise and set harmoniously—
By the recurring seasons, and the swing,
This way and that, of the suspended rod
Precise and punctual, men divide the hours,
Equal, continuous, for their common use,
Not so with us in the immaterial world;
But intervals in their succession
Are measured by the living thought alone,
And grow or wane with its intensity.
And time is not a common property;
But what is long is short, and swift is slow,
And near is distant, as received and grasp'd
By this mind and by that, and by every one
Is standard of his own chronology.
And memory lacks its natural resting-points,
Of years, and centuries, and periods.

It is thy very energy of thought
Which keeps thee from thy God.

SOUL.

        Dear Angel, say,
Why have I now no fear at meeting Him?
Along my earthly life, the thought of death
And judgment was to me most terrible.
I had it aye before me, and I saw
The Judge severe e'en in the Crucifix.
Now that the hour is come, my fear is fled;
And at this balance of my destiny,
Now close upon me, I can forward look
With a serenest joy.

ANGEL.

        It is because
Then thou didst fear, that now thou dost not fear,
Thou hast forestall'd the agony, and so
For thee the bitterness of death is past.
Also, because already in thy soul
The judgment is begun.   That day of doom,
One and the same for the collected world—
That solemn consummation for all flesh,
Is, in the case of each, anticipate
Upon his death; and, as the last great day
In the particular judgment is rehearsed,
So now, too, ere thou comest to the Throne,
A presage falls upon thee, as a ray
Straight from the Judge, expressive of thy lot.

That calm and joy uprising in thy soul
Is first-fruit to thee of thy recompense,
And heaven begun.

III.

SOUL.

        But hark! upon my sense
Comes a fierce hubbub, which would make me fear,
Could I be frighted.

ANGEL.

        We are now arrived
Close on the judgment-court; that sullen howl
Is from the demons who assemble there.
It is the middle region, where of old
Satan appeared among the sons of God,
To cast his jibes and scoffs at holy Job.
So now his legions throng the vestibule,
Hungry and wild, to claim their property,
And gather souls for hell.   Hist to their cry.

SOUL.

How sour and how uncouth a dissonance!

DEMONS.

Low-born clods
   Of brute earth,
     They aspire
To become gods,

By a new birth,
And an extra grace,
And a score of merits,
As if aught
Could stand in place
Of the high thought,
And the glance of fire
Of the great spirits,
The powers blest,
The lords by right,
The primal owners,
Of the proud dwelling
And realms of light,—
Dispossessed,
Aside thrust,
Chuck'd down,
By the sheer might
Of a despot's will,
Of a tyrant's frown,
Who after expelling
Their hosts, gave,
Triumphant still,
And still unjust,
Each forfeit crown
To psalm-droners,
And canting groaners,
To every slave,
And pious cheat
And crawling knave,
Who lick'd the dust
Under his feet.

ANGEL.

It is the restless panting of their being;
Like beasts of prey, who, caged within their bars,
In a deep hideous purring have their life,
And an incessant pacing to and fro.

DEMONS.

The mind bold
    And independent,
        The purpose free,
So we are told,
Must not think
    To have the ascendant.
        What's a saint?
One whose breath
        Doth the air taint
Before his death;
        A bundle of bones
Which fools adore,
          Ha! ha!
When life is o'er;
Which rattle and stink,
    E'en in the flesh.
We cry his pardon!
        No flesh hath he;
        Ha! ha!
        For it hath died,
        'Tis crucified
        Day by day,

20*

Afresh, afresh,
            Ha ! ha !
      That holy clay,
            Ha ! ha !
This gains guerdon,
            So priestlings prate,
            Ha ! ha !
      Before the Judge,
            And pleads and atones
      For spite and grudge
            And bigot mood,
      And envy and hate,
            And greed of blood.

SOUL.

How impotent they are ! and yet on earth
They have repute for wondrous power and skill ;
And books describe, how that the very face
Of the Evil One, if seen, would have a force
Even to freeze the blood, and choke the life
Of him who saw it.

ANGEL.

            In thy trial-state
Thou hadst a traitor nestling close at home,
Connatural, who with the powers of hell
Was leagued, and of thy senses kept the keys,
And to that deadliest foe unlock'd thy heart.
And therefore is it, in respect of man,
Those fallen ones show so majestical.

But, when some child of grace, Angel or Saint,
Pure and upright in his integrity
Of nature, meets the demons on their raid,
They send away as cowards from the fight.
Nay, oft hath holy hermit in his cell,
Not yet disburden'd of mortality,
Mocked at their threats and warlike overtures,
Or, dying, when they swarm'd, like flies, around,
Defied them, and departed to his Judge.

DEMONS.

Virtue and vice,
    A knave's pretence,
        'Tis all the same;
        Ha! ha!
           Dread of hell-fire,
        Of the venomous flame,
           A coward's plea.
Give him his price,
           Saint though he be
Ha! ha!
      From shrewd good sense
           He'll slave for hire;
        Ha! ha!
           And does but aspire
To the heaven above
        With sordid aim,
And not from love.
        Ha! ha!

SOUL.

I see not those false spirits; shall I see
My dearest Master, when I reach His throne ?
Or hear, at least, His awful judgment-word
With personal intonation, as I now
Hear thee, not see thee, Angel ?   Hitherto
All has been darkness since I left the earth;
Shall I remain thus sight-bereft all through
My penance-time ?   If so, how comes it then
That I have hearing still, and taste, and touch,
Yet not a glimmer of that princely sense
Which binds ideas in one, and makes them live !

ANGEL.

Nor touch, nor taste, nor hearing hast thou now ;
Thou livest in a world of signs and types,
The presentations of most holy truths,
Living and strong, which now encompass thee.
A disembodied soul, thou hast by right
No converse with aught else beside thyself ;
But, lest so stern a solitude should load
And break thy being, in mercy are vouchsaf'd
Some lower measures of perception,
Which seem to thee, as though through channels
      brought,
Through ear, or nerves, or palate, which are gone.
And thou art wrapp'd and swath'd around in dreams,
Dreams that are true, yet enigmatical ;
For the belongings of thy present state,
Save through such symbols, come not home to thee.

And thus thou tell'st of space and time and size.
Of fragrant, solid, bitter, musical,
Or fire, and of refreshment after fire ;
As (let me use similitude of earth,
To aid thee in the knowledge thou dost ask)—
As ice which blisters may be said to burn.
Nor hast thou now extension, with its parts
Correlative,—long habit cozens thee,—
Nor power to move thyself, nor limbs to move
Hast thou not heard of those, who after loss
Of hand or foot, still cried that they had pains
In hand or foot, as though they had it still ?
So is it now with thee, who hast not lost
Thy hand or foot, but all which made up man
So will it be until the joyous day
Of resurrection, when thou wilt regain
All thou hast lost, new-made and glorified.
How, even now, the consummated Saints
See God in heaven, I may not explicate ;
Meanwhile, let it suffice thee to possess
Such means of converse as are granted thee,
Though, till that Beatific Vision, thou art blind ;
For e'en thy purgatory, which comes like fire,
Is fire without its light.

SOUL.

His will be done !
I am not worthy e'er to see again
The face of day ; far less His countenance,
Who is the very sun. Natheless in life,

When I looked forward to my purgatory
It ever was my solace to believe,
That, ere I plunged amid the avenging flame,
I had one sight of Him to strengthen me.

ANGEL.

Nor rash nor vain is that presentiment;
Yes,—for one moment thou shalt see thy Lord.
Thus will it be: what time thou art arraign'd
Before the dread tribunal, and thy lot
Is cast forever, should it be to sit
On His right hand among His pure elect,
Then sight, or that which to the soul is sight,
As by a lightning-flash, will come to thee,
And thou shalt see, amid the dark profound,
Whom thy soul loveth, and would fain approach,—
One moment: but thou knowest not, my child,
What thou dost ask: that sight of the Most Fair·
Will gladden thee, but it will pierce thee too.

SOUL.

Thou speakest darkly, Angel; and an awe
Falls on me, and a fear lest I be rash.

ANGEL.

There was a mortal, who is now above
In the mid glory: he, when near to die,
Was given communion with the Crucified,—
Such, that the Master's very wounds were stamped
Upon his flesh; and, from the agony

Which thrilled through body and soul in that embrace,
Learn that the flame of the Everlasting Love
Doth burn, ere it transform. . . .

IV.

Hark to those sounds
They come of tender beings angelical,
Least and most childlike of the sons of God.

FIRST CHOIR OF ANGELICALS.

Praise to the Holiest in the height,
  And in the depth be praise:
In all His words most wonderful;
  Most sure in all His ways !

To us His elder race He gave
  To battle and to win,
Without the chastisement of pain,
  Without the soil of sin.

The younger son He will'd to be
  A marvel in his birth:
Spirit and flesh his parents were;
  His home was heaven and earth.

The Eternal bless'd His child, and arm'd,
  And sent him hence afar,
To serve as champion in the field
  Of elemental war.

To be His Viceroy in the world
    Of matter, and of sense;
Upon the frontier, towards the foe,
    A resolute defense.

ANGEL.

We now have passed the gate, and are within
The House of Judgment; and whereas on earth
Temples and palaces are form'd of parts
Costly and rare, but all material,
So in the world of spirits naught is found,
To mould withal and form into a whole,
But what is immaterial; and thus
The smallest portion of this edifice,
Cornice, or frieze, or balustrade, or stair,
The very pavement is made up of life—
Of holy, blessed, and immortal beings,
Who hymn their Maker's praise continually

SECOND CHOIR OF ANGELICALS.

Praise to the Holiest in the height,
    And in the depths be praise:
In all His words most wonderful;
    Most sure in all His ways!

Woe to thee, man! for he was found
    A recreant in the fight;
And lost his heritage of heaven,
    And fellowship with light.

Above him now the angry sky,
  Around the tempest's din;
Who once had angels for his friends,
  Had but the brutes for kin.

O man! a savage kindred they;
  To flee that monster brood
He scaled the seaside cave, and clomb
  The giants of the wood.

With now a fear, and now a hope,
  With aids which chance supplied,
From youth to eld, from sire to son,
  He lived, and toil'd, and died.

He dreed his penance age by age;
  And step by step began
Slowly to doff his savage garb,
  And be again a man.

And quicken'd by the Almighty's breath,
  And chastened by His rod,
And taught by angel-visitings,
  At length he sought his God;

And learned to call upon His Name,
  And in His faith create
A household and a father-land,
  A city and a state.

Glory to Him who from the mire,
In patient length of days,
Elaborated into life
A people to His praise.

www.ingramcontent.com/pod-product-compliance
Lightning Source LLC
Chambersburg PA
CBHW052347110726
47901CB00005B/1385